Fall From Grace

Tim Weaver

W F HOWES LTD

This large print edition published in 2015 by
W F Howes Ltd
Unit 4, Rearsby Business Park, Gaddesby Lane,
Rearsby, Leicester LE7 4YH

1 3 5 7 9 10 8 6 4 2

First published in the United Kingdom in 2014
by the Penguin Group

A CIP catalogue record for this book is available
from the British Library

ISBN 978 1 47128 293 5

Typeset by Palimpsest Book Production Limited,
Falkirk, Stirlingshire
Printed and bound by
www.printondemand-worldwide.com of Peterborough, England

Mixed Sources
Product group from well-managed
forests, and other controlled sources
www.fsc.org Cert no. TT-COC-002641
FSC © 1996 Forest Stewardship Council

PEFC Certified
This product is
from sustainably
managed forests
and controlled
sources
PEFC
PEFC/16-33-415
www.pefc.org

This book is made entirely of chain-of-custody materials

For Sharlé

AUTHOR'S NOTE

For the purposes of the story, I have made some small alterations to the working practices and structure of the Metropolitan Police. My hope is that it's done subtly enough not to cause any offence.

PART I

1978

CHAPTER 1

It took them an hour to get to the beach, a small, horseshoe-shaped bay on the southern tip of the county. The father had wanted to get there early, to avoid having to fight for a space in the tiny car park, and because someone in their village had told him that there were five spaces – tucked away beneath the slant of a vast, ninety-foot rock face – that stayed in the shade all day. When they arrived and saw there were two spaces still empty, the father drummed out a victory beat on the wheel of the Hillman Avenger and started whistling to himself. His wife, in the passenger seat next to him, broke out into a smile.

'I think we can safely say you're happy.'

'Is it too early for an ice cream?'

She rolled her eyes. 'We've only just had breakfast.'

'That was over an hour ago,' he joked, and after he parked up and turned off the engine he looked over his shoulder, towards the back seat. His son was up on his knees, fingers pressed to the glass, looking out at the cove.

'What do you think, my boy?'

'Are there rocks to climb here, Dad?'

His father laughed. 'Yes, son. There are rocks to climb.'

The tide was on its way out, a swathe of wrinkled beach left in its wake. Beyond the blanket of sand was water as clear as glass, much of it contained within the gentle arc of the cove, the rest out in the channel, where the boy thought it looked like the world went on for ever. Excited now, he helped his dad take two deckchairs and all the food down to the sand, then came back for his bucket and spade, and made a break for the water's edge. Behind him, his mother called after him, telling him not to wander off too far, and he shouted back to her that he wouldn't. As the father set up, the mother continued to watch the boy, a trail of his footprints leading all the way down to the sea.

'He's so grown up now,' she said.

'He's only eight, Marie.'

'I know.' She stopped, watching the boy dipping his toe into the water. 'But don't you think the time's going so fast? I mean, it seems like only yesterday the nurses were handing him to me for the first time. Now look at him.'

'He's fine.'

'I know. I don't mean he's not fine. I just mean . . . before we know it, he'll be married, with his own kids. Maybe he won't even stay in this area.'

'Of course he will.'

'There are no opportunities for him here, Tom.'

'What are you talking about? He'll take over the business.'

'He says he doesn't want it.'

'He's only eight.' He came up behind his wife and put his arms around her waist. 'He doesn't know what he wants. When I was eight, I wanted to be an astronaut.'

'I just don't want him to forget us.'

He kissed his wife on the cheek. 'He won't forget his old mum.'

At the water's edge, the boy turned back to them and waved his mother towards him. 'Mum!' the boy shouted. 'Mum, come and look at this!'

'See?' the boy's father said. 'I told you.'

She smiled again, kissed her husband on the cheek and headed down to where her son was standing in a foot of water, pointing to something out beyond the edge of the cove. At first, as she followed his line of sight, she couldn't tell what had got his attention. But then it emerged, on its own out in the channel, like a lonely, drifting ship.

The island.

She'd tried to forget how close they were to it here.

'What's the matter, sweetheart?'

But she already knew. The island sat like a fin above the water, a craggy sliver of land a quarter of a mile out to sea, awkward, broken, ominous. Even from this distance, even as light bounced off the water and the sun beat down, there remained something dark about it; all the stories it had to tell, all the memories it wished it could forget.

Instinctively, she put a hand on her son's shoulder.

'What *is* that place, Mum?' the boy asked.

She looked out across the channel, unsure how to respond.

'Mum?'

'It's . . . It's, uh . . .'

'What?' the boy said. 'What is it?'

And then slowly, automatically, she brought him into her, pressing him to her hip, and she said to her son, 'It's somewhere bad, sweetheart. It's somewhere very bad.'

2013

CHAPTER 2

The address I'd been given overlooked a railway switchyard in Pimlico. Built from London stock brick, the two-storey building was a quarter of a mile south of Victoria station, almost on the banks of the Thames. There was no signage on it and its windows were dark, giving the impression it was empty. But it wasn't empty. As I got closer, I could see the hardwood front door had been freshly painted in a muted blue and a security camera was fixed to the wall, its lens focused on the entrance. Embedded in a space next to the door was a number pad with an intercom. I buzzed once and waited.

From where I was standing, the river was mostly obscured by the rusting iron struts of a railway bridge, but in between I could see a slow procession of sightseeing trips carving along the water. This close to Christmas, the vessels all had fairy lights winking in their windows, and some of the tourists – braving the chill of winter – stood on the decks, wearing Santa hats. Otherwise, there seemed a strange kind of hush to the morning, a greyness, like the city had slipped into hibernation.

A couple of seconds later, a ping came from the intercom and the door bumped away from its frame. Inside was a short corridor with polished oak floors and a big arched window, light bleeding out across the walls and ceiling. Everything was finished in the same neutral off-white colour, except for two blue doors at the end and a marble counter on the right. Behind it sat a smartly dressed woman in her early twenties.

'Mr Raker?'

I nodded. 'Was that just a lucky guess?'

She smiled, reached under the counter and brought out a visitors' ledger. 'I was told to expect you about this time,' she said, and laid a fountain pen on top. 'If you can just sign and date it, I'll show you where you need to go.'

I signed my name. 'It's 12 December today, right?'

'That's right, sir.' Once I was done, she gestured towards the first blue door. 'Head through there to find our meeting rooms. Yours is Dickens. When you've finished, feel free to use our facilities. We have a bar in the basement, and that second door takes you into our restaurant. We serve food between twelve and four, although you'll need to ensure your representative is with you, as we only serve guests when they dine with a member.'

'Okay.'

'Is there anything else, Mr Raker?'

'No, I think that's fine.'

I headed through the first blue door.

Another corridor revealed eight further doors, four on each side, all closed, all with brass plates. Each was named after a British writer, and Dickens was the fourth down on the left. As I approached, I could hear the hum of conversation in one of the rooms. The others were completely silent. At Dickens, I knocked twice.

'Come in.'

The meeting room was small but immaculate: more oak flooring, chocolate-coloured walls, a twelve-foot table, and floor-to-ceiling windows that looked out over a pristine garden. Above it, I could just make out the railway bridge, but otherwise it was easy to forget that the building was surrounded by industry and roads.

'Mr Raker.'

DCI Melanie Craw got up from a seat at the head of the table, a laptop and a closed file in front of her, and came around to greet me. We shook hands, then she pushed the door shut and directed me to the table. I took a seat, removing my jacket.

'Would you like something to drink?' she asked.

'Water would be fine. Thank you.'

Craw was in her early forties, slim, with a short, practical haircut, and cool, unreadable eyes. No jewellery, except for a wedding band. Never skirts, only trousers, and always the same subdued colours. She was stoic and steady, difficult to break down, but she wasn't unfeeling. She had an understanding of people, of what made them tick. We'd never had a working relationship, just a caustic, often bitter series of confrontations, but I admired her all the same. I couldn't honestly have said if the feeling was mutual.

As she went to a cabinet in the far corner, where a jug of iced water and some glasses were sitting on top, a brief, uncomfortable silence settled between us.

Perhaps it wasn't so surprising. I found missing people for a living, and through my work had come into conflict with Craw when she'd been the SIO on a case that had almost cost me my life. I'd been stabbed in the chest and left to die in the shadows of a cemetery by a man we'd both ended up trying to find. Through luck or fate, or a little of both, I'd been discovered, spent a month strapped to a hospital bed, and the next four recovering at the old place my parents had left me in south Devon.

Afterwards, I'd wondered if I ever wanted to return to London.

In the end, I had, not only because the city was where most of my work was, but because, once the physical pain was gone, the only thing I had to face down were the memories of what had happened to me – and those memories were all here. As she handed me a glass of water, I imagined – eighteen months on – Melanie Craw was different as well. Things had changed for me. It seemed impossible they hadn't changed for her too.

'Thanks for coming,' she said. 'You found it okay, obviously.'

'It looks derelict from the road.'

She smiled, sitting down. 'I think that's why people like it.'

'Are you a member here?'

'Through my husband. These sorts of places . . . I guess it's a male thing. I don't really get it, but it's always made him happy. I find it's useful for meetings like these.'

'Meetings like what?'

She nodded. 'I wanted to offer you some work.' She saw the surprise in my face, nodded again, as if to reassure me, and pushed the file across the table.

I glanced at it, then back to her.

'I want you to find someone.'

It was my turn to smile this time. I had a long and illustrious history of making enemies at the Met, Craw among them, not intentionally and not with any sense of enjoyment, but as a by-product of what I did. In the end, I'd accepted it as collateral damage. I didn't do this job to make friends, I did it in order to bring home the missing.

'I can't see the Met signing off on this,' I said to her.

'Well, you're right about that.'

'So why am I here?'

'This isn't for the Met.'

I studied her, instantly suspicious of her intentions. The idea of Craw asking for my help – even as time dulled the memory of our last encounter – seemed utterly perverse; the type of thing she'd have refused to do, even if someone had held a

15

gun to her head. But there was no movement in her face. No hint she wasn't serious.

So I opened the file.

A man in his early sixties looked up at me, his picture stapled to the front page of a missing persons report. He was sitting on the edge of a rock, somewhere on moorland, a vast green valley sweeping into the distance behind him. It looked like the picture had been cropped: along one edge was the outline of a second person; along the bottom of the shot, I could make out the curve of a rucksack. His name was Leonard Franks.

He'd been missing since 3 March.

He was sixty-two, six foot one, had grey hair and blue eyes – but I knew his physical description wouldn't be what got him found now. Once people were removed from their routines, they changed quickly: sometimes because they wanted to, sometimes because it was forced on them. But mostly, this far on, they weren't making any choices at all – because, by now, the majority of missing people were decaying in a hole somewhere, waiting to be found. Even if I gave the families I worked for the benefit of the doubt, and started from the assumption the victim was alive, Franks had been gone nine months, and after that amount of time, a disappearance was never about the way someone looked. It was about the way they thought. Their exit. Their reasons for going.

Their final destination.

I looked at his address. 'He lived in Postbridge?'

'About a mile north of it, yes.'

That was right in the heart of Dartmoor, about thirty-five miles north of the village in which I'd grown up. And yet, as I returned to his profile, I saw that he'd been born in London and spent his entire life in the city.

'So he retired to Devon?'

She nodded again. 'Two years ago.'

I started to leaf through the rest of the file and saw for the first time that he'd been a police officer, retiring at sixty as Detective Chief Superintendent of the Homicide and Serious Crime Command. It was a senior post, and he seemed to have been highly rated. According to the file, he'd put in for retirement at fifty-five, after thirty years of pensionable service, but had been asked by the Assistant Commissioner to stay on.

'How did he go missing?' I asked.

'He and his wife lived in this place, like an old hunting lodge,' Craw said, 'and there was a wood-shed at the side of the building, and another for tools at the back. Not much else apart from that. They were pretty isolated up there. Their nearest neighbours were about a mile away, there was open moorland in all directions, and it was so quiet you could hear a car making an approach five minutes before it even came into view.'

She looked across the table at the picture of Franks.

'Anyway, the two of them were sitting in front of the fire late afternoon, and it started to die out,

17

so she asked him to get some more logs. It was early March, still pretty cold then, especially up on the moors. She goes to put the kettle on and cut them both a slice of cake, while he goes out to the woodshed. He'd done it a thousand times before; the woodshed was literally at the end of the veranda, less than ten feet from the front door.' She stopped; looked at me. 'Except this time he never came back.'

I frowned. 'He went out to the woodshed and didn't return?'

'Correct.'

'So where did he go?'

She shrugged.

'Did his wife go out and look for him?'

'Yes.'

'And she didn't find him?'

'It wasn't dark, so she could see clearly in all directions. There were no cars. No people. They were up there on their own. It was like he'd just vanished into thin air.'

My eyes dropped to the picture of Franks and, as I studied his face, for the first time something registered with me. A physical similarity.

'So who is he?' I asked.

'His name's Leonard Franks.'

'No. I mean, who is he to you?'

She paused for a moment, eyes still on the picture of Franks, hands flat to the table. 'He's my father,' she said quietly.

CHAPTER 3

Craw was utterly still.

'Dad should have retired at fifty-five, just like he'd wanted to, but they offered him a lot of money to stay on, and I think, deep down, he worried about being bored in retirement. He didn't know anything else *except* the Met. It had been his entire life. So he took the offer, and committed to five more years.' She looked at me, impassive at first, but then shrugged and I could see from her face that, in her opinion, Franks's decision had been a bad one. 'Eighteen months in, he started to regret it. He wouldn't back out – that wasn't the type of person he was; he didn't let people down – but, slowly, he grew to hate London. In those last years, he used to complain about everything: the constant noise, having to live on top of people, the crush on the Tube, city politics. So he counted down the time until he turned sixty, then he and Mum upped sticks and were gone.'

'Why Devon?'

She shrugged. 'They'd just always loved it.'

'You don't have any other family down there?'

'No.' She ran a finger along the edge of her laptop, briefly caught in a memory. Her expression softened for a moment, presumably recalling her father, but then there was a flicker of pain. 'About a year ago, Dad gets chatting to this guy who recently moved to their village with his wife. Derek Cortez. They get friendly and it turns out that Cortez used to be a cop too: he ran CID at Plymouth for a long time. He tells Dad that he's also retired, but that he's doing some consultation work for the CCRU.'

She could see I was familiar with it: the Criminal Case Review Unit. Their official remit: unresolved cases of homicide.

Cold cases.

'Cortez went through files,' she continued, 'gave the police his take on things and then made a little money on the side. All perfectly legit – we do the same at the Met.' Her hands moved to her glass of water. She pulled it towards her but didn't take a drink. 'So you can probably guess what happens next. Cortez says, if Dad wants, he can speak to his guy at Devon and Cornwall Police and get Dad involved too. Dad probably would have said no on the spot, because he was two years out of the force and pretty happy in retirement – *but* he and Mum had this big kitchen renovation they needed to do, and they weren't going to turn away a little extra money to help pay for it. And, at the end of the day, it was cold-case work, so there was no pressure on him. Anything he dug up was a bonus and he knew the veranda was the only office he had to commute to. So he tells Cortez he'll take a few cases. If it goes well, he'll do more. If not, no hard feelings.'

I leaned forward and made a couple of notes.

It had been cold in the room when I'd entered, but now it was beginning to thaw, an air-conditioning unit on the wall humming gently in the silence.

'So what happened next?'

She didn't respond, eyes fixed on a space between us. A memory flashed in my head, of us sitting together in the house of a killer eighteen months before. This was that moment repeated, a point in time relived, just with the two of us on opposite sides. People connected, lives were bound to one another; if this proved anything, it was that.

'He'd been at the Met for thirty-five years by the time he retired,' she said, fingers knitted together on the table in front of her. 'I've been there nineteen this year. But the weird thing is, we never really talked about work. It suited us both: Dad didn't ever bring any of his cases home because he wanted a clear division between his life with Mum and his life in the office; and I didn't want anyone at the Met accusing me of getting special treatment from him. It's why I didn't use the Franks surname when I started as a uniform. Craw was Mum's maiden name. It was better that way. I never expected any favours, and I never wanted them. Everything I've achieved, I've achieved without a single

21

second of help from Dad, *or* from the family name.' She paused, looking at me. The muscles in her face tensed, as if she was trying to subdue her emotions. 'But then something changed. On his sixty-second birthday – this was 23 February – my husband and I took the kids down there to see him, and he started talking to me about this case he'd taken on.'

'What was the case?'

'He mentioned this consultation work that Cortez had put him forward for. We were on our own, just the two of us – Bill, my husband, was upstairs; Mum and the kids were already in bed. I remember thinking I was surprised that he'd considered taking on the work, but I was *more* surprised that he'd even brought it up in the first place. Like I said, we'd never talked about his job before he retired, *ever*, and yet two minutes later he's telling me about this case he was working.' Her eyes flicked to the picture of her father. 'For whatever reason, it had really got to him.'

I saw the subtext immediately: he'd worked at the Met for thirty-five years, he'd run the entire Homicide command, he'd seen everything there was to see, all the misery people wrought, all the darkness – and yet, at the end, there had been one case he couldn't get on top of. All cops had them, and not always because they were the most horrific, or engendered the most anger. Sometimes the case stuck for other reasons.

'In what way had it got to him?'

22

She started at the sound of my voice, my question catching her deep in thought. When she finally regained her composure, a little of the steel returned. 'That's just the problem,' she said. 'I never got those details out of him. He didn't mention a victim, *if* there even was one. He never talked about specifics, never named names. He just said the case had been preying on his mind. In total, he probably only spent a minute telling me about it, but that was a minute more than he'd ever spent talking about anything else he'd ever done at the Met.'

'So he didn't give you any details at all?'

She shook her head.

'You don't remember *anything* he said?'

She grimaced. 'Look, what you have to understand is that Dad opening up isn't like *other* people opening up. Dad opening up is him telling me he was working a case; it's him looking at me the way he did when he talked about it. It isn't him spilling all the details about every investigation he worked in thirty-five years at the Met.'

She paused, frustrated. For a brief moment, I thought she might be about to tell me that maybe this was a bad idea – but, instead, she crossed her arms and leaned back.

'The only thing I can tell you is that, the way he talked about it – or, rather, talked around it – made it sound like it had some connection to a case he'd already worked at the Met. He didn't tell me that outright, but that's what it felt like.

He talked about it like he was already familiar with it. But when I tried to probe, he redirected the conversation, as if it didn't matter. It wasn't the content of the conversation, it was more . . .' She stopped, head rocking from side to side, trying to pull the words into focus. She ran a hand through her hair. 'It was more his tone, this . . . *sadness* he had. In the nine months he's been gone, it's never what he said that night that's stuck with me. It's the way he looked.'

'So you went down to see him on 23 February for his birthday – then, eight days later, on 3 March, he was gone?'

She nodded. 'Yes.'

'Do you have a copy of the case he was working?'

'No.'

'It wasn't at the house?'

'No. That was the first thing I looked for after Mum called me up and told me he was gone. I headed down there, and turned that place over trying to find out where it was.'

'Could he have kept it somewhere else?'

'It's a possibility. But why?'

Except she knew why; we both did. It was just a part of her didn't want to have to think about it: the realization that whatever was in that file might have been enough for Franks to head out to the woodshed and never return. There were all sorts of reasons he might have kept the file somewhere else, away from the house: his wife, his sanity, his protection. Maybe the file had put him

24

in danger. Or maybe he felt so burdened by its contents, so distressed by whatever he'd learned, that he'd been unable to get past it.

But had that been enough for him to walk out of the door, turn his back on his life, leave his wife, daughter and grandkids behind? Given his thirty-five years at the Met, I found the idea difficult to swallow – but I didn't know him, so I couldn't discount it yet.

Everyone had a tipping point.

I looked at her. 'Otherwise, did your dad generally seem okay? You didn't have any other worries about him? Your mum never mentioned him acting differently?'

'You mean was he suicidal?'

She wasn't on the attack exactly, but it was clear what she was telling me: *I've already been down this road, already considered this – and the answer is no.*

'People who instigate their own disappearance aren't necessarily suicidal,' I said. 'Sometimes they do it so they can start again; escape one life for another.'

'That wasn't Dad.'

'Sometimes they do it for the good of their family.'

'What good was he doing Mum?'

'That's just the point, though: we don't know what was in the file. Maybe it was a selfless act. Maybe he felt that, by walking away, he was lessening the risk to you all.'

She didn't say anything, but it was clear she wasn't convinced. I understood her frustration, the doubts she had about him leaving voluntarily – but she, more than anyone, knew everything needed to be considered.

'Financially they were okay?'

'They were fine. He'd taken on the consultation work to help pay for the kitchen renovation – but they could have got by without it. He had a thirty-five-year pension.'

'No problems between the two of them?'

'They were fine.'

'Would they have told you if there were?'

'They were *fine*,' she said, placing her hands flat to the table, fingers spread, her wedding ring making a soft *ping* against the veneer.

'I understand,' I said. 'But would they have *told* you if there were?'

A fleeting smile broke out at the fact that she was the one being questioned now. 'Mum would. Dad was much more private. He internalized everything.'

That sounds familiar, I thought. *That sounds like Craw.*

'Have you got any brothers or sisters?'

'One brother. Carl.'

'Where does he live?'

'He met an Aussie girl eight years ago and emigrated to Sydney in 2010. I can arrange something over Skype,' she added, but we both knew him being on the other side of the world cut down on the likelihood he knew anything or, worse, was involved. As if to confirm as much, she said, 'He hasn't been back to the UK since he moved.'

'Okay. So who set up the missing persons file for you?'

'After Mum called me and I headed down there, I drove her to Newton Abbot. The local copper was a guy called Reed. Iain Reed.' She stopped, watching me make a note of the name, the room so quiet now I could hear the nib of the pen against the paper. 'He seemed pretty bright, and said he'd speak to everyone. But then a couple of weeks later, he called me up and it was obvious the search was already hitting the skids. They'd taken prints from the house, a DNA sample, checked Dad's car, spoken to his friends, to Derek Cortez, to anyone who might be even vaguely relevant – and they'd come up with nothing. So I started calling a few people myself, and I began with Cortez.'

'What did you make of him?'

'I was off the clock, so it wasn't like I could drag him into an interview room and beat it out of him. All I had to go on was my gut. But, for me, Cortez checked out. He was a straight arrow; the sort of old-fashioned copper who probably didn't take a risk in the entire time he was on the force. I seriously doubt he was involved in anything, beyond being the one who put Dad forward to Devon and Cornwall Police in the first place.'

'Did Cortez know what was in the file?'

'No,' she said. 'Cortez said he would never have

been shown the cold-case files Dad was being sent. That's not how the process worked. Only Dad would see them.'

'Does that seem likely to you?'

'It checks out. His part was to pass on Dad's address and a recommendation to his contact at the CCRU – and it was up to the CCRU to engage with Dad individually.'

'So who was your dad's contact at the CCRU?'

'His name was DCI Gavin Clark.'

'Did you speak to him?'

'Yes. He was different from Cortez, more officious – I guess because he was still on the force. I didn't tell him what I did for a living to start with, but when he blanked me, I gave it the whole "blue blood" thing. "Show some solidarity. We're all in this together." Eventually, he went for it.' For a moment it looked like some of the fight had left her. 'Thing is, Clark said he never ended up mailing Dad a single case.'

That stopped me. 'What?'

'Cortez had passed on a recommendation to Clark; Clark had spoken to Dad on the phone and got a good reference from the Met. He said he was keen to use Dad's experience, but he was still waiting on paperwork to be signed off before he could mail anything out.'

'So, wait: your dad *wasn't* working a CCRU case at the end?'

'No.'

'Do you think Clark was lying?'

'No. I don't think he was lying, I don't think Cortez was lying, and I don't think Dad would lie to me either. However this case had got to him, it was real.'

'So you think another cold case just happened to land in his lap at the *exact* point in time he'd agreed to help the CCRU? That he was sent *another* file by *another* cop, who had somehow found out about his availability – and all under Clark's nose?'

She must have seen the incredulity in my face, but it didn't knock her off balance: 'I don't believe that file was sent to him by someone else from the CCRU. I don't think it was even a CCRU file. In fact, I'm not sure it was a cop who mailed it to him.'

'Then who?'

'I think it might have been a civilian.'

I frowned. 'A civilian who had a police file?'

'Maybe it wasn't an official police file.'

She'd never mentioned Franks looking at a *police* file, only that he'd been looking into a cold case. It still felt like a stretch, though. If it wasn't Clark who had sent it, it was someone who knew Franks was open to consultation work, who'd come to him at the same time *and* who had enough authority to entice him out of retirement. Even leaving aside the coincidence of the timing, what civilian had that kind of clout?

I let it go for now and looped things back around to Franks's missing persons file. 'So when this local cop, Reed, hit a dead end, why not go searching yourself?'

A moment of defeat flashed in her face. 'I did. But every database search is monitored and audited. When I got back to the office after Dad went missing, my super called me in. I'd told him what had happened to Dad, and he'd been good about giving me time off, but the first thing he said was, "Print off your dad's file, if you haven't already; keep a copy of it – but don't use any more police resources to find him." I didn't blame him. I would have done the same. A distracted cop with a separate agenda is dangerous.'

'So you just stopped the search?'

'No. I spoke to everyone Sergeant Reed spoke to, canvassed the village in case anyone saw anything, I went through Mum and Dad's house, their finances, their entire life – but I had to do most of it remotely. I tried to get down to Devon, but it depended what shifts I was working and what cases were landing in my lap. When I couldn't get down there, I checked in with Reed, and that went on until about a month ago when it became apparent that the search for Dad was dead in the water. I remember getting down to Devon three weeks ago and seeing Mum's face, and it suddenly dawned on me: we'd be a year, two years, five years, ten years down the line and we'd still be in the same place.' She looked from the file to me. 'I'd searched that database top to bottom before I got told to back off, and I'd found nothing.

Nothing. I'd reached the end of the road and didn't have any more options. So I collected up everything I had – which didn't amount to a hell of a lot, as you can see from what I've given you – and I called you.'

'Why me?'

'What do you mean?'

I smiled, because she knew what I meant. 'A year and a half ago, you were telling me you'd make it your life's work to put me behind bars.'

She nodded. 'Look, there's a bunch of ex-cops who are doing the private thing now. I could have asked them. But it's too incestuous at the Met. I need someone on the outside, with no connections to the force, who I know . . .' She paused, choosing her words carefully. But I saw where this was headed: up until now, the search for Leonard Franks had been played entirely by the book – now it was time for something else. 'I don't necessarily agree with the way you work, and I can't condone it as a police officer. But, as a civilian, as a daughter, I've got to the point where I couldn't care less. You know how to find missing people, you know the Devon area well, and – whatever your methods – you're effective, and you care about people. And that's what I need now.'

I started leafing through the file again. The missing persons report was the only official paperwork; everything else Craw had collated herself. As I came across Franks's phone bills, I said, 'What happened to your father's mobile?'

'He left it at the house.'

'His wallet?'

I could tell before she replied what the answer was. 'Same.'

More dead ends to add to the others she'd collected over the past nine months.

'This file contains everything you have?'

'Everything.'

Her eyes lingered on me, and it was like her thoughts were being projected. She'd made the commitment; now she was wondering whether she'd done the right thing.

A moment later, she said, 'I can't support you with any police resources. If you need to get hold of me, call my personal number, not my landline at the office. I don't want to know what you do, how you get your information or who you talk to. I just want to know what happened to my father.'

'Is your mother still living down in Devon?'

'No.' Craw shook her head. 'She's living with me.'

'Here in London?'

'She started to find their place down there too quiet, too big, too upsetting, so I moved her up here a fortnight ago. It didn't feel like I had much choice. We've put the house down in Dartmoor on the market; now we're trying to get her something in the city.'

'I'll need to speak to her.'

She nodded at the file. 'There's a list of numbers at the back, including Mum's mobile. She knows I've come to meet you today, but if you hit any snags, let me know. I think it's best I'm not around when you speak to her. I'm sure you feel the same way.'

I nodded, respecting Craw a little more for that: retreating from the case probably went against every emotion she felt as a daughter, and every professional instinct she had as a cop. But it was the right thing to do, and she was lucid enough to see it. If she was circling the case, she was trying to influence it, however unwittingly. She'd asked for my take, and she'd get it – but not on her terms, and not based on whatever conclusion she'd already reached about her father's disappearance.

'What about your kids and your husband?' I said.

'What about them?'

'Is it worth speaking to them?'

'You can speak to them if you like, but I think it'll be a waste of time. No one else was there on the veranda the night Dad mentioned the case to me, and Bill stayed here in London and looked after the girls when I went down to Dartmoor in the days after Dad went missing. I can gather them together for you to speak to at the house if you want – but to be honest, if you want a character witness, you'd be better off with the people at the Met who spent thirty-five years with Dad. And if you want to know what actually happened on the day he disappeared, what his life was like at the end, I think there's only one place to start.'

'Your mum.'

She nodded.

'Okay,' I said. 'One other thing. People will ask who I'm working for. I get that you want to keep it on the QT – I see the risks – but if I'm getting answers out of people, I need to be able to give them a name. It's just easier. So how do you want to play it?'

'I guess you're going to have to tell them you're working for Mum.'

'Will she be aware that that's the case?'

'Yes.'

'Okay. What's her first name?'

'Ellie.'

I wrote it down. 'I'll keep you up to date.'

'Thank you,' she said, but there was little of the gratitude in her face that she'd just given voice to. She'd opened herself up – and now she'd closed herself down again.

As I went to stand, she held her hand up.

'Anything you find out, however insignificant you might think it, I'd appreciate hearing.' She stopped again, a flash in her face that, on anyone else, might have looked like vulnerability. 'He's been gone two hundred and eighty four days, so every scenario going through your head now, I've already accepted. I just want the truth.'

I nodded again.

But this time it was me who didn't say anything.

Because everyone wanted the truth until they got it.

CHAPTER 4

Craw and I left together, then headed in opposite directions: she, along the banks of the river, back in the direction of Pimlico station; I, north-west towards Sloane Square, so I wouldn't have to change lines on the way to Paddington. As I crossed the railway tracks on Ebury Bridge, I could hear my phone going off inside my jacket.

'David Raker.'

'It's me,' a female voice said. 'Annabel.'

I smiled. 'Who?'

'Ha ha.'

'How's the journey going?'

'That's what I'm calling about. We've been sitting outside Swindon for the last fifteen minutes. They reckon there's been an accident somewhere. I could be a while.'

I looked at my watch. Twelve-twenty.

'Okay,' I said. 'Don't stress. It's fine.'

'Sorry to mess you around.'

'You're not.'

'I'll give you a call when we're moving again.'

'No problem. I've got plenty to keep me occupied.'

I found a quiet table at the back of a coffee shop at the eastern end of the King's Road, ordered a coffee and a sandwich, and then unclipped Leonard Franks's missing persons file from its binding. Using the table and two unoccupied chairs nearby, I managed to spread everything out in front of me. In total, I counted up fifty-two separate pages.

The actual report itself only accounted for sixteen of those pages. The rest had been attached by Craw in the weeks and months after her father had gone missing: statements, insurance policies, a financial breakdown for the year leading up to him vanishing, and another for the nine months since. I concentrated on the period since.

She must have been searching for anomalies in the time he'd been gone – payments in her parents' joint account that didn't make sense, things that were out of the ordinary – clearly hoping that she could find some evidence of her father continuing to spend money after he disappeared, or an indication of what had happened to him. *Maybe an idea of how the hell he never returned from the woodshed.* As my mind lingered on that last part, I returned to Craw's description of what had happened on 3 March.

It was like he vanished into thin air.

There was something weird and slightly unsettling about Franks's disappearance: the way the house was a mile from the nearest neighbour, how it was so isolated you could hear a car five minutes before you could even see it, and yet, when his wife had been out to look for him, she'd found no trace of him anywhere. He hadn't even been a mark against the moorland. No people. No cars.

No husband.

I cast the thought aside, trying not to let it side-track me, and, as I did, something more pragmatic took hold: if Franks had, for whatever reason, engineered his own disappearance, with his back-ground he was going to be shrewd enough not to leave a trail, either out on the moors, or in the paperwork he left behind.

What I held in my hands seemed to back that up. Craw had made a series of annotations in the margins of the Frankses' bank statements covering the year before 3 March. She'd done the same for her father's pension too, where lump sums had been removed to pay for house alterations. But, in the nine months after that, from 3 March until now, she'd either failed to find anything or begun to lose some of her will. In the end, perhaps it was a little of both: before his disappearance, it was possible to see the intimate rhythms of Leonard Franks's life right here in black and white; after-wards, there was a stark sea change – less money leaving their account, barely any movement of funds, all instigated by Ellie Franks. It was clear evidence he was gone. I'd take a closer look at the financials once I got home, but my gut told me they'd lead nowhere.

Away from their accounts, pensions, insurance policies and financial breakdowns, Craw's instincts as an investigator really started to kick in. It was a reminder of how good she was at her job, and a fascinating insight into her process: itemized phone bills for mobile and landline; a typewritten CV of her father's time at the Met; a list of people in the village and transcripts of interviews she'd done with them; impressions of Derek Cortez, the retired cop who'd floated the idea of cold-case work to Franks in the first place; and then, finally, the same for DCI Gavin Clark, who was set to be Franks's point of contact at the CCRU.

Yet while Craw had added some breadth to the investigation, she'd failed to add much depth. It was of course possible that the cold-case file wasn't the catalyst for his disappearance; that one of her father's other, countless cases, from three decades at the Met, had come back to bite him. It was possible one of the villagers had lied to her, Cortez too, and they'd managed to convince her of those lies. He could have been involved in an accident. His body could be lying in a ditch somewhere, waiting to be found.

In missing persons, all things were possible.

But, deep down, I had a hard time seeing most of those scenarios, apart – perhaps – from the idea of him already being dead. Whatever the truth, my first impression was that the last case was key, and that Franks's disappearance had been as much of a shock to the villagers, to Cortez and to Clark, as it had been to Craw, her mother and their family.

As I scanned the phone bills, I knew numbers alone would mean little: there was nothing incongruous about the fact that some of the calls Franks made and received, in the months before he disappeared, were to and from London area codes, just as there was little to be read into others being Devon-based. The last two years of his life had been spent in a house on Dartmoor – he would have made friends there, and in the local area. The sixty years before that, he'd been living and working in London, so I wasn't at all surprised to see both phone bills weighted in favour of calls to the capital.

However, the detailed annotations Craw had made in the margins of the Frankses' bank statements and financial make-up weren't replicated on the phone bills. She'd either decided it wasn't worth doing, which seemed very unlikely, or, by the time she'd got to the phone bills, she'd been forced to stop her own investigation into what had happened to her father. I remembered what she'd said about her superintendent, how he'd warned her not to use police resources to find Franks. He must have stepped in just as she'd been about to tackle the phone bills.

Craw ran a team of her own, and she was – if nothing else – a pragmatist, so she would have understood the reasons why: her boss didn't want her getting distracted by a case that was outside of the Met's jurisdiction. But it still would have hurt her. She'd have felt angry and bitter that he couldn't let her work the case off the books. In a weird way, maybe it was the reason she'd ended up asking for my help. If I was being kind, the Met were deeply suspicious of me; if I was being honest, they loathed everything I stood for. Coming to me, even if her employers never found out, was a clear act of rebellion.

Grabbing my phone, I scrolled through my address book until I got to the letter S. S was for Spike. He was an old contact from my days as a journalist, a Russian hacker living here on an expired student visa. Back when I'd been on the paper, I'd used him all the time: with a single call, he could get you inside any network and smuggle out as much as you needed to know. I only used him to help me find missing people these days, but I wasn't under any illusions about the nature of his work – or the illegality of me asking.

'David,' he said, as he picked up.

'How's things, Spike?'

'Good, man. How are you?'

'I'm good,' I said. 'I need some help with a phone.'

'You need me to get you a bill?'

'No. I've already got the bill. What I need is names and addresses for the numbers *on* the bill. If I scanned some statements in and emailed them to you, do you reckon you could get me the details on every incoming and outgoing call made to these numbers?'

'Names and addresses for each? Piece of cake.'

'That's the correct answer.'

He laughed. 'How much we looking at?'

'Thirteen months, in two chunks. Chunk one is November and December 2012, January and February 2013, up to 3 March. The second is the period after my guy goes missing, so that's 4 March through to . . . well, I guess today: 12 December.'

I didn't expect there to be many incoming calls after his disappearance on 3 March. Most would be from friends who didn't yet realize he was missing, and were calling up to chat, maybe to organize some sort of social event. What I was certain of was there would be zero outgoing calls. Whatever had happened to him, he'd left his mobile phone behind.

'I'll give you the code for my bank when we're done,' Spike said.

Spike's bank was a locker in his local sports centre. I thanked him, hung up and immediately went to my address book again, searching for a second name: Ewan Tasker.

'Task' was another old contact from my paper days, a semi-retired police officer who'd worked for the National Criminal Intelligence Agency, its successor SOCA, and now the organization's latest incarnation, the National Crime Agency. At the start, we'd built our relationship on a mutual understanding: he'd feed me stories on organized crime that, for whatever reason, he wanted out in the open; in return, I got to break them first. Over

41

time, though, we started to hit it off, and when I left journalism to nurse my wife through her last year, we'd stayed in touch. These days, I didn't have much to negotiate with if I wanted his help, so my reparation was a charity golf tournament he forced me to attend once a year, where he took my money, then got to laugh at how badly I hit a ball.

'Raker!' he said, after picking up.

'How you doing, Task?'

'Well, the good news is, I'm alive.' But even in his mid sixties, Task was big and strong, and still one of the smartest men I knew. 'Wow, it's been a while, old friend.'

'I know. I'm sorry.'

'No,' he said. 'I'm balls-deep in casework, so it's as much my fault as yours. I'm only supposed to be working three days a week – but that seems to have gone south pretty quickly.'

'Your handicap must be suffering badly.'

'Like hell it is! I'm still unbeaten on the nineteenth hole. Talking of which, I hope you haven't forgotten the twenty-eighth. Rain, sleet or snow, you're playing, Raker.'

This year's charity tournament was just after Christmas.

'I haven't forgotten, Task.'

'I know you haven't,' he said. 'So what's new?'

I filled him in on the disappearance of Leonard Franks and how the case had landed with me, and then zeroed in on what I needed: 'I've got his missing persons file here, and there's nothing in it. Nothing in his financials, no anomalies, no red flags. I've got a guy looking into his phone records for me, but I was hoping I might be able to get some sort of steer on what this last case of his might have been about.'

'So this is *the* Leonard Franks?'

'Yeah. You know him?'

'A little. I'd heard rumours he'd disappeared.'

'What else have you heard?'

'Nothing sinister. I think people were just surprised. He was – what? – thirty-odd years on the force. You don't last that long without becoming a minor celebrity.'

'What did you make of him?'

'He had a good reputation. People liked him. Franks was as straight as they come, so there was no wriggle room if you based your police work on Hollywood movies. But if you played by the rules, he had your back, every day of the week. You got any sighters on what happened to him?'

'I've only just started, so it's all still coming into focus. What I'm more certain of is that the file was the catalyst for his disappearance.'

'You said his daughter works at the Met?'

'Right.'

'And her super put the kibosh on a database search?'

I understood what he was driving at: everything was audited and logged, which meant the minute Task went into the database, he'd leave a trail.

Dangerous given the fact that Craw had put her boss, and possibly others, on high alert for searches related to Leonard Franks's disappearance. I thought of what Craw had said about Reed, the cop who had set up the original missing persons file. He'd been unable to find the case Franks had been looking into, or at least one big enough to affect him in the way that it had.

And then I remembered something else she'd said.

Maybe it wasn't an official police file.

She'd floated the possibility that a civilian might have sent Franks the file, one they'd presumably put together themselves. It was an interesting angle. Even if it didn't explain the perfect timing – being given a separate case while waiting for the CCRU to dot the i's and cross the t's – it would explain why the CCRU knew nothing about it, and why Reed wasn't able to connect the case to anything Franks had worked on at the Met.

But if it *was* a civilian, they surely would have known Franks in some way: his background, his time at the Met, cases he'd worked. They'd need the skill to construct a compelling file, something to make him sit up and take notice. It made sense they would have crossed paths with Franks, perhaps known his cases. As I lingered on that last thought, I picked up my pen and made a note: *Was the sender an ex-cop?*

'Raker?'

'Sorry. You can probably hear my brain whirring from there.'

44

Going into the database and searching for 'Leonard Franks' would compromise Task. But then more of my conversation with Craw came back to me: *The way he talked about it made it sound like it had some connection to a case he'd already worked at the Met. He talked about it like he was already familiar with it.* There was a possible workaround.

'Task, do you reckon you could search the databases for any unsolved cases in London, for as far back as you can go? It's broad enough not to set alarm bells off – but it means I can go back through them and look for any involvement Franks might have had.'

'You're going to get a shitload of hits. I take it you don't want me concentrating on stolen bicycles and local shoplifters?'

'No. Just major crimes for now. If things get uncomfortable, abandon ship. I don't want to compromise you – but only because, if you get banged up for aiding and abetting, you won't get the chance to see my new, improved golf swing in a couple of weeks.'

He laughed. 'It's a big ask. It might take me a couple of days.'

'Understood.'

'Depends when I can get some alone time.'

'Whenever you can, Task.'

I thanked him, hung up, and went back to Craw's file.

CHAPTER 5

Inserted into a plastic sleeve taped to the back of the file was a plain DVD with 'Footage of the house' written on it, along with a series of photographs. The writing on the DVD belonged to Craw. I set it aside and concentrated on the pictures. They were all of the Frankses' house on Dartmoor. Craw had taken them herself, printed them out on to A4, then explained which direction she was facing in, in a caption next to each one. Every picture underlined just how isolated the place was. I wanted to take a look at it myself eventually, in the flesh, but these made a useful starting point.

Just as she'd explained, it looked like an old hunting lodge: dark wood, with a big veranda that ran the entire length of the front. There was a slanted roof with a brick chimney on one side, and a plastic canopy attached to it, under which sat an Audi A3. I checked back through the paperwork and saw that it was registered to Franks. I could add the car to his mobile phone and his wallet in the list of things he'd left behind.

On the right of the house was the woodshed. It

was more like a lean-to, really; just a piece of corrugated metal, bolted to the house on one side and to two support beams on the other. Inside were hundreds of chunks of wood, stacked right the way up to the top.

Surrounding the house was rolling moorland, gateposts hemming in yellow and green fields, all of them stitched together like patches on a quilt. Its location, a mile north of Postbridge, meant it was elevated from the village, and in one of the shots I could see rooftops in the cleft of a valley, beyond the curve of a hill. Otherwise there was no hint of man-made structures: just a single-car dirt road snaking off from the front of the house.

I turned to the missing persons report itself.

It had been set up by Sergeant Iain Reed, as Craw had told me already. He was based in Newton Abbot. He had interviewed Franks's wife Ellie, then Craw herself, on 4 March, the day after the disappearance. He had asked the two of them the same questions, before concentrating on their whereabouts on the day of the disappearance, probably so he could cross them both off any potential suspect list. A couple of days later, on 6 March, he had organized for a forensic tech to take a DNA sample from Franks's toothbrush. Craw had already told me they'd found nothing, and the results backed her up.

Ellie Franks's statement offered little insight into her husband's psychology, either on the afternoon he disappeared or in the weeks beforehand. It wasn't a massive surprise: families were still dealing with the fallout in those first few days, angry that they weren't able to see it coming, distraught at the lack of reason. Unearthing useful leads depended on the craft and skill of the interviewer, of being able to manoeuvre around people's grief – and Reed hadn't been able to. He'd compiled a solid report, one that covered obvious and important areas, but it was like a black-and-white picture crying out for some colour.

Craw's interview was different: shorter, because she hadn't been there the day her father went missing, but more textured. Her abilities were right there on the page as she tried hard to steer Reed in the direction she felt an investigation needed to go. But ultimately, even if his police work lacked a little spark, Reed could see the crucial angles, and when it came down to the question of what had happened to Leonard Franks – if he *hadn't* just left out of choice – Craw's hunch saw her on less certain ground.

REED: You don't think he had it all planned out?
CRAW: Had what planned out?
REED: His disappearance.
CRAW: No.
REED: You don't think there's even the smallest of chances that he could have left of his own accord?
CRAW: That doesn't make sense to me. He

left without a change of clothes, without his wallet, without his phone.

REED: So you think someone was responsible for him going missing? Against his will, I mean.

CRAW: I think that's more likely.

REED: But when I spoke to your mum about that, about whether she heard any cars, any voices, disagreements, any sign your dad was undergoing any struggle at all, she said she heard nothing.

CRAW: I don't have an answer for that.

I could understand where Craw was coming from. Franks's life at the end was one he'd spent the last part of his career dreaming about. His remote house in Devon, time with his wife, those were everything he told Craw he wanted as he fell more and more out of love with London. I believed a case could come along that might still affect him, surprise him, perhaps overwhelm him, even after thirty-five years as a cop. But I had a harder time believing it would be enough to have him heading for the nearest exit.

Yet how did you get a car up a mile-long dirt track without being seen or heard by the occupants of the house? And how did you overpower a man the size of Leonard Franks, and do it in total silence, without raising the alarm? In her interview, Ellie said she had gone out to see where Franks had got to after 'about five minutes', which meant, judging by the photographs Craw had taken of the house – and the desolate dips and ridges of the surrounding moorland – she should have been able to see and hear a car winding its way back down to Postbridge, or people leaving on foot with Franks in tow.

But Ellie told Reed that she hadn't seen anybody.

So, in the end, even if her gut told her something more was at play, that someone else was involved, Craw had to go with what her mother had said she'd seen and heard.

No cars. No people.

No explanation.

CHAPTER 6

A lonely shaft of winter sunlight punctured the glass roof of the station as I watched her moving along the platform towards me. She was wheeling a black suitcase and clutching her phone in her spare hand, and when she was halfway along, the light suddenly seemed to get drawn to her, freezing her for a brief second, like a camera flash had gone off.

She hadn't seen me yet, waiting for her on the other side of the ticket barriers, but I could see her clearly: blonde hair at her shoulders; a face full of gentle sweeps; pale skin that seemed to bleach under the light of the roof. She was trim, but not skinny: even through her jacket you could see the definition in her arms, a reminder of how she liked to run, of her days spent on stage, teaching dance and drama to kids. I saw nothing of myself in her and everything of her mother, except for the moments when she smiled. The way her eyes were. The way her mouth lifted. Those were mine, and I loved them.

Once she got to the barriers, she fed her ticket into the machine and then started looking for me.

I waved to her, and began moving closer. As she came through, the smile bloomed on her face. 'Sorry I'm late. I thought you might have given up on me.'

I brought her into me and hugged her.

'Never,' I said.

At the age of forty-two, I found out I had a daughter. She'd been conceived when I was still a child myself, in a moment of immaturity I never looked back on for twenty-four years. In the summer of 1988, I'd left the village in Devon I'd grown up in, not yet eighteen, and sat in the back of my parents' battered Ford Sierra, waving to my girlfriend as I left for London. Because I was going to be at a university two hundred miles away we'd tearfully agreed to end our year-long relationship in the days before, but she never mentioned that she was pregnant, even though she would already have been at the sixteen-week mark then.

I didn't see her again for almost a quarter of a century.

After I graduated, I landed my first newspaper job – on a regional paper in south London – met my wife Derryn, married her and eventually buried her, and I never knew about the girl growing up on a part of the south Devon coast I'd once called home myself. By the time I was carrying Derryn's casket through the cemetery, I'd stopped thinking about becoming a father, accepting that my shot at it had been laid to rest alongside her.

But then, after I was attacked and stabbed a year and a half ago, I returned to Devon to recover, and through a case I eventually took on down there, I met Annabel.

Her first twenty-four years had been equally clouded; a young life built around a lie that everyone involved had been content to go along with for reasons that had probably seemed right at the time. She didn't know about me, didn't know that the people she'd spent her life with weren't actually her parents at all, even though they'd been a mum and dad to her in every way that mattered. So when we met each other for the first time, and especially in the days after, our conversations were quiet, both of us still shellshocked by the enormity of what we'd been told. It didn't help that she was grieving, having to cope with the deaths of people she'd loved, and the demands of an eight-year-old sister for whom she'd suddenly become the most important person in the world. I'd buried my wife, so I knew Annabel's pain, or at least a version of it, and had answers to some of her questions.

But not all.

In the end, some things she'd have to figure out herself.

CHAPTER 7

We walked from the Tube station in drifting rain, catching up on the month since I'd last been to see her in Devon. It was a welcome break from thinking about Leonard Franks.

'How's Liv?' I asked, as we entered my road.

Olivia was Annabel's sister. She was staying with a friend's family for a few days while Annabel came to visit.

'She's good. I'm catching glimpses of a teenager in her, which is slightly *less* good.' She paused, smiling. 'But she's doing really well.'

'Is it like catching glimpses of yourself?'

Annabel frowned. 'No. I was a model teenager.'

I laughed. 'I'm sure you were.'

At home, I left Annabel to unpack and shower while I prepared dinner. I lived in Ealing, in something of a rarity for London: a two-bedroom detached bungalow. The ink had still been drying on the contracts when Derryn, my wife, was diagnosed with cancer, so although we'd got to spend some time enjoying our house together, before she passed on, in reality most of my time here had been spent alone.

But slowly, thanks to Annabel, that was changing.

Once I set dinner going, I headed through to the spare room and scanned in the phone bills Craw had given me. I emailed them to Spike and sent a message to Task with an outline of what I'd asked for: major unsolveds in London, for as far back as he could go.

After pressing Send, I thought again about Franks's disappearance, picturing how those last few moments must have been: what he'd said to his wife; whether – if he knew he was about to walk out for good – he might have acted a little strangely, said something that, in retrospect, could have been construed as a goodbye, or lingered for a moment longer than he might normally, watching Ellie Franks head to the kitchen.

And then I thought about what it would mean if he hadn't. What if he didn't look back? *It meant he'd gone out there expecting to return.*

With that last thought still swimming through my head, I leaned back, the leather chair wheezing beneath my weight, and looked out across the spare room, a place that had, at best, become an office, at worst a dumping ground for my professional life. Shelves full of missing persons files; pictures, cuttings and photocopies trapped inside their covers. Random photographs stacked in piles against the wall, the faces of people I'd found, looking out in poses I'd come to know so well.

And then another shelf full of printouts, most of them police reports, most in my possession thanks to the sources I'd managed to secure during my newspaper days and maintain ever since. There was little room for anything else, although there were some reminders of an old life that seemed so long ago now: photos of me and Derryn on a beach in San Diego; another from an awards ceremony in the late 1990s, a younger, different version of me receiving a statuette; and then a picture of me and a colleague in the searing heat of a South African township.

As my attention returned to the computer, I fired up the web browser and googled Franks's disappearance. There was hardly anything: hundred-word stories in the *Guardian*, *Mail* and *Express* – all culled from the same press release – and a longer version of the same press release in a local Devon paper. Franks's status as a thirty-five-year veteran at the Met counted for little: in the press release, there would have been few details, certainly not an account of how he vanished on open moorland, so all news-desks had to work with was a former cop going missing. It was interesting, just not interesting enough. When people disappeared every minute, media coverage depended on an angle.

I grabbed the file Craw had given me, and opened it up to the list of names and addresses, zeroing in on two: Gavin Clark of the Cold Case Review Unit, and Derek Cortez. Craw had given both the all-clear, but I wanted to be sure.

I called Clark first. The number listed was his landline at work. After thirty seconds, and no answer, it went to voicemail. He sounded stiff and serious, so I kept my message deliberately short, explaining that I was looking into the disappearance of Franks, but stopping short of telling him I wasn't actually a police officer.

When I was done, I hung up and dialled Cortez's number. Unlike Clark, he picked up almost immediately. He sounded old, his voice a little hoarse, as if he was just getting over a cold; and there was a reticence to him initially, like he expected me to be selling him something. But after I explained who I was and what I was doing, he softened up.

'Such a tragedy,' he said in a soft Devonshire lilt.

'Did you know Leonard well?'

'Well enough. He and Ellie kept passing our house in the village, on their walks. We have a house almost on the road, and they'd come down the track from their place up there and take the path that runs just outside ours, down to the moorland behind us. I got to know them through repetition, really. Then we started talking. *Then* we got on to the subject of what we did, and that was when I found out that he'd been at the Met.'

'And after that?'

'After that, we started getting together properly: we'd go up there, they'd come down here, Len and I would go off and play golf. We all got on so well. At some point, I must have mentioned the work I was doing for the CCRU to him. Initially, I'm not sure he could have cared less. That's not to say he wasn't interested in what I was doing, but it was clear that he had no wish to return to that life. But then their kitchen renovations started and, boy, did they have some ambitious plans for that place.'

'So you recommended him to Clark?'

'Yeah. My part didn't last long, though: basically the length of a phone call. I gave Clark a shout and told him Len was up for some freelance work. You can imagine Clark was interested straight away. He's a miserable sod, but he knows when he's on to a good thing. Len ran murders up in London for all those years, so he was a good find.'

'Did he ever talk to you about his cases?'

'At the Met? Never.'

'That didn't surprise you?'

'Not at all. Some officers are like that, especially in retirement. In my experience, you get two types of cop: the ones who seek solace through sharing, and the ones who don't.'

'What about the CCRU?'

'What about it?'

'Did he ever mention receiving a case from Clark?'

'No. And I never asked him. Even when I'd been selling the dream, so to speak, I didn't ever give him details of cases I was looking into – and, to be fair, he never wanted to know. I got the sense we were from the same school of thought: these were cases and victims entrusted to us, and we had to do our best by them. Prudence was a part of that.'

We talked for a while longer, but the conversation started to dwindle, so I thanked him and hung up. On the list Craw gave me, I put a line through Cortez's name. There was a chance that, at some stage down the line, he might come back into the picture. But somehow I doubted it.

In the file Craw had compiled, next to the phone bills, was Franks's email address. A password had been pencilled into the margin alongside it. Craw had written, 'He has an iPad too, which I have at the house. You can collect it whenever you want.' I went to Gmail, put in his address and password, and accessed his inbox. He had two hundred and ninety-two messages. Nine had been sent to him in the days and months after he disappeared, five from friends who didn't realize he was missing, four from others asking him to get in touch. All had been read, presumably by Craw.

I zeroed in on the email conversations Franks had had with Derek Cortez and Gavin Clark. The Cortez email chain seemed to back up what he'd just told me. At one point, Franks had thanked Cortez for recommending him to Clark; Cortez replied, telling him it was his pleasure. *And that's where my part in this ends! Clark will get in touch directly.*

There were several other names I recognized, from the list Craw had already put together for me of Franks's friends and associates. Quite a few were old work colleagues, Franks talking to them about life at the Met post-retirement; and although they replied non-specifically, not referencing individual cases, it was clear they still treated him with reverence, one – presumably from habit, or perhaps as a half-joke – even calling him 'sir'. There weren't any email chains dealing directly with the question of the case he'd been looking at before he'd vanished, but the messages provided a compelling insight into relationships he'd built over a long time. As I worked through them more closely a second time, I drafted a list of ten names that cropped up most regularly.

All of them were cops.

Despite the theory about the file coming from a civilian, I couldn't dismiss the possibility he might have been sent it by someone still at the Met. Perhaps they'd seen it as a favour to him, or as a way to help him reach some kind of closure. That didn't explain how the case had stayed – and remained – off the radar when Sergeant Reed had gone looking for it, why ex-colleagues had never mentioned it in correspondence with him, or why someone else inside the Met might care as much about its contents as Franks. It didn't explain why they might be willing to take such a risk either, especially if they *had* printed off police records and then mailed them out. But just because it was a risk, it didn't make it inconceivable. *Someone* had to have sent it to him.

'Are you in the middle of something?'

I turned. Annabel was standing in the doorway. I hadn't heard her.

'Not at all.' I waved her in. 'Welcome to the nerve centre.'

She smiled and looked at the files, the photographs of the missing, the pictures on the wall. Last time she'd been up to London, she hadn't come in here. I watched her edge further inside, her gaze returning to the files, before sitting on the floor and bringing her knees up to her chest. 'What are all those?' she said, gesturing towards the shelves.

'That's my work. That's what I do.' I looked at the files on the shelves. 'All of those are cases I've closed in the four and a half years I've been doing this.'

'How many have you closed?'

'Sixty-seven.'

'That's a lot of cases.'

'Most are pretty straightforward.'

'So why do you keep all the paperwork?'

I shrugged. 'I guess because things repeat.'

'What do you mean?'

'I've just found that life has a way of tethering you to certain people – to places as well. It's like . . .' I paused. 'Like connective tissue. You're bound to things, whether you like it or not, and it doesn't matter if you fight it, you're always drawn back to them.'

She nodded, but then slowly seemed to drift away.

'Am I getting too mystical?'

A flat kind of half-smile. 'No. I was just thinking about how hard it is for me to leave Olivia alone these days. The crazy thing is, the rational part of me knows she's safe. I only texted her about five minutes ago.'

'She's fine.'

'I know. But every minute of every day, it feels like I'm watching her. And I get scared . . .' She stopped. 'I get scared I can't protect her.'

'You don't have to be scared.'

She glanced at me, her eyes glinting in the subdued light of the room. 'What if it happens again? What if someone comes for us? I couldn't do anything about it last time.'

'They won't.'

'Are you saying that to make me feel better – or do you genuinely believe that?'

'I genuinely believe it.'

'What makes you so sure?'

'I promise you, whatever you do now, wherever you go, I'll have your back. Yours *and* Olivia's. She might not be mine, but that doesn't matter. I have a responsibility to you and, in turn, to her.' I looked at the files, then back to her. 'But what happened to you, it was a one-off. Most people will go their whole lives without experiencing what you two did. What's getting to you, what's making you think like this, isn't reason – it's fear.'

She didn't say anything for a moment. Then: 'Don't you ever get scared?'

'Of course.'

'I don't mean by an unexpectedly large gas bill.'

I laughed. 'Neither do I.'

'So what scares you?'

I briefly considered something soft and re-assuring, something to allay her fears and send her back to Devon with the confidence to push on. But she wasn't seeking fortitude, and I never wanted her to question anything I said.

'Desperate people,' I told her. 'They're what scare me.'

'What do you mean?'

My eyes drifted to the files again, to the sixty-seven cases that had become the only life I knew. 'I mean, sometimes it's hard to believe what they're capable of.'

CHAPTER 8

Before dinner, I'd laid some of my work out on the living-room table, so we ate at the kitchen counter instead. Eventually the subject got back to Olivia.

'How are you finding it?' I asked.

'Looking after Liv?' She rocked her head from side to side. 'It's tiring.'

'Why don't you ask Emily for help?'

She didn't look up, turning her beer bottle gently on the counter in front of her. Emily had been one of the keepers of Annabel's secret – the same secret that had been kept from me – and in the months since the truth had come out, it was clear Annabel was having a hard time looking at her in the same way. Eventually, she just shrugged.

'It's okay,' I said. 'We don't have to talk about it.'

'It's not that. It's just . . .' She paused, then took a mouthful of beer. 'I don't know, I just . . . I can't even look at her. All those years she knew the truth about me, and about you – and she never said anything.'

A second later, I clocked movement out of the corner of my eye. Through the kitchen window,

I watched my next-door neighbour, Liz, moving through her living room. I couldn't see much, but I could see enough: she had boxes stacked up against one of the walls, already taped shut; and then there were more beyond that, in a line, these ones all open. As she toured the living room, she was picking things off shelves and placing them into the boxes. She'd been doing it every night for a week.

I looked from her house to her front garden. It was dark outside now, but all the homes in the street were illuminated by Christmas decorations, Santa smiling at me from the other side of the road, a reindeer two houses down blinking red and green. Along the guttering on the front of mine, I'd hung some blue lights, and when I knew Annabel was coming, I'd gone out and got a tree too. But in Liz's house there was no tree and no lights, only boxes – because at the bottom of her garden was a FOR SALE sign.

I picked at the label of my own beer, attention drifting from the sign, back to Liz's living room. It was almost empty now, a stark, abandoned reflection of what it once had been. A memory formed in my head of us lying together on her sofa.

'You okay?'

Annabel's voice brought me back.

I smiled at her. 'Yeah, I'm fine.'

But she was smart. She could tell something was up. Her eyes moved to Liz's living room and then back to me, and it was obvious something had fallen into place.

'Oh, *right*,' she said. 'That's the neighbour.'

I'd talked to Annabel about Liz. I'd told her how we'd gone out for eight months and been friends for a lot longer, until I'd done what I thought had been best for both of us and removed myself from Liz's life. I'd wondered every day since whether it had been the right thing to do.

'Are you the reason she's moving out?'

'It would be incredibly arrogant of me to think that.'

'Is that a yes?'

I sighed. 'I don't know. Maybe.'

'I'm sorry.'

'I had a meeting today,' I said, trying to manoeuvre the conversation in a different direction. 'It was in the diary before I knew you were coming up, and there are a few things I need to take care of off the back of it tomorrow. I should be done by lunch, but I was thinking maybe tomorrow morning might be a good chance for you to do the tourist thing.'

Annabel had only been to London three times, once while she was still in primary school, once in the months before I'd known her, and once in the year since. We'd seen each other fourteen times in a year, and thirteen of those times I'd been the one to make the trip down to Devon. She'd wanted to come up more – specifically she'd wanted to see the city and take in the sights – but she had Olivia to think of now.

'Sounds good to me,' she said.

'Are you sure?'

'One hundred per cent.'

'I'll give you a shout when I'm done.'

'It's fine. Honestly. I can't wait to be a tourist.'

'Do you like steak?'

She smiled, seemed confused. 'I love steak.'

'Great. There's a fantastic place near Covent Garden that's always got space. I've got to pop down to Wimbledon, but I thought maybe we could meet at the restaurant for a late lunch once you've decided you've had enough of pounding the pavements.'

'That sounds fab.'

I smiled at her and, automatically, without thinking, glanced across to Liz's living room again, just a square of light against the night. Liz emerged briefly, placing some books into a box. She was dressed in tracksuit bottoms and a vest, her chocolate-coloured hair scraped back into a ponytail. I wondered if she'd seen me letting Annabel into the house, and what she must have thought. She didn't know I had a daughter. Since I'd ended things between us, we'd barely spoken. A hello out on the drive; awkward conversations that led nowhere about things that didn't matter. I never wanted it to be like this, had clung on to the idea that our time together might be worth something more, a bind that wouldn't fray, even if our relationship was different.

But, in my life, there would always be the missing. And that would always be the problem.

THE FIRST GOODBYE

The dog died on 7 January. As snow came out of the sky, landing softly on the roof of the house, the animal moaned gently, shuddered on the rug next to the fire and finally became still. She kept her hand pressed to his stomach, felt his belly cease to swell and shrink, but didn't look down at him. Instead, she sat there – cigarette smoking between the fingers of her other hand – and stared out through the rear windows, across a patchwork of muddy-green squares, to the thin, skeletal trees on the ridge of the hill, their last rust-coloured leaves long since gone. Below them were sludgy farm tracks, criss-crossing the fields as they traced the outline of the woods, but there was no life in any of it. No breeze. No movement. No vehicles.

No people.

Just silence.

She dug a grave next to the old well a few hours later, carved a rectangle of mud out of a fresh blanket of snow, digging down with a shovel. When she'd gone about two feet – muscles tired, joints aching

68

– she paused, arm resting on the handle of the shovel, and looked back at him through the French doors. He was still lying next to the fire where he'd died, covered with an old rug from the bedroom. Her vision blurred. She didn't cry much any more – she sometimes wondered whether she was even capable of it now – but she cried then: tears ran down her cheeks, tracking the bones and muscles of her face, her eyes taking in the shape of the dog, so small under the rug, lying there like rubbish waiting to be dumped. When she wiped the first wave away, more came; when she wiped them, they were instantly replaced. After a while, she gave up trying and just stood there, shivering in the cold, alone on the edge of the silent fields, one foot sinking into the damp earth. When she finally placed the body into the hole, she found herself muttering a goodbye to him, over and over – 'Goodbye, my baby; goodbye, my baby' – her words gradually softening as the tears came again and again, her voice drifting in and out like a radio losing its reception.

An hour later, when he was finally in the ground, motionless and cold beneath the earth, she retreated into the warmth of the house. A fire crackled in the front room, the stone chimney licked black, the smell of old wood and pine in the air. She thought about making some food, knew she should probably eat, but decided to grab an open bottle of wine instead and returned to the chair in front of the fire. The flames curled and twisted. Wood popped. Black smoke coiled in the throat of the chimney. The wine passed through her body, warming her from the inside, and, as it settled in her stomach, she removed a photograph from the pocket of her trousers and gently unfolded it on her lap.

Her eyes filled with tears again as she looked at the picture.

'Goodbye, my baby.'

She would miss the dog, the companionship, the sensation of weight at her feet, of being able to reach out and touch something. But she knew, even as she'd had one foot in that grave, snow falling around her, that her tears hadn't really been for the dog.

She looked across the office at Garrick, his eyes on her, fountain pen hovering above the pad in his lap. He had a covering of grey stubble, but otherwise he was immaculately turned out in a royal-blue suit and red tie, the trousers perfectly pleated, his shoes polished to a shine. Above him, on the wall, was a heater, whining gently; on his right was a desk with a computer and an in-tray.

'Why don't you tell me about what happened that day in July, six years ago?' He studied her, and when he got no response, he leaned forward, his shaved head catching some of the light coming through the only window in the office. 'Look,' he said, 'I understand that this must be difficult for you.'

'Do you?'

'Of course.' He set the pad and the pen down. 'You've been seeing Dr Poulter for six years, and now he's retired you have to get used to someone new. I am completely aware of how strange and, perhaps in its own way, frightening that will be. If it helps, I'm a little frightened myself.' He paused, dropping his voice to a pretend whisper. 'I'm conscious that, if I want to keep my job, I have to make a good fist of this.'

'So it's really about your career?'

'Actually, it's about you,' he said, almost as if he'd expected the comeback. He watched her for a moment and then smiled again. 'If I don't do my job properly, if I can't gain your trust, then I've failed, and the people here will replace me with someone else.'

'Why are you only here two days a week?'

'I have other patients in other hospitals.'

'Poulter used to see me three times a week.'

'Dr Poulter said you were getting better,' Garrick replied. 'His recommendation – which I believe he discussed with you – was that, now you're an outpatient, now you're getting your life back on track, you only need to be seen six to eight times a month.'

She didn't offer any reply.

'However, if you feel that's not enough, we can discuss additional sessions. But in order to do that, you need to let me a little way in. How does that sound?'

Again, she didn't respond.

Garrick nodded and reached across to the desk. Next to the keyboard were loose sheaths of paper. He brought them to his lap, leafing past five or six pages, all of them marked in highlighter pen. She watched his long fingers moving left to right, trying to find the part he wanted. After about thirty seconds, they stopped; he tapped a finger on a highlighted paragraph halfway down and looked up.

'I see you worked at a place just off Oxford Street.'

His eyes moved across her face. This was what Poulter used to do when he was trying to get a response from her: he examined her, tried to use her stillness against her. In the early years, it had worked: she'd hated silence then, been frightened of it, because it reminded her of the days, weeks and months after the death. She'd gone back to the house and all she could hear were its beams, its floorboards, its structure, groaning in the heat of the sun, and then – as time slipped by – moaning in the bitterness of winter. Back then, the silence became too much, too frightening, the walls of her home like a mausoleum – which was why she'd tried to kill herself. She'd tried a second time, and third time, until she eventually ended up in Poulter's care. Nearly six years on, she'd gone past the idea of killing herself, even if the memories were as painful as they'd always been.

'You worked in marketing – is that right?'

She shrugged, those same memories playing out in her head. After a while, she realized she'd drifted. Garrick tilted his head slightly, as if trying to read her thoughts.

'My dog died a few weeks ago,' she said.

If Garrick was surprised by the change of direction, he didn't show it. 'I didn't realize you had a dog.'

'A black Labrador.'

'What was its name?'

'His name.'

'What was his name?'

'Bear.'

He smiled. 'Was Bear big?'

'That's why we called him Bear.'

'Who's "we"? You and your ex-husband?'

Her nose wrinkled.

'It wasn't his dog as well?'

'It was his dog in the sense that Bear lived in the same house as we did – but Robert was never a dog person.'

'Robert Collinson. That was your ex-husband, right?'

She nodded.

'You two divorced five years ago – in 2000?'

She didn't respond, looking up to the only window in the office, a rectangle high above the desk where sunlight was streaming in. 'I had to bury him,' she said quietly.

'Bear?'

'Yes.'

'How did that feel?'

She frowned. 'How do you think it felt?'

'Had you had Bear a long time?'

'Yes,' she said. 'Six years.'

Garrick had been busy writing something down, but he stopped immediately, pen paused at the midway point of the pad, and looked up again. 'So you got him back in 1999?'

She nodded.

'When in 1999?'

'August.'

A pause. 'So a month after the accident?'

She nodded again.

'Which means Bear wasn't just a dog to you?'

His words passed through the dust-filled sunlight as if there were a weight to them, and she felt a sludgy, pained stirring in her stomach, a dread at having to retrace the path back to her past. She'd been seeing Poulter for six years, other doctors too, sitting in this same chair, in this same building, letting them into her life as she tried to reclaim a sense of who she might once have been. Now she was going to have to do it all over again. Garrick seemed decent, ingenuous, just like they all did, so sometimes she'd guide them back to that day herself, let them wade around in the shallow waters and ask her questions she knew she could deflect. On those days, she liked coming here, even looked forward to it, because, while she recognized they were being paid to treat her, she found the fact that someone was interested in her, faked or not, oddly comforting.

But then some days she'd slip up or say something without thinking, and suddenly they'd manoeuvred past her defences and she was back beside the pond; and all she could see were arms thrashing around, above the surface of the water, clawing at air, tiny fingers desperately trying to find her as the dome of his head disappeared beneath for good.

And there was nothing she could do.

Before she realized, tears had filled her eyes, and

as she looked over at Garrick, she saw a moment of pity pass across his face.

'I couldn't save him,' she said softly.

'Was Bear a replacement for Lucas?'

She didn't reply.

Garrick came forward. 'Was Bear how you tried to forget him?'

Slowly, she started nodding – and then the words began to fall from her lips again. 'Goodbye,' she said. 'Goodbye, my baby; goodbye, my beautiful baby boy.'

CHAPTER 9

The next morning, I found a note in the kitchen from Annabel telling me she'd braved the rain and gone for a run. I admired her discipline, especially as I'd already told her I had a treadmill in the garage. After brewing some coffee and making some toast, I grabbed the DVD marked 'Footage of the house' that Craw had left in Franks's file for me, and took it through to the living room. The fire was on, and rain was tapping against the windows.

The video started with an establishing shot of the Frankses' place, filmed from about a hundred feet away. It looked like it was autumn, which meant Craw must have filmed it recently, perhaps when she'd made up her mind about bringing the case to me: copper-coloured trees swayed gently beyond the A-frame roof of the house, and the fields around it were dotted with piles of golden leaves, mulched by rain. As she started to move the camera, wind crackled in the microphone, and for the first time I got a clear idea of how isolated the Frankses' house was. It sat midway down a slope: to the left of the house, the incline continued, up towards a tor which was marked with a pile of huge boulders; to its right, the slope fell away like a breaking wave, eventually meeting up with Postbridge. The rooftops of the village – marks of charcoal in the distance – were the only civilization for miles. The rest was fields: segmented further down into the squares I'd seen in the photographs; a rolling carpet of bracken and yellow-specked heather further up.

There were two cars at the house. One, a Mini Cooper – presumably Craw's – was parked on the grass about fifty feet from the front veranda; a second, Leonard and Ellie's Audi A3, was parked at the side of the house, under the plastic canopy. The dried mud track running from the house down to the village started close to Craw's Mini and continued in a straight line across the moorland, carved out of it by years of use, before kinking right and following a treeline down to Postbridge. The trees, beginning to thin out, must have basically fenced the house in during the summer: fully covered, it would have been like a natural wall, preventing anyone beyond them from even knowing the house was there.

A couple of seconds later, the camera cut to a shot of the rear of the house, not visible in the photographs Craw had provided. Here, I could see the toolshed. It was small – no more than five or six feet across – and, although it was padlocked, it was flimsily constructed, attached to the house but gradually leveraging away from it. The woodshed was out of sight, at the side of the house, but the camera briefly passed a tree trunk with an axe embedded in it, where Franks must have cut the wood.

Next, the video switched to the interior for the first time.

Immediately inside the front door was a living room, running the entire length of the house. Off it were three open doors: through one I could see kitchen units; through the next, a downstairs bathroom; through the third, a desk with a computer on it, and two bookcases. The living room itself was neat and uncluttered. Three big leather sofas surrounding a TV. A dining-room table. A sideboard dotted with photographs. A beautiful flagstone fire. As Craw panned from left to right, I could see the photographs were mostly shots of her, her family and their kids. At the back was an L-shaped staircase leading up to a small, open landing area overlooking the living room. Upstairs, I spotted three more doors.

At this point, Craw spoke for the first time: 'This room used to be divided into two, but Dad knocked the wall down when they moved in.' A couple of seconds later, the video jumped again and we were in the kitchen. 'This is the renovation they were in the middle of when he disappeared,' she continued, and it was certainly clear that the kitchen had never been finished. There were spaces where some of the worktops hadn't been placed yet; none of the cupboard doors had been attached;

and the walls were half painted, two in cream, the others in a sickly yellow colour that they must have been in the process of covering up. Craw zoomed in slightly, taking in a long window above the sink that looked out over the back garden. This close, I could see a vegetable patch, a couple of flower beds and a patio. Again, I was struck by how much it seemed a part of its surroundings. Look quickly, and it was like the whole of the moor was theirs.

After that, there was a series of quick cuts, every room shown for thirty seconds. The house was bright and uncomplicated, and followed a similar pattern throughout: neutral walls, bright accessories, family photos, books, indoor plants. There were two bedrooms upstairs and a second bathroom. Finally, Craw returned to the spare room downstairs, which incorporated a prehistoric PC perched on a desk, and a cupboard. They sat either side of a narrow window that looked out across the moors, the edge of the toolshed visible on the left.

Suddenly, on the sofa next to me, my phone started ringing. It was a Devon number, but not one I recognized. 'David Raker.'

'It's Clark,' a male voice said by way of introduction.

Gavin Clark from the CCRU.

'DCI Clark. Thank you for calling me b—'

'Who are you?' he said.

'As I mentioned in the message I left, my name

is David Raker. I'm looking into the disappearance of Leonard Franks. I believe he was in the process of taking on some—'

'I never ended up giving him a case.'

'That's what I was told, yes.'

'By who?'

'By his wife.'

'You're working for her?'

'Yes,' I lied. 'I was hoping to get an idea of the arrangement—'

'We never had an *arrangement* because he never ended up taking on any work for the unit,' Clark said. 'I spoke to him on the phone, I liked what he had to say, he had the perfect CV, so I was in the process of getting him signed off. That's it. End of story.'

'You didn't talk about a specific case to him?'

'Why's that your business?'

'I'm just trying to find him.'

'Yeah, well, so are the police.'

'I think the police have run out of ideas.'

'This is still an active case – you know that, right? Not *my* active case, so you do whatever the hell you like. I don't care. But you buzzing around trying to get answers will make problems for someone somewhere.'

You could never be one hundred per cent sure over the phone, but his annoyance sounded genuine, and the way he'd spoken about Franks backed up everything Craw had told me already: her father had never had a case through from the

Cold Case Review Unit because Clark was waiting for his involvement to be signed off higher up the chain.

I thanked him and ended the call.

Now it was time to speak to Ellie Franks.

CHAPTER 10

Craw lived in a big house on the edge of Wimbledon Park, set back from the road behind solid oak gates. I'd never asked her what her husband did for a living, but as I approached in the car, I doubted the Met were paying her anywhere near enough for a place like this.

Built from red brick, it had gables at either end, with windows in a line under each roof. From the gates, the driveway split. A short left fork dropped away to an open garage door on the lower-ground floor, with the Frankses' Audi A3 inside. On the right, it curved up to where a Mini sat parked. I'd seen the same one on the DVD that morning.

I pulled up at the gates in my creaking seventeen-year-old BMW 3 Series and pushed the intercom. It buzzed once. Ten seconds later, without any response, the gate squealed loudly and began to fan out. I could see Craw standing in a window at the front of the house, directing a remote control at the gate. I parked behind her Mini.

Grabbing my pad and pen, I headed for the front door. It opened as I was about to knock, Craw standing in the doorway in a pair of white leggings and a pink long-sleeved sports top. I couldn't help but be surprised at how she looked. I hadn't ever seen her in anything other than the muted colours of a Met detective: greys, blacks, blues; a procession of identical trouser-suits notable only for their incremental colour changes.

'How are you today?' she asked.

I stepped past her, into the house.

'I'm fine. You?'

'Fine.'

It still felt odd seeing her like this, and talking to her in this way, even after processing it for a day: eighteen months ago we'd been at each other's throats; now I was being invited around for coffee.

She closed the door behind me.

Immediately inside was a sunken living room. Around its edges were bookcases and storage cabinets, coat stands and pot plants; in the middle, three tan leather sofas and a fifty-inch TV. Photographs were conspicuous by their absence, of Craw, of her family, but I didn't read anything into it. This was who she was, and now I understood where she got it from: she was inviting me into her life, but clearly she wanted some of it to remain off-limits. Like her father, she was drawing a clear distinction between work and home.

The only place where she'd had to concede ground was on an oak coffee table in the space between the sofas: she'd left a pile of photographs there, all of her father.

'Can I get you something to drink?' Craw asked.

'Coffee would be great.'

She nodded. 'Take a seat. I'll go and get Mum.'

I sat and started going through the pictures of Leonard Franks. In one of them, he was in running gear at the start of a half-marathon, and above his head, on a banner, I could see a date: 18 September 2006. He didn't look that different from the photo of him I'd already seen in his missing persons file. Maybe the seven years in between had brought a little more wear and tear – a few more lines around the eyes, his grey hair a little thinner – but otherwise time had been pretty kind to him.

When I moved through the others, I found him on a beach somewhere, with a salt-and-pepper beard, his grandchildren around him; in another, he was in uniform at a police ceremony, clean-shaven, arm around his wife. In another, he and Craw were smiling for the camera, beers in their hands and a barbecue smoking in the background. They were both on the veranda of the Frankses' house on Dartmoor.

A moment later, I heard voices behind me and turned and saw Craw and Ellie Franks coming down the stairs and into the living room.

I got up.

'David, this is my mum, Ellie,' Craw said. 'Mum, this is David Raker, the man I've asked to find Dad.' Craw had dropped back behind her mother, and off the back of those last words, her eyes flicked to me as if to say, *I can handle the truth if you find out he's dead. But she doesn't need a reality check yet.*

That wasn't generally how I liked to work. It was important to be honest with the families, to temper expectations, especially after their loved ones had been missing for a long time. Nine months was a long time, and Craw knew that better than anyone. But I let it slide for now. She nodded her thanks, and as her mother got closer, I shook her hand.

'Nice to meet you, Mrs Franks.'

'Oh, please,' she said, 'call me Ellie.'

She was smaller than Craw by about four inches, and dressed in a grey pleated skirt and a cream cardigan, but the physical similarity between mother and daughter was obvious: the same eyes, the same facial lines, the same slightly stiff gait. Just like her husband, Ellie Franks looked good on retirement, and as we chatted politely about the weather, she joked about how she and Leonard had once been trapped in their Dartmoor house for a week because of snow and that he'd almost driven her crazy.

'He just can't sit still,' she said, perching hesitantly on the edge of one of the sofas, a smile on her face. 'By the end, I was ready to tie him to a sledge and send him downhill to Postbridge.' But then the smile started to fall away and a sadness washed across her face.

Craw asked her mother what she wanted to drink, then disappeared into the kitchen, leaving us alone as she'd promised to the previous day.

'How are you finding life back in London?' I asked.

She drew her cardigan around her. 'Oh, you know . . .' She paused, a small, sombre smile forming. 'It's fine.' *But it's not the life I wanted.* 'Where are you from, Mr Raker?'

'David. I live here in London.'

'And before that?'

'I was in south Devon until I went to university.'

'Oh, really?' There was a flash of hope in her eyes. She came forward, hands pressed to the sofa either side of her. 'So you must know the area well.'

'It's a big county,' I said, trying to introduce some realism.

'Such a wonderful part of the country.'

'Yes, it is.'

'Len and I started to fall out of love with the city. It's all noise and aggression. You get on the Tube and it's like a war zone. I just couldn't be bothered with it, and as Len got closer and closer to retirement, we talked more and more about moving away.'

'Why Devon?'

I'd asked Craw exactly the same question the previous day, but I wanted to make sure there was no undiscovered connection to the county. Ellie shrugged. 'We used to go down there a lot, particularly in our fifties. Len loved the peace down there. In our later years, we became big walkers, and Dartmoor was just a place we fell in love with.'

'No family? No other reasons?'

She shook her head. 'No. All our family are here.'

'And you were happy down there?'

'Oh, very happy,' she said.

'No problems?'

'Absolutely none, I assure you. We bought that place about seven months before Len retired, and kept going back whenever we had free time, to get it ready for when we moved. And then, a few months after he turned sixty, we bid farewell to London for good.' She paused for a moment, her eyes moving to the photographs of her husband. 'There's not a single day I regret that move, despite what's happened. I can honestly say the two years we had down there, in that house, that beautiful place, were the best years we *ever* had.'

I gave her a moment to enjoy the memories. Next, we'd be walking over tougher, more painful ground. 'What about in the days and weeks before Leonard went missing?'

She seemed disappointed I'd brought it up.

I pushed as gently as I could. 'Did he maybe mention something that might have been bothering him, or seem in any way different?'

She was already shaking her head, and I realized she'd become so used to the question now, she could almost sense it coming. 'No,' she said, 'he was fine.'

'Melanie said that he'd been talking to a man named Derek Cortez about possibly doing some consultation work for Devon and Cornwall Police. Did he mention that?'

'Yes,' she said. 'We talked about it over dinner one night.'

'When would that have been?'

'Oh, probably mid November last year.'

'And how did that discussion go?'

'It went fine. Len liked to keep his work and home life separate. It was one of the things I loved about him most. As I'm sure you can appreciate, it requires a determined, disciplined mind to do that, but he managed it. I'm not going to pretend that he didn't *ever* bring up his time at the Met during forty-two years of marriage, but it was rare – and he certainly never brought it up in front of the kids. But he'd discuss big changes, and things that might affect us both, and he told me about his conversation with Derek, and how Derek was going to call his contact at the uh . . .' She searched for the words.

'The CCRU,' I said. 'And then they got in touch with Leonard?'

'Derek said Len would have to get some sort of official clearance first. A month or so later – maybe the end of December – Len spoke on the phone to someone at Devon and Cornwall Police. I think they just wanted to get to know him a little better.'

'That was Gavin Clark?'

'Yes, that's him. He spoke to Len, told him they were very interested in using his experience, but that they'd have to wait for everything to get cleared first.'

'Did Clark say how long that would take?'

'I think Len said at least a couple of months.'

This all confirmed what I'd been told by Craw, Cortez and Clark himself. Two months on from that phone call between Franks and Clark would have been the end of February, beginning of March. By then, Craw had been down to Dartmoor for Franks's birthday on 23 February, and he'd mentioned the cold case to her. *Which meant he already had it in his possession by then.* That either meant Clark had got the paperwork signed off in under six weeks, and lied to Craw, and me – for whatever reason – about never sending Franks a file. Or, more likely, the file came from someone else.

'We'd planned a big kitchen renovation,' Ellie Franks was saying, 'and it was going to cost quite a bit more than we'd budgeted. Len used a chunk from his pension to pay for it, but that pension may have needed to last us another twenty or thirty years – so it seemed like a sensible idea, him taking on some stress-free extra work.'

She hung on to that last bit, swaying a little: stress-free work that may have ended up being the reason he disappeared. I gave her a moment.

'So what happened after that?'

'What do you mean?'

'Do you remember him receiving a file?'

'Yes. It came in the post one day.'

'Did you have to sign for it?'

'No, it was just regular first class.'

'Do you remember when the file turned up?'

'I'm not sure.'

'I really need you to think hard about that.'

She took a long breath. 'Maybe late January, early February.'

'How sure are you about that?'

'After he disappeared, Melanie said she and Len talked about the work he was doing, very briefly, when she came down for his sixty-second birthday, and as you might know already, his birthday is 23 February. So it must have been before that. It's difficult for me to remember exactly, but I suppose he must have been working on the file for at least a couple of weeks beforehand. It could have been longer, perhaps a little shorter.'

'Do you remember where it had been sent from?'

'No, I don't.'

'Maybe a return address, or perhaps a postal mark?'

'No,' she said again. 'I never thought to look.'

'So you were the one who took receipt of it?'

'Well, I picked the envelope up off the floor, if that counts as taking receipt of it. Len had gone to Ashburton to get some things for the house. We had a bit of a leaky roof at the time. I picked it up, sorted through our mail and left it to one side for him.'

'That was your only contact with it?'

She paused, nodded. 'Yes.'

It was obvious Ellie was smart enough to have figured out – if Craw hadn't told her already – that, whatever case her husband had been working on at the end had probably been the reason for his disappearance. But I wondered if Craw had mentioned anything about its origins, about the truth behind the file: that Gavin Clark had confirmed to Franks that he'd have to wait until the start of March for his first case – and yet that file had landed on their doorstep several weeks earlier, in late January or early February.

My guess was that Craw had chosen not to tell her. If she had, Ellie would surely have glimpsed the deceit beyond: that taking delivery of the file meant Franks had lied to her about who he was working for – or, at best, chosen not to say anything. Maybe, in the grand scheme of things, not a massive lie, but a lie all the same. Separating out work and home life was one thing, but he'd already blurred the boundaries when he'd talked to his wife about taking on CCRU work to help pay for the kitchen. Ellie knew he was looking at a case – he'd just chosen not to tell her the truth about who had sent it.

'Okay, so what about in the days after?' I asked.

'Days after?'

'Did you ever see him working on the case?'

'Oh yes,' Ellie said. 'We usually had a couple of hours every afternoon where – if it wasn't too cold – we'd put the patio heaters on and sit outside. He'd be at one end of the veranda, at the table, and I'd curl up at the other, on our wicker sofa.'

'So you sat apart when he was looking at the file?'

'What do you mean?'

But then, a moment later, I could see she understood: maybe it was easier for him to work at the table – or maybe he'd chosen to sit at the opposite end of the veranda because he didn't want her to see the file.

'Did he ever look at the file at night?' I asked.

'Sometimes, when I watched TV.'

'Did he sit apart from you then too?'

A flicker in her face. 'Yes.'

There was going to be no way to trace the origin of the file. If it had been sent to Franks by recorded delivery, I might have had a trail, but locking down a location for where a first-class envelope had been mailed from would be like searching for a mote of dust. I looked at the photos of Franks, spread out on the coffee table in front of me, and then back to Ellie.

'You're positive you don't remember seeing anything of the file? Even a brief look while Len was working on it: words, names, details, photographs, anything.'

She shook her head, certain. 'No. I wish I'd taken more of an interest now.'

Briefly, that same sadness ghosted across her face. She reminded me so much of Craw, of the meeting we'd had the day before, of the times we'd crossed swords before that. Ellie was a little warmer, but there had been no tears from either of them, at any point. Yet stoicism could only disguise so much: they were hurting, and every attempt to conceal it just played out more clearly than ever in their eyes.

'Okay,' I said, keeping my voice even, patient, 'so you didn't see the contents, but do you remember what it looked like? For example, was it bound together and relatively tidy? Was it inside a proper hard-backed folder? Did it look official? Or did it look more home-made? Perhaps it was just a stack of paper, or maybe placed in a Manila folder?'

'Like I said, I didn't ever see it close up . . .' She stopped, her eyes fixed on a space between us.

Come on, Ellie: give me something.

I waited her out and, after a couple of moments, she looked back at me. 'From a distance, and from what I can remember, it seemed like the type of file you'd expect the police to compile. I mean, it was in a folder – a beige one, I think; just a standard A4 loose-flap folder – and the paper inside . . .' She paused again. 'It looked pretty tidy and well maintained, but I don't think it was bound.'

'All right,' I said, writing down what she'd said verbatim. 'All right, that's really good, Ellie. Thank you.'

She smiled, and seemed to relax a little. It was clear she hated having to recall the day her husband vanished. Unfortunately for her, this was only the beginning.

'So, I've been going through Leonard's emails, and I see he still kept in touch with some old colleagues at the Met. I know he didn't talk to

93

you much about his job, but did he ever talk about the people he worked with?'

'Oh yes, quite often.'

'Okay. Anyone in particular?'

'Goodness. There were lots. He worked across so many different commands, it was difficult for me to keep up. I guess there were probably four or five who he would have considered to be his best people: Donna Jones, Alastair Jordan . . . uh . . . Tony Mabena, Carla Murray . . . Gosh, I'm trying to think. Jim Paige. Is any of this even vaguely useful?'

I cross-checked with the list of ten I'd made that morning and all five were on it. 'Can you remember what those five did at the Met? Did they work for your husband?'

'Jim Paige didn't. He and Len were about the same age and came up through the ranks together. When Len retired in 2011, Jim was running the sexual assault . . . uh . . .'

'Sapphire?'

'Yes. That's it.'

'What about the others?'

'The rest all worked for him at one time or another, though I guess Carla must have been around the longest. I wouldn't be able to tell you *how* long, but Len recruited her from somewhere up in Scotland – Glasgow or Edinburgh – back in, I don't know, maybe the mid nineties. It could have been earlier. He was a superintendent at the time, covering murders and all that sort of thing.

After that, he went on to run the gang unit, and she went with him, then he moved on to the uh . . . oh, gosh, what are they called?'

I knew from the potted history Craw had given me that Franks ran the Directorate of Professional Standards after leaving Trident, the gang unit. 'The DPS?'

'Yes, that's it. Anyway, after that, he returned to run the Homicide command and Carla moved back with him – and that was where he stayed until he retired.'

'"Carla" is Carla Murray, right?'

'Right.'

I circled her name, as well as that of Jim Paige.

'Did you ever meet any of his colleagues socially?'

'We used to see quite a bit of Jim, as he and Len were old friends, like I said. They talked regularly on the phone too – just catching up with each other – once every couple of weeks. There were a few dinner parties, summer barbecues, that sort of thing. We hosted a couple. I wouldn't say they were super-regular, but maybe a few times a year. Back in his forties and early fifties, he used to go out drinking one night a week with his team. He said it kept morale up, and got everyone together; he'd buy them all a couple of pints and they'd get to know each other, beyond what they knew already through work.'

'Why only up until his early fifties?'

'After he got the promotion to chief superintendent, he started to scale that sort of thing back. I think he felt he couldn't be one of the guys any more, that there had to be a clear line between him and those who worked for him. That's just how Len was. It's what I loved about him. He was good with people, gracious, treated them well whatever their background and however they'd come to him. But when he needed to take tough decisions, he always would. I suppose some people respect you for that and some don't.' She paused for a moment, more of a slump to her frame now. All of a sudden, she looked older, a little frailer. 'I remember he said to me once, "Sometimes you just have to let people go." I think he meant you can't please all of the people all of the time.'

Or maybe he didn't mean that at all, I thought. Maybe he meant something else entirely.

CHAPTER 11

Craw returned from the kitchen, placed a cup of fruit tea down in front of her mother, handed me a coffee and told us she'd be upstairs if we needed anything else. I thanked her and watched her leave, then turned back to Ellie.

'Okay, so tell me about 3 March.'

She nodded, but didn't say anything. For a moment it felt like she was wrestling with her courage as much as her recollection. 'It was a Sunday, and we never did much on Sundays.' She stopped, smiling, then cleared her throat. 'I think we woke late that day, had a cup of tea in bed, read the papers and took it in turns to play around on Len's iPad. Then, later, we went for a walk up to Stannon Tor, which is about a mile north of where our house is. Once you get up there it's so lonely, and the views are absolutely stunning. Then we got back for lunch, and spent the afternoon sitting in front of the fire, dozing.'

'Everything seemed normal?'

'Everything was fine.' But she cleared her throat again, and for the first time there was the merest hint of a flash in her eyes. 'About four-thirty, five o'clock, the fire started to die out and it began to get cold, so I asked Len to get some more logs.'

'It was you who asked him?'

She looked thrown by the comment. 'I'm not sure I . . .'

'You asked him, rather than him deciding to go himself?'

She understood where I was headed now. Was there no intention on Franks's part to head outside until she asked? Or did he instigate the decision himself?

'Yes,' she said.

'You asked him?'

'Yes,' she repeated. 'I asked him to go outside.' The rest of it went unspoken but was basically painted in her face: *I made him go outside – and he never came back.*

'So he went to the woodshed . . .'

She looked up, rocking a little now, like a boxer on the ropes. Then she took a breath and nodded. 'Right. I guess it could have been a touch later than five o'clock, but it was definitely well before six, because the sun hadn't set, and at that time of the year, up there on the moors, the sun goes down between about ten to and quarter past.'

'Do you remember if he said anything to you before he went outside?'

'He complained – tongue in cheek; it was a bit of a running joke – about having to go out into the cold, but I told him I'd put the kettle on and cut him a nice slice of cake as a reward.' A pause. She sniffed gently. 'So he got up and headed outside, and I went through to the kitchen, put the kettle on and grabbed a carrot cake out of the fridge. We'd bought it that morning at a bakery in Widecombe. Len loves his carrot cake.'

Something gave way in her face again. I pulled her back in: 'And you reckon that took about five minutes?'

She nodded. 'At least five. Again, it could have been a bit more. I remember I ended up getting distracted by a story I hadn't got around to reading in the newspaper.'

'And then what happened?'

'I came back through and saw that he wasn't back.'

'How long did it normally take him?'

'A minute. The woodshed was literally at the end of the veranda. All he had to do was go out, grab three or four logs and bring them back. He went outside in slippers.'

Craw hadn't mentioned that.

If I was to run with the theory that he'd instigated his own disappearance, then the fact that he didn't take his wallet or his phone made a certain kind of sense: the contents of his wallet – bank cards, driver's licence – made him traceable, as did the technology on his mobile phone. But if you were planning on leaving, if you knew you were about to exit your life for good, would you really head out on to moorland, in the embers of winter, in your slippers?

It could have been another way of disguising his intentions, and there was nothing stopping him leaving a change of clothes somewhere close by. But something struck me: Ellie had been the one to ask *him* to leave the house, not the other way around. What if she'd never asked? Or what if the fire hadn't gone out as fast that night? What if they'd already had enough logs stored inside the house?

He wouldn't have gone out at all.

Either way, having watched the video Craw shot, I could picture the scene more clearly now: Ellie emerging from the kitchen and realizing he hadn't returned; heading outside and calling his name.

'I know this sounds like a weird question,' I said to her, 'but do you remember if, in the days after he disappeared, you noticed that any of his clothes were missing?'

'Missing?'

'Or maybe a backpack? You said you were both walkers, so I'm guessing you'd have a backpack of some description. Did you ever notice that disappearing before 3 March?'

'No,' she said. 'No, I didn't. I still have it.'

That didn't necessarily discount the idea of him storing a bag somewhere: he could have just bought a new one. 'So when he didn't come back, you headed straight outside?'

'Yes.'

'And what did you find?'

'Nothing. He wasn't at the woodshed. I took a

walk all the way around the house, as he has this rickety old toolshed at the back that he sometimes forgets to lock up at night. But when he wasn't there, I came back inside. I figured I must have missed him.'

'You said the sun hadn't yet gone down by then?'

She was lucid enough to see where I was headed. 'No. The day was overcast, so that made the last hour of the day quite gloomy, but I could see clearly in all directions.'

'Down to the village and up to the tor?'

'In all directions,' she repeated, more forcefully. Again, I glimpsed Craw in her. She was sitting back on the sofa now, mug in her lap, the last cords of steam escaping past her face. 'You can hear cars as soon as they get on the dirt road a mile away in Postbridge. On a clear day, you can see people approaching in whatever direction you're facing. That Sunday was grey, but there was no fog. No mist. The policeman Melanie and I spoke to down in Newton Abbot – Sergeant Reed – asked me if it was possible I might have failed to spot Len, but there's just no way: wherever he headed, I'd have seen him.'

I nodded, but the reality was that something had been missed. I'd have a clearer understanding once I'd been to the house and taken in the surrounding land, outside of the boundaries of Craw's home-made movie. Just because Ellie Franks hadn't seen her husband in the moments after he'd failed to come back from the woodshed didn't mean he wasn't there. In terrain like Dartmoor there were ravines, furrows, clefts, wrinkles, each a place to lay low, waiting for it to get dark.

There were countless places to hide.

Or countless places to be hidden.

CHAPTER 12

After I'd thanked Ellie Franks for her time, Craw returned and led me along the corridor off the living room. There were two further doors, both open: one was a study, the other a plain white room that hadn't been furnished with anything other than a desk and chair.

Sitting on the desk were two cardboard boxes.

As we passed the study, I glimpsed two sets of sofas in an L-shape, a glass coffee table, and a PC on a small desk in the corner. There was no chair under it, but there was a stack of books – too far away to make out – piled on top. I wondered if Craw's husband worked from home – the set-up certainly made me curious as to what he did – but when I thought about bringing it up, a way to show an interest and further smooth our transition from adversary to ally, I knew she would hate it. She wasn't a fan of small talk. It wasn't just that she placed a high value on veracity, it was that she was, in her own way, quite awkward, incapable of feigning an interest in things that weren't import-ant to her. Her husband was likely to be very important to her. My interest in him wouldn't be.

As we entered the room beyond the study, I thought again about Leonard Franks, about how Craw had described him the day before – and how she could have been describing herself. She had a resemblance to her mother as well, in all sorts of ways, but it was the traits she shared with her father that gave me a moment's pause. Breaking down Craw was hard, and after thirty-five years of seeing everything human beings were capable of, I imagined Franks would have been even harder. *Dad was private*, she'd said to me. *He internalized everything.* In the end, that didn't just make him less of a communicator.

It made him harder to find.

'This is all Dad's stuff,' she said, placing a hand on top of one of the boxes. Both of them were big: two feet long by about a foot and a half high. 'Obviously the furniture is still back at the house in Devon. Some clothes too. Other stuff as well: his tools are in the shed, his desktop PC in the lounge, nick-nacks, that kind of thing. But the rest is here.'

'There was nothing on his desktop PC?'

'It's ancient. They used it to print off letters, and as a way to get photos off their camera. You can take a look when you head down there.' The rest was implied: *if you don't believe me.*

I flipped the lid on one of the boxes.

Inside it was like a car-boot sale: photographs, old diaries, some books, DVDs, an OS map of Dartmoor. Basically, an orderless cross-section of his life.

'Have you been through this?'

She nodded. 'Many times.'

I found more of the same in the second box, although there was an iPad this time – which Craw had mentioned in her notes – next to a framed photograph of Franks, in uniform, at another police ceremony. He looked much younger in this one, maybe late forties, and was standing on stage somewhere, shaking hands with a uniformed officer. On the other guy's shoulder patch I could see his insignia: an assistant commissioner.

Next to the iPad was a mid-range SLR camera and shoebox on its side, an elastic band around it. I reached in and brought out the SLR first. As I started to scroll through the photos on its tiny digital screen – beginning with pictures of Ellie standing on their veranda – Craw said, 'All the pictures on there are on the iPad if that makes it easier.'

'All of them?'

'Every single one. I've checked about fifty times. Of course, you'll want to make sure, though.' She phrased it vaguely like an insult, but I let it go, placing the camera back inside, and she gestured to the shoebox. 'All his notebooks are in there. Before iPads and smartphones came along, Dad was a paper man – he wrote *everything* down.'

'That's good for me.'

'The iPad's his, but they both used it. Mum took a lot of video on it, so she could show me what they'd been up to when I went down to see them.

I guess we both kind of forced him into buying it after he retired because they were down there in the middle of nowhere, and Mum worried that he'd go a bit stir-crazy after spending his life in the city.' She pointed at the SLR. 'But the truth was, he was fine. He really got into his photography, followed his sport, planned out hikes, kept in touch with friends.'

'Friends like Carla Murray and Jim Paige?'

She studied me, as if she thought I was trying to play her. 'I suppose.'

'You don't know either of them?'

'I know Jim pretty well, Carla not so much.'

I plucked the iPad out of the box. Franks had synced his Gmail account to the Mail app, and although I'd already been through all the conversations he'd had with ex-colleagues in the police force, I could see more clearly now, after speaking to Ellie, why she'd described Paige and Murray as being her husband's two closest friends at the Met.

In the email chain with Murray, there were one hundred and sixty-seven messages over the course of the two years Franks had been retired. In one, Murray even directly referenced the number of cases they'd worked together. *I reckon it was one hundred and thirty-nine*, she said. I could see the level of comfort they had in each other's company, how they used the same unofficial shorthand ('the hole' was the commissioner's office; the weekly stats they had to compile were 'Dumbers' instead of numbers), and while they both stuck to the same subjects – she: office politics, promotions, government budget cuts; he: renovations, Dartmoor, retirement – it gave a clear sense of their relationship.

The only thing that really caught my attention this time was the frequency of the emails in the five weeks before his disappearance. Before 27 January, they were in touch with each other at least once a week; sometimes second or third emails were only short replies to previous messages, but clearly both Franks and Murray felt compelled enough to reply. And yet, after 27 January, up until his disappearance on 3 March, emails dropped right off: one exchange in the first week; nothing in the second; an email from Murray that Franks didn't reply to in the third week; another from Murray in the fourth week that Franks *did* reply to; and then nothing in that final week before he vanished. The tone of the emails hadn't changed: they were still friendly, and they were both still talking about the same sort of things – so why the sudden drop-off in volume?

I wanted to speak to her, and wanted to speak to Jim Paige too. He and Franks had come up through the ranks together and been friends ever since. A friendship over that period of time forged bonds that couldn't easily be broken, and some-times led along roads you might not travel for anyone else. Their conversations were chummier than the ones with Murray, and less reverent: she still treated him with respect, even while they joked around, whereas Paige called him 'Len' and 'General Franko', and constantly had fun at his expense. Like those with Murray, though, Jim and Franks's conversations had a real warmth to them. And as I moved through the emails with a fresh sense of the role Paige had played in Franks's life before retirement, things began to crystallize further: other colleagues who had been at their pay scale, the social circles they'd moved in, their love of being out on the golf course, memorable tales from a Met skittles league they'd both played in. The emails contained fine detail too, like the name of their local pub, a place called the Hare and Badger, which they both spoke of fondly, and which Paige talked up for serving real ale. It was one of the only times the pair of them got senti-mental. In a conversation from 2012, where Franks mentioned that he missed their 'weekly chinwag at the Badger', Paige said things weren't the same since he'd gone.

'I'd like to speak to them.'

'Murray and Paige?' Craw asked.

I nodded. 'Murray says she worked one hundred and thirty-nine cases with your dad. That's a lot of cases. One of those might have a connection to the file he was sent.'

'That's going to be hard.'

'Why?'

'Why do you think? As soon as I do the intro-ductions, they'll know I've hired you to find Dad. Jim's an old family friend – but he's also part of the Met top brass. One call to my super and I'm on disciplinary. I didn't get into this to end up with the sack.'

'You got into it to search for your dad.'

A flash of frustration in her face.

'Look,' I said, 'I get what the risks are, but if you want to find out what happened to him, you're going to have to help me out a bit.'

She paused, annoyed that I wasn't backing down. Then her faced softened: she'd thought of something. 'Actually, there might be a way.' She stopped a second time, her mind turning over. 'There's a Met charity event tonight at a wine bar on Millbank. It's mostly cops, but there are some Whitehall suits, journalists – you shouldn't look too out of place. Unless, that is, you run into one of your many friends on the force.'

I smiled. 'Murray and Paige will be there?'

'Paige will. I don't know about Murray. Like I say, I don't know her that well – only to say hello to, and only through Dad. Do you want me to get you a ticket?'

'Can you get me two?'

She frowned, instantly suspicious. 'Who you planning on bringing – *Healy*? That should liven things up a bit. I think he's got even fewer friends in blue than you have.'

'No. I haven't seen Healy for over a year.'

Despite the way she'd spoken his name, a sadness lingered in her face. Colm Healy was a failed project of hers, a cop she'd tried to bring back from the hinterland, someone she'd rescued from the ignominy of suspension, but who had ultimately betrayed her trust. I'd known him even longer than Craw, but saw the same person as her: a man full of anger and bitterness, whose aggression was a way to subdue his own failings; and then the heartbroken soul drifting in the shadows beneath, still deeply affected by the death of his daughter, and a case that destroyed his life. I hadn't talked with Healy for a long time; it sounded like Craw hadn't either – but in a strange way he remained the one thing we had in common.

'Any idea what he's up to these days?' she asked.

'No.' But then I remembered something I'd said to Annabel the previous day: *I've found that life has a way of tethering you to certain people.*

It was Healy I'd been thinking of when I told her that. We weren't friends exactly – perhaps never would be, at least conventionally – but there was something between us: a kinship, a connection, some kind of subtle, unspoken duality. After Craw had fired him in June 2012, I'd offered to put him up at my parents' old place in south Devon while I recovered from being stabbed. He'd had nowhere else to go, and – as he was one of the major reasons I hadn't ended up dying that day – I felt I owed him for helping save my life. But then he'd come back to London five months later, in November, and I hadn't heard from him in the thirteen months since. I'd tried calling him, but he'd never called back. In the end, I figured he wanted it that way.

'So,' she said, 'if not Healy, then who?'

'I'd like to bring my daughter.'

She frowned. 'I didn't realize you were a father.'

'Neither did I until a year ago.'

She studied me a moment longer. 'Fine.'

'Thank you.'

'For obvious reasons, though, I can't—'

'I get it. I'm on my own.'

Craw watched as I placed the iPad back and took out the shoebox that had been sitting next to it. I got the feeling that she was wondering what she'd signed herself up for with the charity event, but I didn't say anything; this would probably be my only shot at Paige, and deep down, despite the reservations she had as a professional, her feelings for her father were pulling her in the opposite direction. She knew it had to be done.

I flipped the lid off the shoebox.

Inside was a series of black A6-sized diaries, spines facing up, each with a gold-foil year printed on it. At one end of the box was 1982; at the other, 1994. There were also two bigger A5 notebooks, thicker, with white covers. There were no dates on their spines. I picked one of them out and could see it had been used as much more than a diary: Franks had marked dates off, scribbled in meetings and reminders, sketched out crime scenes, listed theories and stuck in Post-its.

I held the shoebox up to Craw. 'Have you been through these?'

'Yes.'

'And you didn't find anything?'

She shook her head. 'But that doesn't mean there isn't something worth finding. I worry that I'm too close – to him, to the life he led, to his career as a cop.'

'Can I take all this stuff with me?'

'That's what it's all here for.'

Briefly, something passed across her face. She'd probably spent the past twenty-four hours wondering if involving me was a good thing, not because she didn't trust my abilities or my instincts, but because she had to accept her part in this was over. I was talking to her mother and to her. I was taking home the cardboard boxes and being given the keys to the Frankses' house on Dartmoor. All of a sudden, this was my case, not hers.

Now all she could do was wait.

CHAPTER 13

The steakhouse was at the northern end of Long Acre, halfway between Covent Garden and Kingsway. After I left Craw's place in Wimbledon, I called Annabel and gave her directions to the restaurant, and then found a space in a car park close to Waterloo. The walk across the river was cold, wind rolling down the Thames like a wave, and by the time I got to the Strand, sleet was drifting out of the sky and I was chilled to the bone.

The place was called Gustavo's, after the owner. It was at the far end of a long, narrow cul-de-sac and was wedged between a property firm and an advertising agency. Instead of the bland, silver-grey panels of the businesses that surrounded it, its front was mostly all glass, potted bay trees sitting either side of its door, a striped canvas awning pulled all the way down, protecting lunchtime smokers from the sleet.

Inside it was done out in dark wood panelling, booths lined up around its edges, tables in the middle. It was small, but it was warm and the food smelled good. I asked for a booth at the window, looking back up the alley, so I could see when Annabel arrived.

I'd grabbed a backpack from the car and thrown in some stuff from the boxes that Craw had given me, including more photos, Franks's iPad and the two white notebooks. A lot of the contents of the boxes, even at a quick glance, I knew wouldn't come to much – old golf trophies, dog-eared airport thrillers, comedy snowglobes – but the iPad and notebooks were different. I unzipped the bag and took everything out.

The photos were a good spread, but nothing I hadn't seen before. This collection leaned much more towards his work life than his home life: time-bleached shots of him sitting on the edge of a desk in a Santa hat at an office Christmas party; flanked by three other cops, what looked like a CID office in the background, all striking comedy poses; a serious picture of him at his desk; in plain clothes again, arms crossed, on a stage, listening to someone off camera; and an official police photograph, in full uniform.

Midway down the pile, sandwiched between interchangeable pictures of his career, was the only photo that didn't include him. Not him, not his work, not the police, not his family. Instead, it was a discoloured shot of Dartmoor, taken in the depths of winter, the ground covered in a blanket of frost. There were swathes of bracken rising up out of the chalk-white grass and – in the spaces between – huge moss-covered boulders, scattered as if they'd dropped from the sky. Whoever had taken the picture was elevated, maybe even on a tor, looking down a valley between two sweeping hillsides. Nestled in the cleft at the bottom was a tiny stone bridge and, behind that, the silhouette of a spire. The drop from the point at which the picture had been taken, to the bridge, must have been eight hundred feet, and a stream – silvery in the soft morning light – ran almost the entire way.

I turned the picture slightly, holding it up to the light.

On the left, built in a natural plateau on the hillside, was what remained of a tinner's hut, a square of grey rubble embedded in the grass where the foundations of a house had once stood. My eyes drifted to the spire again, trying to imagine where the shot might have been taken. If it was a spire, it was a church. If it was a church, that probably meant a village. It wouldn't have been Postbridge because there was no church with a spire, but it was definitely Dartmoor: the bracken, the hut, the moorland. So why would Franks place this alongside photos from his life at the Met? Or was it here by mistake?

I set the picture aside and shifted my attention to his iPad.

His applications were spread across two pages, but the desktop had changed very little from how it would have looked, box-fresh, from the factory. He hadn't divided any of them into sub-folders or tried to order them in any way, and the few additions he'd made didn't stand out: BBC iPlayer, 4OD, Skype, Sky Go, a rambler's app, maps for walkers. I logged in to Skype to see what his contacts list looked like and found only two names: Craw and her brother. In Videos, he'd added nothing; in Music, there were ten songs, all classical; there were no names in his Contacts, no Reminders or Notes, no magazine subscriptions in Newsstand.

I'd already been through his email, so I moved on to Safari, tracing Franks's web history back. His life on the Internet seemed to reflect his taste in apps: walks around Dartmoor, sport, a little TV and film – and repeat visits to an amateur photography site, specifically their tutorials on how to take better pictures with the type of SLR he had.

Tapping on Photos, I found two hundred and five pictures and twenty-one videos. There were plenty of pictures of the house before and after they'd moved in, some of them renovating it, some of Craw and her family on its veranda, one of Franks at the side of the property, repairing something on their Audi – but mostly they seemed to be landscapes.

Ellie stood in a number of them, framed by stark, stunning scenery: hills rolling away into the grey mist of morning; sun falling out of the sky behind her; open farmland, cows grazing, a tor rising into half-light. I took a second look at the physical photo I'd set aside, of the valley and the remains of the tinner's hut. It was of the same ilk. He was an amateur photographer, interested enough to spend hours on the Internet finding out how to take better pictures. It made sense he'd tried to capture this part of the world.

I didn't have any headphones with me, so I turned the volume down and started to go through the videos. They were dotted among the photos, and it was easy to establish a pattern: all the pictures had been taken on Franks's SLR, transferred to their desktop PC at home and then across to the tablet. All the videos had been taken directly on the iPad.

The first video had been shot two months after their move to Dartmoor, Ellie on camera, Franks putting a sledgehammer through a dividing wall in the living room. I remembered what Craw had said on the video she'd shot of the house: *This room used to be divided into two, but Dad knocked the wall down when they moved in.*

This was the first time I'd seen him in motion, his thinning silver hair – parted to one side – soaked with sweat, his six-one frame still lean, despite a slight paunch. He moved cautiously at first, as if conscious of the limitations of his body, but then – as he began to swing the sledgehammer – he got into a rhythm and his age became irrelevant: even in his early sixties, he was still strong and powerful, returning again and again to the wall until all that was left of it was ragged plasterboard, wooden struts and dust.

'Did you enjoy that?' Ellie said, the microphone

on the iPad distorting slightly as she strayed too close to it. Franks was clearing debris away from what little remained of the wall. He looked back over his shoulder at her and broke out into a smile. I'd seen him smile in pictures Craw had given me, but not like this: sweat glistened on his face, soaked through his clothes, and he was out of breath. But he was relaxed. The smile was real.

He straightened. 'You spying on me?'

'Just a little.'

'I think I preferred full-time employment to this.'

She chuckled and ended the video there.

Others painted an even clearer picture of the Frankses' lives in retirement: movies of the house taking shape, as Franks first finished the donkey work, then a succession of tradesmen came in and transformed the living room; the two of them planning out their next project – the kitchen – talking about budgeting, about how it might look, Ellie always filming, which seemed to confirm her husband's love was in still photography, not in film. There were smaller moments too. Ellie videoing her husband as they climbed a tor, wind crackling in the microphone, disguising their voices; Leonard saying something to her, seemingly having good-natured fun at her expense, then holding out a hand towards her to help her across a stream. Finally, Ellie trying to capture them both, using the iPad's reverse camera function – while Franks pretended to take a picture of her trying to take a picture of them, using the SLR around his neck.

This was where video and photographs were so different. Most photographs only scratched the surface: how a person looked that day, what they were wearing, where the picture was taken. But video was different: these moments between the two of them were everything I needed to know about their relationship, a natural and genuine cross-section of their life, brought alive and played out in front of me. If I'd had any doubts about their marriage at the end, if I'd entertained the idea he might have left without feeling anything for his wife, they'd been extinguished.

This is what photographs can never give you, I thought.

And yet, a few seconds later, my eye was drawn away from the films, back to the physical photograph I'd set aside.

Because I'd spotted something.

CHAPTER 14

Leonard and Ellie had begun using the iPad in April 2011, presumably shortly after it had been given to Franks, and around the time he'd retired. As I scrolled through the list of photos and videos, each broken down by date, I noticed the same picture I'd found in the box – of the valley, the tinner's hut and the church spire – was also in digital form on the iPad.

Except it wasn't *exactly* the same.

The physical copy was old and discoloured. It was impossible to tell how old, but it had been in the box, lost among his other photos, for a long time. Yet even taking into account its age, it was clear that the picture had originally been taken on 35mm film, not digitally. It wasn't an ultra-crisp image constructed from tens of millions of pixels. It had the slightly smeared, tinted quality of film – or, at least, film in the hands of an amateur.

However, every picture he had on his iPad was digital: high quality, pixel-perfect. *Every* picture. That included the one of the valley, although it was subtly different from the physical version: it was taken from *almost* the same angle but not quite; it was framed the same way, but zoomed in a fraction more; there was frost – just not as much; and, on the right-hand side, further down the valley, was something new: fence posts. I checked the date it was last modified: 12 April 2012. The year after they retired to Dartmoor.

It's the same location – but years later.

He'd been back to the valley, for whatever reason, and tried to take a like-for-like photograph. But why? Because the physical copy was degrading? My eyes moved over the newer, digital version and recalled my conversation with Ellie: *We used to go down to Devon a lot, particularly in our fifties. Len loved the peace down there. In our later years, we became big walkers, and Dartmoor was just a place we fell in love with.*

There were all sorts of reasons there might be two slightly different versions of the same valley, taken years apart. Perhaps it was a place that was special to them, and Franks wanted to remember it. Maybe this was the place Ellie talked about, the place that made them fall in love with Dartmoor. Or maybe it was their favourite hiking spot.

I grabbed my phone and dialled Craw's home number, banking on her mum still being home. Ellie answered after five rings. We talked politely for a minute, and then I asked her about the photograph. She seemed to miss the point initially.

'Oh, Len loved photography. After he retired he said he wanted to spend more time getting into it.'

'I'm thinking of that one picture in particular.'

121

'Why that one?'

I didn't know why, I just knew something about it – and the fact that there was a newer, almost-duplicate version – didn't sit right. Without all the facts to hand, it felt like it wasn't worth leading her down that road yet, so I massaged the truth. 'I'm pretty sure I know where most of these pictures were taken. But not this one. I don't think it's taken at Postbridge. There's a valley with a church spire in the distance, and a tinner's hut on—'

'A what?'

'A tinner's hut. Those piles of rubble you see out on Dartmoor, they're what the tin miners used to live in, before the industry collapsed.'

'Ah, right. Yes, of course.'

'Anyway, this shot I have, it's got a church spire in the distance, and a tinner's hut on the left. Does that ring any bells? Maybe this was a place you and Leonard loved?'

'I'm not sure.'

'That doesn't sound familiar?'

'It's hard to say without seeing it.'

'Okay. Are you on email there, Mrs Franks?'

'Ellie. Yes, I am.'

'Could I email the picture to you, just to be sure?'

'Yes, of course.'

She gave me her email address.

I took a camera-phone picture of the photograph and emailed it straight through to her.

'Would it be possible for you to have a look at that right now for me?' I asked.

'Yes. Okay.'

'That's great. Thank you.'

After I hung up, I put the physical version of the picture next to the iPad version and took them both in. The differences seemed even starker now.

A couple of minutes later, Ellie called back.

'No,' she said. 'I don't recognize that at all.'

'You never went there with Leonard?'

'No. Not that I remember, anyway.'

'You don't know what church that is in the background?'

'No. Sorry.'

I looked at the pictures. 'Did he ever go hiking by himself, without you?'

'Very rarely.'

'But it happened sometimes?'

'Yes,' she said. 'Sometimes.'

'Was it generally when you were busy doing other things?'

'Generally.'

'But not always?'

'No.' And then she said quietly, 'Sometimes he just liked to be alone out there.'

CHAPTER 15

A couple of minutes later, as I was finishing my coffee, Annabel arrived, face red raw from the cold, hair matted to her scalp by the sleet.

'I look like a drowned rat,' she said.

'You look fine to me.'

'You're biased.'

'Well, that's true. How was the big city?'

She smiled. 'I ended up having to imagine what the London Eye looks like from the top, because I didn't want to remortgage my house in order to pay for a ticket.'

'But everything else?'

'Everything else was great. The bus tour was fun, the Tate was *amazing*. I loved riding the Tube too, though I'll never understand how people put up with it at rush hour. There must be nothing worse than having to spend ten minutes sniffing a stranger's armpits.'

'You're lucky if you've got a commute that keeps the pit-sniffing to ten minutes, believe me.'

We both ordered a steak, and she asked about my morning, so I told her how I'd been down to

Wimbledon, but kept the rest of it deliberately vague; not because I didn't trust her with the details, but because I didn't want her to know Leonard Franks was still buzzing around my head, or to think that this meal, and her visit, weren't important to me. But then I started to feel guilty, and remembered how I'd vowed never to lie to her or keep anything back. So I told her how he'd gone missing, and what I'd been asked to do.

'He walked out of the house and never came back?'

I nodded.

'So where did he go?'

'I don't know.' I pulled a glass of water towards me. 'You know Dartmoor just as well as I do. That place is vast, but it's desolate. You get the right spot there, you can see for miles. From the photographs I've seen, it looks like they had a clear, unimpeded view of the surrounding valley. So if Franks was out there in the minutes after he decided to make a break for it, or somebody decided to do it for him, he should have been visible.'

'But he wasn't visible?'

'No.'

'Don't you think that's a bit . . .'

'Weird?'

She shrugged. 'I was going to say "creepy".'

I looked at the picture of the valley. 'Yeah, there's definitely some of that.' After I'd returned the photographs to the backpack, along with the iPad and the notebooks, I said to Annabel, 'Look, I've been invited to a charity event in central London this evening. For the police. I feel I ought to go. It's kind of a two-birds-one-stone thing.'

'Work *and* pleasure?'

'Mostly work.'

She smiled. 'That's fine.'

'I feel bad about it.'

'No, you must go.'

'I was thinking maybe you could come too.'

As our waiter brought a couple of beers over, I studied the expression on her face, the fascination in it, the excitement of being let inside a case, and realized how alien it felt. Derryn had gone before my missing persons cases had got into double figures, and for Liz it had all been too much, and we'd got to a point where I stopped talking about my work altogether. She'd watched me tortured, arrested and left to die, and for her there was no logic in returning to a job like that, a job that had almost cost me everything.

After Derryn and until Annabel, I'd had no one to share my cases with, and I often wondered whether it was part of the reason the missing had become so important to me, why I still kept them stacked on a shelf at home. Often, in my quieter moments, when I had nowhere else to go, I found myself returning to the faces of people I'd helped, an unspoken ritual where I sought inspiration in cases I'd already put to bed. In a small way, perhaps that made me more like Leonard Franks than I'd ever given thought to.

Because we both had secrets.

Except my history, my secrets, were up there on that shelf.

His were somewhere out on Dartmoor.

CHAPTER 16

O nce we got home, Annabel said she wanted to call Olivia, so I gave her a little privacy, grabbed Leonard Franks's boxes from the car and took them through to the spare room. Craw had given me contact details for her brother, so I fired off an introductory email, prepping him for the fact that I might call as part of a follow-up. I'd also told her to let her husband know I might be in touch at some point. But as he'd been left at home with the kids the night Franks disappeared, and in the days afterwards, and her brother was in Australia, it felt increasingly unlikely I'd need to pick up the phone to either of them.

I created a document on the computer and catalogued everything in the boxes, right down to golf trophies and snowglobes. Craw had told me her father's desktop PC was still on Dartmoor, and I'd seen it myself in the video she'd shot, so I still wanted to take a look at that. But for now, as I set the box to one side again, I'd narrowed things down to three clear items of interest: the notebooks, the iPad and the photographs.

This time, I concentrated on the notebooks.

I'd been through the other, more traditional black diaries at Craw's house – the ones covering the years 1982 to 1994 – and they'd been used as straightforward planners. The white notebooks were more than that. As well as being used as a way for Franks to schedule appointments and recall important dates, they'd also developed into a dumping ground for theories, names, crime-scene sketches, printouts, Post-its and receipts.

They were both the same. White, 350-page Moleskines, with an elasticated red band, and an inner pocket stitched into the rear cover where he'd put even more stuff: notes he'd made on separate pieces of paper, presumably when he hadn't had the notebooks to hand; lists of questions; a graph about police stats cut out of a newspaper. It wasn't a diary exactly, because he didn't always add days and months, and he sometimes went weeks between entries, but it was close enough. There were no printed dates inside, just lined pages, but the whole thing was structured with a vague chronology, the first notebook starting with his first day as a superintendent in May 1995. It wasn't all work, either; it had been used for personal reminders too.

'Why the sudden change?' I'd asked Craw at her house.

'What do you mean?'

'Before May 1995, he was using these black diaries,' I'd said, picking one of them out of the box. 'After that, he switched to these white ones and filled them full of anything and everything.' I'd flipped open the inner pocket at the back. 'Look at what he has in here: paper he's sketched ideas on, things he's cut out – there's even a napkin with a list on it.'

She'd shrugged. 'Like I said to you earlier, he was old school. He grew up in a world where paper was the best weapon a cop could have. He always made notes, about everything, even when the Met started to modernize. If he hadn't been given that iPad at the end, he probably would have single-handedly destroyed the rainforest.'

'So he switched to these in May 1995 . . .'

'Because that was when he was promoted to superintendent. I think, when he got that promotion, he felt he needed to step things up even more. Impress the top brass. He could see he'd need to bring his A game, every hour of every day.'

The two notebooks were certainly going to keep me occupied: the first Moleskine covered 1995 through to 2004, and although some of it – like birthday ideas for Ellie – I could immediately discard, it was still nine years of his life. The second covered 2004 through to the day he disappeared, entries getting thinner and less frequent as technology became more prevalent, and especially in the years after he retired in 2011. The last entry, the day before he vanished, was a list of items he needed to collect from a home-improvement store in Ashburton. I remembered Ellie saying they had a leaky roof.

It instinctively felt like there might be answers here; that, even eighteen years after that first entry, some event or bad decision could have come back to haunt him. The biggest secrets were always the ones buried the deepest – but they could still be found. History was fragile. There only needed to be one mistake, one oversight, one misstep, for the entire narrative to crumble. You just had to find the right crack to prise open.

I unclipped the inner pockets at the back of the notebooks, sorting the contents into two piles: 1995–2004 and 2004–13. Each pocket contained a mixture of pages torn from other pads, the backs of letters that Franks had used to jot down notes on, decade-old receipts; in the 2004–13 notebook there was even a birthday card. I started to go through them but soon got lost. In the notebooks themselves there was a logical route, from one date to another, but here there was no order at all: phone numbers without names, names without phone numbers, lists that didn't make sense, receipts for lunches he'd bought or snacks he'd grabbed. The only picture it painted was of a hoarder, someone who was unable to discard, either out of habit or because of some innate fear of losing something important.

It could have been a time issue too: maybe, because of his schedule, he'd got into a routine of putting anything he deemed vaguely important into the notebooks, with the intention of coming back to sort them later. But the longer he went without sorting them, the harder it became for him to remember what mattered and what didn't, and the trickier the system was to understand.

If there was even a system at all.

I went back to the start, and began going through the notebooks again, more methodically this time, adding names and numbers that repeatedly came up to the document I'd catalogued everything else in. After a while, despite some numbers not having names attached, or vice versa, I started to get an even clearer sense – from accompanying notes, from locations he'd included – who the people were he'd worked with, at what point in his career, and in what meetings or cases their paths had crossed. I ignored personal entries for now: social functions, dates spent with Craw and her family, lists of items he needed for home improvements, a kind of ad hoc diary he'd written on a trip to see his son in Australia. I'd come back to those things, because everything needed to be looked at and processed, but for now I concentrated on names and events from his day job, across the eighteen-year period the two notebooks covered.

An hour later, Annabel came through and said she was going to get ready for the police charity event. I told her I'd soon be doing the same. Afterwards, I returned to his diary system, this time concentrating on cases Franks had made a direct reference to.

When he hadn't listed enough specifics for me to get a clear idea of exactly what the case involved,

I cross-referenced what details I *did* have with news stories of the time to get a better overview: using Internet reports, I was able to trace the path of the case, from the first time the story broke, to a suspect being charged, to the day it arrived in court, and then to its conclusion. I kept my notes about each case brief and in shorthand and, by the end, had listed one hundred and forty-four of them, which wouldn't have been anywhere close to every case he worked during the eighteen-year period the Moleskines covered, but it was every case listed inside their covers and it was a decent starting point.

The reason for making the effort was clear: if, as Craw suggested, that last case seemed to affect him somehow, it seemed a reasonable bet that he would have committed some of its details to paper, tried to work out his questions and frustrations inside the covers of the notebooks. Which meant, if true, I just had to locate it in the list.

I went through the cases again, trying to familiarize myself with names, phone numbers, crime-scene locations and investigating officers. I remembered something Ellie had said to me and flipped back through my own pad to part of the conversation I'd had with her earlier. I'd written down verbatim what she'd said: *From a distance, and from what I can remember, it seemed like the type of file you'd expect the police to compile. I mean, it was in a folder – a beige one, I think. Just a standard A4 loose-flap folder.*

It wasn't an official police file – that much

seemed obvious now. But then my eyes moved to a note I'd made the day before: *Was the sender an ex-cop?* That would explain it being tidy and well put together. It explained how someone could compile a compelling case, know what they were doing, what details to make available to Franks – and what might get him to sit up and take notice. The alternative, of course, was that it wasn't an *ex*-cop at all – it was a serving cop, working something off the books.

Serving cops like his friends Murray and Paige.

I studied the document I'd put together and zeroed in on their names. There was no doubt that – just as in his email inbox – those two were the most dominant forces in his diary system. Mentions of Carla Murray mostly seemed to be in relation to individual cases, first as Franks's number two, then – as the years went on and Franks started climbing the ladder – as his most trusted investigator; Jim Paige was referenced mostly in social events – golf days and fund-raisers – but also in a series of meetings between command leaders.

Returning to the contents I'd removed from the inner pockets of the Moleskines – the scraps of paper, the Post-it notes, the birthday card, lists, everything he'd scribbled on to – I did what I hadn't done first time round: I dumped anything that didn't feel relevant. The two piles were a graveyard of random ideas, snatched moments, of things Franks had probably thought were important to note down – there and then in someone else's office, or in a meeting – but which he most likely never looked at again. In truth, it wouldn't have surprised me if, a week after adding something to the diaries, he forgot what they were even in reference to. Even so, by the end, a couple of things had caught my eye: one from the 1995–2004 notebook, and one from the second.

The first was a scrap of paper with a drawing on it.

The second was a pub flyer.

The scrap was a piece of torn, lined paper about four inches across. On it, Franks had drawn something in biro:

Next to that, he'd written, 'BROLE108'. There was no date on it, no indication as to when it might have been added, other than at some point between 1995 and 2004. When I checked it against the document I'd created, of all the crime scenes he'd listed in the notebooks, I didn't find a single case that featured the name 'BROLE108'.

I grabbed my phone, took a photograph of the sketch and dialled Craw's mobile. She didn't answer, so I called her home number. Ellie picked up. After a brief conversation, I said to her, 'Does the word "BROLE108" mean anything to you?'

'No. Whatever is that?'

'I just found a reference to it in Len's notes.'

'Do you think it's a code for something?'

My eyes flicked between the scrap of paper and the pub flyer. 'Maybe. Difficult to say at the moment. What about the number 108 – does that have any significance?'

'One-oh-eight? No.'

'The letters B, R, O, L and E. Could they stand for something?'

'They could do, I guess.'

'But nothing Len ever mentioned?'

'No.'

'I've just sent you another email. Could you take a look?'

She put the phone down. About a minute later she was back on the line, having looked at the sketch. 'What's that?'

'You don't recognize that either?'

'No.'

I set the scrap of paper away from everything else and moved on to the pub flyer. It was for a place called the Hare and Badger. I instantly recalled the name from an email that Franks and Paige had passed back and forth in 2012. It was on Broadway, close to the entrance to St James's Park station and within spitting distance of Scotland Yard. Paige had talked it up for its ales, and then the conversation had got softer and Franks had said he missed their weekly pint. Paige responded by saying things hadn't been the same since Franks retired. That exchange stuck with me because it was one of the few times they'd tried to articulate their friendship. It suggested the pub held good memories for both of them, that it had become special, a part of their routine.

The front of the flyer was advertising a promotion. *Banish those New Year blues!* it screamed. *Our mighty triple-decker sandwich on home-made rustic bread, plus an ale of your choice, only £7 – this lunchtime and every lunchtime this month!* Below were the terms and conditions. The promotion ran from 1 February to 28 February 2013.

I still had Ellie on the phone, so I said to her, 'Do you remember if you and Leonard travelled up to London back in February? Maybe you came to see Melanie?'

'February . . .' A pause. 'Uh, I'd have to check my diary.'

'Can you do that for me?'

'Yes. Okay. If you think it might help.'

I heard her place the phone down again. As I waited, I returned my attention to the flyer and flipped it over. The reverse was unprinted and blank, except for random doodles Franks had made – yet something about them caught my eye.

'Got it.'

Ellie was back on the line.

'Any luck?'

'Yes. That second weekend in February. We spent a couple of days with Melanie. On the Monday, there was a lecture at the Black Museum that Len said he wanted to see. It was an all-day thing, so

I dropped him off and then picked him up again later on.'

The Black Museum was the nickname given to Scotland Yard's Crime Museum. It wasn't open to the public, but police and invited personnel could attend lectures on forensic science, pathology and investigative techniques, and see the murder weapon of Jack the Ripper, or the protective apron worn by the acid-bath murderer John Haigh.

'Did Len go to the lecture with Melanie?' I asked.

'No. She was busy at work.'

'So he went on his own?'

'No,' she said. 'He met Jim Paige there.'

I thanked her and hung up, then returned to the flyer and to the doodles Franks had made on its reverse. He could have made them during a break in lectures, when he and Paige had headed across the road to the Hare and Badger for a drink and a bite to eat. Or he could have made them later on, somewhere else, having taken the flyer with him. But, whenever he began drawing them, it was clear – that day – something else was preying on his mind.

Because in among the doodles was a two-line list.

1. *Milk?*
2. *Double-check 108.*

'One-oh-eight,' I said quietly.

Years before, he'd written the same number on the scrap of paper.

THE BOYFRIEND

July 2005 | Eight Years Ago

T he corridor was sterile and cool, walls painted a neutral white, doors a uniform blue for as far as she could see. This part of the hospital was always quiet. Whenever she sat and waited for her appointment, she'd hear occasional hushed conversations, doors opening and closing, trolleys being wheeled along the linoleum, but not a lot else. When two nurses emerged from either side of her, saying something to one another as they passed, it felt out of the ordinary. Mostly, whenever she waited for Garrick, she waited in silence.

Her eyes returned to his door.

He had his name stencilled on it now: Dr John W. Garrick.

It had been six months since Garrick had replaced Poulter, and she had to admit that slowly, perhaps reluctantly, she'd found herself taking to him. In a way, they were all the same, piling questions on top of questions. And yet what she liked about Garrick, what made him different from Poulter, and from the others she'd seen, was that he wasn't a complete blank: he didn't shut her down the moment she asked him who he was, what his opinions were, what mattered to him. He didn't give much of himself away either, but he at least met her part of the way. That was enough. She didn't want to feel like she was returning to this place to talk to a blank wall. She wanted the comfort of another voice.

A few minutes later, he came to the door.

'How have you been feeling this week?' he asked, beckoning her in.

'I've been feeling good,' she said.

Garrick watched her sit down opposite him, and then seated himself in his black leather chair. He crossed one leg over the other, put one hand on the arm of the chair and laid the other flat to the desk next to him. She looked at his desk. There were never any pictures on it.

'You've been feeling good?' He smiled. 'Well, that's excellent.'

He watched her get comfortable, pulling a pad across the desk and flipping open the front page. He removed his fountain pen from the spiral binding. Right down to his choice of pen, he had an old way about him, older than his fifty-something years. He moved smoothly, purposely, was quick-witted and smart, so it wasn't physical.

It was something else.

Sometimes she wondered whether the fountain pen was him trying to recapture the feeling of some past point in his life. Maybe it was a line in the sand for him, an anchor, something to connect him back to a longed-for notch in his timeline. She wondered these things because she was the same. She'd frequently thought about getting another dog, the same breed and colour as Bear, a living, breathing memory that might tether her to a time in her life when things had been better.

'Are you okay?'

She looked at him, realizing she'd drifted off. He shifted in the chair, his slight frame coming forward, the pad on his lap now, pen in his long fingers, a half-smile on his face.

'Yes,' she said. 'Sorry.'

'You don't have to apologize.'

'I was just thinking about the past.'

'Past regrets?'

She rolled her head from side to side. 'I suppose.'

'We've talked a lot about those regrets over the past six months. Lucas's death. The impact that had on you. Your suicide attempts. Your divorce from Robert.'

'I wasn't thinking about Lucas, or Robert.'

'So, if not your son, or your ex-husband, then what?'

There was a single window in the office, about two feet above their heads. She couldn't see anything from where she sat, but there were birds out there, swipes against the blue, drifting in the cloudless sky.

'It doesn't matter,' she said.

He didn't say anything. She knew all their tricks by now: his silence was a way to coax the information out of her, or to tell her he didn't agree. But she didn't fold.

Instead she changed the subject.

'I've met someone,' she said.

Garrick seemed surprised. 'Really?'

'He works on a building site.' Her eyes fell from the high window and, before she knew it, a smile had crept across her face. 'Not where I usually look for my men.'

Garrick laughed. 'But that's okay.'

She nodded.

'How do you feel about it?'

'Feel about it?' She shrugged. 'I haven't been with anyone since Robert and I got divorced, so I suppose I'm nervous. What if dating has changed over the past five years?'

'I'm pretty sure it hasn't.'

'Yeah, but when was the last time you dated?'

'Admittedly, quite a while ago.'

She smiled again. 'Well, we'll see.'

'How did you meet him?'

'He gets the same bus as me in the morning.'

'You just got chatting?'

'Yes.'

'Are things going well?'

She shrugged. 'It's only been a few weeks, but I think it's going okay. He's rough around the edges, but he seems quite fun. I figure I probably need a bit of fun in my life.'

'Of course. What's his name?'

'Simon.'

'What have you and Simon done together?'

'He took me for a curry on our first date.'

Garrick nodded, a knowing smile moving across his face. In one of their sessions a few months before, they'd ended up talking about eating out and she'd told him she wasn't a big fan of Indian food.

'Why didn't you tell him you preferred to eat somewhere else?'

'I felt sorry for him.'

'Why?'

'He was trying so hard.' She looked down into her lap. 'Like I say, he's rough around the edges; different from the sort of men I've dated before. Usually I wouldn't even contemplate going out with a man who thinks Da Vinci is the name of a pizza restaurant, but when he started talking to me at the bus stop . . .' She paused. 'I felt like I wanted to take a risk.'

'A risk?'

As her fingers laced together in front of her, she looked up at Garrick again. 'I get the sense there's something up with him; that he's carrying something . . .'

'Something he's not telling you about?'

'That's what I want to find out.'

'Why?'

'I like to know who I'm dating.'

Garrick paused, his eyes fixed on her, his forefinger tapping out a gentle beat on the fountain pen. 'So you're dating him in order to find out what secret he's keeping back?'

She shrugged again. 'I don't know.'

'Do you find him attractive?'

143

'He's okay.'

'You don't find him stimulating.'

'I never said that.'

'You said he thought Da Vinci was a pizza restaurant.'

'That was a joke.'

Garrick watched her for a moment more, then noted something down. When he was done, he sat back. 'So what happens when you find out?'

'His secret? I don't know. Maybe I won't.'

'But if you do?'

Her eyes drifted to the high window again, to the square of blue sky visible beyond the room. 'I guess it depends on what kind of secret it is he's keeping from me.'

CHAPTER 17

Four-Seven-Four, the location of the Met charity event, was on Millbank, overlooking Victoria Tower Gardens. Through what remained of the rust-coloured trees, we could see the Houses of Parliament, brightly lit against the dark of a freezing December night.

Inside, the event was in full flow: the buzz of conversation; music playing in the background; a line of televisions above the bar, showing pictures of police officers. Some were in uniform, some plain clothes; some were posing for shots in hospital wards, others out on the streets. I led Annabel through clusters of people I didn't recognize to the bar.

The dress code was smart-casual, but a lot of what I imagined were CID officers had come straight from the office, undone their top button and lost the tie. Most uniforms seemed to have traded in their garb for jeans and T-shirts, and the Whitehall contingent were visible a mile off: suited, mannered, stiff, caught in conversations with cops neither side really wanted, given that budget and manpower cuts were the elephant in the room. I bought us both a drink, then fished out one of the tickets Craw had emailed through.

'Maybe smart-casual means really smart or *really* casual.'

She smiled. 'I feel overdressed.'

She was wearing black heels with a subtle pattern on them that matched her top, mauve trousers and a stylish fitted jacket, buttoned up at the front.

'You look great,' I said. 'I don't know if that's what a father is supposed to say to his daughter, but I'm learning on the job here.'

She smiled again. 'Thank you.'

Although I hadn't admitted as much to Annabel, I was frequently conscious of saying the wrong thing. She was twenty-five, years out from childhood, and I was finding the balance difficult: when you'd been a part of your child's life, when you'd watched them grow, you could grab them and hug them, tell them they were beautiful, that you loved them. There was little to be misconstrued in that. But when they were her age and there was only an eighteen-year gap between you, when you'd spent most of your lives apart, compliments might be felt as improper and hugging her might sometimes be inappropriate.

It was clear Annabel was struggling too, maybe even with the same issues, but definitely with other, smaller things: in the year I'd been taking trips cross-country to see her, she'd yet to call me anything. Not David, certainly not Dad. I didn't expect the latter: for her, it was near-impossible to make that adjustment after a quarter of a century calling someone else that. But, at the very least, I'd hoped for David. I understood the reasons for her reticence, for the conflict that must have arisen in her, but although I liked to suppress it and pretend it wasn't a problem, it hurt just a little. Without a name, it felt like I was just drifting aimlessly through the space between us.

'Are you okay?'

'Sorry,' I said, looking at her. 'Caught in a moment.'

I scanned the room for any sign of Craw, or of Carla Murray and Jim Paige. I'd googled both and had managed to find pictures of them online, Murray sitting in front of a nest of microphones at a press conference, Paige in uniform in a press release, when the Met announced he was heading up Sapphire. The downside was that neither picture was recent, so my idea of how they looked was based on a version of them that had existed six or seven years ago: Murray, a stout, blonde-haired woman in her early forties, with flint-grey eyes and a small mole on the ridge of her jaw; Paige, the total opposite – stick thin, no more than eleven stone, with a shiny, hairless head and warmer, blue eyes.

'I promise I'll make this quick,' I said to Annabel and, as I looked out again, I was surprised to see Melanie Craw break from behind a cluster of people and make a beeline across the room towards me. As was her style, she'd left the dress behind – if she even owned one – and gone with a charcoal-grey trouser-suit, but she'd added a red blouse and red heels. The only time I'd seen her with more colour on was when she'd answered the door to me at her home. In her hand was a glass of red wine. She stopped short of me, nodded once, then introduced herself to Annabel. The two of them chatted politely for a while about Annabel being in London.

'Paige is at the other bar,' she said, turning to me.

'And Murray?'

'She's not here.'

I nodded, looking out across the room to where a second, smaller bar was built in the far corner. Two men were leaning against it, one of them side on to me – his chubby frame straining inside a tight pinstripe jacket – the other slightly turned away, elbows resting on the counter, dressed in a black suit minus the tie. It was Paige. He was in his early sixties, five foot eleven and, except for a tan, looked exactly like the photo I'd seen of him.

'I thought I was on my own tonight,' I said, turning to Craw.

'You are. I'll keep Annabel entertained.'

I looked at Annabel. 'I won't be long.'

She nodded. 'I'll be fine.'

I headed across the room towards Paige.

CHAPTER 18

Paige had the build of a marathon runner, his jacket hanging off him at the shoulders and sleeves, trousers sharply pleated down the front, giving them a comically big look. Physically, he seemed the exact opposite of a man who might run an entire Met command, dealing daily with its complexities, yet what he gave away in size, he made up for in other, less tangible ways. Even as he leaned against the bar, the man in the pinstripe jacket bending his ear about a meeting they'd had, it was clear he had a presence about him, something impossible to pin down, and even harder to teach.

I ordered a bottle of beer and stood at the bar, looking out across the room. The guy in the jacket was talking about statistics, half drunkenly, Paige making the occasional non-committal noise. I waited sixty seconds and then looked over again, and this time Paige met my gaze and his eyes widened into a barely concealed *help me* expression.

This was my in. 'Chief Superintendent Paige?'

The man in the pinstripes stopped mid-sentence, looked back over his shoulder at me and frowned.

'Hold on a minute, pal, I'm right in the middle of something here.'

'It's okay, Al,' Paige said.

'But I wanted—'

'We can talk about this in the morning.'

Al hesitated, his face dissolving into wounded anger, and then nodded to Paige. Flashing a look of disgust at me, he headed off.

I moved into the space he'd occupied.

'Thanks,' Paige said.

I held out my hand. 'David Raker.'

He took it, a crease to his face. 'Raker. Where have I heard that before?'

'Probably alongside a swear word.'

His frown deepened.

'I find missing people. And, often, that means picking up—'

'Where the Met have failed.'

'Your words, not mine,' I said, smiling.

He nodded in return. 'So, given your line of work, I'm assuming you're here tonight because someone's gone missing and we've failed to find them.'

'Actually, no. I'm pointing the finger of blame at Devon and Cornwall Police this time.' I smiled again, trying to keep him onside. 'The person I'm looking for disappeared down on Dartmoor. He left his house to go and get some firewood, and never came back.'

He knew instantly who I meant.

Something changed in his face.

'I'm trying to find Leonard Franks.'

'I realize that.' He studied me. 'For who?'

'His wife.'

'Does Melanie know about this?'

'You'd have to ask Ellie. But given that DCI Craw and I don't have the happiest of histories, and the fact that she's seen me here and hasn't strangled me yet, I'd suggest Ellie's kept it quiet for now. Or, at least, Craw's choosing not to ask.' The only truthful thing in all of that was that Craw hadn't strangled me yet, but I kept my expression neutral. 'So, have you got a moment to talk?'

He eyed me for a second. 'Talk about what?'

'I just wanted to find out—'

'You want the inside track?'

He kept his voice even and controlled, but it was clear his guard was up and instinct had kicked in. When a cop got cornered, this was what happened: they went into lockdown until they figured out if there was an immediate threat to them.

'Have you found out where he went?' he asked.

'No. Not yet.'

'What about why he left?'

I shook my head. 'I've only been on this a few days.'

'You'll be on it a week, a month, a year, believe me. People who get paid to do this for a living couldn't find a trace of him.'

'I don't do this for free.'

A humourless smile. 'I'm sure you don't.'

'Look, I'm not going to endanger your pension

pot here. I just want to talk to you about Leonard Franks. As I understand it, you and he were friends for years – I think you can give me a unique perspective on him. Ultimately, you might help me find him.'

He just looked at me.

'I don't know you from Adam,' he said finally.

I reached into my jacket, got out a business card and held it out to him. 'You won't have to search too hard.'

'You think I care what it says about you on Google?' The atmosphere had soured. He didn't take the card. 'I met you for the first time two minutes ago, now you're trying to screw up an *official case* involving my *best friend*. You think, for one minute, I'm going to jeopardize the search for him by talking to someone who corners me at a bar?'

He wasn't going to play ball because, in truth, he was right: he didn't know me, and had no idea whether he could trust me. I didn't blame him. Problem was, I might not get another chance alone with him, so I either wrote off any potential contribution he made – or I tried to create a common cause. My mind looped back to the pub flyer I'd found; to the lecture that Franks told Ellie he and Paige were attending at the Black Museum.

'Do you remember going to the Hare and Badger on Broadway back on 11 February? I know you two used to like it there. I've seen your email conversations.'

He looked at me. 'Is that right?'

'You remember meeting him that day?'

'That was *ten months* ago.'

'He told Ellie he was going to a lecture with you.'

He didn't say anything.

'At the Black Museum.'

A pause – and then his eyes narrowed.

Something was up, and, inside a couple of seconds, I realized what: Franks had been to the pub that day, but it wasn't to meet Paige. He hadn't been to a lecture with him either. I could tell from his face that the first Paige had heard of any lecture, of any lunchtime meeting with his friend, was now. At best, that meant Ellie had misunderstood what Franks had told her when she'd dropped him off on the morning of 11 February.

At worst, it meant Franks had told her a bare-faced lie.

'What's going on, Mr Raker?'

I saw a subtle shift in Paige's expression. Some of the animosity had dropped away as he realized he wasn't the only one who'd been taken by surprise here.

'I was sitting on a sunlounger on a beach in Tenerife on 11 February,' he said. 'If Len told Ellie otherwise, then I'm afraid . . .' He faded out.

We both knew what it meant.

'I think you can help me,' I said.

His eyes moved from me, out into the room,

his defences up again. He scooped a bottle of beer off the bar counter and started picking at the label. 'How do I know you're not some shithouse reporter?'

'Because I gave up journalism in 2009.'

He looked at me. 'So you *are* a journalist?'

'Was.'

A long, resigned sigh. '*Great.*'

'You can find out everything you need to know about me on the web – or you can log into the police database and get the full A to Z from your fellow boys in blue. I'm not hiding here. This isn't some elaborate ruse. All I want is thirty minutes of your time.'

He sighed, running a hand through his hair, his gaze flicking between the faces gathered around him. He went to speak, stopped himself and looked at me again. Then, finally, he committed, voice suddenly quiet, his attention fixed once more on the crowds. 'I've spoken to Melanie a few times since Len disappeared, and it's the same for the both of us. We're hamstrung. She got read the riot act about using police resources, day one. If I go searching and get found out, I've got even further to fall. So one thing I need to be absolutely clear on is that, if we talk, it's off the record. This stays under lock and key.'

'I can guarantee that.'

'Yeah?' He turned to me. 'I don't know anything about you, so your guarantee is worth absolutely zero to me. With that in mind, let me also give you a guarantee in return: if you cost me even a *second's* sleep, if you drop me in the shit with anyone, even if it's with the guy who cleans the toilets in Scotland Yard, I will make you pay for it. I'm not one for threats, but I mean this: number one priority for me is Leonard Franks.'

'Same here.'

'I need to be insulated.'

'You will be.'

'If it all goes to shit, and there are reasons it might, we never spoke.'

I looked at him. 'Why would it go to shit?'

He emptied the last of his beer, placed it down on the counter and turned to me. 'I'm prepared to tell you, but I'm not doing it here. There's a hotel on Horseferry Road called The Neale. It has a bar in the lobby. I'll meet you there in an hour.'

CHAPTER 19

Annabel and I left the event and grabbed something quick to eat, then I paid for a taxi to take her home and headed south along Millbank. The Neale was a tiny boutique hotel overlooking St John's Garden. Inside it was all marble and brushed steel. I headed past the reception desk towards a semicircular bar area, done out in charcoal sofas and mauve accessories.

Paige was right at the back in a booth.

He had someone with him.

At first, as I approached, it was difficult to see who – they were facing Paige, legs under the table, hand around a beer bottle, mostly disguised by the high back of the booth – but, as I got closer, I realized it was a woman. I could see her nails had been painted a subtle pink, and she was wearing an engagement ring on her left hand. Paige was talking to her, gesturing, but then broke off as soon as he saw me enter the bar.

A second later, she came into view.

It was Carla Murray.

She'd undergone much more of a change than Paige, shifting a ton of weight and growing her hair long. There was still a toughness about her, those grey eyes studying me as I approached, her hair scraped back into a functional ponytail. She must have been five foot nine, perhaps just shy of ten stone, but she'd never be petite, even if she wanted to be: whatever size she'd given away in the time since the photograph of her at the press conference, she'd now replaced with sheer muscle power in the gym.

Paige gestured for me to take a seat opposite him, and Murray shifted along her booth. She introduced herself in a broad Glaswegian accent, but didn't offer her hand.

'Well, this is a surprise,' I said.

Paige nodded. 'I take it you know Carla already.'

'Only from what I've read.'

'Then I guess that'll have to do for now.' He stopped, looking out across the bar, his gaze flicking between tables, ensuring we weren't being watched. 'I realized why I recognized your name earlier,' he said, eyes back on me, a hint of hostility in them. 'I was just telling Carla: you were the one who was all over the Snatcher case Melanie had last year.'

'I'm not sure I was all over it.'

'You ended up getting stabbed because of it.'

'Well, that much is true.'

He watched me for a moment, like he expected me to add something else. When I didn't, he said, 'Lots of people at the Met don't like you, David. You know that, right?'

'I'm not here to make friends.'

'You're here to find people?'

'Right.'

'People like Len Franks?'

I nodded.

He studied me for a moment more, glanced at Murray, then leaned back in the booth, shrugging. 'I care a great deal about finding Len.'

'Then we're all on the same page.' Neither of them made a move to continue, so I turned in the booth and looked at Murray. 'I didn't realize you two knew each other.'

'I've got to know Carla since Len disappeared,' Paige replied for her.

'How come?'

His eyes pinged to Murray and then back to me.

'How come?' I repeated.

Again, Paige didn't reply, and Murray made no effort to fill the silence.

But then Paige started turning his beer bottle and looked up at me. 'There are some things you should know. Things that might help you find Len. Given what you've found out already, what I've read about you, and what people at the Met have told me about you over the phone in the last hour, it's safe to assume you'll keep digging until you get to what we know, anyway. So I'd rather you heard it from me.' Paige gestured to the bar. 'Can I get you a drink?'

'I'm fine, thank you.' When neither of them made an effort to continue, I said, 'Look, anything you tell me will be in complete confidence. I know all you've got to go on is my word, but while I doubt you've heard anything positive about me from whichever colleagues you spoke to at the Met during the last hour, no one there can accuse me of not being able to keep my mouth shut. Whatever you've got doesn't go any further.'

'David,' Paige said, 'if I didn't think that was the case, we wouldn't be here.'

I reached into my pocket and got out my pad and pen, setting them down on the table. When I looked up, Paige and Murray were staring at each other. They didn't try to disguise it. Instead, it was like they were still undecided about whether to move forward.

'There's one thing I need to be *really* clear on,' Paige said finally. 'When we met earlier, I promised I'd come after you if you dropped me in the shit. I meant that. I've had a look at your cases, at some of the places you turned up and people you found, and while everything looks watertight on the surface, I'm confident I could find some anomalies if I chose to look a little harder. This conversation goes anywhere beyond this booth, I'll find holes in those cases, and I'll take you to the cleaners. That's a promise.'

He needed reassurance. 'Understood.'

'Len was, *is*, my best friend. But he made some decisions that were . . .' Paige cleared his throat. 'He made some choices that might have conse-quences. I don't want to speak for Carla, but I know she feels the same way. He was her commanding officer, her mentor, her friend. The choices he made, we need to ensure . . .' He stopped again. 'We need to ensure we don't give them oxygen. Or, at least – if they *are* to be made public – we need to ensure it's an abridged version.'

'So this is a skin-saving exercise?'

'No,' Paige said. 'Far from it. Nothing you find out about Len will have any effect on us. Len's choices are his choices. We were never involved in them. Not at any point.'

'So you're saving *his* reputation?'

'I'm trying to help you find him.'

'Why haven't you tried to go after him yourselves?' I looked between them. 'If you know something, something that will get him found, why not make that available?'

Paige held up a hand. 'It's complicated.'

'So Craw doesn't know about these "choices" Franks made?'

'No.'

It seemed unlikely she wouldn't have asked Paige some questions, though. She knew about Paige and her father's friendship. She'd have asked Paige if he knew why Franks left. She'd have sought him out.

'So,' I said to him, 'what you're saying is you lied to Craw?'

'I chose to keep some things back.'

'Why?'

'For her protection.'

'Craw doesn't strike me as the type who wants to be protected.'

'No one *thinks* they want to be protected. But Melanie has a career, a family. She has a professional obligation to the Met. Her commanding officer told her *specifically* not to use police resources to go after Len, but if I gave her what I had, the pull to find her father would be such that she would go against those orders and get herself fired. You, David . . .' He paused, a wrinkle of distaste in his face. 'You have no obligation other than to yourself. You have nothing hemming you in. This is your entire career. *This* is your family. That makes you impossible to police, and that's why I invited you here. Because this is the only way I can, at least in part, try to limit the damage you'll undoubtedly do. I care about what happens to Melanie because I care about Len Franks. Less kindly, I wouldn't give a shit if you disappeared off the face of the earth tomorrow.'

I couldn't pretend it was the first time I'd heard that. 'So you're the only two who are in on this?'

He nodded.

'Why only you two?'

He nodded a second time, expecting me to ask. 'At the end of January, Len got in touch – separately – with Carla and with me. Afterwards, we both agreed he sounded quite . . . distressed. He said he'd been looking at a cold case and he wanted our help.'

'Okay, hold on. What was the case?'

'He didn't say,' Murray replied.

It was the first time she'd spoken since she'd introduced herself.

'He didn't mention anything about it, to either of you?' I glanced at Murray. She shook her head. 'Did he hint that it might have been an old case he worked here?'

'He didn't say,' Murray said again.

Which meant he'd only referenced the fact that he was working some sort of cold case. Same story he'd spun for everyone, including his family. Craw really hadn't been exaggerating when she said he internalized everything.

'So why did he choose to ask only you two?'

Paige this time: 'I'd known him thirty-odd years. Carla was a trusted lieutenant and worked the most number of cases with him. I think it's pretty obvious why.'

'Why not Craw?'

'Clearly, he didn't want to involve his daughter.'

I thought about what Paige had said earlier in the conversation: *The choices he made, we need to ensure we don't give them oxygen.*

I looked between them. 'So if he didn't call to tell you what case he was looking into, what did he phone up to talk about?'

Paige looked at Murray. She adjusted her sitting position, so she was against the back wall, able to take us both in.

'He didn't say much,' she said. 'The Boss was

never one for flowery language or drawing things out. He just said he was looking into a case, to help pay for his kitchen renovation at the house. "You might be able to help me," is what he said.'

'Help him how?'

'He asked me if I remembered another, separate case we worked together back in 1996. I didn't, not off the top of my head. Seventeen years is a long time in any walk of life, but it's a whole lot longer if you've spent every single day of it standing over dead bodies.'

'Did he try to jog your memory?'

'Yeah. He mentioned the victim's name.'

'Which was?'

'Pamela Welland.'

I wrote it down. 'You remembered her?'

'Yeah, I remembered.'

'What happened to her?'

'She was murdered. Her body was dumped in a patch of wasteland near Deptford Creek; eleven stab wounds to the stomach, one to the back. Pretty frenzied. She'd only turned eighteen a couple of weeks before.'

There was a heavy, funereal pause, as if we were all paying our respects to the girl's memory.

'This was in the days before everyone owned mobile phones,' she went on, 'before online dating – I mean, no one in Pamela's family even owned a computer – so it was much harder to trace a victim's movements. But it looked like she'd been on a date two nights previously, to a bar in Soho.

That was the last time anyone saw her alive. We had a couple of eyewitnesses, including one in the bar that night, and they said they saw Pamela talking to a guy in his early twenties: blond hair, six foot, stacked. Could have been some sort of weights junkie. The witness in the bar said the guy was obviously trying to crack on to Pamela, but she didn't seem to be playing along. I think the exact quote was something like, "She didn't seem to be all that into him." So we go to the bar and secure the CCTV footage, and we grab a list of calls made from Pamela's parents' landline in the days before she meets this guy. A couple of days after that, we've identified the suspect: Paul Viljoen.'

I added his name to the list.

She continued, 'We brought him in. The Boss and I did the interview, and this Viljoen falls apart. He was Dutch, but spoke good English. I think he was here on some sort of work placement scheme. I can't remember exactly. Anyway, he starts out all calm and collected, but once the Boss gets at him, Viljoen starts wrapping himself up in lies. Eventually, he realizes he's in deep, deep shite, so he starts to slip into Dutch, pretending he's not properly making himself understood in English. But it's too late by then. He's already dug his own grave. An hour later, he confesses. Basically, he was just a stupid kid: full of booze, whacked out on steroids. He kept apologizing to us, kept apologizing to her like she was in the room with him, saying he got angry because he thought she'd been

164

laughing at his technique. I guess we'll never know the whole truth. Pamela apparently didn't look interested in him, and the CCTV backed it up. But she must have been interested enough to leave with him.'

'So you charged him?'

'Yeah. He ended up getting twenty years.'

I made a couple more notes, then looked up at her. 'So Franks asked you if you remembered the case. Once he jogged your memory, what happened after that?'

Her eyes moved to Paige, like she was seeking his permission to continue. Paige nodded.

'He asked me if I could get hold of the footage of Pamela Welland.'

'Footage?'

'The footage of her from the bar, the night she was murdered.'

'Why?'

'He seemed reluctant to say why exactly.'

'You didn't ask?'

'I *asked*,' she said, as if I were painting her as an amateur, 'I asked plenty of times. But the Boss just kept saying the same thing: that it had to do with this cold case he was working. Whenever I'd tried to probe further, he'd always find a way to dance around it.'

My mind was already moving: what relevance did the murder of Pamela Welland have to Franks's cold case? Then I thought of the scrap of paper and the pub flyer.

'Does "BROLE108" mean anything to you?'

Murray frowned. 'No.'

'Wait a second,' Paige said, holding up a finger. 'What relevance has that got?'

'I don't know.'

'We're supposed to be *sharing* here.'

'I don't know what it means,' I said, looking at him. 'Franks has got it written down a couple of times in his diaries. I haven't figured it out.'

Paige eyed me with suspicion.

I grabbed a napkin and a pen from my jacket and then drew the sketch that Franks had made on the scrap of paper.

'What about that?' I asked, showing it to them both.

'What about it?' Paige asked.

'Does that seem familiar?'

'What is that – some sort of stick man?'

'I'm not sure.'

I looked at the drawing: the body, arms and legs of the 'stick man', the triangle on its left shoulder, and the oval encasing it all. There was a part of me that felt like I might have seen it somewhere before, but I couldn't put my finger on where. Franks had also written 'Milk?' – above 'Double-check 108' – on

166

the back of the pub flyer, years after he'd made the sketch on the scrap of paper. Weirdly, that had begun to worry me: did a bland reminder to pick up milk mean the sketch and '108' reference were just as unimportant? What if the sketch was just another doodle? What if none of it meant anything?

I pushed the doubts aside and moved on. 'So did you send Franks the footage?'

She shook her head. 'Absolutely not. I'd do anything for the Boss, but I wasn't about to put my job on the line to fish out some seventeen-year-old CCTV film.'

Paige moved his beer bottle across the table, the remains sloshing around at the bottom. He'd peeled away most of the label. 'A day after he called Carla, he got in touch with me. Asked me to do the same thing: see if I could source the footage of Pamela Welland from the pub. He asked Carla as a colleague, as someone who worked that case with him; he asked me as someone he'd known for a long time. I guess, cynically, he played on our friendship.' He paused. 'I found it difficult to say no to Len. But then I went into the system, had a look around and saw Carla had logged in the previous day and been looking at the exact same case. So I picked up the phone and called her.'

'That's how you two got to know each other.'

He nodded. 'She came up to my office, we chatted about it and decided that this should all be kept on the QT. What he was asking was illegal, and could place us both in a great deal of harm.

167

Look at me: I'm fifty-seven years of age. I wasn't about to get caught with my hands in the till when I'm six months away from retirement. I wouldn't expect Carla to either. She still has many important years ahead of her. Helping Len would have been career suicide. So I called him up, and I said we couldn't do it. He was still a friend, so we wouldn't tell anyone about what he'd asked us to do, but we wouldn't be sourcing any CCTV footage, *or* passing on anything else from the database.'

I remembered the drop-off in email frequency between Franks and Murray in the five weeks before he'd left. The tone of the emails hadn't really changed, but their regularity had. In that third week, Franks hadn't even bothered replying to Murray.

Now I understood why.

He was angry, or hurting. Or both.

He hadn't been emailing Paige anywhere close to as often as he had Murray, so if there had been a similar drop-off in the frequency of their contact, it wasn't as noticeable when I'd looked. However, it explained why, in both cases, I hadn't spotted anything out of the ordinary in any of the messages that had moved between Franks and Paige and Murray: no tension between them, no mention of specific cases, no indication there were any problems.

Because they'd hidden it all.

Meanwhile, the most interesting conversation

remained unspoken: why Franks had asked for the footage in the first place.

'Did the Welland murder have any links to his new life in Devon?'

Murray shook her head. 'No.'

'You sure?'

'Why do you think I went hunting around in the database?' she said. 'I wanted to see what his sudden interest in her was, seventeen years after Viljoen went down for her murder. I wanted to see what other case – especially an unsolved – could possibly tie into her death, or whether we'd missed something first time around.' She started shaking her head, ponytail swaying from side to side. 'I went through the file, back to front, front to back, but it was a rock-solid conviction. The police work was perfect. Viljoen was guilty. He *confessed*. There were no mistakes, no slip-ups. There was no reason for the Boss to want to see that footage. Viljoen isn't even up for parole for another three years.'

Murray glanced at me.

She wasn't done, so I didn't interrupt.

'Except the Boss . . .' She stopped again. Some of the steel left her eyes, a sadness emerging for the first time. 'He always took cases like that one hard. Kids. Women. I don't know whether it was a paternal thing, maybe something you get once you've had kids of your own. But as I started to look at the paperwork again, at the way the case played out, I started to recall how invested he'd become in that particular one.'

'Invested how?'

'After he called me in February, I began to go back through the case and I started to remember more and more about the Welland investigation. Little things. Things I'd dismissed as unimportant at the time.' She paused again and looked towards Paige. He didn't move, didn't try to stop her. 'One day, a few weeks after the Boss disappeared, I was sitting around, thinking about him, and this clear memory came to me: of walking into his office – like, five years after Welland died – on a completely different case, with Viljoen already banged up, and finding him watching an old movie on this portable TV he had.'

'What was the case?'

'I don't know. It was unrelated.'

'To Welland?'

'To anything. It's not the *case* that was important.'

I looked at her, momentarily confused.

'It was the movie he was watching,' she said.

Suddenly, it clicked. 'He was watching the CCTV footage?'

Murray nodded. 'Five *years* after that case was put to bed, I walked in and found the Boss watching footage of the night Pamela Welland disappeared.'

RETREAT

July 2008 | Five Years Ago

Crying, she retreated to the loft. She opened the hatch, slid the ladder down and climbed up into the shadows. At one end was a window, looking out over the fields at the back of the house, but otherwise it was dark. There were no bulbs, and she never wanted there to be. She liked its silence and its gloom. It reflected her mood whenever she came up here.

They'd been fighting for a while now. In truth, they'd fought almost from the time they first got together, but at the beginning it was every so often; a blowout followed by a short stand-off, before they came together again, laughed things off, returned to normal.

Or as normal as they got with Simon.

But this one had been bad.

Perhaps the worst yet.

It had started just after breakfast. They'd overslept, which hadn't helped. Her mind had been drifting over the past few months, and she'd spent most of the night lying awake in the dark, listening to the sound of him

171

snoring. He'd come home stinking of booze, and had rolled into bed next to her and immediately fallen asleep. He'd sweated through his clothes, and she could see blood under his nails and a cut down his arm.

She'd seen this same thing over and over during the three years they'd been going out, and had often thought about leaving. She'd told Garrick once that she'd gone out with Simon because he represented a risk, because he was different from the other men she'd dated – and because he was holding something back. Some kind of secret. At the start, she'd had a romantic vision of it being a secret like hers – a loss, an emptiness that could only be filled by someone who recognized it – but instead it was much more base than that: he was stealing building supplies from his employers and selling them on – and he was an aggressive, drunken cheat.

Even so, she wasn't scared of him. She hadn't stayed because she was frightened. She absolutely believed him capable of bad things, had figured out early on that he wasn't just earning money from his job on the site. But it wasn't the fear of his lies, of who he was, or what he might do to her, that kept her here. It was the fear of being on her own. She didn't need to go and see a psychiatrist to know that, and didn't need to look in the mirror to see it in her face. She could feel it deep down in her bones, like a quiet murmur, constantly vibrating.

That's what loss felt like to her: an endless hum.

You had to have a clear sense of your own mortality, of its boundaries, of the risks to it, to fear someone might hurt you or, worse, take your life. She'd lost that when Lucas had died, arms thrashing around above the surface of the pond.

Her beautiful, beautiful boy.

But at least here, in this relationship, the hum was suppressed. When they fought, she stopped being able to hear it. When they made up, it remained muffled. It was only in the quieter moments before and after, the moments when she was alone, that she heard it clearly, and felt it, and she realized she needed company, even if it had to be someone like Simon.

She needed Simon in order to forget Lucas.

So, as the first brave stabs of daybreak edged across the sky, her thoughts finally began to drift, and she'd managed to fall asleep. When she'd woken again, it was after eight and the sun was already up. She shoved Simon, telling him he was going to be late, and he rolled out of bed – shoulder-length hair licking at the side of his face, greasy and unkempt – and glanced at the clock. 'What the fuck?' he'd growled. 'Look at the time.'

And that had been the start of it.

As she'd stood there at the kitchen counter, preparing sandwiches for them both, he'd said something under his breath. She'd turned back to face him and asked him to repeat himself. He was wound tight, from waking up late, from not being able to find his work boots, from a night full of booze and whatever else he'd been up to. He found his work boots where he'd kicked them off the night before, outside the back door, and as he sat down at the kitchen table and started to lace them up, he said, 'What do you need sandwiches for? You planning on going to work today?'

She stepped away from the counter, kitchen knife in her hand. He glanced at it briefly.

'It's Tuesday,' she said quietly. 'You know I have an appointment with Dr Garrick today.'

He shook his head. 'Garrick.'

'You don't have to pay, so what do you care?'

No reply. He continued lacing his boots.

'Huh? What do you care?'

He finished one boot and looked up at her, laces of the other between his fingers. 'I don't,' he said. 'But you've been seeing him – what? – three and a half years and it's made zero fuckin' difference. You still mope around like it's everyone else's fault but your own.'

'What?'

'You heard what I said.' He finished the second boot and stood, facing her across the kitchen, using his height advantage to assert his authority. 'You know what you might want to give some thought to? Getting a decent paying job. I'm out there busting my arse, trying to bring home a living wage, and you're swanning around like royalty, wasting your money on this useless fuckin' shrink.'

'I've never asked you for anything.'

A snort. 'You're living under my roof.'

'I pay my way.'

He nodded, kept on nodding, as he removed a high-vis jacket from the pegs at the front door. 'You think a three-day-a-week job in a poxy shoe shop is going to help us?'

She just looked at him.

'Whatever,' he said. 'I don't give a shit.'

'That sounds about right.'

She could see him colour instantly.

He stepped towards her, finger in her face. 'You think anyone else would put up with all your shit, you snarky bitch? Do you? I'm a fuckin' saint. It's a miracle I haven't hung myself from the rafters listening to you mope around like you're the only person in the entire fuckin' world who ever had a problem.'

'That's what you call it? A "problem"?'

'It's been nine years.'

'So?'

'So get over it.'

Anger rose in her throat. '"Get over it"?'

'Yeah. Get over it.'

'He was my baby.'

'He's dead.'

'You're talking about my son.'

He didn't respond this time, shrugging on the high-vis jacket.

'That's my son,' she said, trembling with rage, and she realized how hard she was gripping the knife; could feel sweat on her hands, licking against the handle of the blade.

Simon took his sandwiches and bagged them.

'How dare you talk about him —'

'Fuck your son,' he said.

A moment later, he left.

In the loft there was a series of boxes stacked against one of the walls, each one marked so she could remember what she'd put inside. This was where most of her stuff stayed now. She didn't bring it down into his house, because he complained about her cluttering up the living room with pictures and ornaments, and after their argument, after what he'd said to her at the end, she was never going to share a single important moment with him again in her life. Not her day, not her thoughts, certainly not photographs and memories.

Most of what she'd collected over the years, she'd dumped. When she hit a low, it became a cleansing ritual, a slow, painful sanitization process: she'd take everything that represented that stage of her life and she'd cast it aside. Clothes. Pictures. Music. Films. Books. But some things she found hard to let go, even as she recognized how dangerous it was to hang on to them. There were things in her possession that she'd promised she'd got rid of. She knew the risks in keeping them, but the risks always seemed worth it at times like this.

These things were her anchor.

Her constant.

So she wiped her cheeks, shifted two of the boxes off the pile and on to the floor, and opened the lid on the one marked '1996'.

On top were the newspaper clippings.

'Hello, Pamela,' she said softly.

PART II

CHAPTER 20

F lakes of snow were drifting out of the night sky by the time I left the hotel. I zipped my coat up, wind ripping along the street, and tried to plan a logical route through what I'd just been told. A file had turned up for Franks in the post, almost certainly in late January. It had something to do with Pamela Welland, or with Paul Viljoen – or both.

Several days later, he calls Murray, because they worked the case together, and tries to get her to source the footage for him of Welland and Viljoen at the bar the night Welland was killed; footage he'd taken out of evidence once already, five years after he and Murray had originally put the case to bed in 1996. When she refuses, he goes to Paige, playing on their friendship. Paige also refuses, realizing Franks is endangering himself, and tells him to back away. A month later, Franks has vanished.

As I walked, I went to the browser on my phone and put in a search for Pamela Welland. There were a few stories about her murder, mostly covered by true crime sites, but 1996 was when the Internet was in its infancy, which meant newspaper accounts from the time were mostly front-page scans. What I managed to find backed up what I'd been told by Paige and Murray. I'd floated the idea of them getting me Welland's file, but Paige had shot it down. There were other ways to secure a copy, through someone like Ewan Tasker, but if Paige or Murray went back in to look at the Welland case, for whatever reason, they'd find Task's search for Pamela Welland logged – and that meant compromising one of my best sources.

I wrote the idea off and clicked on one of the images of Welland. She was sitting on a whitewashed stone wall outside a Spanish hotel, probably sixteen when the picture was taken, blonde hair in a plait, eyes disguised behind mirrored shades. The newspaper that had run the picture had called her 'tragic and beautiful', and it was hard to disagree with either of those sentiments. I felt a pang of sadness, for her and her family.

When I reached Millbank, flanked by the hardwood skeletons of Victoria Tower Gardens and the relentless grey of the MI5 buildings, I thought of Ellie, and then Craw. The worst she probably imagined was Franks in a hole somewhere, wrists cut, whatever he'd known about the Welland and Viljoen case, about everything else, lost on his lips for ever. She'd looked at me the day before, over her mother's shoulder, and I'd seen as much in her face. She was prepared to accept that fate for Franks, if it came to it.

And yet while Craw was realistic, her working life shaped by human tragedy, there were lies and there were lies. After nineteen years, the ones told to her by countless suspects in unending interviews passed right through her.

But the ones told to her by her father wouldn't retreat so easily.

Those would feel like a knife in her back.

As I entered Westminster Tube station, my phone started buzzing, so I double backed to preserve the signal and found a place in the shadows, behind the pillars on Bridge Street.

'David Raker.'

'David, it's Spike.'

I'd almost forgotten I'd called him. He'd been tasked with getting the names and addresses of all the people who'd made or received calls to and from Franks in the phone statements Craw had handed over. I'd also asked him to do the same for the rest of 2013, from 3 March through to now.

'Spike, thanks for calling me back.'

'Sorry it's so late.'

I looked at my watch. 'Ten-fifteen? You call this late? I'm just getting started. So what have you got for me?'

'Okay,' he said. I heard a couple of taps on a keyboard. 'Thirteen and a half months of phone statements – the first batch covers 1 November 2012 through to 3 March this year, as requested. The second will take you through to yesterday, 12 December. I've grabbed you names and addresses for each and every caller. That's what takes time. Once you've got one number, it's just a copy-and-paste job. But it's the actual process of finding out who the number belongs to and then accessing their address which is the ball-breaker. Anyway, it should be all there.'

'I appreciate it. Did you spot anything unusual?'

'You're not looking at a hell of a lot after your guy leaves on 3 March.'

'Am I looking at anything?'

'A few incoming calls, which I guess is to be expected, right?'

Family and friends would have been calling him in the days and weeks after he disappeared, trying to find out where he was. Calls after that were likely to be from people he wasn't as close to, who were unaware he was gone.

'Any outgoing?' I asked.

'Outgoing calls from his mobile after 3 March?' A pause, as he checked the statements. The answer came back quickly. 'No,' he said. 'Not a single one.'

CHAPTER 21

An hour later, after a delay on the tube at Earl's Court, I arrived home. As I approached the house, I saw movement through the corner of my eye and turned to see what it was. Liz was coming up her driveway, dressed smartly in a long black raincoat, dark hair swaying against her back, red scarf in a knot at her neck. She was carrying a slipcase in one hand and checking her phone with the other, her face illuminated by its blue light.

For a moment, I paused there, watching her. She was oblivious to me, hidden on the other side of the wire fence that separated our properties. But, ten feet short of her house, the security light came on, flooding her approach, and she saw me paused halfway between my house and the road. She stopped, phone dropping to her side, and we looked at each other, stillness and silence the only things between us.

'Hey, Liz.'

'David. I didn't see you there.' Her eyes moved to my house, a light on inside. I could see Christmas decorations down the street, beyond her, blinking against the black.

'How are you?' I said.

'I'm fine.'

'Looks like you've had a long day.'

A flat smile inched across her face. 'I had one of those cases I used to hate, where the person I'm defending . . .' She stopped, rolling her eyes. *I don't really like.* Even alone, she rarely bad-mouthed her clients. It was one of the things I'd always liked about her.

'What are you doing for Christmas?' I asked.

'Katie's coming to stay for a few days.'

Katie was her daughter. In the time Liz and I had been dating, I'd never got to meet her, and I doubted I'd been painted in my best light in the year since we'd split.

'That's unless I get a flurry of viewings.' We both looked at the FOR SALE sign. 'I'm picking her up tomorrow, so I'm praying that doesn't happen quite yet.'

'I hope you're . . .' I paused. 'I hope you're not . . .'

I didn't know how to phrase the question without making myself seem arrogant. I hadn't ever asked her if she was moving out because of what had happened between us, but she had never expressed any desire to move before then – in fact, quite the opposite – so it always seemed the most likely explanation. As she watched me flounder, she didn't step in, and the corner of her mouth twitched in something approaching a genuine smile.

'Help me out here,' I joked.

'Why would I do that?'

But then the smile fell away as her eyes drifted across my shoulder to the house. I turned. Annabel had come to the door to see who it was, before disappearing back inside.

I looked at Liz. 'It's not what you think.'

'It's none of my business.'

'She's my daughter.'

Her eyes narrowed and I realized I'd done the opposite of what I'd hoped: she looked at me with renewed mistrust, unsure of whether I was telling the truth. These were the moments that had driven a wedge between us at the end, and the reason I knew we could never go back. This was the look in her face every time I talked about work, about the cases I took on and the people I found. And I didn't blame her for a single second of it: I'd lied to her about the things I did in order to protect our relationship. But all it had done was undermine every conversation we had.

'I mean it,' I said.

'It's none of my business,' she said again, and moved the rest of the way up the driveway to the front steps of her house. I watched her go, realizing that this might be the last conversation we would ever have. She turned back to me, as if she realized the same.

But neither of us said anything more.

Maybe because we knew we were irreparable.

Maybe because this was what happened at the end.

CHAPTER 22

After Annabel went to bed, I moved to the spare room, shut the door and woke the MacBook from its slumber. Logging in to my email, I found Spike's message and dragged the PDF attachments on to the desktop. There were two, separated into landline and mobile. In turn, they'd then been subdivided into pre- and post-disappearance.

Landline calls, over the course of the year I'd asked for, totalled twenty pages; mobile phone calls accounted for even more at thirty-nine. Spike had ensured each number that had dialled into either of Franks's phones had a name and address marked against it. He'd also listed the recipients of every call Franks made *out* of his phones. I had to accept a fair proportion of the calls from the landline, before and after 3 March, would have been made by Ellie, but this would still help map out a trail.

Before loading up the PDFs, I picked up the Moleskine covering 1995–2004, and opened the computer document that I'd created earlier, cataloguing every name and case Franks had listed in the notebooks. I zeroed in on 1996. The case of Pamela Welland was mentioned – but not anywhere near as much as I'd expected. In fact, it was one of the least detailed of any of the cases he'd made notes on in that first Moleskine notebook. I felt deflated as my eyes moved down the information he'd included.

His notes ran in two separate clumps, one dated 12 April 1996, which was the day after her murder, the next a month later – 14 May – when Viljoen was under arrest. The first entry was just a basic listing of the facts; facts that I'd already gathered from Murray. In the second entry, on 14 May, Franks referenced Murray, saying she was leading the interview, and he had written down a series of questions, presumably so they could discuss them beforehand. He'd also written down a series of notes about Viljoen being refused bail, being remanded into custody, and then the date of his first appearance at the magistrate's court. Nothing in it added anything to what I'd already found out.

You're still hiding from me, Leonard.

I tried not to linger on the disappointment, and turned to the scrap of paper with the sketch and 'BROLE108' written on it, and then the pub flyer. I'd set them away from the other junk he'd stored in the Moleskines. If I was to accept that the scrap of paper came first, because I'd found it in the diary covering 1995–2004, I also had to accept that, years later – in the Hare and Badger pub on 11 February 2013 – the significance of the '108' was still preying on his mind, whether he was in there on his own or with someone else. Again, my eyes lingered on the mention of 'Milk?', right above the number on the flyer – and, again, doubts began to creep in, a small, destructive voice trying to convince me that this was just some kind of shopping list, a reminder to pick something up.

And yet I refused to let it take hold: the fact that the sketch held some distant kind of familiarity to me was one thing – but it was the repetition of the number '108', years apart from the first mention, that felt most compelling.

Snow scattered gently against the window, making a soft noise like fat crackling in a pan, and, as I looked out, I could see it swirling around in the glow of the street lights. A set of fairy lights winked from the guttering of a house opposite and, briefly, I wondered what Christmas at the Frankses' house would have been like this time last year. Whatever it was like, a month later the file turned up – and everything changed.

I returned my attention to the PDFs.

I concentrated on the landline calls first, working in chronological order, from the first day the statements began – 1 November 2012 – all the way through to the date of Franks's disappearance on 3 March. The same names came up time and again: Craw, at home and on her mobile; three long-distance calls to their son in Australia; Jim Paige at work and on his mobile; Carla Murray's mobile; Derek Cortez; the main line at Franks's local golf club, and the people he'd played with there, all of whom had already been checked out. Then a succession of builders' merchants, plumbers, plasterers and decorators.

Nothing rang any alarm bells. The conversations between Paige and Franks seemed to stick to a fairly similar routine: fortnightly, between fifteen and twenty-five minutes. Ellie had mentioned the chats the two men had enjoyed when I'd spoken to her.

The only time the pattern changed was at the end of January: on Thursday the 31st, they'd spoken for fifty minutes, two or three times longer than usual. This must have been the call Paige had told me about earlier: *A day after he called Carla, he got in touch with me to see if I could source the footage of Pamela Welland from the pub.*

When I backtracked twenty-four hours, I saw Paige was right: at 15.34 on Wednesday 30 January, Franks had called Murray. Their exchange had lasted twenty-two minutes. After that, there were a few short, sharp calls between Franks and Paige, again backing up what Paige had told me about trying to talk Franks down. Then their calls returned to normal, although notably didn't last as long. The drop-off in duration mirrored the drop-off in email frequency to Murray in those last five weeks.

In the days after Franks's disappearance, the landline statement took on the pattern I'd expected it to: frenetic phone calls from Ellie, first to Craw, then to the police, then to friends of Franks, trying to work out if anyone had seen him. Then a gradual reduction to the point at which she was hardly making any outgoing calls at all. On 27 November 2013, they stopped altogether, coinciding with Ellie's return to London.

I moved on to the mobile records and immediately found a lot of duplication: the same numbers I'd already seen on the landline statements, the same people making and receiving those calls. I worked my way through November and December, then January and February as well. As Spike suggested, calls didn't stop entirely once Franks disappeared: people he didn't keep in touch with as regularly were obviously unaware he was gone and continued to phone, but from 3 March the records began to thin out until, in the autumn, no one was calling his phone any more and Franks had been forgotten.

But as I moved back through the mobile calls, I realized I'd missed something. On 10 March, seven days after the disappearance, a London number tried to get in touch with him. The call had lasted only two seconds, suggesting that whoever had made it had hit Franks's voicemail and hung up. Typed in the margin, adjacent to all the numbers, were the names and addresses of the callers. Except there was no name for this one – just an address.

It was a public payphone.

A road called Scale Lane in SE15.

191

I scrolled further up, an immediate sense of recognition taking hold, and on 24 January I discovered why. Franks had received a call from exactly the same phone box.

Except this call had lasted seven minutes.

I minimized the PDF, fired up the browser and found the phone box on Google Maps. It was on a narrow side street which came off the Old Kent Road in a vague zigzag. The phone box itself was easy to miss, tucked away between a takeaway and a nail salon. Even in winter, with surrounding leaves stripped bare, it would have remained partially hidden, cast into shadow by nearby roofs. And, as I inched the view through a full three-sixty, I realized something more significant: there wasn't a single CCTV camera within a hundred yards.

It had been purposely chosen.

Pulling my pad across, I wrote down a brief timeline:

Late January – Franks receives a cold-case file in the post. Sender: unknown.

24 January – Franks receives call from phone box in S. London. Same person who sent the file to him?

30 January – Franks calls Murray, asking for Welland footage.

31 January – Franks calls Paige, asking for same footage.

11 February – Franks meets someone (who?)

at the Hare and Badger pub for lunch; tells Ellie he's meeting Paige.
23 February – Franks mentions cold case to Craw.
3 March – Franks disappears.
10 March – Franks receives call from same phone box. Call lasts two seconds. Caller doesn't know Franks has disappeared? Or knows he has and is trying to find out where he is?

Suppressing a prickle of unease, I called Craw. She didn't bother with small talk, and asked me about the Met charity event: 'Did you get what you wanted from Paige?'

'I'm not sure yet.' I left it at that. 'I've got a quick question: your dad received two separate phone calls from a public payphone just off the Old Kent Road.'

'Yes, I remember.'

'Did you look into them?'

'Yes. There didn't seem much point in bringing it up with you – it's just another dead end. I should know because I chased my tail on that for a week. The call box is two hundred and fifty feet away from the nearest CCTV camera. I went down and checked.'

'Did he know anyone who lived in that area?'

'No.'

'What did you make of it?'

'I asked around among his friends, trying to see if any of them lived in the area, and the caller wasn't anyone he knew. I looked through his recent cases and found nothing. I was about to prep a request to requisition the footage from two cameras on the Old Kent Road, but then my super shut me down.' A long, melancholic pause. 'I don't need to tell you it would have been a waste of time, anyway. You only need to see the location of that box to know why it was chosen.'

Anonymity.

I was starting to realize why, in her interviews with Sergeant Reed in the days after Franks disappeared, Craw had suggested her father might not have left of his own accord.

She didn't say anything else, but it was clear she was thinking about the call, about what it meant, about whether something had been missed. That wasn't unique to missing persons: relatives clung to the unexplained, whatever the crime, because in the unknown there was hope, maybe answers, maybe some kind of resolution. Except, given what Paige and Murray had told me, I was starting to wonder what kind of answers Craw would end up with – and whether finding Franks could bring her any kind of comfort, or just another twist of the knife.

CHAPTER 23

The next morning was beautiful. The snow had settled on rooftops, in gardens and streets, on windowsills and fence posts, its stillness reducing London to a hush. Cars remained on driveways, people remained indoors and, above, the sky was a vast sweep of blue without a single cloud to blemish it. I took my breakfast through and sat at the rear windows, looking out at a garden undisturbed by anything but bird tracks.

A couple of minutes later, I watched my mobile buzz across the table towards me. It was Ewan Tasker. Forty-eight hours earlier, I'd asked him to use the police database to look into any major unsolveds in London, in an effort to narrow down Franks's cold case. That was before I knew about Pamela Welland. Now the question wasn't who had got to Franks at the end, because it seemed likely – if Paige and Murray were correct – that the answer was Welland. Instead, it was why her death meant so much to him.

After we'd chatted for a while, I steered the conversation around to what Tasker had found.

'I don't know if you'll be thanking me or cursing

me,' he said. It was Saturday, and he was at home, so there was no office noise behind him. 'In a city of seven million people, across an unspecified time period, you're looking at a shitload of hits, just like I said you would. I found ninety-eight unsolved cases that I would personally class as "major". But if you're talking about including people being held up at knifepoint, or beaten up getting the last tube home, then you're going to have to widen the search, and that's going to take more time. For now, though, I've just stuck to the really big stuff.'

'That sounds great, Task.'

I grabbed the Moleskines from the spare room as well as the document I'd created and printed out: it gave me a full overview of every case, name and extraneous item – like the pub flyer – that Franks had made mention of, or included as part of the diaries.

Gradually, we started navigating through the ninety-eight unsolveds, Task giving me a brief account of what had happened – date, crime, victim, circumstances – before moving on to the next. I cross-checked each one with the printout. Where Franks had noted down a case that Tasker also mentioned, even only in passing, I asked for it to be set aside so we could come back to it. Fifteen minutes in, I'd finished my coffee. Twenty minutes after that, I heard Annabel get up and head to the shower.

By the time we got to the end, we'd been going at it an hour. I could hear Annabel pottering around in the kitchen and I'd narrowed down ninety-eight cases to just four.

Momentarily, I paused. The rational part of me knew there was no guarantee any of this meant anything. As much as I'd suspected that within the pages of the notebooks Franks might allude to an investigation that was important to him, it was just as likely that he'd opt not to write *anything* down. Pamela Welland had clearly been incredibly important to him, for whatever reason, but his notes on her case – and on Paul Viljoen – ran to two small clumps on a single page in the first diary. Maybe he'd gone in totally the opposite direction with cases that meant the most to him.

Maybe he didn't include those at all.

I decided against worrying about it for now, and returned my attention to the four I'd asked to be set aside. If nothing else, I could confirm Franks had some involvement in these, either as an investigator, or as a command lead, overseeing the Met's Murder Teams.

'Okay,' I said, 'let's go back over them.'

'You want me to go in chronological order?'

'Yeah, that would be great.'

A couple of taps of the keyboard, then: 'First one: guy from King's Cross named Burgess Smith tells his wife he's heading to the shops to get milk. He never comes home again. Next day, his body is found floating in the Grand Union Canal about half a mile from the train station. Smith was dead before he hit the water. Got stabbed in the neck.

Looked like a robbery – his wallet never turned up, even when police sent divers in.'

I cast my eyes down the other details I'd managed to extract from the diaries and subsequent searches I'd done online. They didn't add much. The case was from August 1997; the killer was never found; Franks was the lead, Murray working alongside him.

'Okay. Next?'

'Next is a 21-year-old woman called Mary Swindon heading back to her car near Kensal Green Cemetery after a night out. Some guy comes out of nowhere, grabs her, pulls her into a side street, rapes her, bashes her head in. The killer's DNA was all over the body, but nowhere in the database. They never found out who the guy was, even retrospectively. This was 2002.'

I used the printout to remind myself of what Franks had written down concerning the case. He'd listed its headline details – all of which matched what I was having confirmed by Task now – but under that, in the diary, he'd also written, 'We need to find this asshole NOW.' As I read that back I remembered what Carla Murray had told me the night before: *The Boss always took cases like Welland's hard. Kids. Women.* I'd added some other details too, based on what I'd found out through media reports. This one was roughly in the same ballpark as Welland.

But, for now, I moved on. 'What about the third?'

'A man gets stabbed in the chest outside The

Knight in Mile End. I assume that's a pub. I probably should have checked that. Anyway, he dies in hospital later. Witnesses say he was arguing with someone on the phone while he was there, but when police got hold of his bill, they found the caller had dialled in from a stolen handset.'

'Who was the victim?'

'Uh, Bryan Calhoon. Hold on.' He paused for a moment as he read on down the file. 'Building contractor. Apparently he was in some kind of major dispute with one of his rivals – a Dean Ireland – after Calhoon allegedly, *illegally*, got hold of a proposal and quotation that Ireland had given to the council, and then massively undercut him to secure the contract himself. Ireland obviously looked good for it – but he had an alibi.'

A dispute between two rival builders seemed about as far away from what I was looking for as it was possible to get, and by 2007 – when Calhoon was killed – Franks was already running the entire Homicide command. That put him way beyond cases like this one, something his diary notes backed up: he'd noted down the name of the victim and the people in his Murder Team, but beyond that there was nothing suggesting any kind of connection with Welland's death.

'And the fourth?'

'Unidentified victim,' Task said. 'Thirty-something. White. Five foot eleven. He was killed in March 2011. This guy must have *really* upset the wrong people. Someone broke into his home, tied him up and slit his throat, ear to ear. Likely drug murder. The vic was found with five grand's worth of coke tucked away in the kitchen.'

I circled the case on the printout. 'No dental records?'

'His teeth were removed.'

'Really?'

'Really.'

'And his prints didn't lead anywhere?'

'No. Prints, DNA, nothing.'

Just like the builders' dispute, Franks had only mentioned it in the loosest possible terms. His notes said, 'UnID'd victim + CB?', and he'd listed the home address for the victim: a council estate in Lewisham. When I'd filled in further details the previous evening, using what little there was online about it, I'd been unable to find out what the *CB* part related to. Still, it was difficult to picture Franks becoming so affected by a drug murder, two years after it happened, that it ended up being the reason he left.

I looked at what I'd written down.

The murder of Mary Swindon seemed the most immediate fit but, in truth, when I looked closer, there were few similarities between the two killings. There was certainly no question that Viljoen was involved. The DNA at the scene didn't belong to him, and by the time Swindon was killed in 2002 he'd already been locked up for six years.

'You got any idea why he was running the case?' Task said.

I tuned back in. 'Sorry, what?'

'Franks.'

'What about him?'

'Says here he was running the case.'

'Running what case?'

'This drug murder.'

Task was talking about the fourth case: the unidentified white male who'd had his throat cut. 'Wait, Franks was *running* it?'

'Yeah. Franks was the SIO on it. The file indicates that he was running point, and that it was his last ever case at the Met. Bit below his pay grade, I'd have thought.'

'What else does it say?'

Silence.

'Task?'

'Shit. I've just seen the time. I'm supposed to be meeting some friends for lunch.' Another long pause. 'I'm going to have to go, Raker. You want a copy of these files?'

My mind was already ticking over. 'Where are you meeting them?'

'What do you mean?'

'I mean, could I come and collect the files from you?'

'Why, are you in town?'

'I can be.'

'We're having lunch at a place near Waterloo.'

'How about we meet on Westminster Bridge?'

'Fine,' he said. 'I'll see you there at one.'

CHAPTER 24

By the time I'd finished up with Tasker, Annabel was sitting at the kitchen counter, eating breakfast. I poured us both some coffee and perched myself on a stool opposite.

'Ready to get back to Devon?' I asked.

She shrugged. 'Yes and no. I'm looking forward to seeing Liv. We normally go out for a milkshake on a Saturday afternoon.' A pause, and then a second, smaller shrug. 'But sometimes, returning . . . I don't know, it brings back a lot of bad memories.'

I nodded. 'It'll get easier.'

She looked up at me, and then her eyes moved around the kitchen. 'Do you ever feel that way about this place? I mean, this is where you were supposed to, you know . . .'

When she didn't continue, I let her know that I understood what she was asking. 'Some days, I imagine what it would have been like to share this place with Derryn. I often think about how she might have done things differently, in the garden, in the house, whether – if we'd ended up having kids – we would have even stayed here long term.'

'It's not painful living here?'

'It was to start with.'

'But not now?'

'Over time, the pain dulls. It doesn't go, but it dulls.'

After that, without my intending it to, the conversation moved on to my work, and to Colm Healy. He was the former cop I'd been talking to Craw about the previous day.

Annabel's train back to Devon left in two hours, and the knotty nature of Healy's and my history felt too ambitious for the time we had left. Yet, as I tried to move the conversation forward again, her eyes lingered on me and I got the sense that, once more, she'd glimpsed where my thoughts were. All I could see of myself in her, physically, was a smile. But beneath the surface there was something more, some kind of instinct, a sense of people that seemed to echo who I was more closely than anything aesthetic.

'Why don't you call Healy?' she said.

'I've tried before.'

'Do you think it might be worth trying again?'

'You sound like my conscience.'

She smiled. 'He's a cop, right?'

'Ex-cop, yeah.'

'Does he ever make an effort to call you?'

'Only when he's in trouble.' I looked at her for a moment, realizing what sort of picture that must have painted for her. 'All I mean is, social calls aren't exactly his style.'

'Has he always been like that?'

I cast my mind back across the two years we'd known each other, and then to everything I'd learned about his life before that. 'Not always. People at the Met tell me he was up there with the best of them once. But then he had this case, and after that it all kind of . . .'

'Unravelled.'

'Yes,' I said, 'that's exactly the right word.'

'What sort of case was it?'

'Three murders. A mother and her daughters.'

'Daughters?'

'Eight-year-old twins.'

Something moved in her face, and as she placed her hands flat to the kitchen counter I realized what: Olivia was the same age as those girls. This was everything she'd been talking to me about the day before. *I get scared. I get scared I can't protect her.*

'Maybe this is something for another day.'

'What happened to them?'

I hesitated for a moment, keen not to play on her insecurity – perhaps, deep down, instinctively looking to shield her – but then reality hit home: she was twenty-five, and she knew as well as me that this was how the world was, even if it was hard to stomach.

'He talked about it once,' I said. 'He told me the hunt for their killer consumed him to the point where he couldn't think of anything else. Every second of every day. It cost him his marriage, it cost him his kids. Literally in the case of his daughter, Leanne.'

'She was murdered as well?'

'Different time, different case – but yes.'

'That's awful.'

I nodded again. 'Leanne and Healy had this massive row the day she disappeared, and the next time he saw her she'd been left in a place so terrible sometimes I wonder how he ever sleeps at night. He's got so much anger, bitterness and grief, all he knows how to do is hit out. But you know something? Sometimes I don't blame him for that.'

'And the twins?'

I looked across to Liz's garden, bereft of furniture and pot plants, and wondered if there was a way of cushioning the truth. 'Nothing ended up the way it should have done,' I said, imagining the horror that Healy must have walked into the day he found those girls and their mother. When I finally turned back to Annabel, there was a flash in one of her eyes. 'Are you okay?'

She blinked. 'I'm fine. I just . . .'

I slid an arm around her and brought her into me. 'I'm sorry.'

'You don't have to be sorry,' she said.

'Olivia's fine.'

She nodded gently.

'You're both safe. I promise.' We stayed like that for a moment, the house quiet, the world beyond even quieter, its noise quelled by the snow. 'I shouldn't have talked—'

'Was the case taken away from Healy?'

When I didn't reply, she looked up at me. Despite the tears forming, there was an unexpected determination to her now, a sudden fortitude.

'Was it taken away?' she asked again.

'Yes.'

'Did anyone solve it?'

I looked at her, but didn't reply. I didn't know how to make this better. She wiped the tears away, and for a second I could see my reflection staring back at me.

'*Did* they?'

'No,' I said, shaking my head. 'There was no happy ending.'

CHAPTER 25

There was barely any evidence of snow out on the main roads, pavements almost cleared, roads slick with water and crumbs of grit – but it was still bitter. By the time Annabel and I had got to Ealing station, I was cold right through to my bones, skin raw and aching from where the wind kept snapping at us. We rode the train to Paddington and, at the gateline, I hugged her and told her I'd see her soon.

After she'd boarded, I headed back to the Tube and worked my way down to the District line platform. The snow had long since ceased to fall, but as I stood there in the freezing cold, it blew in through the open spaces above: off the rooftops and windowsills high up on Praed Street, and from the arches, closer in, that ran along the back walls of both platforms. I moved for cover, where an arced roof straddled the line, perched myself on one of the benches and started checking the messages on my phone.

A couple of minutes later, I looked up again.

Instinctive.

Automatic.

An odd sensation ghosted through me – a brief shiver, but not instigated by the cold – and as I looked from my phone, along the platform, I realized what it was.

It feels like I'm being watched.

The platform was busy, lined three-deep with people waiting for an Earl's Court connection: mostly tourists, clumped together, and businessmen in interchangeable suits. My eyes moved between faces. No one seemed to be paying me any attention, either on this side or across the line. I stood, giving myself a better view of the crowd, but as the train squealed to a stop, I started to doubt myself and eventually cast the thought aside.

I found a café, nursed a coffee and an overcooked melted cheese sandwich, and watched traffic feed off Westminster Bridge for forty-five minutes. I thought of Annabel, of what we'd talked about, and vowed – once this case was over – to give Healy a shout. Then my mind switched to the cases I was about to pick up from Tasker. Four unsolveds Franks had a confirmed connection to, one of which didn't sit right at all: the drug murder.

Why did Franks decide to step in and run it himself?

I'd made a timeline of events for the start of the year – from when the file arrived with Franks, to that last call from the phone box – but now I constructed one in parallel:

Between May 1995 and May 2004 – Franks writes 'BROLE108' and makes 'stick man' sketch on scrap of paper.

April 1996 – Pamela Welland is murdered by Paul Viljoen.

May 1996 – Viljoen arrested and charged by Franks/Murray.

1997 – Viljoen sentenced to 20 years.

2001 – Murray finds Franks watching CCTV footage of the night Viljoen picked Welland up in a bar. Unrelated to case they were on. So why was he watching it? Why after all that time?

March 2011 – Unidentified victim is found dead (apparent drug murder?) in Lewisham. Franks writes 'UnID'd victim + CB?' in notebook. What is CB? WHY WAS FRANKS SIO ON THE CASE?

February 2013 – Franks writes 'Milk?' and '108' on flyer.

As I looked at the timeline, I thought again about Franks acting as SIO on the drug murder. By March 2011, he was weeks away from retirement and had already spent years as command lead, way beyond the day-to-day running of individual cases like that. Why not leave it to Murray, like he'd done with countless other cases in the years before?

Grabbing my phone, I dialled the Met and asked to be directed to Murray. She answered after a couple of rings. I told her who it was, and I could immediately sense her stiffen.

Her voice dropped to a whisper. 'What are you doing?'

'I've got a question.'

'Don't *ever* call me here.'

'It's about another case.'

A pause. 'What are you talking about?'

'Does this case from March 2011 ring any bells with you? A guy had his throat cut in what looked like a drug-related killing. Cops found about five kilos of coke in his flat.'

Silence.

'Murray?'

'It rings a bell. So?'

'So I've been going through Franks's notes and I've found mention of it. Weird thing is, he seems to have taken the lead on it. Why would he take the lead on a case?'

'Why *wouldn't* he?'

'Because he'd stopped running cases ten years ago. He was the command lead, not a foot soldier. Plus this was six weeks before he retired.'

'*So?*'

'The murder of this guy wasn't high profile. The media didn't care. The general public barely bat an eyelid at that type of crime. I find it hard to believe that Franks was actually *asked* to step in and run it by the top brass. And yet he stepped in nonetheless.'

'I don't know.'

'You don't remember?'

She sighed. 'Let me tell you how these things work, okay? Someone gets killed, we get assigned cases, that's it. This isn't like clothes shopping. You don't take one case off the rack, decide you don't like the look of it and then put it back again. So did I ever question what I got given? No. Did I ask the Boss the reasons why he decided to deal with the fallout from some random drug murder? No. Here's what I was thinking: the recession was in full swing, we were underfunded and understaffed, we were all waiting for the axe to fall. I cared about keeping my head down and not getting my P45.'

I made a couple of notes.

'Did he take on many cases himself?' I asked.

'No.'

'That's what I figured. So this was pretty unusual?'

'The Boss mucked in when he needed to, especially around that time when the government were busy ripping the heart out of the force. Now, are we done?'

'Can I just—'

She hung up before I could finish.

Scooping up my pad, I headed out into the cold again, down to the western end of Westminster Bridge, where Task was already waiting. At six-three and sixteen stone, he was still a powerful man and easy to spot among the Christmas crowds. He produced a newspaper, folded in half, and handed it to me.

'Printouts of the four unsolveds we talked about on the phone,' he said.

I took the paper from him. 'Thanks, Task.'

'Burn them when you're done,' he said. His eyes lingered on the newspaper. A corner of a brown file was visible now, up beyond the edges of the broadsheet. 'You're not going to get yourself killed again, are you, Raker?'

'I never got myself killed last time.'

He smiled. 'Just be careful.'

'Do you know something I don't?'

He shook his head. 'No. But I know you. Trouble follows you around.'

BOX OF REGRETS

July 2008 | Five Years Ago

'I have this box I keep in the loft,' she said, looking across the office at Garrick.

He was more casual today – open-necked shirt, woollen sleeveless jumper, black denims, black brogues – but they were all name brands. She'd asked him what he earned once, which made him laugh, but he never ended up telling her. He pushed his glasses up the bridge of his nose and came forward slightly.

'And what do you keep in the box?'

'Memories.'

'What kinds of memories?'

'Some good.'

'Some not so good?'

She nodded.

'Some you regret?'

She nodded a second time.

He flipped to a new page of his pad, picked up his fountain pen from the edge of the desk and then inched off the lid with his thumb. 'We've talked about this before, of course. You hold on to a lot of regret.'

'I've done a lot of regretful things.'

'Like what?'

'I've told you what.'

'Indulge me,' he said.

'Like get together with Simon.'

'You don't want to be with him any more?'

'I hate him.'

'Then why stay with him?'

'Because what else is there?'

Garrick frowned. 'What do you mean?'

'What if there's no one else out there for me? What if arseholes like Simon are as much as I can expect? Maybe my chance has gone now. Maybe this is all I am.'

'Do you really believe that?'

She shrugged. 'Simon and I . . .'

'What?'

'I look at him sometimes, and I wonder . . .'

Garrick studied her. 'What?'

She swallowed, flicked a look at Garrick and then dropped her eyes to her lap. 'I had a massive row with him last week, and as we were standing there, screaming at one another, I realized I had a kitchen knife in my hand. I'd been making the sandwiches.'

For the first time in a long while, she noted a flicker of concern in Garrick's face.

'And what happened after that?' he asked evenly.

'He was disrespectful to Lucas. He said, "Fuck your son."'

'That must have hurt.'

'Yes. It did. At the time, I was conscious of

having a knife in my hand, but after Simon left, I sat there in the loft, with my box of regrets . . .' She paused, a smile ghosting across her face at the name she'd chosen for it. 'I sat there in the loft, and I thought to myself, "I wonder what he would look like with this knife in his eye?" I imagined it. I imagined stabbing him over and over, until his face became a mess of blood and bone and pulp. And do you know what the worst bit was?' She looked up at Garrick. 'I actually felt better afterwards.'

He leaned forward. He had a new pair of glasses, and he'd allowed what hair he had left to grow in a horseshoe shape around the dome of his head. She thought it made him look older than fifty-three.

'I think your relationship with Simon may be having a detrimental effect on your recovery,' he said, rolling his pen between thumb and finger.

'I think you're probably right.'

'So why not do something about it?'

She shrugged. 'I've done a lot of things in the past that I thought were right, and look where it's landed me. I've spent the last nine years being psychoanalysed.'

'That makes it sound bad,' Garrick replied. He was smiling, trying to make her feel comfortable, to get her to open up, to listen. When the smile finally dropped away, he rephrased the question: 'If you could go back, what changes would you make?'

She looked at him but didn't respond.

'You don't want to answer that?' he said.

'Are there things you would change in your life, Dr Garrick?'

'John,' he said. He put down his pen. 'Of course.'

'Like what?'

'Well, we're not here to talk about me.'

'Indulge me,' she said, echoing what he'd said to her earlier on.

He smiled briefly, then glanced at the fountain pen, balanced on the pad now, as if he was searching for some sort of inspiration in it. I knew it, she thought, I knew that fountain pen meant something to him. She'd seen its importance in one of her earliest sessions, the way he handled it so carefully, the way he seemed so attached to it.

'You can always harbour regrets,' he said. 'Always.'

'You don't seem the type.'

He broke out into that big, reassuring smile again. 'Why don't we get back to you?' It was clear that he wasn't going to go any further down this road.

'I wish I hadn't stopped painting,' she said.

'You painted?'

'Yes. I used to paint a lot.'

'That's wonderful. What sort of things?'

'I was never very good.'

'But it made you happy?'

'Yes,' she said. 'Yes, it really did.'

'Why don't you paint now?'

She shrugged. 'It just doesn't feel like the right environment.'

'That's a shame.'

He wrote something down.

'I wish I hadn't taken my eyes off my son,' she said. Garrick looked up at her.

She took a long breath. 'Ten seconds was all it was. I wish I could take those ten seconds back.' She stopped again, trying to suppress the tremor in her throat. 'I regret that neither Robert nor I could deal with the aftermath as well. He blamed me, and I blamed myself, and it took us to the divorce courts – and then it took me to this place.'

A long silence.

'Pamela Welland,' she said finally.

Garrick nodded again. 'She's the girl who was murdered?'

She stared off into the space between them, tracing her life back nine years, to the days and weeks after police found Pamela on wasteland near Deptford Creek. She'd read about it the next day in the papers, seen the photo of the girl – beautiful, unblemished – perched on the wall outside a Spanish hotel, hair plaited, mirrored shades, barely even an adult. And as she'd read the story, her chest had filled with a desperate, cloying sense of anxiety, fear clawing its way up her throat until she could hardly breathe any more.

Why me? Why me?

'Why me?'

Garrick leaned closer. 'Sorry?'

She didn't reply.

'Why you?' he said.

She realized she'd said it out loud. 'Why did it have to be me?'

'I'm not sure I follow.'

'My life could have been different without her.'

'If you hadn't read about her in the papers, you mean?'

Her thoughts wandered again, this time to her dog, Bear, to the moment when she'd first touched his coat, run her hand through it, felt the rise and fall of his belly.

'Maybe in some ways.'

'What ways are those?'

A small, anaemic half-smile. 'Every way that counts.'

After her session with Garrick was over, she sat on one of the stone benches at the side of the building and waited for the bus. She watched a gull climb thermals, all the way up to where the fence traced the circumference of the hospital. Once the bird passed across the razorwire and on to the roof of the building, she couldn't see it any more, only hear it, squawking in the muted hush of the morning as other, more distant noises played out beyond that. The purr from one of the generators. The gentle drone of a vacuum cleaner. The soft sound of music from the day room.

Someone screaming on one of the wards.

She unzipped her handbag and pulled out her phone, checking for messages. There were none. She never went out. She hated her job. She hated her life. She barely spoke to Simon any more. Garrick kept saying the relationship might set her back; that Simon could prove a destructive influence on her, sending her into another spiral. He was worried she'd end up back at the start, as low as she'd been in the days and weeks and months after Lucas had drowned.

But what Garrick didn't know was that there were other spirals she could ride. Moments she'd kept back from him that had ripped her heart out just the same.

There were other, even bigger secrets in her box of regrets.

CHAPTER 26

In total, I wasn't gone longer than two and a half hours – but I knew something was wrong as soon as I got to the front gates of my house. Here, snow was still everywhere, matted to the road and pavements like a layer of white tar, and on my driveway a path had been carved in footsteps: Annabel's and mine, as we'd made our way out that morning.

And now a third trail.

I could see the imprint from my boot, the swirl from Annabel's shoes too. The third was bigger than both of ours: size twelve or thirteen, the manufacturer's mark at the centre of the shoe perfectly replicated in the space between the blanketed flower beds and my BMW. For a moment, I dismissed it as nothing: the postman, someone delivering leaflets, people coming door to door. But then reality kicked in: the footsteps moved parallel to the edge of the drive, all the way up to the front steps of the house.

They didn't come back again.

I looked around me. The street was muted, unmoving, the hum of traffic out on Uxbridge

Road still audible, but suppressed by the snow. I'd seen kids heading out that morning, but there was no one now, and the only cars were the ones parked and paralysed by the weather. As I began to move, unease curdling in my stomach, I quickly realized the screen on the porch had been forced open and the front-door lock was smashed. It was most of the way shut, giving the impression from the street that the house was still locked. But, as the breeze picked up, it gently fanned back and forth, bumping against the frame.

I gave it a shove.

It swung back into the shadows of the hallway. Off to the left was the kitchen. The door at the side of the house, leading directly into it, remained locked. Ahead of me the hallway opened into the living room. I edged forward, the controls for the alarm on the wall to my right. A green LED should have been visible at the top of the pad, and the numbers should have been illuminated. Instead, both were off, and the sensors – watching me from the corners of the house – didn't blink into life as I moved. In the kitchen, on the stove, I could see the clock was still on, and showing the right time. The microwave too.

Which meant the electricity was still on.

But the alarm had been cut.

As I got to the living room, my heart dropped: furniture had been moved, shoved aside and thrown around. Pot plants had toppled over, spilling dirt across the carpet. The doors of the

TV cabinet were open, films cascading out. To my right the house changed direction, heading along another hallway, where the bathroom and two bedrooms were.

I inched along it, hands against the walls either side of me, wary of making too much noise, in case someone was still here. I got to the bathroom first. Except for an open cabinet, it was mostly intact. But in my bedroom everything had been pulled out of the cupboards, drawers from my bedside cabinet on the floor, their contents scattered.

In the spare room it got worse.

My files were all over the place, paperwork everywhere, photographs littering the room like confetti. Everything I'd kept separate – Franks's file, all the notes I'd made, photographs I'd collected, the DVD of the house that Craw had shot, the scrap of paper with the sketch and 'BROLE108' on it, the pub flyer – were gone. So were the Moleskine notebooks and the printout on which I'd logged everything. So was Franks's iPad. Even my Mac-Book had been taken. Its power lead snaked across an empty desk, no longer tethered to anything. I used a mouse instead of the laptop's trackpad – that was now on the floor next to the chair. Anger fizzed through me as I looked at the walls: every photo frame had been smashed, the photos that had existed inside them only hours before – of my paper days, of Derryn – removed and deliberately ripped up, then left among the debris on the floor. As I looked at them, an image formed: standing on the freezing cold platform at Paddington station two hours before, feeling as if someone was watching me.

Then: a noise, like splintering wood.

I backed out of the spare room and looked along the hallway. Listened again. There was no sound now except for the gentle whine of a breeze. When I returned to the living room, I could see the front door beating smoothly against the frame, massaged by the wind. And something else: a breeze at ankle level, passing from front to back. Suddenly, I recalled the footsteps out on the driveway.

They'd come in.

But they hadn't come back out again.

At the rear of the house, there were a set of patio doors on the right which led out to a small decked area, built on three-foot stilts, leading down – via a set of four steps – to the garden. The doors were ajar. I slid the files Ewan Tasker had given me, still inside the newspaper, under the TV cabinet. It was the only thing that hadn't been moved.

Stepping over fallen furniture and scattered DVD boxes, I pushed the rear doors all the way open. Cold air escaped inside, whistling softly as it was drawn in through the house. Immediately beyond the doors, footsteps moved out across the decking, down the steps and over the garden. At the bottom were a set of fir trees, standing sentry behind a six-foot-high fence that marked the boundaries of my property. A gate was built into the fencing at the right-hand edge, which I always kept locked. Except it was open now, its padlock cast off into the snow, one of its wooden panels broken.

That was the noise I'd heard.

I moved quickly across the garden and through the gate. A path ran north to south, fir trees on one side, fence panels on the other. If I headed south, I'd end up at a railway bridge, crossing the tracks close to South Ealing Tube station. If I headed north, the path eventually curved east into a swathe of allotments. I could only see three other people: a father pulling his son along on a sledge, heading down towards the allotments; and a man – hood up, almost out of sight now – heading the other way, towards the railway bridge.

He was carrying a backpack.

A couple of seconds later, as I started to move after him, it was like he sensed me behind him. He looked back, over his shoulder – and I saw he was wearing a balaclava.

I started to up my pace.

He looked again, seeing that I was closer.

Then he broke into a run.

CHAPTER 27

Snow kicked up in front of me as I headed after him. He looked back again, once, twice, before rounding a bend in the path and disappearing from sight. When he came back into view, I saw that I'd closed the gap: the ground between us was marked with evidence of where he'd stumbled, where his feet had hit an icy patch, where he'd planted a hand in the snow. He was maybe forty feet in front, about to enter a short, dark section of the path, where trees on either side met in the middle, creating a ceiling of branches and leaves.

He was dressed in black denims and a black polar fleece, the balaclava a dark blue, the backpack a muted red. Suddenly, like a mouth, the path swallowed him up, the colour of the backpack registering briefly in the shadows before he disappeared entirely. I slowed down briefly, wary of what might be waiting for me – but underneath the twisted arms of the trees there was nothing but mulched leaves. There was no snow, which aided my speed, but the path was slick with icewater. I slipped once, and again as I tried to regain my balance, and as I emerged from the other side – the path splitting in two: left towards the railway bridge, and right towards a housing estate – the snow seemed to get thicker. For a second, I lost him completely. On the left-hand fork, the path just continued, enclosed on both sides by property boundaries and trees. On the right, there was a series of bricked-up railway arches, vines crawling their way up the front of it.

A flash of movement to my right.

The railway arches cast equidistant shadows across the snow, as if black paint had been spilled. He tore himself from the gloom, thirty feet from me. Trees disguised most of what lay ahead, but above the canopy I could see top-floor flats, a series of red-bricked buildings reaching for the sky. Inside twenty seconds, the path ceased to exist and we were heading into a concrete maze: four five-storey blocks, sitting adjacent to one another. Except for their placement, they were identical. Snow lay thick on the ground here, ungritted and dangerous, and as the man darted along the centre of the road, his feet hit a patch of ice and he staggered forward, hitting a parked car. I slowed slightly, wary of doing the same thing, and noticed people watching us from the walkways higher up.

He scuttled around the car and made a beeline for an alley, running between two of the buildings. I followed, snow to concrete and back to snow, as it opened up again into a kind of courtyard. There was a raised hexagonal bed in the centre, the skeleton of a sycamore in it, and kids having a snowball fight. They stopped as we approached, paused like waxworks at the sight of us, and – as we whipped past – I saw where he was headed: a stairwell decorated with graffiti, boring up through the centre of one of the buildings, connecting to floors either side. He was going to try to lose me in the maze of homes.

He disappeared from sight as he took the stairs, and when I saw him again he was a floor above me, his footsteps echoing against the walls. I upped my pace. The stairwell was completely enclosed, protected from the snow, but water still ran down the steps from somewhere and there was an over-powering stench of decay. I looked up again and saw the backpack slapping against him. *He's got the notebooks with him. He's got my laptop.*

He's got my entire case.

But, as he rounded the next corner, disappearing from sight, the footsteps stopped. I slowed, heart thumping. Above me, I could see the twist of the stairwell, circling back on itself all the way up to the fifth floor. But no sign of the man. Not any more.

Either he'd stepped back from the railings, out of sight.

Or he'd exited on to the third floor.

I moved quietly, step by step, keeping my back to the wall. The building played an incessant beat the whole time: dripping water, the industrial whir of a generator, music and voices from the flats. I stopped at the last bend before the third-floor exit, readying myself for impact. But he wasn't there. As I inched forward, I could see the stairs looped up and around to the fourth floor, or continued on to a balcony, where a relentless procession of flats rolled out, coloured doors running all the way down until the walkway eventually kicked left and vanished. Exiting the stairs, I moved quickly past the flats, glancing behind me and then looking out at the view: a snow-covered graveyard of 1960s architecture, the apartment blocks facing in at each other, as if trying to hide themselves.

Where the hell did he go?

Then, around the bend in the walkway, I got my answer.

He was standing with his back to a concrete wall – a dead end – looking at me. In front of him, pinned to him, was a boy. No more than six. The boy was still holding a snowball, clutching it in his gloved hands. His beanie had fallen away to the floor, and his scarf had begun to unravel, hanging lopsidedly at his shoulders. The look on his face was awful: eyes wide, mouth covered by the man's hand, tear trails carving down both cheeks. Against the boy's throat, the man held a knife, its blade glinting in the sunlight.

I inched forward.

'Stay where you are,' the man said.

His accent wasn't local. *Mancunian, maybe. Definitely north-west.* I heard a sniff, looked at the boy and realized it hadn't been him. For the first time, I noticed one of the doors was open and a woman was standing there watching. *His mother.* I saw her lean forward slightly and peer around the frame at me, tears on her face, hand on her mouth.

Her eyes said everything: *Help us.*

'Let the boy go,' I said.

'Or what?'

I took a step forward. 'He's got nothing to do with this.'

'Come any closer and I'll cut his throat.'

The boy's mother started sobbing again, but my eyes didn't leave the man. There was about twenty feet between us now, and – beneath the balaclava – I could see him more clearly than ever: his skin was pale, unbroken, like a smooth alabaster mask, but his eyes were the opposite – perfectly dark, like blobs of oil. As he re-established his grip on the boy, a smile cracked on his face. One of his incisors was chipped.

'Let him go.'

He shook his head. 'Let me tell you how this is going to work, *David*.' He flicked a look at the boy's mother, then his eyes returned to me. 'I'm going to take this kid with me until I'm absolutely one hundred per cent sure you're not following me. If you try anything, *anything*, I promise you: I'll cut his fucking throat. That clear enough for you?'

His mother whimpered again.

'*Is* it?'

229

I nodded. He studied me for a moment.

And then he started to move.

He inched forward, the boy starting to cry again. The man ignored him and, as he passed the mother, she stepped out of the flat, and I saw she was in her mid-twenties, still in her dressing gown, hair tied up, face puffy and lined with tears. I saw a moment, a kind of stutter in her movement, where it looked like she was about to go after them both – but then her eyes met mine and I shook my head at her. A fresh wave of tears came and she paused there, out on the freezing cold walkway, watching her boy being taken away.

The man was a couple of feet short of me when he stopped again, eyes flicking to my feet, my hands and then back to my face. 'You make any move and the kid dies.'

I backed up against the balcony.

They started edging past.

A smell filled the space between us, a sour mix of tobacco and mildew, and then he was beyond me, spinning the boy around in front of him and reversing towards the stairwell. I shuddered in my skin, fighting against the instinct to intervene, and as they got to the stairs, I heard his mother behind me, muttering, 'Joshy, don't hurt my Joshy.'

Then they were gone from view.

The mother broke down completely, shouting out her son's name. I turned round, grabbed her and brought her into me, then looked over the walkway balcony as she cried into my chest. 'It'll be all right,' I said to her, empty words, worthless the moment they came out.

But then the man emerged below. He looked up once, his eyes trying to find me above him, and then cast the kid aside. The boy stumbled forward, into a car – hitting it hard – and its alarm burst into life, shattering the silence.

The man's gaze lingered on me for a moment – fierce, animalistic – and then he took off across the courtyard, back towards the alley.

Seconds later, he was gone.

CHAPTER 28

After returning the boy to his mother, I called the police – reporting my own burglary at the same time – and waited down in the courtyard for them to arrive. As I did, I accessed a device location app on my phone. I'd registered my mobile and laptop on it six months ago for just this reason: I'd been burgled before, had things stolen, watched men come to my home to take more from me than just my belongings. This was how I began to fight back.

A couple of seconds later, I had him: he was moving along the Mall, south of Ealing Broadway. The MacBook had tapped into WiFi coverage, and with WiFi came a location. I watched a green blob slowly inch its way towards the Tube station.

Once he was inside, the signal died.

When he'd taken the Mac, it was in Sleep mode, and as long as it remained that way and he kept hitting WiFi spots, I could follow him across the city. But sooner or later, he'd realize his mistake. I just had to hope it wasn't before he got to his destination.

★   ★   ★

An hour after that, I was home again. I'd given a statement and the mother had backed up what I'd told police. It wouldn't have taken much to convince them, even if I hadn't been telling the truth: the house was strewn with wreckage like the aftermath of an earthquake.

I listed what items had been stolen, including the MacBook, and an officer said they'd do their best to trace it – but, he pointed out, there were obviously no guarantees.

I decided not to tell him I was already on it.

'Why would someone want those white notebooks?' he said.

He hadn't asked me what I did for a living yet and, when I told him, it was likely the tone of the conversation would take a nosedive pretty quickly. Cops didn't like investigators, and they liked them even less when they had the kind of history that I did.

'I find missing people.'

He looked up, over the edge of the pad he was making notes on. 'What, you're some kind of private investigator?'

I nodded, leaving it like that.

He nodded back, writing something else down. When he was done, he said, 'Have you got any idea who this guy you pursued was?'

I shook my head. 'No.'

His eyes narrowed.

He was in his fifties, greying and weathered, but I could tell he was sharp. The irony was, for once

I wasn't lying to the Met: I genuinely had no idea who the man was.

But I was going to find out.

After they were gone, I grabbed my phone and attempted to zero in on the location of the laptop. It had been almost two hours since I'd last checked in. As I waited for the app to update, I returned to the moments before he'd escaped, the way he looked as he shuffled past me on the walkway. Well built but pale. Dark eyes, a cracked smile, a chipped tooth. I remembered the way he'd smelled too, of tobacco and mildew. Unwashed. Unclean.

Everything I had at home on the Franks case was gone: the document I'd created on the Mac; the printout I'd made of it; the Moleskines; every item that Franks had tucked into the back of the notebooks, including the scrap of paper and the flyer. The police had asked me if any cash, any jewellery or anything expensive was missing. But he hadn't taken anything like that. He'd come for one thing, intent on a single outcome.

To stop me finding out what had happened to Franks.

The phone updated with a gentle buzz. There was no signal now. Either he'd shut the laptop down or headed somewhere that didn't have an Internet connection. I kept the programme running, grabbed the landline phone and dialled Craw's mobile.

'It's me,' I said, when she answered.

234

'What's up?'

'I'm going to give you a physical description, and I need to know whether it rings any bells.'

'You'll have to make it quick.'

'Are you in the middle of something?'

'I've got to run to a meeting.'

I gave her the man's description, concentrating on the chipped incisor. That was what would get him found. 'Do his details tally up with anyone you've met or known?'

'No. Why, who is he?'

'He broke into my house.'

'What?'

'Your dad's things are gone.'

'What?'

'His iPad. My laptop. All I've got left is a notepad, which I had on me.'

The whole point of Craw coming to me was because she couldn't go the official route. But now we needed her access. Specifically, her access to the police database.

'So what are you asking me?' she said, but she knew where this was heading.

'I wouldn't ask if it wasn't important.'

Nothing.

'Craw?'

'No way.'

'The guy's in the wind,' I said to her, and then glanced at my mobile phone, the location app still ticking over. It wasn't strictly true – not yet, anyway – but if he didn't resurface in an area where the MacBook could access public WiFi, it soon would be.

'And if he happens to be some long-lost pal of my dad's?'

I didn't reply, but that was where the risk lay: her being caught searching police records after she'd been told to back off – and finding someone linked to her father.

'This is my *career*, Raker.'

'I know. Look, if it can't be done—'

And then my phone buzzed once.

Next to the MacBook listing, a green light had appeared. I tapped on it and the app transferred to a map screen, tagged with street numbers I didn't recognize and side streets that meant nothing.

I zoomed out.

Waiting for it to fill in, I heard Craw saying, 'Raker?'

'Hold on a second.'

The green blob reappeared at the end of a small, unidentified road just off the A2. *Where the hell is the A2?* I zoomed out a third time, and the map began to fill in, this time loading in street names. But the blob didn't move.

Because he's reached his destination.

I switched to a satellite view and saw he was inside an industrial unit, one of four crammed together in a cluster. The signal lasted about a minute before it went dead.

But by then he'd put himself on the map.

He was in a warehouse on Bayleaf Avenue, just off the A2 in south London. The A2, I discovered, was the Old Kent Road – and two streets down from that was Scale Lane. That was the address of the phone box I'd seen on the records that Spike had got me.

The phone box Franks had been called from.

CHAPTER 29

At eight o'clock, night long since having taken hold, I made my way south along Bayleaf Avenue, a single-lane street that hit a dead end four hundred feet down. There were two units on either side, their corrugated-iron exteriors an exact match. The only difference was that the one furthest along had no signage on it and its windows were whitewashed.

It was empty.

His signal had come from inside.

I walked about fifty yards and looked back over my shoulder, to the glow of the Old Kent Road. It was like dropping into the shadows of a cave. There were no lights on inside any of the units any more, no security lamps to herald my approach, no cars or vans or delivery trucks. Halfway down, I had no choice: I checked no one was following me, removed the flashlight I'd brought, and switched it on.

Closer to the empty unit, I saw that a set of arches – sixty feet high – had been closed off with huge metal grates, and could hear the metallic whisper of a railway line above me. As the beam cut across the night, shadows danced in the ridged exterior of the unit. Close up, all the buildings seemed in various states of decay, but the vacant one was worse: hairline cracks had formed on its front, some of its roof tiles were missing, and the ground in front of the cargo doors was swarming with weeds.

The doors were padlocked to a metal plate, screwed into the ground. But on the side was a regular door, six feet off the ground and sitting at the top of a rickety wooden staircase. I made my way around, stepping over fallen pieces of masonry and a twisted, writhing mass of weeds. As I took the first step, I felt it bend gently under my weight, the wood warped and old. On the second, something snapped, so I moved as quickly as I could, taking the rest of them two at a time. At the top, I could see the door was equally neglected: its paint was blistered, it had bent slightly against the frame, and its single glass panel had cracked through the middle. But not everything had been allowed to rot.

The lock was new.

Removing a pick and a tension wrench, I spent the next ten minutes trying to feel my way along the pins, torch between my teeth, hands getting colder, breath steaming up the glass panel on the door. I hated picking locks, the patience it required, the absolute precision, and, in truth, I wasn't particularly good at it. But, finally – on a fourth attempt – I heard a soft *dumph*, and the door gently kicked away from the frame, squeaking on its hinges.

A corridor stretched ahead of me, a door on the left leading into an office, another at the end pulled shut. Next to the one on the left was a window, creamy and smeared. There were the ghosts of old furniture visible through the smoky glass. As I stepped into the building, a fine layer of debris crunched under my boots – and then the temperature started to change. Subtly at first, barely there, the bitter cold still rolling in from behind me. But when I pulled the main door shut, the chill of winter died away and it became instantly, oppressively warm. On the wall beside me was a small, four-bar radiator. I touched a hand to it.

It was cold.

I continued moving. The further I got, the hotter it became. On the window into the office, condensation had formed, trails of water running down the edges of the glass.

Now I could hear a noise too.

A faint repetition, like a machine ticking over.

I stood there, hesitant, some part of me instinctively sounding an alarm. But then gradually I began moving again, inching deeper into the warehouse. I tried the office door, checking the interior. It smelled of damp and cigarette smoke, the odour ingrained in the walls and furniture. But it was cooler than the corridor.

Because the heat wasn't coming from here.

I turned to face the other, closed door.

240

There was a slim gap at the bottom. Where it wasn't quite flush to the frame, a soft wave of light escaped under it, washing out across the floor in front of me. The closer I got, the more heat I could feel. It pressed hard at the door from the other side, and when I touched the handle it was warm. I realized then that the noise I could hear, the mechanical repetition, was actually popping.

The kind of sound you get when something is burning.

I pushed at the door and it opened out into the main warehouse. Most of it was cast into darkness, its ceilings too high for light to claw at, two of its walls a swathe of black. The room was divided up by banks of stand-alone storage units, their shelves cleared out. On the left was an L-shaped wall, about five feet high, its brick crumbling. It sectioned off a space behind which I could see a dirty silver metal hood, bolted to the wall ten feet up, and a series of ventilation pipes.

Underneath was a kiln.

As I approached, I saw the remains of a previous life, a time when this building had housed a glass-works. A set of callipers – almost rusted through – was discarded on the ground. A set of hand shears. A blistered blowpipe. The heat was intense, even from twenty feet away, but as I got closer, the popping noise got louder and I realized the kiln was full of debris: wood, brick, cardboard, plastic, anything at all.

Anything that needed getting rid of.

Something fluttered in my stomach.

Stopping at the brick wall, six feet from the door of the kiln, I looked back over my shoulder. The warehouse felt even bigger now, as if the shadows had spread. When I turned back to the fire, the same anxiety hit me again, thick and congealed in my guts.

From this distance, I could see the remains of the Moleskines, shreds of paper – reduced to specks of ash – being drawn upwards, into the neck of the kiln. Another step closer, and I saw my laptop, sitting on its side among a knot of wood and brick, half of it already melted, splashed across the walls of the kiln like it had detonated. Had he dumped it in here after realizing I'd been tracing him? Or was it always the plan to dispose of the laptop and what was on it? My eyes moved again and I spotted a backpack – the one the man had carried all my things in – and the clothes he'd been wearing: the black trousers, the black fleece, the navy-blue balaclava. There was Franks's iPad too, fused to the rear of the kiln, the screen cracked, its casing reduced to a molten silver pool.

He'd got rid of everything.

I leaned as close to the mouth of the kiln as I could go without scalding my face, trying to get a better view. Inside it was like a dumping ground: the gnarled skeletons of mobile phones; some sort of piping, coiled like a black snake; a pair of blue jeans, caked to the dome of the kiln, as if they had been painted on; countless other items long since burned, unrecognizable as they fused together in the heat. I half expected to find bones in it too, but if there had ever been bodies dumped inside, they had become memories long ago.

Clunk.

A deep, resonant sound echoed across the warehouse.

I swept the flashlight out, to the spaces around me, to the way I'd come in, to the cargo doors. Nothing moved. I shifted the torch on to the shelves, wondering if something had fallen off. But then I remembered the shelves were all empty. I paused there for a moment, waiting for the sound to come again, but all I could hear now was the kiln: crackling, popping, burning.

I felt a trail of sweat run down my back, tracing the ridge of my spine, and then the torch hit an area on the far side. An old table, awash in empty food cartons and beer cans. Discarded magazines. A paint-specked radio which had fallen on its side. A torch.

There was a laptop too, ancient and battered. The electricity had been turned off in this place, so there was no power cord for the laptop, no plugs nearby to even charge it, no modem.

Yet, as I flipped the lid, it sprang into life.

It had been charged somewhere else, and brought here – and now it was leeching off the WiFi from the unit next door. There was also a thin, five-pin lead coming out of one of the USB slots, unattached to anything external – or, at least, not at the moment.

The desktop was clean in a way that could only have been intentional. There were no folders or files, no programs beyond what existed on it when it had first been shipped. I went to the menu and selected Documents and Pictures, and there was nothing in those either. Even the Recycle Bin was empty. The laptop was registered to '334', which had to be deliberate: he'd left his name off, presumably as insurance against just this sort of thing.

His web history went back half a day. Prior to that – presumably prior to using it at lunchtime – there was no evidence he'd ever been on the Internet. He'd cleared out his cookies and cache, and there were no bookmarks.

He repeatedly wipes it clean.

I went through what he'd been looking at today.

Various newspapers. Football sites. Late afternoon, he had spent two hours looking at porn, his history logging a succession of images where women were outnumbered by gangs of men. The more he watched, the darker and more aggressive the content became. But then, in the hour after that, things calmed down, and I found something else, another webpage he'd looked at. It was a tech site titled: 'Do Mac files work on a PC?'

I realized then what the five-pin lead was for.

An external hard drive.

I looked back at the kiln, at the remains of what had once been my MacBook. He'd copied every-thing on my Mac and on Franks's iPad across to the hard drive. The next step was to move them across to his PC.

Then: another noise.

I pushed the lid of the laptop back down. It wasn't the same sound as before – the clunk. This one was softer, less industrial.

I listened.

The hum of the laptop.

The soft crackle of the kiln.

And then a click.

I paused, eyes moving to the kiln, the shelving, the cargo doors; to the door that led back into the corridor.

Then I realized what it was.

Someone's inside the warehouse.

CHAPTER 30

I moved quickly, across the floor of the warehouse, in the opposite direction to the exit. Where two shelving units had aligned in a T-shape, I dropped down and killed the light.

The door opened.

A shape emerged from the corridor, dark against it, the kiln painting one side of them in a soft orange glow. Beneath the hood of their top, I glimpsed a face: it was the man I'd chased; the one I'd tracked here. His skin looked like snow, pale and bloodless, but his eyes were the opposite, reduced to smooth discs like holes in his skull. His clothes from earlier were burning in the kiln, but this new set was basically the same: black hooded top, black trousers, black boots, a blue body warmer, zipped up.

The side door had had a cylinder lock on it – once I'd pushed it closed, it clicked shut and there was no evidence anyone had ever been here. Except, as he stood there in the doorway, I noticed a glitch in his movement, a momentary hesitation, and he paused – fingers still wrapped around the door handle – staring across the warehouse at the kiln.

Slowly, he looked out across the room.

His movements were sharp, robotic, like a machine scanning its surroundings. In the lack of light, there was something more menacing about him, his rigidness, the way he seemed to sense something was off, like an animal. I felt myself tense as he looked at me, towards the area on my left, and then on to the loading doors. When he came back again, the tiniest pinpricks of light registered beneath the hood – his eyes connecting with the kiln – and then they were gone again, reduced to an oily black.

As he finally moved and turned to face the kiln, I saw he was holding another backpack at his side, partially hidden. He took a further step, into the warehouse, and kicked the door shut behind him with his heel. Then he stopped again, as perfectly still as before, the hood covering his face. The only thing moving was the backpack, gently swinging back and forth beside him like a metronome. Now it was like he was listening.

I'd chased him down earlier, got within feet of him, been confident of taking him if I'd ever been given the opportunity. But not now. There was something different about him: quiet, controlled, menacing. I'd surprised him earlier. He hadn't been prepared.

But he was prepared this time.

About ten seconds later, he moved again, across to the kiln, looking in through the door at the fire. As he watched the flames burn, eating their way through all the evidence he'd dumped, he flipped back his hood and I got my first proper look at him, without the hood, without the balaclava.

He was in his early forties, shaved hair, light from the fire glinting in the dome of his head. Five-ten, five-eleven, a little overweight, but not enough to slow him down. He had the build of a lapsed bodybuilder, muscle indent still evident, even as his shape had started to change. But there was a weird dichotomy to him: he looked like a nightclub bouncer, all brawn, like he should have been slow and cumbersome. Yet as I recalled him out on the walkway of the tower block – his small, aggressive movements – and now watched him again here, I realized that was exactly why he was so unnerving.

He hid who he really was.

Automatically, I felt myself stiffen as he left the kiln and came across to the table. It was about thirty feet to my left. He placed the backpack down on top and began to unpack it: a six-pack of beer, a sandwich, crisps, a magazine. He set the fallen radio the right way, then flicked it on. It was tuned to a station playing heavy metal, volume down low. He didn't adjust it. Instead he continued to unpack the bag. More food: chocolate, tinned fruit, cereal, milk. But then the food stopped coming.

A hard drive.

Duct tape. Rope.

He pushed the tape and the rope to one side, checked to see if there was anything else in the bag, then tossed it aside. Unzipping his body warmer, he went to the inside pockets. From one he took out his mobile phone. He checked the screen, the light briefly illuminating his face and surroundings. I silently edged back into the darkness, trying not to get caught in the glow, and then looked off across the warehouse to the only way out. I could make a break for it, perhaps get a two-second head start on him – but I'd have to avoid shelving units on the way, would waste a second opening the door, then another at the exterior. By that time, he'd be on me. *Or you could try to take him.* I turned back in his direction and saw he had his hand in the pocket on the other side of his body warmer.

He brought out a gun.

I felt myself tense again, a ripple of alarm following it. He placed it down next to the other items, its casing making a soft thud, and then started to unpack the sandwich. I looked between him and the door. If he was settling in for the night, I didn't want to get caught here. But, equally, I didn't want a bullet in the back either. All I had as protection, as a way to fight back, was the rubberized casing of the flashlight. My wallet. My phone.

Nothing else.

I'd walked into a dead end.

I shifted slightly in the dark, trying to get further away from him. He wouldn't be able to put the lights on because they weren't working, but he already felt too close. I edged to my left, moving on my haunches, and came to rest next to another shelf. I adjusted quietly beside it – and the metal zip on my jacket tapped against the shelving.

It pinged.

He turned immediately, eyes on my position. I quickly shifted again, further back. Apart from the kiln popping and crackling, the warehouse was silent. Picking up the gun, he stepped away from the table, shed his body warmer and let it drop to the floor behind him. His head tilted slightly, trying to see beyond the shadows, and then he took a step forward, his back to the kiln, and instantly became a silhouette. I couldn't make out his face at all now. Not where his eyes were, not even in which direction he was facing.

I was blind.

My heart banged against my ribcage.

Turn around.

And then his phone erupted into life.

It buzzed across the table behind him in a series of robotic beeps – a mechanical heartbeat – light strobing across the walls, a pale green glow thrown along one side of his face. I saw his eyes move inside the shadows of his eye sockets, catching the light like a mirrored panel: there, gone, there, gone. He stayed in the same place, unmoved, ignoring the phone, his gun up in front of him.

Ten seconds. Twelve. Fifteen.

When he finally came to life again, he turned halfway – side on to where I was – and glanced at the phone, before his eyes flicked back towards me. Brow furrowed.

He knew something was up.

He could sense it.

But then, as the phone stopped ringing, he shuddered out of his stillness, turned back towards the table and picked the mobile up. He looked at the screen, clicked a couple of options, then tossed it back on to the table. Picking up his sandwich, he pulled a chair out from under the table, slid in, and started using the laptop.

After a couple of minutes, a thought occurred to me: *What if my own phone goes off?* As quickly as I could, I reached into my pocket, felt around for it and turned it off.

When I looked back, my heart dropped: the man had turned slightly and through the corner of his eye he was looking off into the dark, to the position I'd been in when I'd brushed the shelving unit. A video was playing on the laptop, but he wasn't paying attention. Instead, he started looking for something else. A second later I realized what.

The torch.

I moved again in the direction of the loading doors, quickly and silently, using the nearest shelving unit as a guide. Dust kicked up, getting into my throat, and I had to cover my face to subdue any noise. I heard a clatter and looked up in time to see the man placing the gun down and picking up the torch. He flicked it on, stood where he was and shone it into the space I'd first occupied. I kept moving, slower now, as he swept the cone of light from left to right, a spotlight tracking my route. Out of the dark in front of me came the loading doors, a thin glow escaping under it. I'd gone as far as I could.

Shit.

But then the cone of light stopped five feet to my right, the torch dropping away to his side, light skittering back across the warehouse and forming a pool next to his leg.

He switched it off.

After a brief pause, he returned to the kiln, opened the door and stood there, face lit, eyes lucent, as if thinking. A moment later, he walked back to the table. Putting his body warmer back on, he checked his phone again, packed everything into the bag, including the gun – and then he left.

CHAPTER 31

I heard the main door close, then footsteps passing outside the loading bay, crunching on compacted snow. Getting to my feet, stiff from keeping so still, I took off after him, leaving the heat of the warehouse behind me. In the corridor, it was a relief to feel a slight drop in temperature – and it felt even better hitting the sub-zero chill of the night air.

He was already at the top of the road.

I moved quickly along the pavement, trying to keep noise to a minimum. I didn't want anyone out on the Old Kent Road to hear my approach, or to place me at the scene if things went south. It was only nine-forty, so the main road was still busy: traffic passed easily across trails of grit, people too, following pavements where snow had been pushed into piles, or reduced to slush. At the mouth of the road, I paused: I had a gap of about ten seconds between passers-by. Slipping out of Bayleaf Avenue and into the pedestrian flow, I spotted him about a hundred and fifty feet ahead of me. He had the hood up on his top, body warmer zipped up, hands in his pockets, heading north towards Walworth.

I powered on my phone and picked up the pace. Ahead of me, three identical eighteen-storey tower blocks rose like fingers out of the earth, hundreds of windows illuminated against the black of the sky.

A couple of minutes later, as the man continued along the Old Kent Road, he looked back over his shoulder. I took a subtle half-step to the left, moving in behind a couple a yard in front of me. Anything more, any great shift into the shadows at the edges of the pavement, and he'd notice. After a few seconds, I leaned – peeking past the couple again – and saw him passing a Chinese takeaway flanked by stone dragons. He'd slowed down a little now, head bowed, fiddling with something in front of him. As he came to a junction, he stopped, still concentrating on what he was holding. I slowed, using the shadows of a building, set back from the street, as cover. Then I saw what he had in his hands.

His phone.

Is he texting someone?

Or is someone texting him?

He passed a burnt-out building, sandwiched between an English-language centre and a vacant record shop. Windows were boarded up. Graffiti adorned the lower floors. Charred tongues of smoke licked their way up the paintwork. And then, suddenly, as we moved left on to New Kent Road, I saw where he was heading: towards the Tube at Elephant and Castle. Up ahead, framed by the grim shell of the shopping centre, were the grey-green glass panels it was housed in. Above that, the sky was black, light rain starting to drift in. The drizzle was barely visible, but I could feel it against my face and hear it against the buildings around me. It beat a soft tempo, like a distant chant.

Inside the station, he took the escalators down into the earth, heading for the northbound platform on the Northern line. I hung back, conscious of being seen. It was after ten now and the platform was almost empty. Hovering in the gangway between the concourse and the line, I held my position, the man about thirty feet further down, on the platform edge. Over his shoulder, along the gloom of the line, headlights started to burn holes in the dark, the tracks making an electrified twang, brakes starting to squeal. Then, finally, the train entered the station, whipping past the man, his face reflected in the glass over and over, countless windows forming and re-forming him. I edged closer, his features replicated more fully as the carriage slowed to a halt. Inside the hood I saw the paleness of his face and eye sockets reduced to black puddles under the overhead lights.

As he boarded, his back to me, I did the same, casually striding through an open door, at the end of the next carriage down from his. I looked through to the next car and could see him clearly, half turned towards me, muscular arms reaching to a handhold. After a couple of seconds, he seemed to sense someone watching him and started to turn in my direction. I backed away from the glass, out of sight. The door closed. The train juddered into motion. I grabbed a handhold myself, deciding not to look again for now.

But then he came into view again.

He was back out on the platform.

His eyes moved along the passing carriages, one to the next, until he found me. I stepped forward. When his gaze met mine, a smile splintered across his face and he followed me with his eyes, all the way along the station until we finally disappeared from each other's line of sight. And then the darkness of the tunnel claimed back the train.

Shit.

He'd figured out I was tailing him.

But I hadn't made any errors, any slip-ups.

It was a textbook tail.

My thoughts quickly came together, as I remembered him using his phone on the walk up from the warehouse. Had he been warned I was on to him? If he'd been warned, it meant someone had been stalking me while I'd been shadowing him. But that didn't make sense to me either: I'd been so conscious of my surroundings, of him, of other people, it seemed impossible I'd missed a tail.

Unless the tail wasn't physical.

I got out my own mobile phone.

Unless they never had to move at all.

CHAPTER 32

By the time I got to Borough, I'd removed the battery and SIM card from my phone. I double backed to Elephant and Castle, then exited and returned to where I'd left my car. As I slid in at the wheel and fired up the engine, I popped the SIM back in and powered on the phone briefly, to check if I'd missed any messages. A few seconds later, it buzzed.

Craw.

I quickly called her back.

'Let's cut to the chase,' she said, and immediately it was clear that something had got to her. 'I might as well go out with a bang before I get the sack in the morning.'

'What are you talking about?'

'I did your database search.'

I thought of the man I'd just lost on the Tube. She meant she'd gone against all her instincts and put his description through the computer. I couldn't say I was disappointed.

'And?'

'And you were right.'

'About what?'

'The chipped tooth got us a match.'

I grabbed my notepad. 'Who's the match?'

'It's complicated.'

'Everything's complicated.'

'It is when you're involved.'

She was on the defensive because she felt I'd forced her hand; that I'd made her go searching in the database against her will. But she wouldn't have gone searching if she didn't want answers. Craw was one of the most uncompromising people I'd ever met.

'Remember, it's *your* father I'm trying to find here.'

'I know.'

'Are you sure?'

A pause that doubled as an apology.

'He was a cop,' she said finally.

'Who?'

'Chipped incisor.'

I thought of him standing on the platform. Looking off into the dark of the warehouse. Holding a knife to the boy's throat. 'So he's not a cop any more?'

'No. Reason he's on the database is because he got done for speeding on the M25 two years ago. Like, *really* speeding. One hundred and thirty-two miles per hour. It was his second serious speeding offence in as many years, so this time he got twenty hours' community service and a five-year driving ban.'

'What's his name?'

'Neil Reynolds,' Craw said.

'Have you heard of him?'

No response.

'Craw?'

'Yeah, I've heard of him.'

'How?'

'Jim Paige pushed him out.'

'Of the Met?' I took that in. 'When?'

'June 2011.'

'Why?'

'I don't know. Never met him, never worked with him. Reynolds is so far off my radar he's just a blip. All I remember is overhearing a couple of the lads on my team talking about him in the kitchen at work one morning. There were whispers about him.'

'What sort of whispers?'

'People said he was on the take.'

'When was this?'

'I don't know. Like I said, all I've heard are vague whispers.'

'So he was part of Sapphire, working under Paige?'

'For a while. Then he worked murders. After Dad retired in April 2011, Jim was made acting chief of the Homicide command for six months, so he became Reynolds's boss a second time.'

I paused, one hand on the wheel, one on the gearstick, my mind moving ahead. So why would Reynolds care that I was looking for Franks? He'd broken into my house, stolen my casework, copied what he'd needed and burned the rest. That spoke of a man trying to hide something – or get to something first. Could he be looking for Franks as well?

'Raker?'

'So Paige sacked this Reynolds guy two months after your dad retired?'

'Yeah.'

Had the whispers about Reynolds being on the take turned out to be true? Or had Reynolds done something even worse two months into Paige's stint as Homicide chief? I'd need to speak to Paige again, even if the idea didn't make me comfortable: he'd been hard to chisel away at first time around, and if my phone conversation with Murray was anything to go by, I'd have to work even harder to get anything more out of him.

'I'll give Paige a call in the morning,' I said.

No response on the line.

'Craw?'

'Maybe there's a workaround.'

'Workaround?'

'Maybe there's someone else you can talk to instead.'

'Who?'

'Someone else who worked with Reynolds.'

'*Who?*'

A long pause. 'Colm Healy.'

CHAPTER 33

I parked the car a couple of streets away from my house, and approached from the south, coming in via a series of alleyways. I'd gained a clear enough view of Neil Reynolds – from the knife he'd held, without blinking, to a six-year-old's throat; even from just being inside the same four walls as him – to know I couldn't write off the possibility that he might come back to my house again and wait for me. He was violent, merciless, unpredictable – and he was smart. He'd messed up the first time and left a trail all the way back to the warehouse, but I doubted he would make the same mistake again.

The night was colder than ever and the side roads hadn't been gritted. I moved as quickly as I could, Santas and reindeers in gardens all the way down, lights winking from drainpipes and fascia boards. A couple of times I could feel my feet slide, but I managed to spot most of the ice before I hit it. As the house came into view, I slowed, looking up and down the street. Curtains were pulled. Blinds were shut.

The whole road was quiet.

I moved up my driveway to the front door. It was still locked. Letting myself in, I kept the lights off and grabbed a torch from the kitchen. I checked the rooms one by one.

There was no one waiting for me.

I packed a suitcase, grabbed a spare phone I kept in a drawer in my bedside cabinet, and an old laptop I'd had as a journalist and never given back, and moved through to the living room, untouched from the way it had been left by Reynolds. On the drive home, I'd bought a new SIM card. I put it into the spare phone, powered it on, and texted Craw to let her know that I'd be on this number now if she needed me. I let Annabel know about the change as well. Pocketing it, I slid out the files Ewan Tasker had got me from under the TV cabinet, and checked them briefly.

The three other unsolveds I skim-read and then immediately set aside, feeling certain now that they weren't going to open doors for me.

But the drug murder was different.

It felt like there was something in it.

As I leafed through the pages, I got my first official confirmation that Franks had indeed acted as SIO on the case, and my first look at the unidentified male victim. He was lying on a mortuary slab, a photograph that must have been taken in the days just after his death. The file listed him as thirty-nine but he looked at least ten years older, gaunt and hoary, hollow dents in his cheeks, skin drawn so tight his jaw was as sharp as a razor's edge.

I looked out across the back garden, checking for signs of movement, but save for the fir trees – swaying gently in the breeze – everything was still. I'd managed to pull the broken gate back into place and secure it with a new padlock, but everything else would have to wait. My furniture, my things, my memories, would remain strewn across the rooms of the house like rubble until I found the time to align them again. The alarm would remain unconnected too. The only thing I'd moved was a picture of Derryn and me – one of the few Reynolds hadn't ripped up – which I'd put inside a book, to keep it flat, and slid under the mattress.

I snapped the file shut and returned to my conversation with Craw.

Healy.

He'd worked with Neil Reynolds.

Digging out his number, I tried calling him, but it quickly went to voicemail. 'Healy, it's Raker. I just wanted to . . .' I paused. He'd hate thinking this was some kind of charity call, so I made it clear it wasn't. 'I wanted to talk to you about a case.'

I hung up.

He'd never been able to solve the case that had broken him; never found the man who'd killed the twins. He'd carried demons for so long – fought them, been beaten by them and dragged himself out the other side – it was a miracle he was even still able to function. But if there was something Healy recognized, it was a monster.

And Reynolds was one of them.

CHAPTER 34

Armed with Reynolds's home address, I headed back into the heart of London. Craw said he lived in a house at the southern end of the Old Kent Road, half a mile from the warehouse. I'd hunted around on websites that handled industrial properties and discovered that the warehouse had been unoccupied for almost two years – which meant he'd been using it illegally. I toyed with the idea of calling the police anonymously and giving them the warehouse, and especially the evidence of what Reynolds was disposing of in there, in an attempt to head him off. But while it would give me some wriggle room, and it would be hard for him to get at me from the inside of a custody suite, it was too risky for now.

If I gave the police Reynolds, I also gave them Craw and me. He had copies of all my notes, of my case, of Craw's part in it. It would jeopardize her career, and it would halt the forward motion of the case – and I wasn't prepared to let the police dictate the pace and direction of my search for Franks. With the cops between us, I'd be unlikely to *ever* get at Reynolds, at his motivation, at the reasons why – as seemed likely now – he'd called Franks from the phone box on Scale Lane. He'd turned over my house, sacked it, tried to dismantle my case. I wanted to know why, even as the idea formed that Reynolds was yet to *really* come at me. He'd destroyed my belongings – but he'd stopped short of actually harming me.

That was before I went after him.

Before he knew he'd been compromised.

Now the game had changed.

An hour after leaving home, I reached a parking lot opposite Reynolds's place. It was gone midnight, his windows were all dark, so there was a chance he was already inside, asleep.

But somehow I doubted it.

Pulling into a space that faced the front of his house, I checked for signs I was being followed. The only pair of eyes I could make out was a CCTV camera on a lamp post sixty feet from his front door.

The house was in a row of brown two-storey buildings, the ground floors home to beauty salons, betting shops, newsagent's and corner shops, the first floor a series of matchbox flats. Some had net curtains, some no curtains at all. The doors up to the flats sat in between the shopfronts, almost like they'd been squeezed in at the last minute, each door painted a different colour.

On the way down, I'd picked up a coffee and a bacon roll at a petrol station. I began unwrapping the roll, eyes fixed on the front door of Reynolds's place.

Then my phone started ringing.

I scooped it up and looked at the display. A central London landline I didn't recognize. Slotting the phone into the hands-free, I pushed Answer.

'David Raker.'

'It's Healy.'

I'd been half expecting him not to phone back at all, so the call took me by surprise. I glanced at the clock on the dashboard. Twelve-fifteen.

'Healy. How are you?'

A pause. 'Okay. You?'

'Yeah, not bad. It's been a while.'

'Yeah.'

'Almost thirteen months.'

'Yeah.'

'What have you been up to?'

'Not a lot.'

I looked at the clock again. 'You got a job?'

'Yeah. Twelve-month contract.'

'Doing what?'

No response. I'd first got to know him over two years ago, and Healy's default mood was pissed off, so the terse answers didn't throw me. But there was something else hidden in the shadows, something weary and sad about his lack of reply.

'Healy?'

'I'm working as a security guard,' he said, his Irish accent softened by years in London.

'How's it going?'

'How do you think it's going?'

He said it quietly, but he failed to disguise the resentment in his voice. I imagined the man I'd known – angry, bitter, overweight – sitting behind a desk in the front entrance of some office building, clock-watching his life away. Eighteen months ago, he had been Craw's right-hand man, helping to spearhead one of the largest manhunts in Met history.

'You said something about a case?' he asked.

'Yeah. You remember a guy called Neil Reynolds?'

Silence. 'What's he got to do with anything?'

'Craw told me you worked with him.'

'*Craw?* You working for *her* now?'

'She came to me. Her father is missing.'

Another, even longer silence. I glanced at the clock in the car again. Either he was at work, at the end of a shift, or he was having trouble sleeping. Given everything that had happened to him – the case that had torn his life apart, the death of his daughter, his dismissal from the Met – I sometimes wondered how he slept at all.

'Healy?'

'So you're looking for Leonard Franks?'

'Yeah. You know him?'

'I know him enough.'

'What do you make of him?'

'He's a decent guy.'

He didn't say anything else, but that was high praise from Healy. I steered the conversation back around to the reason I'd wanted to speak to him. 'And Reynolds?'

Another long pause.

'I've got to do my rounds in five minutes,' he said finally. 'Let me give you a call when I'm back at my desk.'

He hung up without stopping for an answer.

While I waited, I returned to my bacon roll, my eyes on the house. There were two windows on the first floor, still no lights on in either. I reached into the back seat, unzipped the suitcase I'd brought with me and got out the file on the drug murder.

A few pages in, my mobile sprang into life again.

'What's your interest in Reynolds?' Healy asked, after I answered.

'His name came up.'

'In relation to what?'

'In relation to Franks.'

A deliberate pause, as if he was threatening to hold back whatever he'd found out. But then, quietly, slowly, he started again. 'Reynolds was in Trident, working gangs, then moved to Sapphire, under Jim Paige. After *that*, he became part of a Murder Investigation Team in Lewisham. I was working in an MIT in Southwark, and the two commanders organized this tie-up where we'd share resources across borough lines. I met Reynolds a few times, sat in on a lot of meetings he was in, but never worked directly with him.' He stopped. 'They used to call him Milk.'

Milk.

Despite the doubts that had threatened to take hold, my instincts had been right: when Franks had written 'Milk?' on the pub flyer, it wasn't part of a shopping list. It was a nickname. Which meant Reynolds had been on Franks's radar that day in February. I felt a charge of adrenalin grip me: if 'Milk?' was relevant, then the sketch and '108' had to be too.

'Raker?'

I tuned back in. 'They called him Milk because he was pale?'

'Right.'

'Craw said Reynolds got fired in June 2011?'

'Right again.'

'For what?'

'Why don't you ask Craw? Sounds like she's got all the answers already.'

I ignored the jibe. 'I want to hear what you think.'

'All I've got is rumours and whispers,' he started – and then stopped again. In the background, I heard another voice. 'All right, pal,' Healy said, his voice slightly muffled now. 'See you in a bit.' He waited another couple of seconds, then came back on the line, his voice as clear as before. 'The guy I work with here is a major pain in the arse. Likes checking on me more than he likes checking on the bloody store.'

'You were telling me about Reynolds.'

'Yeah.'

'He got the boot.'

'Right. This is all second hand.'

'That's fine.'

A momentary pause, as if he was gathering his thoughts. 'Basically, the way I heard it was that Franks started seeing a few wonky details in some of Reynolds's murder cases. Tiny things. Indiscrepancies. And when he questioned Reynolds about it, Milk's explanation didn't do much to calm Franks's nerves. Rumours started getting around about Reynolds being in the pocket of a guy called Kemar Penn. You ever heard of him?'

'No.'

'K-Penn. Real nasty piece of work. Penn ran the show at the Cornhill estate off Blackheath Hill. People said he'd buried a few bodies too – but he was smart. Just what the world needs: a psycho with brains.' A snort of disdain. 'Anyway, trying to convict him was like trying to make shit stick to a wall. He didn't use his phone, didn't use the Internet – basically, he made sure he never left a trail. Cops at the Met talked for years about K-Penn being able to see things coming, like he had some kind of sixth sense. Then a few of them started wondering if his sixth sense might be called Neil Reynolds.'

I paused, processing it all. 'But Franks didn't have enough to fire Reynolds?'

'No. From what I heard, Reynolds covered his tracks. But while the brass might not have been able to pin anything on him, they knew something was up. Franks expected his teams to be squeaky clean – to do things by the book – so he had a hard-on for Reynolds a mile long. One of the guys I knew on Reynolds's Murder Team said Franks pulled Milk into a meeting room one day and ripped him a new arsehole. This guy I know said Franks was so angry, they could hear him from the other side of the floor. So when Paige took over after Franks retired, Reynolds was on Paige's radar from day one.'

'And, two months in, Paige fired him?'

'Yeah. But you can bet Franks was watching from the wings, even in retirement. He hated any sort of corruption. Any whiff of it got stamped out. He would have prepped Paige in the weeks and months before he retired, as part of the changeover, and then all Paige had to do was wait for Reynolds to slip up. And that's exactly what happened.'

'How?'

'Rumour was, it had to do with Franks's last case.'

That stopped me. Healy was talking about the drug murder. I looked down at the case in my lap, at the face of the victim. A ghost haunting the pages of the file.

'What about it?' I asked.

'Again, this is all second hand,' he said, but for the first time I could hear a subtle change in Healy's voice, a buzz, as if this return to his days at the Met had brought him a sliver of salvation. 'Franks retired having never found out who the victim was in this drug murder he was working – or why this guy had been killed. I remember chatting to a couple of informants I was using at the time, and they all got dragged in for interview, as suspects. Franks had a line-up with more lowlifes in it than you'd find at an EDL rally, but these snitches, they got the sense that K-Penn was always his number one suspect. Eventually he brought Penn in, grilled him over and over, but *still* couldn't put him at the scene. So when he retired, the case was dead. Franks had worked all the angles, exhausted all possibilities. Yet, a few weeks later, Jim Paige finds Reynolds with his nose in Franks's casework. I remember everyone at the Met was talking about that: Milk finally slipping up. Because why would he be doing that? Why would he be so desperate to get a look at that file?'

I got where he was headed. 'Kemar Penn.'

'Right. People reckoned Reynolds was trying to find out whether Penn grassed him up in interviews with Franks. The stakes were high for Milk: he probably *was* on Penn's payroll, and Penn probably *was* involved in that murder. Cutting someone from ear to ear, and removing the guy's teeth? That's *exactly* the sort of shit Penn would pull.'

I made some notes, but didn't interrupt.

'Franks was gone by then, but everyone knew him and Paige went way back. Reynolds knew it too. He must have figured out that Paige would be all over him like flies on shit from the minute he took over Franks's old job. So the most common theory was that Reynolds found the case on the computer and started going through it, trying to ensure he was still watertight after Penn's interview. But when Paige found him looking through the case file, all he ended up doing was confirming the suspicions Franks and then Paige already had about him: that he was K-Penn's man on the inside.'

'So *that* was what got him fired?'

'Apparently – and, again, this is just what I heard – Paige made him a deal: walk, and we don't dig down into all the cases you've worked. We don't go after you. Fact is, no cop wants to have to deal with Professional Standards – or, worse, the fucking IPCC.'

All of which made sense, but still didn't explain why Franks had taken on the role of SIO on the drug murder. Why *that* particular case? Why return to the front line at all?

I looked down at the file. 'And no one ever found out who the victim was?'

'All I remember is people thought the vic was a drug dealer – but someone new on the scene. Apparently, identification was made harder by the fact that the dump this guy was killed in was being paid for in cash, he was renting it under a false name, *and* through some two-bit landlord who didn't give much of a shit, as long as he got paid.'

'What name did the victim use?'

'I'm trying to remember. Marvin Roberts. Or Robinson. Something like that.'

I looked at the photograph of the victim again. *Who are you?*

'I better go,' Healy said finally.

'Yeah. Okay. Look, I appreciate your help.'

He didn't reply.

'Maybe, when this is done . . .'

'Yeah,' Healy said.

A brief, uncomfortable silence.

'All right, Healy . . . well, we'll meet up for a drink in a couple of weeks. Make sure you keep your phone on this time, okay?'

Silence.

'Healy?'

'Yeah,' he said quietly, 'see you around, Raker.'

CHAPTER 35

I started going back through the file. As that same gaunt face stared out at me, I recalled something Carla Murray had said when I'd called her at work to ask her why Franks had taken the lead on this particular case: *Did I ask the Boss the reasons why he decided to deal with the fallout from some random drug murder? No.* Her choice of words hadn't lodged with me earlier on in the day, but they did now: *why he decided to deal with the fallout.*

He'd taken it on from someone else.

As I flicked through the file, I could see the investigation had been split into two distinct sections: the two days after the victim was found dead, when a cop called Cordus had been running the show; and the six weeks after that, leading up to Franks's retirement, when he'd chosen to lead the investigation himself. Ultimately, the end result was the same: they never found the killer, and they never identified the victim.

There were clear differences in the two men's police work. Franks was more exhaustive, his interviews slower and more temperate. The key question remained the same, though: why Franks had chosen to get involved in *this* case. He wasn't just in charge of the Lewisham Murder Team at the time, he was in charge of *all* London's MITs. This kind of investigation was a decade behind him. In March 2011, he was sitting in on meetings with Met commissioners, which – weeks short of retirement – meant he shouldn't ever have been close to running an actual case.

I looked up and across at the house.

It remained quiet, unlit.

Given his position at the top of the Homicide command, it made sense that Franks would have been drafted into meetings about Reynolds, especially if there was possible corruption in one of his teams. It made sense that he would have been the one to give Reynolds the dressing down that Healy had described, because all murder detectives were ultimately his responsibility. Everyone I'd spoken to had said Franks was a straight arrow – if he'd been unable to trust Reynolds, if he'd had any doubts about his integrity at all, it didn't surprise me he'd have tried to get rid of Reynolds immediately. So were his suspicions about Reynolds why he chose to take over the case from Cordus?

I checked the house again as I finished my coffee, and tried to clear my head. According to Paige and Murray, it was cases with women and children that Franks could never let go of. This case was the complete opposite. So did he take on the running of the case in order to make sure their pursuit of Kemar Penn was done by the book? Was it his one last job for the Met before he headed off into retirement? That sounded like the sort of thing Franks might do – especially as the force had been after Penn for years.

And yet something didn't feel right.

I just couldn't put my finger on what.

What's going on, Leonard?

On 11 March 2011, neighbours found the front door of the victim's house in Lewisham unlocked – when they ventured inside, they discovered him in the middle of the room, gagged and bound, his throat cut. There was five kilogrammes of cocaine in the kitchen, stored behind cereal boxes, and a stolen phone was on the floor next to him, his prints and blood on it. The place was dusted down, and a partial footprint was found inside the front door. Forensics said handles, work surfaces and door frames had all been wiped down.

Cordus, in his original assessment, noted that the place had been broken into. The front door had been forced open with a crowbar, the wood at the side of the frame split. In his assessment, Franks agreed, but went a stage further, proposing the suspect had broken into the house at night: the partial footprint had been formed from rain-soaked mud, and when Franks got in touch with the Met Office, he'd discovered that it had rained for three hours the night of 9 March 2011. Throughout, Franks's police work was high quality, but it hadn't brought him the answer he'd sought:

by the time he retired, a man was still dead, and the killer still out there.

At the back of the file was an interview Franks had conducted with three female students who lived opposite the victim – but, as I began reading it, I noticed something.

The road had become quiet, a hush settling as the rain continued to fall lightly, chattering against the roof of the car. Slabs of grey slush had started to form at the edges of the pavements, pockmarks gouged out of them by the rain.

And someone was approaching the house.

It was Reynolds.

CHAPTER 36

He came from the right, hood still up on his top, backpack on his shoulder, dressed the same as when I'd followed him earlier. He looked behind him, then across the road in the direction of where I was parked. I slid further down into my seat but his eyes were already past me, out along the road. As he stood there, trying to find the right key from a bunch in his hand, the light from one of the shop windows poured across him, and I could see the left sleeve of his top had burned away, reduced to thin, sinewy strings of material. He must have caught it dumping items into the kiln.

Letting himself in, he paused in the doorway, nothing visible beyond, and looked both ways again, up and down the street. Then he stepped inside – and closed the door.

I waited.

About thirty seconds later, directly above the betting shop, a light came on. For the first time I noticed the window had a plastic sheet taped to the glass. Briefly, I saw his silhouette, hunched over something, arms moving, before he disappeared again. After ten minutes, I glimpsed him a second time, closer to the window, facing off to his right. He was stationary now, hands gesturing. *Is he talking to someone on the phone?* He stayed like that for sixty seconds, before stepping away from the window completely.

Then the light went off.

A minute passed. Two. Five.

As I started to wonder whether he might actually have called it a night, the door to the house opened again. He emerged on to the icewater-slick pavement, breath gathering in a cloud above his head. He had a new beanie on, a new top too, but the rest of him was the same. He looked up and down the street, the paleness of his face like a moon inside the blackness of his hood. Logically, I knew he couldn't see me: I'd parked behind a four-foot concrete wall, obscuring the make and registration of my car, and there were trees close to me, their branches clawing at the windscreen and touching the roof. And yet, as his eyes shifted left to right, passing my position, there was a sudden rigidity to him, as if he'd deliberately tensed, ready to go on the attack.

He senses he's being watched.

I slid even further into my seat.

But then his attention shifted. After locking up the flat, he stood there, fiddling around in his pockets for something. Eventually he brought out a cigarette packet. He removed one, propped it between his lips and sparked up – and then he headed off south, moving through pools of light cast by the shopfronts. Briefly disappearing from view, he emerged again, this time in the brightly lit car park of a toy store. Cigarette smoke cast off into the night around him, once, twice, three times – and then, finally, he was gone.

I got out of the car and set the alarm.

As I moved, drizzle dotting my face, I thought about what I was about to do – but not for long. The more thought I gave it, the greater the doubts, and I didn't want those now. Instead I headed around to the back of the row of houses that Reynolds lived in.

At the rear was a narrow one-way street. Grubby six-foot walls enclosed the gardens, and on the other side of the street was the south face of a twelve-storey block of flats, windowless and vast, like the hull of a supertanker. I'd thought about picking the lock at the front, but it was too exposed, plus there was a CCTV camera sixty feet from his front door. Here, there were no cameras, no people, barely any sound: this far back from the main road the snow hadn't been cleared yet, the covering still thick and tumescent, like stepping into a different city in a different part of the world.

I moved level with Reynolds's garden, checked I wasn't being watched, then hoisted myself up and over the garden wall, dropping into a swirl of shadows.

Pausing there in the dark, I scanned the windows in the terrace.

Blinds had been closed, curtains pulled. I was hidden. Immediately in front of me was an extension with a slanted roof, a window showing through to a tiny staff room.

This was the back of the betting shop.

I used the drainpipe and windowsill to haul myself up on to the slanted roof beneath Reynolds's first-floor window, and tried to lever it open. It was old-fashioned, fixed to runners, and as I applied some pressure, it shifted in its frame.

There was a latch inside, which hadn't been secured. Beyond that, I could see the vague outline of a television and light from the Old Kent Road peeking through the curtains on the far side. I tried pushing the window up again and this time it juddered on the runners, forming enough of a gap for me to feed my fingers inside and force it upward. I ducked under the window, into the flat, and pulled it shut behind me.

Grabbing a penlight from my pocket, I shone it into the dark.

It was the living room. A small TV on a cheap piece of flat-packed furniture. Some DVD boxes stacked against the wall. The other way was an old-fashioned gas fire, with a black hood and scorched metal frame. A three-seater sofa, which had lost its shape years ago, with a pillow on it. Adjacent to that was a cardboard box, acting as a makeshift table, and another full of electrical wires, circuit boards and dismantled pieces of plastic.

On top, half broken, was an old-fashioned wiretap.

As I edged closer to the sofa, a smell began to emerge. Unwashed sheets. Mould. *Mildew.* Reynolds's smell. I pointed the torch towards walls that hadn't seen a coat of paint in a decade, and a naked light bulb, its cord dangling down like a hangman's knot.

I checked out front, making sure Reynolds wasn't approaching, then moved from the living room into a short hallway. It smelled vaguely of damp. Off to the left was a windowless bathroom, the extractor fan still humming. On the right were stairs down to the ground floor and then a tiny kitchen with a skylight in the ceiling that was covered in moss and birdshit. At the other end of the hallway was a second room, door open.

It was a bedroom.

Inside was a bed, tidily made up with sheets and a duvet. A bedside cabinet. A chest of drawers and two wardrobes. This room smelled better, of deodorant and clean sheets.

I started opening the wardrobes and going through the clothes hanging up inside. A couple of suits, jeans, sportswear. At the bottom were shoes, and a few cardboard boxes. I pulled one out and flipped the lid. A mountain of movie DVDs to add to the ones in the living room. In the second box were more clothes.

And then a series of printouts.

They were folded over, so I opened them up. The front page was blank, but the rest of it I instantly recognized.

Leonard Franks's missing persons file.

At the top was the database ID number of the person who'd logged in and printed out the file. Next to it was the date: 12 March 2013. *Nine days after Franks vanished.* Reynolds was long gone from the Met by then, but he'd still managed to obtain the file somehow. He'd still found a way.

A sudden heaviness took hold as I looked down at the account of Franks's disappearance, at the face I'd seen countless times over the past three days. Was all of this about Franks and Paige firing Reynolds? Was that really what it came down to?

I knew it would be worth checking the ID number at the top, so I noted it down and placed the printouts back where I'd found them, turning to the drawers of the dresser. More clothes, and then some electrical equipment: a portable DVD player, an electric shaver, an old mobile phone. I got the phone out and powered it on, but there was no SIM and it had been restored to factory settings. I put it back exactly where I'd found it.

Despite the cracked ceiling and threadbare carpet, Reynolds had treated this half of the flat better, as if he cared more about its contents. He'd started smoking as soon as he got outside, but it was clear he never smoked here. The way everything was boxed and lined up spoke of a different side of him. More ordered. More precise. And both of those things were frightening – because those things made him more dangerous.

In the last wardrobe, standing on its end, was a

plain grey notebook. I removed it. As I brought it towards me, two photographs fell out.

I picked them up and opened the notebook.

There was nothing written inside. The only thing it was being used for was to store the pictures – to keep them flat and prevent them from fading.

Because they're important to him.

The first was a shot of an imposing stone building, with a series of vertical stained-glass windows. It wasn't the whole building, just a portion of it: an arched front entrance, a studded oak door, a semicircular sweep of steps leading up to it. Above the entrance, the building tapered into a spire.

A church.

Except it was a church in desperate need of repair: one of the stained-glass windows had been smashed – leaving a jagged mouth of broken glass behind – and a path to its left, tracing the slight curve of the cracked cream exterior wall, was overgrown and wild. On the very edge of the picture was something else: a fence, knotted with tendrils of long grass, and a river – or maybe a lake.

My first thought was that it could be the church I'd spotted in another photograph: the one Franks had two copies of in his possession. His had been a shot of a valley, with a spire in the distance, the rubble of a tinner's hut embedded in the hill on the left.

Setting that thought aside, I went to the second

photo in Reynolds's possession. It was of a long corridor, windows on the left and right, each window made up of twenty separate glass blocks segmented by thin metal strips. The glass remained intact, but the rest of the corridor had long since begun the decaying process.

Paint had begun to peel away from the ceiling, mottled and coarse, like skin sloughing away from old bones. Big wooden boxes that had once protected radiators were stripped and fractured. Walls, rubbed raw of paint like the ceiling, had returned to the starkness of the concrete beneath. And, at the other end, was another door, arched like the one at the front of the church, two stained-glass windows flanking it. The door was slightly ajar, and through the gap the next part of the church revealed itself: a glimpse of what looked like benches, a shaft of light from a high window – and then some sort of tall metal stand, covered in cobwebs, looking somehow out of place.

As my eyes moved between the two photographs, I tried to imagine where this place was located.

If the spire in the valley belonged to *this* church, it meant both Franks *and* Reynolds were interested in it. If it didn't, I now had two churches circling the case.

And no apparent connection between them.

I thought briefly about taking the photos with me, but it was clear from this side of the flat – by the way Reynolds had kept it – that he would notice if something was out of place. So I grabbed my camera phone, photographed them both, and then returned them – and the grey notebook – to the wardrobe.

That was when I heard a thud.

I stepped away from the wardrobe and listened. Nothing. Closing the wardrobe, I headed through to the living room and looked out on to the Old Kent Road. There was no sign of Reynolds. But then I heard the same noise a second time.

Shit.

It was the sound of a door shutting.

He was already back inside the flat.

CHAPTER 37

I headed straight for the window and tried to inch it up on its runners. It made a soft squeak, juddered, and then jammed on the left side. Behind me, out in the hallway, the light had come on. Footsteps were coming up the stairs. I loosened it, trying to free the jam, and as it finally started to move again, it made a louder, deeper noise, like a painful groan.

The footsteps stopped.

Pushing at it more frantically, I continued shifting it up, conscious of the noise but even more conscious of being caught inside the flat. Behind me I heard another creak on the stairs. Then another. As soon as he got to the landing, the floorboards would let me know he was there – but by then he'd only be the width of a room away from me.

I pushed again. Despite a fresh wave of resistance, this time it shifted upwards, once, twice, leaving enough of a gap for me to get through. I ducked under the bottom edge of the window and out into the bitter cold. Rain fell against my face, melting ice too, falling from broken drainpipes further up. I grabbed the edge of the window and forced it down – back along its runners – until it hit the lip of the sill with a dull thump.

A second later, the light came on.

I whipped back, out of sight, inches from the window itself. Initially there was no noise from inside: all I could hear were cars on the other side of the house, passing on the Old Kent Road, and the gentle patter of rain against the window. My hand was flat to the slanted roof, in a patch of freezing snow, but as I thought about moving – about trying to adjust position – a shadow shifted inside and I could see someone come to the window.

Reynolds.

He leaned right into the glass, almost pressed against it, his skin like flour, pale and powdery. I'd never been this close to him, even when he'd had a knife to the boy's throat, and suddenly he seemed bigger and more muscular than ever. He looked down to the street below, studied it, as if trying to draw something from it. From beyond him, I heard something else – a low, inaudible noise – and realized it was Reynolds's mobile phone. He couldn't have stayed there for longer than fifteen seconds, but it felt like hours, his eyes shifting left to right, back and forth along the same patch of road. Eventually he stepped away from the glass.

'Hello,' he said quietly, his accent deadened by the rain.

I stayed exactly where I was.

Not moving an inch.

Listening to his side of the conversation.

'*What?*' He paused again: five seconds, ten seconds. 'What help can that possibly be?' Another, shorter pause. 'Are you fucking *insane*? Now he knows all about me.' A long silence – before, finally, Reynolds spoke again: 'Yeah, well, you better hope so.'

There was a subtle change in the light.

He's moving.

A creak close to the window, before his movement became more distant. He was crossing the room. Quickly, the sound of his footsteps disappeared altogether, and all that was left behind was the rain, beating out a pulse on the walls, the roof, my coat.

I risked a look.

The living room was empty, light passing in from the hallway, out across the colourless carpet. *Time to go.* I slid forward, off the edge of the roof, and landed with a thud on a bare patch of cracked concrete. The impact tremored up my legs, settling as a sharp pang in one of my ankles. I pushed the pain down and made a break for the back wall, hauling myself up, easing over it and dropping down on to the other side.

Back at the car – cold, tired, aching – I slipped in at the wheel, fired up the engine and turned the heaters all the way up. As I slowly began to thaw out, the light in the bedroom came on and

Reynolds's silhouette passed against the thin curtains.

I glanced at the clock.

One-fifty.

Then, at the very periphery of my vision, I noticed something else for the first time: another vehicle on the far side of the car park, partially hidden next to a bent tree, its branches weighted with snow. The car was facing in my direction, motor running, a shadow sitting inside at the wheel. The driver's side window was open, an elbow resting there, an orange glow winking in the black of the front seat as the person smoked a cigarette.

Casting my eyes out across the rest of the cars in the parking lot, I saw that all of them were empty. There were no all-night shops here. No ATMs. No reason to be here this late. I hadn't seen the car when I'd parked up. I hadn't even seen it when I'd left for the house.

Which meant it had just arrived.

I got out.

As I stood there, my eyes on the other vehicle, I could feel the warmth from the heaters take off into the night, dying instantly. A biting wind drifted in from my left. I glanced across the road, aware that this could be some kind of trap, but Reynolds had returned to the living room, its light on. When I looked back at the car – red, its make indistinguishable in the shadows – nothing had moved: the engine was running, the person inside was still smoking, their elbow was on the sill of the open window, clouds of cigarette smoke taking off into the cold and rain. I pushed the door of the BMW shut, and took three or four steps in their direction, expecting the driver to react in some way.

But they didn't.

The car kept running.

The driver carried on smoking.

So I started moving. I headed as fast as I could in the direction of the car, careful to land my feet where there was no ice, determined not to let them get away. But the closer I got, the less concerned the occupant seemed to be, arm moving inside the car, bringing the cigarette up to their mouth, up and back, up and back, like a pendulum.

Twenty feet short of the car, I stopped again.

It was a woman.

She turned to face me, shadows shifting, and the faint orange glow from a nearby street light swept in across the driver's seat. Her grey eyes were fixed on me and her hair had been pulled back from her face into a bun. After flicking her cigarette out into the snow, she zipped her leather jacket all the way up to her chin, the collar fitting snugly along her jaw, and then her eyes returned to the empty space beyond me, where her cigarette was a gently dying light.

'We need to talk,' she said.

It was Carla Murray.

CHAPTER 38

I followed her north, across the river at Tower Bridge and then east along Whitechapel Road. Rain continued to fall, getting harder and more opaque, Murray's headlights fading and re-emerging as we continually hit traffic. When we passed the Royal London Hospital a police car whipped past us, flashbar throwing blue light into the shadows, revealing the vague shapes of the homeless, camped in doorways among black rubbish sacks. Eventually, as Whitechapel became Mile End Road, she pulled a right.

A couple of minutes later, a bank of six terraced houses emerged from the night. They faced out at a row of trees, stripped for the winter, and backed on to a series of council garages, its maze of doors zigzagging off in the direction of Stepney Green.

Murray drove on to where a line of parking bays had been created for an estate further down. I pulled in next to her and buzzed down my window. She lowered hers.

'How long have you been following me?' I asked.

'Not long. Since you called me.'

'Why?'

She glanced in her rear-view mirror.

'Murray?'

'I don't want to talk here.'

'Where do you want to talk then?'

She shifted in her seat and looked back up the road to the row of houses. 'The one on the end, with the window boxes.'

'That's yours?'

She nodded.

I switched off the ignition and followed her up the short concrete path to her front door. As she unlocked it, she looked both ways along the terrace, checking we weren't being watched, before gesturing for me to enter. As I stepped up into the warmth of the house, I saw her check her surroundings a second time. I wasn't sure what worried her more: whatever she was about to reveal, or being seen at her house with me.

Inside was a small hallway, a kitchen directly ahead of us and what I assumed was the living room off to my left. It was hard to tell for sure. She'd pulled the door shut. When I looked up the stairs, I could see she'd done the same to the ones up there too.

'Follow me.'

We headed up.

When we reached the landing, there was the scent of perfume, of fresh sheets and bath salts. The walls were decorated in a soft eggshell colour, the doors and frames newly painted. I glimpsed a photograph of Murray and what must have been

294

her fiancé, a guy in his forties with the build of a rugby player, but otherwise there was no hint at what might have gone on in the house, of who else might spend time here. Instead the rest of the wall space was filled with paintings that all looked the same.

At the furthest room around, the one that faced off to the front of the house, she paused. It was the only interior door with a lock on it. 'We have an hour before my partner gets home,' she said, fishing in her pocket for a key. 'I want you gone by then.'

It wasn't the warmest invitation I'd ever had, but I said nothing, intrigued by what might lay beyond the door.

Finally, after a moment's hesitation, she unlocked it, pushing the door back into the darkness. At first, it just looked like an empty room. There were curtains at the window, but she hadn't bothered pulling them across. Instead, she'd taped thick black card to the glass, so no light escaped in.

Or, more likely, to stop anyone seeing in from outside.

But then I realized it wasn't empty. As I followed her in, I saw the wall behind the door was covered in something, half hidden. She flicked on the light.

It was a ten-foot-by-ten-foot map of London, tacks pinned to it, thin pieces of string running from individual tacks to the edges of the map, where Murray had stuck photographs, newspaper clippings and photocopied pages.

I took another step closer.

One piece of string connected a house in Lewisham to a photograph of the victim in the drug murder.

Another ran from the spot in Deptford Creek where Pamela Welland's body had been found to the same picture of her – mirrored shades, perched on the wall outside a Spanish hotel – that had appeared in the newspapers.

There was a third, pinned to the Hare and Badger pub on Broadway, just down from Scotland Yard, where Leonard Franks had met someone, and lied to Ellie about going to the Black Museum with Jim Paige.

And then there were various shots of Neil Reynolds, long-lens photography – presumably taken by Murray herself – of him leaving his house, or sitting in the window of a café. From each of them came pieces of string, pinpointing the locations of the pictures: the Old Kent Road, Rotherhithe New Road, entering the Tube at New Cross Gate.

Finally, there was a picture of Franks; a picture of the place he and Ellie had lived in on Dartmoor; and then a third photo.

Another house.

One I didn't recognize.

The room we were in was small, pokey. For most people it would have been a study, or a nursery. Maybe one day it might still become that for Carla Murray. But for now it wasn't either of those things.

It was her own personal incident room.

'What's going on?' I said to her.

She unzipped her jacket, removing her phone and an A6 notebook. 'You're not the only one trying to find Leonard Franks.'

CHAPTER 39

She opened her notebook at the middle and then held it in place with her thumb and forefinger. Her eyes moved from what was written, to me, to the photos on the wall, then back to me.

'I couldn't say anything to you in front of Paige,' she said.

I glanced at the map. 'I'm not surprised.'

Her jaw tightened, throat muscles flexing. She looked conflicted again, decades of instinct – of interview-room sobriety – difficult to shake off. 'I need to know that you—'

'You don't have to ask for my discretion.'

She looked at me for a moment more, then at the spaces around us, at this place she'd brought us to, and she seemed to realize there was no backing out now.

'I never really stopped wondering why he disappeared,' she said. 'He wasn't just a boss to me, a mentor. He was a friend. My father upped and left when I was three, so I never really had a dad.' She paused. 'I'm a walking cliché, I guess, but he was something like that to me. Not a father, but something close.'

I nodded, shrugging off my coat and laying it on the floor. It was warm in the house. Out on the landing, I could hear the boiler ticking over.

'Anyway, when he called, asking about that CCTV tape of Pamela Welland, it was obvious he was upset about something. I worked with him for years – *years* – and after you've been around a person for that amount of time, you get to know their patterns and their rhythms. You get to see what upsets them, what makes them happy, their view on things. And the Boss was one of the most composed men I've ever known in my life.'

'But he wasn't composed when he called?'

'No.' She shook her head. 'Far from it. I'd rarely heard him like that. Maybe once or twice in twenty years. You remember the Richmond Park Rapist? That got to him.'

I recalled the newspaper coverage: ten women raped, the first two in Richmond Park itself, the rest on its fringes. Police failed to catch the man responsible for twenty-seven months, by which time the press and public were in a feeding frenzy. But the Met had refused to serve up a sacrificial lamb. Which had been lucky for Jim Paige: he would have been running Sapphire – the rape and serious sexual assault command – at the time.

'Sapphire wasn't even Franks's command, though,' I said.

'So he's only allowed to feel something for murder victims?'

'That's not what I meant.'

She took a long breath. 'That was just the type of person he was.'

Certainly there was a pattern forming: for whatever reason, Franks couldn't let go of cases where women were involved. Craw was probably a major reason for that: having a daughter of his own would bring everything into focus. He could put himself at the scene and see her there. He could imagine the feelings of the family. He could understand the vengeance they sought. Recently, it was a feeling I'd begun to recognize myself.

And yet those themes weren't prevalent in the case he worked at the end. The murder of a drug dealer, trying to nail Kemar Penn – that had been Franks's encore.

'Anyway,' Murray went on, 'there were a few cases, but not many. Most of the time, if he felt anything, he internalized it, because you never saw it on his face, in the way he treated you or in the way he spoke. That's not to say he didn't lose his rag from time to time, but when you worked for the Boss, you knew what you were getting from him: candour, loyalty, trust. If you went at cases hard, honestly, properly, he'd be with you all the way. The whole journey. You couldn't have anyone better at the helm.' She stopped, rubbing an eye, her face a little greyer all of a sudden. 'But if you were sloppy, if you didn't do the best by the victims – and especially if you lied, or compromised the integrity of a case – he'd shut you down, without even blinking.'

I glanced at the picture of Reynolds. 'Like he did with him.'

'It's obvious that you know a bit about that arsehole already.'

'I'm certainly learning quickly.'

'Milk just had this way about him. This weirdness. He'd look at you, but for a bit too long. You'd turn around in a meeting and find him watching you, or be sitting on your own in the cafeteria and he'd wander over and sit right beside you, even if every other table was empty. His real gift – if you can call it that – lay in surveillance, in watching and listening to people, and that just made him . . . I don't know . . . creepier.'

I thought of the old-fashioned wiretap I'd found in his flat, and then the way he'd been able to trace the signal on my phone. Clearly, they were skills he was still putting to good use.

'I used to think he was playing at being an oddball,' Murray went on, 'but after a while I started to realize that he wasn't playing. He just *was*.'

Her hair had been tied into a bun, but it had started to come loose, and as she tried to address it, her eyes fell on one of the pictures of Reynolds.

'Maybe that set alarm bells off with the Boss,' she continued, 'I don't know. Or maybe it was the fact that some of Milk's cases just never got solved, even when it looked like he was sitting on a cast-iron conviction. Suddenly a lead would evaporate or a witness would never resurface. People reckon it started when he was still working gangs, that that was when he first established contact with Kemar Penn. But there was never any talk of him being dirty then; not really any talk of him being dirty in Sapphire either, when he worked for Jim Paige. I mean, there was a lot of smoke, but no fire. Once he was put on a Murder Investigation Team, though, things changed. Rumours started.'

'How did they start?'

'I don't know. They just started. The thing about that drug murder was that no one could connect Reynolds to it and no one could say for sure that he had tacit knowledge of it – or, worse, was involved. But it *felt* like it, you know? I mean, he was interested enough to dig it out of the computer after the Boss retired, in order to take a closer look.'

I nodded. 'Why did Franks choose to run that case?'

'What do you mean?'

'I've read the paperwork, and it says he took over the running of the drug murder from a detective called Cordus two days into the investigation. You told me on the phone that you didn't know why he chose this case in particular . . .' I gestured towards the wall. 'But then I find myself standing in your house in the middle of the night in front of a map you made and photos you took.'

She didn't respond.

'Look, for what it's worth, I don't care that you lied, to Paige *or* to me. I don't care what secrets are swilling around the Met. All I care about is finding out what happened to Franks. So why'd he take the lead on the drug murder? Why not another case? Why *any* case? Did it have something to do with Reynolds?' I paused, waiting for a response, but then a second, clearer thought hit me: 'Or Pamela Welland?'

If I'd hit on something, Murray didn't react. Instead, her eyes slowly returned to the map, to the photographs and newspaper cuttings.

'You told me earlier on that you'd been following me since I called you,' I said to her, trying to head off any thoughts she might have of backing away now. 'But it looks like you've been watching Reynolds for a lot longer than that.'

A hesitant pause.

'Murray?'

She watched me for a moment longer. 'There's this pub just down the road from the Yard. The Hare and Badger. I met the Boss there for a drink when I shouldn't have.'

Something snapped into place. 'So it was *you* he met there.'

'You knew about the meeting?'

'I just didn't know who it was with.'

For a second that seemed to knock her out of her stride. Then she steadied herself. 'This was in the days after he'd already asked Paige and me – and we'd already refused – to get hold of the footage from the night Pamela Welland died. The Boss . . . when he asked to meet up, he called me from a phone box near his house in Devon. A *phone box*. That set alarm bells off, minute one. It meant he didn't want the call on his phone records.'

'Or it meant he didn't want Ellie to hear him.'

She nodded. 'Yeah. I guess there's that.'

'So what did he say?'

'He told me he understood about the footage, that he wasn't going to press me on getting hold of it, but that he wanted to meet me all the same. He had some questions.'

'About what?'

'He started telling me he was going to be up for the weekend seeing Melanie and her family, and that he'd have some free time on the Monday. He asked if we could meet in the pub for lunch. So we did. We took a seat as far away from the action as we could possibly get – and, out of the blue, he starts asking me about Neil Reynolds.'

'Reynolds? Why?'

'He wanted to know what Reynolds was up to; whether I'd heard what he'd been doing since he got the boot from the Met. This was, like, *two years* after Milk got his P45 from Paige. I had no idea where Reynolds was. The question came totally out of left field. A couple of weeks before, the Boss was asking me to de-archive footage from a seventeen-year-old case, now he wanted the whereabouts of *Neil Reynolds*. I mean, what the hell? Reynolds wasn't even a *cop* when Welland was murdered back in 1996.'

304

That confirmed something, at least: the mention of 'Milk?' on the two-line list he'd made on the back of the pub flyer. Now all I needed was a steer on the second part, the 'Double-check 108', and how it was linked to the scrap of paper with the sketch on it – if it was linked at all.

'You remember I asked you and Paige about "BROLE 108"?'

She nodded.

'Were you telling me the truth or trying to avoid a situation with Paige?'

'Telling the truth.'

'You don't have any idea what that means?'

'No,' she said. 'Why?'

'It's just a loose end I haven't been able to tie up yet.' My eyes drifted to the pictures of Reynolds, and I said to her, 'Franks didn't ask about anything else that day?'

She shook her head. 'Just Reynolds.'

I tried to piece it together from what I knew, tried to work out why Franks might have wanted the footage of Welland in January and the where-abouts of Reynolds in February.

'What happened when you asked him why he wanted to find Reynolds?'

She shrugged. 'He kept fobbing me off, trying to reassure me that none of it really mattered. I told him I could speak to Paige about it, and he told me not to. He said Paige wasn't to know that he'd called to ask another favour. No one was. In the end, I asked him outright if he thought he was in some kind of danger.' She paused, her gaze fixed on a space between us, her recollection of that day painted in her expression. 'But he said no.'

'Did you believe him?'

A flicker in her face. 'Not really, no.'

I gave her a moment, both of us taking in those last three words.

Her eyes were back on Franks, tracing the outline of his face, and for the first time I could read her as clearly as if she'd spoken the words.

Did I ever really know him at all?

'So, since that meeting, you've been slowly trying to piece it all together?'

'Yeah. One thing the Boss taught me, almost from the moment I arrived at the Met, was to write everything down – and *never* throw it away. He taught me to keep *everything*. That was what he did. It was an old-fashioned way of working – even back in the nineties – but I wanted to impress him, so I did what he asked. And I got into a routine of doing it, every case, every victim, every beat in an investigation . . .' She faded out. 'Especially the parts of an investigation that didn't feel right.'

I understood what she was driving at: what didn't feel right was Franks's requests for the Pamela Welland footage – and asking the whereabouts of Neil Reynolds.

'After I met him that day at the pub,' she continued, 'I went home and dug out my notes from the time of the drug murder. I didn't work that case, but the Boss asked my opinion about it, like he always did, and handed me the file so I could give it a pass. I noted down some thoughts at the time, and when I went back over those notes at the start of this year, I began remembering more and more about what had happened back then.' She paused for a second, gathering herself. 'How much do you know about it?'

'The drug murder? Not much.'

'The victim may as well have been a shop-window mannequin. His teeth had been removed, his prints went nowhere, he used a false name, and had a landlord happy to just take the cash, no questions asked. Again, when I checked my notes I found reference to a meeting I'd had with the Boss on 13 March 2011 where he'd briefed me on it, and told me that he was going to take over the running of it from Cordus. I can tell you *exactly* what his reasons were, because I wrote them down verbatim. He said it was "because of cutbacks, because I can't pile another case on teams that are already stretched to breaking point, and because I'm the only warm body left". And you know what? I didn't think twice about it. I was up to my neck in other cases, like everyone else. So we all thanked him for mucking in, we all went back to our desks, and no one gave it a second thought.'

She faded out. In the silence, I heard a car pass on the road outside.

'But now . . .' she said softly, her neck chain pinched between her fingers. 'Now I'm pretty sure that wasn't the truth.'

'Maybe he thought Cordus wasn't up to running the case?'

'No. Cordus was one of the Boss's go-to men. The Boss trusted Cordus like he trusted me. Cordus was whip-smart, had everything the Boss looked for in a murder cop.'

There was no desk in the room, no chair, just the map on the wall, and a series of box files stacked up on the floor beneath. Murray laced her hands together and leaned against the windowsill, her eyes not meeting mine. It was clear she still didn't fully trust me, but I was in her house now, involved as much as she was.

'I wrote some other things down too,' she said finally. She flipped forward in her notebook. 'The victim told the landlord that his name was Marvin Robinson. But some of the dead guy's neighbours – these stoner party girls studying at the UEL – said he once got drunk with them and ended up confirming that – *surprise* – that wasn't his real name at all.'

While waiting in the car, I remembered being about to read the interview with the students across the hall when I'd spotted Reynolds approaching.

I watched Murray's eyes return to the map, to the photographs and cuttings, and then to the picture of the second house I hadn't recognized, pinned to the wall on its own.

'You know where that is?' she asked.

I looked at the house. 'No.'

'Devon.'

I took a step closer, taking it in properly this time. It was a shabby-looking semi-detached backing on to fields that rolled up and away into an indistinct distance. Murray pressed a finger to the bloodless face of the victim in the drug murder, both his eyes closed, the mortuary slab a muted blue-grey behind the creamy dome of his skull.

'It belongs to our victim,' she said.

'The house in Devon does?'

'Yeah. Or at least it did.'

She turned back to the photograph of the dead man.

'And according to those students across the hall, "Marvin Robinson" told them his real name was actually Simon.'

SIMON

September 2010 | Three Years Ago

Simon left on a Thursday. She woke one morning to find him packing a suitcase in the spare room, clothes strewn around him. He stank like the morning after the night before, of booze, of sweat, of other women, and had a greasy sheen to his chest and back. As she approached, she thought he looked more at home than ever among the damp wallpaper and the musty stench of old carpets. At the window, instead of a pair of curtains, there was a tatty, mud-streaked orange blanket.

'What's going on?' she said.

He didn't answer.

'Simon?'

'Like you give a shit.'

The truth was, she didn't. He'd fitted what she'd needed in the years after Lucas had died, in a way she could never fully articulate in sessions with Dr Garrick.

'Are you going somewhere?'

'Yeah,' he replied. 'You could say that.'

'Where?'

310

'I'm moving out.'

'What?' Her first thought was of losing the roof over her head, of no longer knowing she had a place to come back to. 'Why?'

'Why not?'

She frowned, taking a further step into the room. He watched her come in, his eyes lingering on her.

'What's going on?' she said again.

'Are you deaf?'

'What, you suddenly decide you want to move out?'

'Yeah. So?'

She looked at the suitcase. 'So you're going to need a lot more than a suitcase full of clothes. What about all this?' she said, gesturing to the room, to the space around her, to the walls in need of paint, and to the cheap, faded furniture. 'What about the house?'

'What about it?'

'What do you mean, "what about it"?'

He smirked. 'It's already sold, you stupid bitch.'

Her heart sank. 'What?'

'It's been on the market for six months. I got an offer on it two months ago and just signed the contracts yesterday.'

She felt like she'd been punched in the stomach.

'And you didn't think to tell me?'

'What the fuck's it got to do with you?'

She backed up a little, hitting the panels of the door, her hands flat to them. 'When were you planning on telling me that you were leaving me homeless?'

He shrugged.

'That's it? A shrug?'

'You bring me down,' he said, closing the suitcase. 'You're like a walking fuckin' raincloud. All you do is piss and moan, and mope about because you've had a few tough breaks. We've all had tough breaks. We're all dealing with the shit life throws at us.'

'Yeah?' she said, regaining her composure, anger suddenly burning in her throat and chest. 'What tough breaks have you had, Simon? Not stealing as much as you'd like from work? Not making enough from stolen goods? Getting the clap from some skank you've been screwing?'

He took a sudden step towards her. 'What did you say?'

'You heard what I said.'

He grabbed her by the arm, his fingers digging into her flesh, pressing so hard it was like he was clawing his way through to the bone. 'Don't ever talk to me like that.'

'Or what?'

'Or I'll fuckin' kill you.'

'Yeah? Maybe you shoul—'

He pushed her hard against the nearest wall, one hand instantly on her throat, the other still clamped on her arm.

'You think I won't do it?' he spat through gritted teeth.

He pressed harder, as if trying to force a response out of her, but his grip was too tight: air ceased to ebb and flow and her vision began to blur, Simon starting to fade into a spill of muted colour, like she was seeing him from the other side of frosted glass.

With one last push, she fought back at him, her nails brushing the front of his shirt, then again, then again. Finally, they glanced the side of his face, digging in and ripping their way downwards. He yelled and stumbled back, clutching his face, blood spilling out between his fingers. He hit the bed, the suitcase rocking behind him, and fell on to it.

'You stupid bitch!' he screamed, looking down at his hands, blood on his fingers, on his face, smeared along the ridge of his jaw.

She roused herself from the haze, the feeling of his fingers still burning on her throat, and ran downstairs, her hand gripping the banister, making sure she didn't fall. She heard him behind her, on the landing – quick footsteps, floorboards creaking – and upped her speed, along the hallway, into the kitchen. She yanked open a drawer and grabbed a knife, six inches long with a serrated edge.

Except, when she turned around – backside against the knife drawer so he'd have to go through her to get one himself – he was standing in the doorway, leaning against the frame, as if something had occurred to him. Blood ran in four separate trails down his face – but now he didn't even seem bothered. She held the knife up in front of her, moving it in the air from side to side. He didn't react. Just watched it.

'Don't come any closer,' she said.

He didn't say anything.

'I should call the police.'

This time he smiled, pushing away from the door

frame. She jabbed the knife at him, but he wasn't coming for her. He was going across the kitchen, to the phone.

He picked it up. 'Give them a call.'

She looked from him to the phone, confused.

'Give them a call,' he said again. 'Go on. Tell them what happened. Tell them everything. They can come around here, or we can go to the station, and then you can tell them all about who I am. And I can tell them all about you.'

She frowned.

Another smile, even wider than the last. 'You don't know anything about me, really. If you did, you'd know I gave up stealing from my boss years ago. I'm into drugs now, honey. There's more money in pills and coke than I ever earned siphoning off timber and fuckin' metal sheets.' He paused for effect, fingers touching the marks on his face. 'And you know what? Because of that, I'd been thinking about getting the hell out of Devon for a while. Being in the arse-end of nowhere is a pain. The drugs are too much of a hassle to get hold of. I've screwed every skank in the county. It's all fudge shops and cream teas. But you know where I could make a fuckin' killing? London.'

He studied her, as if expecting a reaction, but she didn't give him anything. And yet still the smile didn't drop from his face.

'Anyway,' he continued, 'after I got an offer on this place, I started thinking about all the stuff I'd need to take with me to the Big Smoke, and I thought, "I

wonder if I ever left anything important in the loft?"
So I went up there, and remembered that was where
we'd stored most of your shit when you moved in.
You always told me that they were boxes full of
worthless tat.'

Now she felt a flutter of panic.

'But they're not – are they?'

She watched him place the phone back on the
cradle, his eyes returning to her. Without even realizing, she'd dropped the knife to her side. Confusion
and panic had taken over. He'd finally got at her –
and this time he hadn't had to lay a finger on her.

'What do you want?' she said.

'What do I want?' He smirked, taking a step
towards her. 'I want you to tell me everything – and
you can start with Pamela Welland.'

CHAPTER 40

We both stood in front of the map, our eyes on the victim in the drug murder. *Simon.*

He had a first name now, even if we didn't know anything else about him. Yet something was troubling Murray. I saw a flicker, almost a grimace, in her face as she traced the piece of string connecting the crime scene at his house in Lewisham to the photo of him on the mortuary slab.

'Where in Devon did he live?' I asked.

'Kingsbridge.'

I watched her. She was still caught somewhere, still troubled by something. I gave her a moment more, then pushed her on it: 'Is everything okay?'

She glanced at me, almost jolted, and then her eyes shifted across from the photos of Simon, of the house, to where Franks was pinned up.

'Not really,' she said finally.

'What's up?'

She took a long breath. 'Given everything I knew about the Boss, the way in which I'd seen him work across twenty years – this incredibly detailed, tireless crusade to do right by victims – what I

316

would have expected him to do, when he found out from those students what this guy's real name might be, was take that information and run with it. I would have expected him to use "Simon" as a jumping-off point; to use it as a basis to explore other drug-related cases in the computer, involving men with that name.'

'But he didn't?'

She shook her head. 'No. Nowhere in that case file will you find mention of the Boss putting in a search for a "Simon". Like I said earlier, I never looked closely at the investigation he was compiling at the time – I had my own cases, my own problems. We *were* stretched thin. We *were* under-resourced. And then, shortly after he hit a dead end on it, he retired, and when he retired, everything got forgotten. But after I met him in that pub back in February, after the weird request for the Welland footage, and the questions about Reynolds, I went back through my notes and started to do a little digging.' She paused, flicking a look at me. 'A few days later, I pulled the file on the drug murder.'

'What did you find?'

'To my face, the Boss told me back in 2011 that the "Simon" lead was a dead end. He said he'd never been able to find out if the victim had been lying when he told those students his real name. I remember that, because I wrote it all down, just like he'd always taught me. He said he couldn't find any connection to other drug-related cases, using the name "Simon". But do you know how long it took *me* when I decided to put in a search back in February?'

I shook my head.

'Half a minute.'

We both hung off the back of that. Despite how many times she must have processed that since Franks had disappeared, it was like she was still coming to terms with it for the first time. Franks had never been able to find a connection to a 'Simon'.

She'd found one in thirty seconds.

'In January 2011,' Murray went on, 'two months before this guy was found dead, cops down in Lewisham interviewed a Simon Preston after he was stopped and searched. They found an ounce of weed on him. They let him off with a warning, so there's not much else in the computer on him, *except* in the PNC, where a search for his full name brings up a driver's licence, and housing records.' She pointed to the picture of him on the wall. 'It's him. The picture on his driver's licence matches the guy on the slab there.'

I looked at Simon Preston.

Franks chose not to go looking for him.

'Have you read the transcript of the Boss's interview with the students?' Murray asked. When I shook my head, she continued, 'Try and find the bit when they mention to the Boss that this guy referred to himself as Simon. They *don't*. The Boss never included that part of the interview in the paperwork. The name Simon got mentioned in the office, verbally. That was why I wrote it down. But it never got included in the file itself. Instead, in his official conclusions, he said the students were "unreliable witnesses" – doped up, immature.'

'So he lied?'

'No. The girls *were* unreliable. The evidence of that is right there on the page. Their interviews are a mess. A high-ranking cop with thirty-five years' experience dismisses a lead put forward by a bunch of potheads – so what?'

'But he deliberately didn't follow up—'

She held up a hand. 'After I pulled the file, even as I tried to process the fact that he'd chosen not to look for this Simon guy at the time, I was thinking, "I trust the Boss. I trust him completely. There must have been a reason he didn't look harder for Simon."'

Murray wasn't seeing straight – or, at the very least, choosing not to. Franks had wanted to take the helm so he could control where the investigation went – and how he controlled it was by preventing it being linked to Simon Preston.

But why?

What was so special about Preston?

I glanced at my watch. We'd already been going thirty-five minutes, which meant we were running out of time before her partner got back. Gesturing to the photograph of Simon Preston's house in Kingsbridge, I said to her, 'So Preston was originally from Devon, but moved to London?'

Murray nodded. 'In September 2010.'

'And before that?'

'As you can see, I found the house he sold before he moved. I also traced him to a job he used to have on a building site. Nothing there. He paid his taxes and didn't seem to get into any trouble while he was in that part of the world. If he was in the drug game before he came here, he did a good job of keeping it all on the QT.'

'So is it possible that Franks knew Simon Preston *before* Preston died?'

'Maybe. The problem was, by the time I'd plucked up the courage to ask the Boss why he'd overlooked this Simon lead, to question his decision-making at the time he worked that case, he'd already disappeared.' She paused, eyes narrowing, as if she'd seen some accusation in my face. 'You don't understand what our relationship was like. I never questioned a *single decision* he made in the entire time I worked for him. Do you know why I didn't? Because he always made the *right* decision. *Always.*'

'And this time?'

A brief moment of fire, as if she was going to come back at me again – but then she started rubbing at her eyes, and a sudden, overwhelming sadness seemed to freeze her. She retreated to the windowsill once more, feet pressed into the carpet, looking down.

In the silence, I tried to align my thoughts. Franks. Reynolds. Simon Preston. Pamela Welland.

Everything was connected, I knew that for certain – but I still couldn't work out how or why. Then I realized Murray was watching me, head tilted to one side, shadows marking her face.

'Care to share your thoughts?'

I turned to her. There were so many layers to this case, I had to be careful it didn't become a blur. 'Okay,' I said. 'It seems highly likely Preston was in the drug game, given the stop-and-search two months before he died, and the fact that five kilos of coke were found in his flat after he was killed. It also stands to reason that Kemar Penn wouldn't much like someone else muscling in on his territory either. So, leaving aside the idea that Simon Preston and Leonard Franks somehow knew each other *before* Preston's death, what if the reason Franks fudged the case was because he saw something else in it?'

'Meaning?'

'Meaning Neil Reynolds's involvement.'

Murray frowned. 'You're accusing Reynolds of *killing* Simon Preston?'

'He was K-Penn's inside man. Does that seem so unlikely to you?'

I glanced at the photographs of Reynolds leaving his house, getting into his car, standing in the fuzzy half-light of a petrol station. Then I remembered him with a knife at a boy's throat. I remembered watching from the shadows of the warehouse, his face lit by the molten glow of the furnace. He was capable of it. He was capable of killing someone.

Preston. Franks. Anyone.

When I turned back to Murray, she was looking at the same photographs as me, and something had changed in her.

'No,' she said finally. 'No, it doesn't seem unlikely at all.'

CHAPTER 41

We had twenty minutes left.

'The day Franks met you at the pub,' I said, trying to maintain the momentum, 'he asked if you knew where Reynolds was, right? So maybe whatever cold case he was working on in retirement, in the month before he disappeared, had some connection to that drug murder. What if it *was* the drug murder?'

I paused, remembering Craw's words: *The only thing I can tell you is that the way he talked about it made it sound like it had some connection to a case he'd already worked at the Met. He talked about it like he was already familiar with it.*

'Maybe he requested it,' I said to her.

'The file on the drug murder?'

'Yes.'

'From who?'

'I don't know.'

She looked at me, and I could see her mind ticking over. 'What if . . .' She paused, a moment of uncertainty. 'What if the Boss had been using Simon Preston as some kind of . . .'

I saw where she was going. 'Informant?'

323

She nodded. 'We all have them.'

'So you're suggesting he buried the connection to Simon Preston because he didn't want to reveal Preston as an informant?' I stopped, considering it. 'Why would he go to such lengths? Preston was dead. What did it matter if somebody found out he was a snitch?'

'Because maybe there were others.' She stopped, shrugged. 'I'm thinking aloud here, but maybe the Boss had a few more scattered around, and if the secret got out about Simon, the secret got out about them all – and that meant *no one* informing on K-Penn.'

'And that meant—'

'There was no one to inform on Reynolds. *That* was what the Boss *really* cared about. He knew Reynolds killed Simon Preston, but didn't have the evidence, so the Boss fudged the case in order to come back to it. He fudged it so that Reynolds wouldn't know he was a suspect. Reynolds got enough of a look at the file on the Preston murder – before Jim Paige caught him with his nose in it – to think he was safe. But he wasn't safe. Even in retirement, the Boss was waiting for Reynolds to slip up. And when Jim Paige gave Reynolds the push from the Met, and he no longer had the protection of the force, it gave the Boss the opportunity to *really* go at Reynolds – so that's what he did.'

'But what about Pamela Welland?'

'What about her?'

'Where does she fit in?'

'Maybe she doesn't.'

'Then why was Franks calling you and Jim Paige, asking for a copy of that CCTV tape?'

Murray took a long breath. 'I don't know.'

I looked at the wall again, trying to pull it all together. Murray's theory made a certain kind of sense. The concept of Reynolds killing Simon Preston on behalf of Kemar Penn I could definitely believe. The idea of Preston being an informant also explained the connection, at least latterly, between Franks and him. And yet something wasn't sitting right with me. Why would Franks – a straight arrow, a man of honour and integrity – put his entire career on the line to falsify a case? Why would he put himself, and his new life in Devon, in danger? He loathed Reynolds for being dirty and getting away with it, but I couldn't believe he loathed him that much. What bugged me more was that at no point in the two years they'd been retired had Ellie *ever* mentioned Franks looking at a police case, let alone working one – not until that last one had turned up in the post. He left the Met at the end of April 2011, and was sent the cold case in January 2013. So if he was so obsessed with nailing Neil Reynolds, why hadn't he done anything about it for almost two years?

I tried to clear my head again, my eyes returning to the map, string criss-crossing it like a loom, photos tacked to the crumbling plaster. Newspaper cuttings lifted away from the wall as warm air continued its journey through the house. For the first time, I noticed how exhausted I was. As my adrenalin started to fizzle out, as reality took hold and I felt frustration at not being able to get at all the answers, my body shivered, goosebumps scattering up my arms and tracing the ridge of my spine.

'What about his life down in Devon?' I asked, trying to stay focused.

'Simon Preston?'

'Do we know anything else about it?'

'In what sense?'

'In *any* sense. You said he worked on a building site?'

'Yes.'

'Did you speak to his boss?'

'Yes. The business closed in 2012, but I managed to track him down. He said Preston had a bit of a temper on him, but that he turned up on time, worked hard, et cetera, et cetera. After I finished there, I moved on to the local cops. They had nothing. He wasn't anywhere close to their radar.'

Turning to face her, we watched each other in the semi-darkness, and then I said, 'Are you going to slap the cuffs on me if I admit to some mild trespassing?'

The hint of a smile for the first time.

'Reynolds broke into my house and stole everything I had on Franks.'

'*What?*'

'So I got inside Reynolds's place tonight.'

'You broke into *his* house?'

'When you saw me returning to the car, that was where I'd been.'

I could see the conflict playing out in her face: her instincts as an investigator, the rule of law, versus the need to know what I'd found.

Then she said, 'And?'

'He had Franks's missing persons file among his things, with an ID number at the top. We should find out who it belongs to.'

'You mean *I* should find out?' She studied me for a moment. 'Okay.'

I nodded my thanks as slivers of street light peeked through the gaps between the black card and the window frames behind her.

Then Murray said, 'There's one other thing.'

'What?'

'I found out where the house was, mapped it' – she nodded at the wall, at the picture of Simon Preston's former home – 'and printed it out. It's a tiny cul-de-sac of ten semi-detached houses on the eastern fringes of Kingsbridge. At the back, they look out on to these fields that run parallel to the Plymouth road.'

'So?'

'So, anyway, two or three months back, I started calling the people in the other houses, hoping to find someone who remembered Preston. And I got talking to this guy who lived next door to him. Andrew Stricker. When I asked him if he recalled Preston, he was, like, "Are you kidding me? Of *course* I remember him." So I asked him what he meant, and he said to me, "They fought so often, they're impossible to forget.""

'"They"?'

'Preston lived with someone.'

I glanced at his picture. 'Who?'

'I asked this Stricker guy and he said he never spoke to her for more than a couple of minutes the entire time she was there. He said she seemed pleasant enough, that she'd always say hello if they passed each other, but that she seemed to want to deliberately keep herself to herself. "She didn't really seem his type," is what Stricker said to me.'

'In what sense?'

'I asked him that, and he said, "Simon was pretty rough and ready. He'd come home drunk at night, the whole street could hear him swearing when something wasn't going his way, but she seemed a lot softer. Not a mouse. Not someone who could be pushed around. But quieter." He said you could tell she was smart. "You could tell she had a lot going on up top" are the exact words he used. So I asked him, if she was so smart, why was she shacked up with a scumbag like Simon Preston? He said he didn't know, but when they were arguing – and this was often; like, blazing rows once or twice a week – he said she never backed down. Not ever. I asked him if he ever saw evidence of physical abuse, and he said no – not anything obvious, anyway. He told me, if he had, he would have called the police.' She shrugged, a twist of frustration. 'To be honest, it would have been better if he *had* called the police. Then we would have had her name.'

'Stricker didn't know her name?'

'He said he overheard Preston calling her Kay.'

'K-A-Y?'

'Presumably.' She took a long, deep breath. 'The only other thing Stricker said he could recall clearly was this one fight they had, just before they moved out in September 2010. He said he remembered overhearing an argument about going to a hospital.'

'Hospital? Was Preston ill?'

'No. I looked through the autopsy notes. He was on his way to screwing up his liver and lungs with all the shite he was putting in his body, but he wasn't hospital bad. So maybe they were talking about the woman he lived with.'

'Who we can't find.'

'Right.'

But then, unexpectedly, I felt a buzz of familiarity, the sense that I'd made some sort of connection without knowing it. Slowly, the outline of a memory emerged from the darkness. My eyes drifted back to the wall, to the board full of faces, to the house on the Old Kent Road where Reynolds was holed up. *What is it? What am I seeing?* Murray was studying me now, as if she'd noted the realization in my face, the shift in my thoughts.

And then it hit me like a train.

The two photographs Reynolds had in his flat. One had been of a cavernous, abandoned

Victorian building, with a spire and stained-glass windows, fenced in, with a glimpse of a river or a lake in the background.

The second was of a corridor with glass blocks either side of it, its walls peeling, a thick arched door partially open at its end. Through the doorway, there had been some kind of metal stand, coated in cobwebs. Somehow, it had looked out of place in a church, as if it didn't belong there, but I hadn't been able to put my finger on why at the time.

Now I knew: it was a stand for an IV drip.

Because it wasn't a church in the photographs.

'It was a hospital,' I said quietly.

'What?'

'Did you do a search for "Kay"?'

She nodded. 'Yes. I didn't find anything.'

'Nothing related to Preston, or Reynolds, or Franks?'

'No.'

'What about when you searched for "Kay" and "hospital"?'

'Nothing,' Murray said again. 'This woman's a ghost.'

'No,' I said. 'We can find her.'

A frown. 'Why, do you know her?'

I removed my notepad, trying to zero in on the drawing that Franks had made on the scrap of paper. I'd copied down a rough approximation of it – and now, finally, I knew why, every time I'd looked at it, a vague sense of recollection hit me.

'You remember I asked about this?'

I turned the sketch to Murray, so she could see it.

She nodded. 'Yes.'

'Paige thought it was a stick man.'

'It's not?'

'No,' I said. 'This rogue triangle on the top there – I know it. I recognize it. I think it's a greenhouse. This is the layout for a building.'

As I said that, my mind flooded with memories: a fuzzy, sun-bleached flicker of images from an August in 1978 when my mum and I had stood on the edges of the sea, looking out into the English Channel.

'What is that place, Mum?'

She looked out at the channel, unsure how to respond.

'Mum?'

'It's . . . It's, uh . . .'

'What? What is it, Mum?'

And then slowly, automatically, she brought me into her, pressing me to her hip, and she said to me, 'It's somewhere bad, sweetheart. It's somewhere very bad.'

I looked at Murray.

'Whoever Kay is,' I said, 'I think she was a patient at Bethlehem.'

BETHLEHEM

November 2010 | Three Years Ago

The sea lapped at the wheels of the vehicle as it crossed the causeway. Further out, it was choppy, waves rolling in, ceaseless, unyielding, consuming each other as they raced for the shore – but here, on the other side of the sandbank, it was almost still, like a sheet of frosted glass. The only thing disturbing it was the vehicle's wake, fanning out in a cone.

She looked ahead of the ferry, to the hospital.

Bethlehem.

This early in the morning, most of it was just a silhouette, grey and indistinct against the sky, its T-shaped wings gripping the curves and chasms of the tidal island. As the sun rose to the east, the colour drained from its western side, and the banks of windows – running in three lines, one on top of the other – somehow seemed to blend with the walls and appear to fade from view. Once they did, she always thought the western wall became more ominous: black, monolithic, sinister.

Mesh fencing traced the entire circumference of

the island, side to side, north to south, its undulation, its flow, and was topped with two cords of razorwire and a guard tower, giving it the feel of a prison camp. At the jetty, security guards stood sentry at the main gate; another two were stationed fifty feet further in. Beyond that, the road snaked around a knot in the island and up to the front of the main hospital building.

There were no cars parked outside.

There were never any cars. The hospital had been built at a time when most people didn't have a vehicle to get around in. It wasn't a problem one hundred years ago.

It was now.

These days, most employees crossed the causeway on a second, separate vehicle – both vehicles referred to as ferries, even though they weren't boats – once in the morning, once again at the end of the day: it came across twice, specifically for them, and was kept at a farmhouse half a mile inland. The patients never got to ride that one.

Theirs – the one she was on at the moment – was more stripped back, basically just seats and windows, everything screwed down and reinforced to ensure it couldn't be used as a weapon. It was almost comical to look at – a reconditioned bus carriage sitting on top of a huge trailer, pulled by a tractor with over-sized wheels – but she'd been coming here so long, it didn't seem strange any more. Despite how it looked, it was effective: she'd read that they'd only had one serious incident in the entire forty-six years the ferry had been crossing the causeway – which was just as well because, once a week on a Friday, they ran the secure transfer. That was different from the days she came. That was when they brought in the killers, the people who were never going to be released. In hushed whispers, she'd heard some of the non-medical staff call it 'Psyday' instead of Friday.

Because that was when the psychos arrived.

Back at the start, she'd spent almost a year at the hospital as an inpatient, looking out across the sea from the inside of those windows, listening to her first doctor – Poulter – trying to talk her back from the edge. After she got better, she began returning to Bethlehem as an outpatient, three days a week to start with – and when Garrick replaced Poulter, it was reduced to Tuesdays and Wednesdays because that was when Garrick was in. He'd speak softly to her, like she was easily frightened, trying to get her to talk about Lucas, about her divorce from Robert, about her suicide attempts. Despite everything, she enjoyed the routine, coming back to this place when he was in, having a conversation with someone who wanted to listen. Sometimes she'd held things back from Garrick, other times she'd tried to trade with him, telling him she was ready to open up if he told her more about him. She trusted him, but there were still things – even five years on – that she'd chosen not to tell him.

'So, it's been two months since Simon left.'

She roused herself from her thoughts and looked across the room at Garrick. He was leaning forward, one hand clutching his fountain pen, one handing her a glass of water. She thanked him and took the glass, placing it down on the table between them.

'How would you say that time has been?'

She shrugged. 'I don't miss him, if that's what you mean.'

'I didn't really expect that to be the case.' He smiled at her. 'Has Simon been in touch with you since he moved to London?'

She shook her head. 'No.'

'How do you feel about that?'

'I couldn't care less.'

Garrick nodded, and noted something down. 'You told me once that you never loved him. If that was the case, why did you stay with him for five years?'

'I suppose he helped numb my pain.'

'You mean Lucas?'

'I mean, Lucas, Robert . . .'

'What else?'

She stopped; a small, sad smile. 'My dog.'

'How did he help you forget those things?'

'By just being himself. Simon was a snide, selfish bastard, so when I was with him, that took my full powers of concentration. It was good for me. It stopped my mind from wandering. Plus I got a roof over my head. I paid him a little rent, from the money I earned working at the shoe store, but it wasn't much. As I'm starting to find out, even if you want to live in abject squalor, you still have to pay for it.'

'How is the new place?'

'It's been two months. It's not so new any more.'

'Of course. So how is it?'

'It's okay. As much as you'd expect when you're renting a small room in a small house. Four walls. A bed. It's better than being on the streets. The old woman who rents it to me is deaf as a post, though, so I sit in my room at night and have to listen to her guessing answers on game shows.'

Garrick nodded. 'It's an adjustment.'

She didn't say anything.

'Is there something else bothering you?'

She glanced at Garrick. She shouldn't have been surprised that he'd read her so easily – not after all this time. At the start, even until recently, she'd been able to hold her thoughts back from him, disguise them, and he'd always fail to see the concealment in her face. But not now. Now the two of them were so familiar with each other.

'Simon . . .' She stopped. 'Simon found something.'

'When was this?'

'Two months ago. Before he kicked me out.'

'What did he find?'

'My box of regrets.'

If Garrick was surprised by the news – by the fact she hadn't mentioned anything until now – he didn't show it.

'Did he actually open it up and go through your things?'

'Yes.'

'How did that make you feel?'

'Annoyed. I'd got sloppy.'

'What do you mean?'

'It was tucked away, into a corner of the loft, and he never went up there because that was where all my crap was dumped, and all he cared about was that none of it took up space in his house. But then, when he put the house on the market without even telling me, and especially after he sold it, he started to prepare for the move, and he went up there . . . and he found it.'

Garrick shrugged. 'He knew about Lucas already, though.'

'That's the thing . . .'

'What?'

'That box was about more than Lucas.'

'So what else was it about?'

She paused. 'It was about Pamela Welland.'

Garrick sat back in his chair, a frown creasing his brow. 'I don't understand why that should matter, though? I think I understand why you stayed with Simon. I get that your relationship with him was . . .' He took a long breath as he tried to find the right word. 'Convenient, for whatever reason. I hope, one day, you will share more on that particular subject.'

She didn't reply.

When it became clear she wasn't going to help him out, he continued: 'I get that you didn't trust Simon enough to share all of your past with him. But he knew about Lucas. He knew you lived and worked in London before you moved down here to Devon.

What difference does it make if he knows about Pamela Welland? That case is over. The man who killed her is in jail – and has been for fourteen years.'

Again, no response.

Garrick tilted his head. 'Kay? Why is that girl's murder so important to you?'

She glanced at Garrick.

'Why does it matter if Simon found out about Pamela?'

'It's not her,' she said.

'Not her what?'

'None of this is about Pamela Welland. Not really.'

'What are you talking about?'

She looked up at the window, at the endless sky, at the seagulls squawking as they glided past. Then she turned back to Garrick. 'Pamela Welland's just where it starts.'

PART III

CHAPTER 42

The tidal island was six miles from where I'd grown up in south Devon, and about two miles west of Start Point lighthouse. Between them was a gentle, V-shaped bay, gouged out of coastline at the tip of the county, and surrounded by blue water and jagged rock. Before the construction of the lighthouse, the whole area had been a graveyard for ships.

But that wasn't what made the island famous.

Once a monastery, and then a small fishing village, in the early 1850s the tidal island, and what remained of the buildings that existed on it, were razed.

In its place, a psychiatric hospital was built.

When it first opened its doors, institutional psychiatry didn't even exist as an idea, so locals just called it the asylum, even though its actual name was Keel Point, after the region in which it had been built. But in 1897, a minister from Salcombe called Balthazar Rowe was put in charge, in an effort to bring an overcrowded, dangerous and fractious patient population into line with some old-fashioned fire and brimstone. Inevitably it failed: five years later, Rowe was killed by what modern doctors would probably call a schizophrenic – but not before he'd renamed Keel Point 'Bethlehem'.

The name stuck.

As the building was six hundred yards across and a quarter of a mile from the mainland, the original thinking was that it would be easy to contain patients and prevent escape when the tide was in. But to ensure the place remained secure, even when the tide was out and the causeway between the mainland and island could be crossed – albeit with difficulty – on foot, a three-metre fence had been erected around the circumference of the island. I'd read about Bethlehem many times, seen articles about it in the local press, subconsciously absorbed its unique layout – the 'stick man' and the triangle – over and over again, without even realizing it. I would pass it in the back seat of my parents' car when we took the coastal road, the glass panels of the greenhouse winking in the sun as they funnelled to a point at the south of the island. But I'd only ever been close to it once: my parents had taken me to Keel Point beach at eight years old, and I'd looked out to where it was perched on the undulating grass like the broken claws of a bird, and thought it was a prison camp.

It's bad, sweetheart.
It's somewhere very bad.

The catalyst for Mum's warning had, most likely,

come four years before, when a patient called William Silas ran amok in the place. Silas had murdered three men in a bedsit in Bristol in 1974, and stored their bodies in an outhouse at the bottom of his garden. Over the course of the next three weeks, he repeatedly returned to where he'd left them, cutting pieces from their bodies and cooking them. He'd eaten two of the men before neighbours started to become suspicious about his journeys to the outhouse in the middle of the night. Silas was told he would never be released, and sent to Keel Point.

On the ferry trip across to the island, he managed to break his thumb and two of his fingers, and slip one of his handcuffs. Once he was off the bus, he made a break for it, taking a guard hostage, killing another, then murdering four kitchen staff once he found a secure space to hole up. When armed response units finally got to him, he was sitting in the middle of the kitchen in a pool of blood, carving chunks off the people he'd killed.

After that, there were always stories about Bethlehem.

Locals would talk for years after about how blood from Silas's victims washed up on the shore that day, but while that seemed unlikely – even if my mum believed it – there were other stories that were harder to dispel: the accounts from people who lived nearby who said, on a still night, you could hear screams carry across the water; the way that, when the sun set in the summer, it looked like the walls of the hospital were bleeding; or how the three banks of windows on its eastern wall – built so patients could look out to the channel – darkened like the eyes of the dead when the sun went down.

But then, in November 2011, all of it was consigned to history.

Unable to afford the running costs, criticized for security measures that didn't come up to modern standards, and under pressure from locals who hated having it so close, Bethlehem closed its doors. Since then, there had been talk about tearing it down – countless, endless discussions about it – and yet still it remained: a ghostly, decaying memory on a slab of land a quarter of a mile out to sea.

CHAPTER 43

As the sun came up four hours later, bleeding across a cloud-streaked sky, I arrived at the beach I'd been on thirty-five years ago. The drive down from London had been quick, the motorway empty, concrete giving way to fields, then fields giving way to coastline.

The snow had all but gone from this part of the country, pulped by the rain, but it was colder than ever. I got out of the car and wandered down to the edges of the sea, to where I'd stood with my mum what felt like a lifetime ago. Additional eight-foot walls had been erected around the circumference of the island now, obscuring most of the hospital. But not everything could be disguised: as the day broke beyond Bethlehem's lonely spire, I could see graffiti on the perimeter, some on the actual building itself too. Smashed windows. Crumbling masonry. Holes in the roof. It was the kind of slow decomposition only a building could go through: solitary, silent, arrested.

People were already out walking dogs, or running across the sand, earphones in, breath forming above their heads. As I watched them, I thought again about the pictures of Bethlehem that Reynolds had been keeping. I thought about the reasons he might have them. I thought about Preston's former girlfriend, about who she might be, and whether she might be relevant. And I thought about the sketches of the hospital layout that Franks had made, some time between 1995 and 2004. The question was why he'd drawn it.

And whether the answers might lie across the water.

Even if they did, they would have to wait for now. With the sun up, crossing the causeway on foot was going to be too much of a risk. I needed to travel at low tide and under cover of darkness and that meant either four-fifty tonight, or five-twenty in the morning. The issue with tonight was that, despite the winter gloom, people would still be around, walking dogs on the beach, coming home from work. At five-twenty tomorrow morning, it would be quieter, but the risk remained the same: if I was even *slightly* longer than an hour out there, there was the potential to get caught on the island. An hour either side of low tide, the water level could rise by as much as a foot – and the higher it got, the choppier it got, and the more difficult it became to navigate without a boat.

Rowing across gave me more options and would allow me to leave at any time I wanted. But for that I needed a decent boat, and there was nowhere to hire them on this part of the coast. The best I could lay my hands on at such short notice was a dinghy at my parents' old cottage, and I seriously doubted it would be able to cope with the rigours of anything other than low tide. Plus, if I bought a bigger boat, I had to transport it, and then I had to find a way of securing it out of sight once I got across to the island.

That, in truth, was the real issue: not getting over there, but remaining unseen during daylight hours. If I got caught going out to the hospital – or coming back – by a passing boat, or people on the beach spotted me and reported me, I risked derailing the entire case. At best, I'd return to the loving arms of the local police force and get a ticking off. At worst, I'd be dragged into an interview room and charged with trespassing.

I also felt like I needed a clearer sight of where Bethlehem fitted into Franks's life. It closed in 2011 – the year Leonard and Ellie retired to Devon – and Ellie had said Franks never came down to Devon, separately from her, in the years before they moved. It seemed likely she would have noticed if he had. And yet a conversation I'd had with her stuck with me. She'd said that, after they moved down, they liked to go hiking together.

Did he ever go hiking by himself, without you?

Very rarely, she'd replied.

But it happened sometimes?

Yes. Sometimes. Sometimes he just liked to be alone out there.

What if, when he went out alone, he wasn't going hiking on the moors? What if he was heading to the coast? What if he was journeying across the channel? From the pictures in Reynolds's flat, it was clear *he* thought there might be answers in the hospital, but what could possibly have been so important to Franks that he'd risk rowing across the causeway to a closed hospital complex? Whatever the answer, if Neil Reynolds had taken those photographs himself, it meant he had *also* been inside the hospital at some point since its closure. But nine months after Franks disappeared, he remained missing, which seemed to suggest Reynolds had found nothing, otherwise Franks wouldn't still be in the wind.

Yet I wanted to make the crossing myself.

One of the two photos Reynolds had in his possession had been of the entrance to the room with the metal stand in it. Why photograph that entrance? Why that room? The hospital was a spectre, forgotten and empty – but Reynolds had gone anyway, and he'd chosen to take that shot.

He hadn't found Franks.

But maybe he'd found something else.

CHAPTER 44

An hour later, at just gone nine, I finally reached Dartmoor. Winter had robbed it of its colour, reducing its bracken to a scorched brown, its trees to corpses, its views to a fine grey mist. As I came in on the B3212, caught in a conga-line of cars, I could see snow in the craggy folds of the hills – but mostly it was wet, drizzle dotting the windscreen, obscuring the road ahead, slowing my progress even more into the heart of the park.

My thoughts shifted to Craw.

For the moment I decided against calling her, not until I had a clearer sight of how things fitted together: Preston, the woman he'd been living with, Bethlehem, Welland. But, even without calling her, I could guess how these latest revelations might feel: like her life was coming off the rails. The man she'd modelled herself on – her beliefs, her career, her family life – had spun a succession of lies to keep anyone from finding out who Simon Preston was – and, in doing so, he'd cheated the same system he demanded others uphold so aggressively. Given all that I'd learned about him, Franks was certain to have done it for what he thought to be the right reasons – but that didn't change his actions.

Or the damage it might do to his daughter.

At nine-thirty, I finally reached Postbridge. It was still and silent, seemingly in hibernation, little sign of life except for the gentle, almost serene ascent of smoke from chimneys. There were six, maybe seven buildings visible from the road, and by the time I'd passed the last of them I'd left the village and could see a wooden sign ahead marked 'Franks'.

I pulled off on to a mud track awash in water and grey slush. It rose sharply across the face of the moors, the house not yet visible from the bottom. On my left, I followed the treeline I'd seen in the video Craw had shot, a procession of old, gnarled trunks, their leaves long since gone. Halfway up, an A-frame rooftop emerged above the brow of the hill, and then the track started to veer right. As it did, more of the house came into view, perched like a bird in a nest, fields rolling off either side, the moor continuing its flight upward, beyond the boundaries of the property to where a tor – a third of a mile further up – was marked by a collection of huge boulders. Everything was just like it had been in the video, except film had failed to fully grasp how removed this place was: a tiny house set among endless fields, under the shadow of a tor, below perpetual sky.

I parked up and got out.

Standing in the drizzle at the front of the house, I knew answers were unlikely to be here, even though it was the scene of the crime. It was the reason I hadn't already been down, why I'd relied on Craw's video: if Franks had left of his own accord, I felt certain he would have covered his tracks; if he'd left because Reynolds had come for him, it was even less likely mistakes would have been made, let alone missed by Craw. Reynolds had been flying below the radar for a long time, and even when questions were raised about him – as they had been constantly, from the moment he came under Franks's command – there was never enough to pin on him. He was slippery. But, worse, he was clever.

That was what made him frightening.

I did a circuit of the house.

The woodshed looked even less sturdy in the flesh, a lean-to with warped, misshapen support beams and a corrugated-iron roof that had rusted in the middle. Chunks of wood remained inside, but the nine months since Franks's disappearance had seen them gradually succumb to moss.

I continued around to the back of the woodshed, where I found the tree stump I'd seen in the film. The axe that had been embedded in it was long gone.

A few feet further on was the toolshed.

Its door was padlocked. I opened it up with the keys Craw had given me, and looked inside. It smelled of old wood and oil, and Franks's tools had all been removed, except for a shovel, a brush and a rusting lawnmower. No hammers. No screwdrivers. No chisels. I went through pots of nails, wall plugs and curtain hooks, and found nothing.

There was a small porch at the back, leading into the kitchen. Through the glass I could see glimpses of the Frankses' half-finished renovation. In the parts that had been fully fitted, drawers were empty and shelves were bare. As I rejoined the front side of the house at the end of the veranda, I looked up to the tor, two hundred feet higher than me. The boulders that had marked out its peak had now been consumed by mist.

Inside, I walked the rooms, opened the cupboards and the wardrobes, and found nothing. Franks's old PC was still in the study, but the electrics had long since been switched off. Craw had told me that would be the case, so I'd brought an extension cable and an adaptor. Setting the engine of my car running, I slotted the plug adaptor into the cigarette lighter, and the extension cable to the plug, then ran the cable all the way through the house to the study. But Craw had warned me about the PC too and after ten minutes all I found were duplicates of the pictures Franks had uploaded to his iPad.

Then I heard something.

I got up from the PC and wandered into the living room.

It had sounded like a series of clicks.

Now, though, there was nothing: the house was utterly silent. I retraced my steps through both floors again, listening out for the same sound, but all that came back was the patter of rain on the roof. After a moment more, I began looping up the extension cable.

As I closed up the house and returned to the car, I paused for a moment midway across the lawn and looked back at the woodshed.

An odd feeling ghosted through me.

I'd just spent an hour searching the place, opening every door, checking every loose floorboard, making sure nothing remained hidden.

And yet something unsettling clung on.

A sense that I'd missed something.

I watched clouds pass in the windows of the house. Listened to the soft moan its wooden bones made as the wind pressed against them. My eyes traced the spaces beyond the building, across the rolling moorland, falling on three paths that had been carved – through seas of heather and bracken – by walkers over the years. They moved parallel to one another, like claw marks, until they finally faded from view.

Maybe it's nothing.

Maybe you just want something to be here.

I headed back to the car.

CHAPTER 45

My parents' old place was west of Dartmouth, off the coastal road that eventually wound its way to Kingsbridge. It was part of a small settlement built on a curved bay, although – of all the houses in the village – theirs was the most physically removed from it, perched in the hills above: the kitchen looked out over a line of fishermen's cottages butting up against a sea wall, and to the beach beyond, boats moored on its shingle. At night, when the wind passed through, sometimes you could lie in bed and hear their masts chiming. Other nights, the sound of laughter from the Seven Stars, a shabby, salt-blanched pub that sat among the cottages. But, mostly, all you could hear was the sea, relentless, metronomic, the gentle chatter of pebbles in summer and the boom of breaking waves in the winter.

I let myself in, turned on the electrics and the water, then sat at the table in the kitchen, listening to the kettle boiling. There was no mist here but the skies were equally oppressive, and as I nursed a mug of coffee, rain began peppering the glass, and it was like moments in time had become teth-ered. Thirteen months earlier, I'd been in the same position, with the same drink, looking out at the same weather.

Another time. Another life.

Connected to each other by the missing.

I woke to the sound of my phone. For a moment I was disorientated, unsure of where I was. But then slowly, as I crawled from the depths, everything shifted into focus.

I glanced at my watch.

Ten past five.

I'd been asleep for six hours.

I brought the mobile towards me and looked at the display. Annabel. Taking it through to the kitchen, I sat down at the table.

'Hey, sweetheart.'

'Hey. Are you okay?'

'Catching up on some sleep.'

'You burning the candle at both ends again?'

'Not in a fun way.' It was dark outside now, the village reduced to dots of light. 'Actually, I'm back in the motherland.'

'Oh, cool. Are you coming to see us?'

'Definitely. I just need to take care of a couple of things first.'

'You still trying to find that guy?'

'Still trying.' In the background of the call, I could hear Olivia laughing at something. 'How's Liv?'

'She's good. Glued to the TV.'

'And you?'

'I'm fine.'

But, as she paused for a moment, I sensed she wanted to give voice to something. 'You sure?'

'It's Emily,' she said. 'She keeps trying to call me.'

Emily: the woman who'd kept Annabel's real parents a secret from her, from me, from anyone. She'd had her reasons, good reasons some of them, but it didn't make it any less painful for Annabel. It pained me too – some days a great deal – because I'd spent twenty-four years not knowing my daughter. But I was older, a little more sculpted by life. Maybe, in a strange way, I was even expectant of lies now, because of the nature of my work. Annabel would come around – but in her own time, and on her own terms.

'Things will get easier between you,' I said.

'I don't want to speak to her.'

'I understand that. But if you think, even for a moment, that you can make it work, I'd pick up the phone to her. Emily's just like the rest of us.' I looked out across the table, at the pictures I'd laid out, of Franks, of Ellie, of Craw. 'We all just want to be surrounded by the people we love.'

CHAPTER 46

lthough Franks's iPad – and the photographs on it – had been destroyed, in a moment of what was either fortune or foresight, I'd removed the SD card from his SLR camera when Craw had first handed me Franks's boxes at her house. I'd left the camera with her, but taken the SD card with me, ostensibly as back-up in case I ran into any problems with the pictures on the iPad. I hadn't been expecting the kind of problems Reynolds had brought me, but when he turned over the house, he missed the SD card, as I'd left it in the car.

After I was finished with Annabel, I went out to the BMW and retrieved the old laptop I'd brought from home, returned to the house, and slotted the SD card into it. A minute later, the pictures were copying across to the desktop.

As I sat there waiting, I still couldn't shake the feeling I'd missed something.

Maybe something Murray had said.

Maybe something at the Frankses' house.

Using the trackpad, I double-clicked on a picture of their home, taken by either Leonard or Ellie in the months after they'd moved in. Next to the laptop, in two rows on the table, were colour printouts of the photos that Craw had given me, which I'd asked her to resend after Reynolds had taken the original printouts from my house. Craw's were different shots, taken over two and a half years later, but of the same house from the same angles.

The house is empty.

You didn't miss anything.

My eyes drifted back to the photograph on the laptop, of the home when Leonard and Ellie had first moved in. I'd looked at it countless times. When I compared it with the ones Craw had taken in the months after Franks went missing, they appeared identical. Same A-frame roof. Same veranda. Same woodshed. The same sense of complete isolation.

I moved through the photographs on the PC desktop, then through the hard copies on the table. Outside, through the rain, the beach was barely visible now. Inside, my work was lit by a single table lamp and accompanied by the gentle hum of the central heating.

After ten minutes, I got up and filled the kettle again.

Clear your head.

I walked to the kitchen door and opened it up, letting the bitter air ghost past me. The rain made a soft sound on the gravel of the drive, like a gathering of voices. As I listened, I thought of another picture, also taken on Dartmoor: the one Franks had two copies of – the shot of the valley with the remains of the tinner's hut in it, and the church spire in the distance. This one was a real church spire built on top of a real church, not the kind I'd seen on the hospital at Keel Point. But I was yet to narrow down the location, and still hadn't been able to figure out why Franks had two versions of the same shot: one taken on film years ago, and one taken in the time after he retired to Devon.

As the kettle came to the boil, my thoughts shifted again, back to Bethlehem, and to my plan to get across there in the morning, at low tide. I wasn't sure what I expected to find, but I knew there was *something* there, my mind returning over and over to the room with the IV stand. Why was Reynolds so interested in it? Why that room, of all the hundreds of rooms there must have been in the building? What did it represent?

If I was going to do it, I had to be at the beach for 5 a.m. I'd bought a wetsuit on the way down from Dartmoor, and had packed that, a change of clothes and a torch into a waterproof backpack and left it in the boot of the car. Deep down, I knew a boat would be more practical, safer too, but it would also be harder to hide once I got across – and that just gave me one more thing to worry about.

I closed the door and poured myself a coffee, returning to the pictures.

I moved from the front-on shot of the house taken two and a half years back, around the time the Frankses had first moved in, to the one Craw had taken on a grey autumn day only a few months ago. The only change was in the colour of the structure itself, a subtle, imperceptible difference, the wood lightening by a couple of shades as sunlight bleached it over time.

What aren't I seeing?

I went through the other pictures. The back of the house, the porch, the rooms, the unfinished kitchen, returning to that shot of the front, feeling that if there was something, it was here. I'd stood in the same position, in the rain, facing the house, earlier, and I'd got exactly the same sense that something was up.

A murmur of conviction.

A certainty.

So what the hell is it?

The old pipes creaked and shifted behind the walls of the cottage as the central heating fired up again.

The house is empty.

You didn't miss anything.

'The house is empty,' I repeated quietly.

And then, in an instant, I saw it.

I've been looking at the wrong part of the picture.

As I'd stood there earlier on, I'd seen three paths beyond the back garden, carving their way through carpets of heather and bracken – almost parallel to one another – as the moor rolled on past the boundaries of the house. They were trails imprinted on the moor by walkers, by years of passers-by rounding the property as they skirted the tor. Except in the picture the Frankses had taken when they'd first moved in, there weren't three trails.

There were only two.

In Craw's photograph – two and a half years later – the third trail was less defined than the other two, still covered in a flat layer of bracken, but it was there nevertheless, bearing slightly right as the other two remained straight. I let rationality kick in, trying to convince myself of the reasons why: maybe walkers had begun to carve out a new path for themselves in the years in between, keeping to the gentlest contours of the slope as it dipped and then rose. An easier path. A tamer, less demanding route across land that could be craggy and hard.

Or maybe it wasn't walkers who had made it.

Maybe it was Franks, after he moved in.

And maybe it led somewhere.

CHAPTER 47

The weather got worse the moment I hit the moors. By the time I reached the house it was 10 p.m. and rain was coming down so hard it was like nails were falling from the sky.

I pulled as close to the house as I could get, headlights flooding the veranda, and kept the engine running. Everywhere else, the moors were utterly, perfectly black: there was no definition to anything, no sense of where its lines moved and fell. Outside of the headlights, it was a vast, endless void. As I got out, wind whipped in, pressing hard, rocking the car on its springs.

From the boot, I grabbed the extension lead I'd used earlier, connected it to the car and began unravelling it, moving across the front lawn – just a fenced-in continuation of rolling moorland – and up on to the veranda. I unlocked the house, grabbed a tatty lamp that had been left behind by Ellie, and plugged it in. Light spilled out across the living room and ran through to the kitchen. With no electrics to call on, it was as good as it was going to get. More importantly, it would help anchor the house in the darkness while I headed out into the night, following the third trail. After I was done, I returned to the veranda, immediately under attack from the wind and rain again.

Continuing around the woodshed, I swung my flashlight across the spaces beyond the back garden and found the three trails. In the months since Franks had vanished, the third trail had started to become less defined, fresh roots growing out of the trampled bracken, callow heather closing in from both sides. The other two – established over decades – remained flattened yellow pathways, clearly demarcated across the grass.

Rain came again and again, pounding my face and jacket. I stood at the start of the third trail and shone the flashlight along it. Behind me, the picket fence that the Frankses had used to segregate their land creaked and popped in the wind. To my left, somewhere in the darkness, and a third of a mile above me, was the tor. To my right, I could see the very faintest of lights – a square of window – from one of the houses in Postbridge.

Otherwise, except for the lamp in the house, there was only darkness.

Tilting the flashlight down, I started along the trail.

It was uneven and difficult to judge. When I almost turned my ankle in an animal burrow, I slowed down even further, and started to feel the toe of my boot hitting gashes in the earth, hidden beneath blankets of bracken. There were sudden, unexpected slants in the topography too, knocking me off balance and forcing me away from the path. When I got back on to it, I tried to concentrate on where I was stepping, but it became more and more difficult: not only was the path becoming less defined, the rain was getting harder, pelting against my face in pellets as hard as gravel. Finally I had to stop – adrift in a sea of total, impervious darkness – pull up the hood of my coat and zip it to my chin.

Now all I could hear was rain.

As it drummed against my hood, I pushed on. Ahead of me, mud trails – slick with rainwater – winked in the glare of the flashlight, and the path disappeared for a moment, overrun by bracken. I stopped again, raised the torch, tried to angle it beyond the growth – and then I picked up the trail on the other side, zigzagging slightly and bearing right.

I glanced over my shoulder, back towards the house.

It was why I'd used the lamp: to act as a beacon. Even so, it was like being out at sea in the middle of the night, the shore reduced to a pinprick of light. Except I'd gone further than I thought: I'd dropped about three hundred and fifty feet, the house above my eyeline, and I was a quarter of a mile away already. The light from the living room and the kitchen seemed to drift in and out as rain ran into my eyes.

I pushed on, down further and further across worsening terrain, until I realized I'd lost the trail. I stopped and swung the torch around, back up the way I'd come. Rain had turned the slope into a mudslide, but – among it – I could just about make out a line of trampled bracken. I traced it with the flashlight from about sixty feet back, following its movement in my direction. And then, thirty feet from where I was, I noticed something.

The path stopped.

It ended in a small clearing about three feet across, free of bracken or heather. As I got closer, I could see the clearing hadn't been created by foot – it had been burned away, with something like weedkiller.

But too much had been used.

The grass had scorched.

Five feet from the clearing I saw it had a molehill in it, a flat plate of mud, sitting there like a cake. The wind whipped in through the valley again, funnelled by the incline of the hills either side, and I was forced into a sideways step, rain jagging into my hood. Then, as the light drifted across the molehill again, a sudden realization struck me.

It isn't a molehill.

Someone had buried something.

I moved quicker now, dropping to my knees in the clearing, not caring about the wet grass soaking through my trousers, or the rain pelting against my face. With the torch on the ground, directed towards the hole, I started grabbing handfuls of dirt, throwing it aside, clawing at it, digging down into the moor. Half a foot down, I paused for breath, warm inside the coat, cold on my exposed skin. Then I started again, down further and further, until I was a foot in. Two feet into the earth, I started to wonder if I'd called it wrong, or misunderstood what this was.

But then my fingers glanced something.

It was loose in the hole.

I reached in, picked it out and held it up to the light.

A strip of plastic.

It was about two inches long and half an inch high, and – with a circle punched in the end of it – looked like it might once have been attached to a key ring. I turned back to the hole I'd dug, shining the torch into its corners, wondering if I'd managed to miss a set of keys buried in the mud. Then I stopped, a thought gathering pace.

The keys aren't here, because they've been removed.

The tag was dropped by accident.

I turned the plastic tag over and looked at the other side.

Adrenalin fizzed in my guts.

Something was printed on it: the same thing I'd seen written on a scrap of paper, next to the map of Bethlehem, in Franks's first Moleskine notebook; the same number he then doodled on to the bottom of a flyer, years later, when he met Murray for a drink.

It said, 'BROLE108'.

CHAPTER 48

I pocketed the plastic tag and started to fill in the hole. As I was finishing, beyond the glow of the torch, something shifted in the darkness. I stopped.

Shone the torch out to my right.

Either side of me, the moor continued to slope away, its gradient getting sharper as it dropped further into the valley. The cone from the flashlight carried about forty feet, out to where a sea of ferns moved in the wind. When I shone it the other way, it carried an even greater distance: across a patch of moorland undisturbed by plants or trees, the gentle roll of the hill partly disguising the dots of light from Postbridge that I'd been able to see higher up.

Getting to my feet, I started the climb.

I kept the torch tilted downwards, trying to ensure I didn't lose the path this time, but it was still hard going: the grass had become slick with rainwater, the mud moist and difficult to grip underfoot. A couple of times I slipped, the flashlight tumbling out of my grasp and rolling off into the undergrowth. By the time I retrieved it, I'd retreated another five or six feet. Halfway up, I stopped and looked towards the lights of the living room, to see how far I had to go.

Something moved inside the house.

Killing the torch, I let darkness settle around me, a flutter of unease passing through my chest. I scanned the area, trying to force myself to see, but all I could make out was the vague, grey shapes of ferns close by and tiny blobs of light from the houses in the village. As I turned and faced up the hill, my foot slipped on a band of mud and I had to reach forward, to a raised knot in the path ahead of me, and grab it. I stayed like that for a moment and closed my eyes.

Listen.

Beyond the pulse of the rain, the wind whined like an animal, making it hard to hear anything else. Any footsteps. Any approach. *Anyone close by.* When I opened my eyes again, I could just about make out the shape of the house, eighty feet further up the slope, its outline like a smudge of grey paint against the blackness of the moors.

Inside the light was still on.

At the front, my car headlights too.

I pushed on, more slowly this time, conscious of making a noise the closer I got to the house. When I finally reached the brow of the hill, the picket fence only a few feet in front of me, I could hear something: an uneven banging, loud, louder, then nothing at all.

The front door of the house.

I'd pushed it shut.

Now it was open.

Flipping the flashlight and gripping it like a weapon, I came around the edges of the property, as close to the house as I could get. Halfway along, I checked back the way I'd come: the garden, picket fence, everything that lay beyond it, had disappeared now. All I could see, feel and smell was what immediately surrounded me: the southern side of the house, against my back; the distant hint of Postbridge; the whiff of sodden bracken.

I edged to the corner of the property.

The veranda, built three and a half feet off the ground, was level with my hip. I peered past the woodshed, along the boards of the veranda, to the front door. It was slowly fanning in the wind, knocking against the frame. Someone had opened it and failed to close it again after they'd left. Or they'd opened it up, gone inside – and they were yet to come out.

I looked to my car.

The driver's side door was pushed to, but not closed. Whoever it was had opened it up and had a look around inside. As I paused there, trying to think whether I had anything in the boot of the car I could use as a more effective weapon, the door flapped again in the wind, clattering against the frame and whipping back in my direction. This time – in the light spilling out from the living room – something caught my eye.

It was attached to the door itself.

A thin length of wire.

It snaked off from the underside of the door, all the way along the veranda, into the woodshed. I checked behind me again, making sure no one had approached from the back of the house, and then reached through the rails and grabbed the wire.

It was as thin as a thread of cotton.

Barely visible, but tough and unbreakable.

I leaned right into the woodpile.

In the darkness at its centre, hidden inside the crisscross of logs, something red winked at me. Once. Twice. Three times. *Something electronic.* There was a small space on this side of the pile – enough for me to slide a couple of fingers into – so I fed my hand into the gap, trying to grasp at whatever it was.

I felt my forefinger brush a hard plastic shell.

This time I forced my fingers even further inside, feeling the jagged edge of a log prick the skin at my knuckles. Wind roared across the front of the house, carried down the side of the tor, rain pummelling my face and escaping into the hood. With my cheek pressed against one of the logs – the smell of damp wood forced into my nose – I tried again to grip whatever it was, and felt my fingers trace the bumps and indentations on it.

A series of LED lights.

A plastic grille.

It felt like a walkie-talkie.

But then, as I tried – and failed – to get at it a third time, my eyes returned to the length of wire, attached to the unit and connected to the underside of the door, and my mind spooled back to earlier in the day: as I'd been going through the house, I'd heard a series of clicks.

Shit.

I whipped my hand out of the woodpile. *When I'd come up here earlier in the day, when I'd opened the door and walked through the house, I'd tripped it.*

It was a makeshift alarm system.

CHAPTER 49

I tried to force myself to hear movement from inside the house – confirmation I wasn't alone – but the rain made it hard, suppressing and deflecting the sounds of the moor. In the centre of the veranda, the door flapped like a tongue, the wooden structure of the house creaking as the wind gathered pace. I watched for any change of light, any gentle flicker of a shadow, but the weather was the only thing that moved. The house was still.

At the rear, the picket fence groaned in the wind. When I looked back along the veranda, my eyes fell on the alarm system again, the wire snaking from left to right in the wind and the rain, like a beached fish.

It had been set up to let someone know when the house had a visitor.

Double-checking I still had the plastic tag on me, I moved around to the rear of the house. Fifteen feet along, attached to the back of the building, was the toolshed. On the other side of that was the rear door, leading through to the kitchen. I ducked beneath the first set of windows

– light spilling out from the living room – and headed across the garden to the shed. At the door, I dropped to my haunches, below the padlock, looked both ways along the house and popped the lock. It fell away.

I caught it and set it down.

Easing the door out from the frame, as gently as I could to reduce noise, the smell of oil, old cloths and damp wood poured past me. I reached inside, grabbed a shovel and went to push the door shut again. But then I noticed something through the corner of my eye.

A disturbance in the light from the kitchen.

I brought the shovel towards me, pushed the toolshed door closed and clipped the padlock back through its loop. And then I watched. But there was nothing more: no sign of anyone inside. No shift in the light. No shadow.

Keeping the shovel low, clutching it midway down the shaft, I moved forward, across the garden, towards the door. A couple of feet short of it, I stopped and watched its glass panel again. Still nothing. Inching forward, I slowly rose to the lip of the glass and looked in. Despite the glow from the lamp in the living room, great swathes of the kitchen were still black, the edges of the units closest to me just about visible. Where the renovation hadn't been finished, there were shadows. On the wall I could just about make out a clock.

It was dead.

Tucking the flashlight into my back pocket and gripping the shovel with both hands, I carried on past the kitchen, to the corner of the house. At this side was a small, flattened strip of concrete on which Franks and Ellie had once parked their Audi.

Suddenly: movement.

At the periphery of my vision, I saw a flash of colour beyond the beam of the BMW's headlights. Briefly, everything was shadow and darkness again – and then I saw the same flash of colour, moving off towards the treeline. Someone was heading away from the house.

They had too much of a head start.

I wouldn't catch them on foot.

Dropping the shovel, I headed to the car, yanking open the door and sliding in at the wheel. Freeing the plug adaptor from the lighter, I slammed the car into reverse and whipped it around, the tyres briefly losing their grip on the wet grass before grabbing at the track and jolting me forward. Straight away, it felt like something was wrong, but as the headlights fanned right to left, carving through the darkness like a knife through a curtain, I saw the figure again, and focused all my attention on that. Grey hooded top. A blob of light shining on his shaved scalp.

Reynolds.

He looked back over his shoulder at me, sixty feet in front – and then, weirdly, began to slow up. As I closed in on him, I became aware of a heaviness in the steering, as if the car were being pulled right.

I had enough time to see the half-smile on his face – enough time to wonder why he'd chosen to run and not attack me – before I realized what he'd done.

He'd punctured one of my tyres.

I jabbed at the pedal – instinctive, desperate – pushing so hard it felt like I was kicking through the chassis. The car swerved, snaking off the mud track on to the grass, the treeline looming in front of me. When I realized it wasn't going to stop in time, I yanked at the belt, drew it across me and clicked it home. A second later, the car hit a ridge in the track and smashed into a grass bank. As the belt locked like a vice, pinning me to the seat, the impact sent the car into a tilt and my head lashed sideways, into the window. The glass cracked, splitting against my face.

Darkness.

CHAPTER 50

I woke inside the house, lying in the middle of the living room, next to the lamp. It was still on, although it had been tipped on to its side. I could taste blood in my mouth and feel it running down one side of my face. My arm was caught under me. As I tried to shift my weight and free it, I felt a stab of pain in my shoulder. Whiplash. Bruising. Every time I moved, my chest went into spasm.

A noise.

When I craned my neck to see what it was, nausea swept up through my throat. I listed, rolling on to my back, and when I regained some control, looked again, trying to trace the origin of the sound.

It was my mobile phone.

I gritted my teeth, forced myself up into a sitting position at one of the sofas and watched the phone continue its gentle journey across the floor: slowly, steadily, moving an inch in my direction every time it buzzed. When I looked the other way, I could see my crumpled car through the open front door: hazards flashing, a single headlight still working but pointing off at a forty-five-degree angle, through the treeline to the moors on the other side.

Why am I back here?

Momentarily confused, I looked around the room again. The house was empty, although – with the lamp on its side – the lighting had changed. Shadows crept in around doorways and windows, and into the far corners. Everything was suddenly under-lit, the brightness fading halfway up the walls.

Did Reynolds bring me back here?

My head was swimming.

Pounding.

Unable to find reasons or connections.

And the whole time my phone continued ringing, edging closer to me. After a couple of seconds, I tried to grasp at it, fingers brushing its casing, but the movement sent a stab of pain along my breast-plate that almost took my breath away.

I let my body settle again.

Five seconds later the phone drifted into reach, so I tried scooping it up a second time. I managed to get a finger on it – without moving my shoulder – and pulled it in against my leg. The clock read eleven-thirty. The caller was unknown.

I pushed Answer and slowly brought it up to my ear.

'Welcome back,' a man's voice whispered.

Mancunian accent.

It was Reynolds.

As I tried to adjust my position, I caught a whiff

of something for the first time. I scanned the room again, a prickle of unease forming, my eyes falling on the stairs on the far side. There was almost no light in that part of the living room.

'I imagine you're not feeling too special at this point.'

'No, not really,' I said.

The house was silent now, as quiet as it had been at any point. The rain had stopped. The wind had died down. Now the building was settling again: the occasional creak, a groan, the snap of wood as the walls softly contracted in the cold.

'That whole thing with the tyre, that wasn't supposed to go like that.' A pause. His words were incredibly quiet, but they were uniform, automated, like he was reading from a script. 'I wasn't banking on you belting across moorland at forty-five miles per hour. That's not how people usually drive up here. Don't get me wrong, I wanted you to crash your car. I wanted you to hurt yourself, maybe hurt your ego too. I needed you to understand that I was on to you, and I was in control. But you weren't supposed to find out about the tyre until *after* I was gone. You weren't supposed to have seen me.'

'Looks like your plan's changed,' I said. The line glitched and there was a slight echo; what sounded like contamination from another call. 'What do you want?'

'Stop looking for Franks.'

I didn't reply, but my mind was already shifting

forward: whose side was he on – and why would he be asking me to stop? Because he was protecting Franks? Or because he wanted Franks for himself? I found it hard to swallow the idea of him working with Franks: their relationship had been poisonous. The two of them hated each other.

'I tried to play nice with you, Raker. I turned over your house, I took your casework, I left you alive. At that point, I thought that I'd done enough to disrupt your . . . what would you call it? Case? Mission? Or is this another lost soul you feel responsibility for? Whatever it is, honestly, I didn't want things to go this way. *But*, having found out a little about you since, perhaps I should have expected it.'

'Why should I stop?'

'Why? Because next time it won't be your tyre I'm sticking a knife in.' A pause. 'Believe it or not, I'm not in the business of killing people. That's not what this was supposed to be about. This whole thing . . . think of it as a public service. But, even so, I'll make you this promise: if you don't pack up and return to London immediately, I will kill you, and I will kill everyone you care about. That includes your daughter.'

'Don't ever—'

'Don't ever *what*?'

And then, on the back of that, something clicked with me: *the smell.* I looked across to the far side of the room, at the dark of the stairs. I knew what it was now.

Mildew.

Instantly, as if my thoughts had been projected, something moved in the shadows. And then, out of the blackness, came the toe of a boot. Black. Mud-specked. Worn.

Reynolds.

He leaned forward, elbows on his knees, pale face like a silver smudge against the night. He was cloaked by the darkness, almost wearing it. After watching me for a moment, he rocked forward, a shape ripped from the shadows, and stood, eyes never leaving mine. I could see dust and mud on his hands; my blood too. He came across the room – muscular, but with those same small movements – and stopped just short of me. There was a mobile phone in his right hand. He pushed a button on it and it chirped gently.

'If you're not back in London within twenty-four hours, telling Melanie Craw that you can't work her case any more, I'll kill your daughter in front of you.' He stopped, eyeing me. He sounded different now: harder, his accent more pronounced, his words more severe and carrying a greater threat. 'Do you want to watch your daughter get her throat cut?'

Her throat cut.

Just like he'd done to Simon Preston.

I fixed my gaze on him. 'You even as much as look at her, and I'll—'

'You'll *what*? You think I'm *scared* of you? I've been watching you for a while now, and you've

380

never had a clue. So maybe *you* should be the one that's scared.'

I didn't respond.

'For your daughter's sake, I hope you are.'

Again, I said nothing.

'You've got twenty-four hours.'

His eyes lingered on me for a moment more, a hint of a smile on his face – and then he headed out of the living room, on to the veranda. Light drizzle drifted past him, right to left, caught in the soft light spilling from the house. I watched him take the steps, slowly, his stride almost mechanized.

At the bottom, he looked back at me once.

Thirty seconds later, the moor swallowed him up.

CHAPTER 51

As soon as Reynolds was gone, I hoisted myself up, using the sofa and a nearby wall to steady myself. Some of the discomfort in my shoulder had subsided, but it was still throbbing, sharp pain shooting downwards in a diagonal across my chest. I checked the kitchen for painkillers. I didn't expect to find any, and I wasn't disappointed. Bringing my left arm across my waist and pinning it there, I returned for my mobile phone.

Annabel.

I dialled her number.

Waiting for her to answer, a new thought came to me: what if Reynolds had already been to her house? He probably expected me to call her straight away, expected me to try to move her, and after the tenth unanswered ring, an awful, gluey dread took hold. *He's already been there. He's already got her.*

But then, finally, she picked up. 'Hello?'

'Annabel, it's me.'

'Hey, how are you?'

'Are you and Olivia okay?'

'Fine. Wow, it's late.'

'Where are you?'

A concerned pause. 'Just at home. Why?'

'Listen to me carefully, okay? I need you and Olivia to get dressed, get in the car and take the M5 north. I want you to keep driving until you get to the services at Bristol.'

'What? But I thought you were coming to see us?'

'I'll explain later. Just do this for me, okay? When you get to Bristol, park up and go inside, and wait where you can be seen. I'm going to send someone to meet you.'

'*What?* I don't . . . Are we in danger?'

She was panicked now. So I lied: 'No. Something's come up. I can't get to you for the time being, and I just want to make sure things are watertight. I'm probably being paranoid, but that's a father's job, right?' I tried to make light of it, but she wasn't taken in by it. I looked at my watch. Midnight. 'The man you're going to meet there is called Ewan Tasker. I'll send a picture of him to your phone. You *only* leave with him. No one else. Everything's going to be fine, but I need you to do this one thing for me, okay?'

'Okay.'

'Thank you, sweetheart.'

I told her I'd call back in ten minutes when she and Olivia were dressed and ready to leave. In the meantime, I dialled Task. He didn't sleep much, so he answered after a couple of rings, and when

I explained what I needed from him, he didn't acknowledge the hour, the distance I was asking him to travel or the size of the favour. He'd long since passed the stage where he asked the reasons why. Perhaps that was what every relationship I had in my life was damned to repeat. When we were done, I thanked him, hung up and called Annabel again. She picked up after a single ring.

'Are you all right?' I asked.

'I suppose so.'

I got her to talk me through them leaving the house, locking it and getting into the car. When they were inside, she switched to speakerphone, and I listened to her guide me through her next movements: out on to their lane, exiting the village and picking up the A38. Once they hit the main road, I relaxed just a little. In the background of the call, I could hear Olivia singing to herself, and the *beep beep beep* of a videogame.

I said hello to her.

'Hi, David,' she said.

'How are you?'

'I'm good.'

'Great. You look after your sister, all right?'

'She should look after *me*.'

'I know. You look after each other then.'

'Okay.'

A brief silence.

'Belle says you've put us in danger.'

'*Olivia*,' Annabel said, her voice close to the phone's speakers, the volume sending a crackle of static along the line. 'I didn't say . . . She doesn't . . . I didn't say that.'

'You did,' Olivia countered.

'*Shut up*, Liv.'

'It's okay,' I said. 'I'll send you this picture now, then call me when you get to Bristol. Call me before if you need to. But just keep going until you get to the services.'

'Okay.'

After I hung up, I looked around the empty house, darkness licking its walls, the lamp still on its side, to my smashed, broken car, its front embedded in a grass bank, and knew that Annabel was right: I'd put them in danger. The two girls were on my radar now, they were part of my life. *This* life. Whatever they did, however geographically distant they were to me, their lives could still be reduced to this, any time, by anyone.

I'd told Annabel when she'd come to stay with me that I would protect them both. I told her they were mine now, and they were stronger with me around.

But that wasn't the reality.

The reality was, I didn't make them stronger.

I made them victims.

CHAPTER 52

O nce I'd taken care of Annabel, I thought of something else: the plastic tag I'd found discarded in the hole. I checked the pockets of my coat.

It was still there.

Briefly, I considered 'BROLE108' and what it might mean, then I switched off the lamp, set it down on the table and headed outside. As I pulled the front door closed I felt a twinge in my shoulder, but I'd mostly been able to subdue the pain by keeping my arm pressed in place. Drizzle dotted my face as I locked up and headed across the moors. This wasn't how I'd imagined I'd be leaving the house – injured, cornered, under threat – and as I got beyond the boundaries of the property, the wind made a noise like an exhalation.

You make people victims.

I pushed the thought down and used the flashlight to direct me along the track, down towards my car. The damage to it was bad, but not as bad as it could have been: the bumper was hanging loose, the grille bunched, the shattered plastic from one of the headlights scattered across the grass in front of it. Plus the tyre needed changing. There was probably internal damage too, none of which was going to become clear until I got the car back out on to the road. I wasn't exactly sure how I was going to drive back to the cottage. I wasn't exactly sure if the cottage was even the best place to go any more.

I've been watching you for a while now.

Maybe you should be the one that's scared.

As Reynolds's words echoed in my head, I pushed them down with everything else, yanked open the door and slid in at the wheel. Inside, the car smelled of fried electrics. In the ignition, the keys moved gently as a breeze passed through the front. I tried the engine once and it failed to fire. The second time, it coughed and choked, but then came to life. Pushing it into reverse, but unable to comfortably look back across my shoulder, I used the rear-view mirror as my guide and jammed the accelerator to the floor.

The functioning front wheel spun, mud spewing off ahead of me.

Then it gripped.

The car shot back. When I slammed on the brakes again, the movement juddered through the vehicle and I felt another tremor of pain pass across my body. I gritted my teeth, tensed my body, sucked it up.

Getting out, I walked around to the boot, popped it open and grabbed the spare tyre. It felt like a concrete block. I hauled it half the way out, readjusted my arm so it was even tighter against my stomach, and yanked the tyre the rest of the way. It fell to the ground with a dull *whumph*. I righted it, and clumsily wheeled it around to the front of the car with one arm. *How the hell am I going to change this?*

As I got there, I heard something.

The rumble of another car.

I let the tyre fall flat against the track, grabbed the flashlight – which I'd placed on the bonnet – and directed it down the slope, back in the direction of Postbridge.

Darkness.

No sign of a car.

Yet I could hear it more clearly than ever.

I paused there for a moment, my own car on the track behind me, its one working headlight cutting through the treeline to my right. The rain had started to come again, its clamour gradually increasing as it moved from drizzle to downpour to deluge. A minute later, the heavens opened, and I stood there in the pouring rain, watching nothing but the blackness that lay ahead of me.

It had to be Reynolds, driving away.

He must have left his car at the bottom of the track earlier, before coming up here, knowing I'd hear his vehicle approaching otherwise. Except the noise from the car engine wasn't getting softer. It wasn't the sound of someone driving away.

It was the sound of someone getting closer.

Turning and heading back up the track, I went

to the boot and used the torch to find a crowbar I kept taped to the underside. As I ripped it away I felt a twinge in my upper arm, my elbow, in my collarbone. It delayed me for a moment, the pain becoming more and more difficult to ignore, but then I slammed the boot shut, got in at the wheel and cranked the car into gear. As quickly as I could, I reversed back up the slope.

After hitting the grass, I kept going, further and further back in the direction of the tor. When I was forty feet from the track, swaddled in the night, I killed the lights and the engine, got out and hurried back to the treeline. Suddenly the crowbar felt heavy in my hand – maybe because of my injury, maybe because I didn't know what was coming in my direction – but the tyre was still sitting in the middle of the road. And as I found a space behind an old, crooked oak tree, I knew that was exactly where I needed it to be.

Ten seconds.

Twenty.

All of a sudden, headlights seemed to appear from nowhere, a quarter of a mile down the track. They swept across the treeline as the road snaked from left to right, but it was impossible to tell what car it was, or who was at the wheel. The lights were too bright, the inside of the car too dark, the rain too heavy. As the car got closer and closer, I could see huge fists of water pounding against the windscreen, each one opening like a lesion on the glass, before running off again.

Maybe it's Reynolds.

Maybe he's forgotten something.

But then, finally, the car stopped, the door opening, and the soft sound of music carried off, through the rain to where I was crouched behind the tree.

The driver got out, eyes on the tyre in the middle of the road.

It was Melanie Craw.

CHAPTER 53

I moved out from behind the trees and down on to the track, Craw silhouetted briefly by her headlights. When she formed again, she was watching me through a wall of rain, her eyes moving from the cuts on my face, to my arm, then off to the dark of the house.

'What's going on, Raker?'

She had to shout above the storm. I moved closer to her, trying to think about the reasons she might have come all this way. 'Craw. What the hell are you doing here?'

'What happened to you?'

'What are you doing here?' I said again.

'You ever answer your phone?'

I frowned, confused, then felt around in my pocket for my mobile. Rain splashed against the display as I checked it – but I could read it clearly enough.

No missed calls.

'You never even called me,' I said.

She looked taken aback. 'I called you three times today.'

I looked at the phone again. 'No.'

'Yes. Three times.'

She dug around in her own pocket and brought out her phone, holding it up for me to see. I took a step closer. In her Recent Calls list was my name: once at two-forty this afternoon; the second time an hour later at three-thirty-one; the third time at five-ten.

I checked my phone again.

Nothing.

'I didn't get a single call from you,' I said.

She studied me, a flicker of suspicion in her face, then put her phone away again and pointed to my arm. 'What happened?'

'What are you doing here?' I said again.

'I got a call from Derek Cortez at lunchtime.'

Cortez: the retired cop in the village.

'Cortez? Why?'

'He said he saw someone coming up to the house.'

'Yeah. Me.'

'Well, I know that now.'

'So you came all the way down here, just to be sure?'

She looked at me, and it was clear that wasn't everything. 'He said he saw someone up here three days ago.'

Reynolds.

He'd come to set up his makeshift alarm system. But three days ago, the case had barely even started. Three days ago, I was only just arriving at the members' club to meet Craw. Yet he already had knowledge of our meeting, even then. He'd already been a step ahead. Then I remembered something he'd said to me back at the house, less than thirty minutes ago: *I've been watching you for a while now, and you've never had a clue.*

'What happened?' Craw asked, her eyes back on my injuries.

'Did you pass anyone on your way up here?'

She frowned. 'No. Why?'

I glanced at the house. 'Let's go somewhere else.'

'What's wrong with here?'

Maybe you should be the one that's scared.

'Here's not safe any more.'

My car was battered, broken, and the engine had developed a gentle tick, but it worked – just about – so, after Craw helped me to change the tyre, I led her back into Postbridge, and then south-west towards Princetown. Staying on the moors was a risk: it was lonely and isolated here, and I could be got at again without anyone noticing. But that was also what gave it its edge: with no one else around, it would be easier to see someone coming.

My first priority was to stay off the radar until I knew Annabel and Olivia were definitely safe. Nothing mattered but their sanctuary. Once Task had them secured, then I'd think about my next move.

Given everything I'd found out about him, even if I decided backing down was the best way to survive, the reality was Reynolds wasn't going to want a loose end. Even if Franks was still alive, even if Reynolds did to him whatever it was he was trying to do – find him, kill him – Reynolds would be back for me. I fought now or I fought later, but either way I fought. When it came down to it, Reynolds would never let me just walk away.

As the lights of Princetown emerged from the blackness of the moors, we traced its northern fringes, rain lashing at our cars, sheep scattering in the fields either side of us, and I kept returning to the same questions. Why would Reynolds let me go? Why not take me out of the equation tonight, at the house, while he'd had the chance?

Eventually, the answer came to me.

Even if I didn't have a clear sight of his motivation yet, I realized Reynolds was in the same position as I was: he didn't know if Franks was dead or alive. He hadn't found him yet. All he had was a series of dead ends. What he needed was a fresh approach. Someone with new ideas.

That was where I came in.

By telling me to stop, he probably banked on me reacting. He'd expect me to do the exact opposite. He'd know enough about me to realize I wouldn't just down tools and walk away from a case. That wasn't how I was programmed.

So now he was going to try to use me.

Watch me.

Tail me.

He was going to let me lead him to Franks.

And then, once he had the truth, he would bury me in the ground.

CHAPTER 54

There was a small twenty-four-hour service station on the Plymouth road, just south of Tavistock. At the smeared windows of its café was a series of moulded plastic booths, each one occupied by lorry drivers making the journey from north to south, loaded up with deliveries for a new week. I pulled into the car park and headed right to the back of it, using the shadows and the lorries as cover from the road. Craw followed. After I switched off the engine, it ticked over, rattling as if something had come loose.

We made our way around to the front. Inside it was quiet but not empty: a couple of people looked up, but most didn't even acknowledge us, the majority with cups of tea in their hands and newspapers laid out on the table in front of them.

The decor was tatty: worn, laminated surfaces; paint-blistered walls. There was a scratched counter behind which a grey-haired man in his sixties stood, half turned towards a serving hatch. A woman of about the same age was talking to him from the other side. The whole place was like a time warp, perfectly encapsulated by the fact that the radio was playing songs from the seventies.

We ordered coffees.

In a broad Devonshire accent the guy said he'd bring them over, so I led us to the far corner of the café, as far away from the windows – and everyone else – as possible, and claimed the space against the wall. It allowed me to keep an eye on the doors.

I turned my attention to Craw. Clearly, I wasn't the only one who hadn't been sleeping well. Her eyes were ringed by soft grey lines, her skin pale. She'd had the hood up on a black parka, but as we sat down she removed it and unzipped her coat, running a hand through her short, rain-slicked hair. She was wearing a charcoal jumper with a black-and-white pattern on it that looked like a shattered chessboard.

'Are you okay?' she asked.

I nodded. 'It's been an interesting night.'

'Shouldn't you see a doctor?'

My shoulder was feeling easier now, the process of changing gear on the drive down working some of the stiffness out of it. 'I think it's just bruising.'

'Your car looks pretty bruised as well.'

I smiled. 'Yeah. That'll definitely need a doctor.'

The guy brought our coffees over. After he was gone, Craw emptied two sachets of sugar and a ton of milk into hers. In a strange way, it surprised me: if I'd had to guess, I would have had her down as black, no sugar.

'I think you might have been trying to call my old number,' I said, showing her my phone. 'I sent you a text with the new number in it.'

She frowned. 'Really? When?'

'Yesterday.' I checked my watch. It was one-thirty on Monday morning. 'Or maybe it was the day before yesterday. Anyway, I had to change my phone. Reynolds was tracking my movements through my old one.'

She seemed genuinely shocked. 'In order to do what?'

But she knew already, and – unsurprisingly – that seemed to knock her off balance. The confirmation that there was a hunt for her father. The implication of what was to come if Reynolds got to him – if he even found Franks alive.

'What does Reynolds want with Dad?' she asked.

My eyes moved out to the café, ensuring we weren't being watched, and then out the front, into the night. Thick condensation had gradually taken hold at the windows.

'There were these two cases your dad worked. The murder of an eighteen-year-old girl called Pamela Welland back in 1996, and the murder of a drug dealer called Simon Preston in 2011. I think they might be connected to his disappearance somehow. Maybe they're even connected to each other.'

'How?'

I paused, thinking back to what Murray had told me: that Simon Preston had been living with someone.

A woman called Kay.

I recalled the map of Bethlehem that Franks had drawn, and the photos Reynolds had in his possession too – and then the argument Preston's neighbour had overheard about a hospital. But what, if anything, connected all of that to Pamela Welland? Was it Preston? Was it his girlfriend? Was it the hospital? Whatever the truth was, it was clear some part of the answer lay at Bethlehem, and as that idea began to solidify, it struck me that, in four hours' time, it would be low tide at Keel Point beach. I rolled my shoulder and felt a twinge next to my breastplate. It was easier.

But not as easy as I needed it to be.

Plus there were other, more immediate issues.

I had to ensure Annabel and Olivia were safe before I did anything else, let alone getting across to Bethlehem. But even once Tasker called me to tell me they were fine, I'd have to think through every move. Because, with every move, I had to be prepared to fight: Reynolds was going to try to follow me, try to use me as bait to draw out the truth about Franks. If he thought I'd figured him out, or even if he thought it wasn't working in his favour, he'd put me down.

'Raker?'

I looked back at Craw, realizing I'd drifted off. Her head was tilted slightly, some of the hardness gone from her face. Maybe it was the hour, or my lack of sleep, maybe the pain in my shoulder or the adrenalin draining away, but I thought, perhaps for the first time, how attractive she was. She'd always tried to hide it away, and I understood the reasons for that. She'd built her reputation on exactly the right qualities: talent, intellect, instinct, understanding the psychology of people, a refusal to retreat. In an environment like the Met, dominated by men, she'd beaten them at their own game.

'Your girls,' I said to her. 'I never ended up speaking to them. I'm not sure you even told me their names.'

She eyed me. It was clear she hadn't been expecting this, and it was equally clear she wanted to protect them from whatever was going on with their grandfather.

'Maddie and Evelyn,' she said finally.

'How old are they?'

'Thirteen and ten. Why?'

'Do you ever feel like you're putting them at risk?'

Frowning, she leaned back in her seat. 'At risk?'

'Doing what you do.'

Her arms were crossed, fringe in a diagonal sweep across her forehead. No make-up except for maybe a hint of mascara. No earrings, even though her ears were pierced.

'No,' she said.

I nodded.

'Why, do you feel like you're putting your daughter at risk?'

Belle says you've put us in danger.

'I hoped I wouldn't,' I said to her. 'But I think maybe I have.'

Craw was still eyeing me, the hardness back in her face; the mix of impassiveness and suspicion I'd got to know so well. 'The work you do, it comes with a risk.'

'And yours doesn't?'

She shrugged. 'Police work has its risks. I've been physically attacked. I've been threatened countless times, and not just by scumbags out on the street. Sometimes by my own people. But, most of the time, the rule of law helps protect you. You do things in the right way, at the right time, with the right preparation, you lessen the risk to everyone.'

I didn't want to go over old ground with her, fighting her on the reasons why I did what I did; my justification for sometimes ignoring the rule of law. I didn't break the law often, but when I did, it was because the law didn't work. I broke it because it got in the way of finding innocent people. Deep down, she knew my way was just as effective as hers. Perhaps even deeper down than that, she could see the ways in which it was better. If that hadn't been the case, she never would have asked me to find her father.

And yet I couldn't deny its risks.

Especially now.

It had never really mattered before Annabel came along. I wasn't unconcerned about my safety, but the pull I felt to the lost, to the families of the missing, drove me forward. Despite everything that had happened to me, all the devils I'd had to face, all the darkness in men, I'd never regretted a single moment. And yet I regretted what happened tonight. I regretted compromising my daughter.

'What do Maddie and Evelyn think about your work?'

She shrugged. 'That's not who you are to your kids. When I was still going off to work in uniform at the beginning, they were too young to notice. Now they're older, they have their own lives. I doubt they give it a second thought.'

'And your husband?'

'I don't know what Bill thinks any more.'

She gave me a look that said everything: *There are problems in our marriage – and I don't want to discuss it.* I nodded, looking out at the café.

When I turned back to her, she was still staring at me, obviously angry and upset about being drawn into a conversation about her personal life.

'How are those two cases connected?' she asked.

'Pamela Welland and Simon Preston?'

A nod of the head.

Before I could answer, my phone started buzzing. I picked it up and looked at the display. *Murray.* I glanced at my watch again. One-forty-five. Either she wasn't sleeping, or this couldn't wait.

'Sorry,' I said to Craw. 'I need to take this.'

She looked annoyed, but opened her hands out and sunk back in her seat.

'Evening,' I said, pushing Answer.

401

'Did I wake you?'

'No.'

'You need to hear this.'

I glanced at Craw, who was looking down into her mug of tea, gently turning it with both hands. She gave the impression she wasn't listening, but I knew her well enough by now: she was taking in every word.

'What have you got?' I asked.

'That place you talked about. Bethlehem. Something about it rang a bell. I've just been back through my notes, and . . . it's in there.'

'What do you mean?'

'It's from a while back, May 2000, but I remember it now. The Boss must have been out of the office, I guess, maybe in a meeting, maybe on a case. Somewhere.' She was talking quickly, frantically. 'Anyway, he got this call, and I took a message for him. I didn't have anything else to hand, so I took down the message in my notebook. I knew it wouldn't get lost that way.'

She paused, making no move to continue.

I prompted her: 'Okay. So what was the message?'

'This guy who called, he said his name was Poulter.'

I pulled out my own notebook, wedged the phone between my ear and shoulder, and flipped to a new page. I could see Craw watching as I wrote the guy's name down.

'Who is he?'

'He didn't leave a number, but I wrote down

the message he asked me to pass on: "Tell Mr Franks that I'll be at the hospital until 7 p.m. tonight."'

Bethlehem.

I tried to think logically. 'He could have been calling from any hospital.'

'No. I, uh . . .' Murray paused, her silence heavy with guilt. 'Look, I know I betrayed the Boss's trust, but I thought at the time he might be ill. I was concerned.'

'Are you saying you then tracked this guy down?'

'Yes. To the hospital. That's why the name Bethlehem rang a bell with me.'

'What did Franks say when you passed on the message?'

Craw had been looking out at the room, at the drivers gradually drifting out into the night to continue their journeys. But, at her father's name, she snapped back to me.

'I've been trying to remember,' Murray said. 'But, honestly, I don't think he really said anything. I think he just thanked me.'

'That's it?'

'That's how I remember it going.'

'He didn't look at you strangely?'

'This was thirteen years ago. I don't remember *how* he looked at me. It just says in my notes that this guy was called Poulter, and he'd called the Boss from that hospital.'

'Okay.'

'Obviously Bethlehem has closed down now, so

the number I had for him there is dead. But I did a little digging and have managed to find a home number for him.'

She read it out to me.

'Thank you,' I said. 'This is great.'

'Yeah, well, maybe not.'

I paused. 'What do you mean?'

'There's something else you should know.'

'What?'

Hesitation on the line.

'Murray?'

'You remember you asked me to check that police ID number you found at the top of Franks's missing persons file? The one you came across at Reynolds's place?'

'Yeah.'

'I got a name.'

'So we know who passed him that file?'

'Yeah.'

'Who does it belong to?'

A long silence.

'It belongs to Melanie Craw.'

CHAPTER 55

I looked across the table at Craw, her eyes on me again.

'Okay,' I said to Murray. 'I'll give you a call in the morning.'

She could immediately sense something was up. 'Are you all right?'

'Yeah. Fine. I'll phone you later.'

Ending the call before Murray could ask me any other questions, I placed the phone down on the table and then casually closed, and pocketed, my notebook.

'Who was that?' Craw said.

She asked the question flatly, as if she had no investment in its answer, but there was a kind of narrowness to her face now, like she was holding her breath. *Like she knows something's changed.* I paused, giving myself a moment to think.

She pushed her cup aside. 'Raker?'

I was seeing the cracks in the wall.

She'd driven two hundred and twenty miles when she could have just sent Derek Cortez to check on the house. She'd appeared only minutes after Reynolds, telling me she hadn't passed him on the way – and yet, given the remoteness of the house, and the single-track approach, that seemed impossible. Then there was all the crap she'd spun about me not answering my mobile. *Because she'd deliberately called me on my old phone.* I'd dumped that handset days ago, after I found out Reynolds was tracking it – and the first person I texted with the number for the replacement was her. Now it seemed clear: she'd chosen not to call me on the new one because she didn't *want* me to answer.

What she wanted was an excuse to come down here.

'Raker?'

I'd never seen her cry once when talking about her father. She'd never got *close*. What kind of daughter showed zero emotion when describing her dad going missing?

One who was working against him.

I looked at her, and then out into the café, moving between faces. Was it just her, or were other cops involved too? Could they be here, at the other tables? I'd told Craw where we were going before we'd left Dartmoor. She could have phoned in the details to whoever else was involved while we were driving down here. But then my gaze finally returned to her and I thought of something worse: *I've been watching you for a while now, and you've never had a clue.* Maybe the reason Reynolds was on to me so early was because he'd been prepped by someone before the case had even started.

Maybe I was sitting with her.

'Raker?' she said. 'What the hell's the matter with you?'

She seemed agitated now, on edge, and suddenly this whole thing made perfect sense: what better way was there to watch me? And as I thought of that, something hit me hardest of all: *listening to Reynolds on the phone at his flat.* I'd been out on the roof, him at the window, only able to hear his side of the conversation. *'What?'.* . . . *'What help can that possibly be?'.* . . . *'Are you fucking insane? Now he knows all about me.'.* . . . *'Yeah, well, you better hope so.'* He was being told his file had been accessed. He was being told I knew some of his history now. And he was being reassured it was part of the plan.

'*Raker?*'

I held up a hand. 'I'm just thinking.'

'About what?'

About you being the one who accessed Reynolds's file for me. About what your plan is. About why you and Reynolds would work together in order to find your father.

'About *what*?' she said again.

'Is it easy to gain access to the database?'

As soon as the words were out of my mouth, I wanted to pull them back in. My shoulder pinged with pain and my guts began churning at the thought of being set up, of being betrayed by the daughter of the man I was being paid to find. Yet even as the truth began to form in front of me, a

407

part of me still fought against the idea. I didn't know Craw. Not really. In reality, no one knew anyone. But I hadn't expected this. At no point had I ever seen this coming.

'The database,' I said.

'Are you talking about the *police* database?'

'Yes.'

'Hard.'

'It's hard to access it?'

'What do you think?' she said, a look of contempt in her face. 'It's not open to the public, if that's what you mean.'

'Could someone log in with your ID?'

A frown, but no response.

'*Could* they?'

'Technically, yes.'

'But only if you told them your number?'

She nodded. 'What the hell's going on?'

'Is that the done thing?'

'What?'

'Telling people your number?'

'Absolutely not.'

'Does anyone know yours?'

She studied me for an instant – a split second of confusion – and then it was like a light switched on. She shifted back in her seat, hands flat to the table.

Something had changed in her.

'Why?' she said.

I didn't reply.

Instead I felt a pop of pain at the back of my

head and, for a moment, white spots flashed in front of me. When they were gone, a fresh spike of nausea bubbled in my throat. I tried to ignore it, watching Craw's eyes move out to the café. I turned and looked myself. Almost unnoticed, it had become just us and a driver in a green tracksuit top.

On cue, he glanced in our direction.

He was in his forties, bearded, overweight, but big and powerful. He looked from me to Craw, his eyes lingering on her, and then returned to the newspaper he had out in front of him. *He could be working with her and Reynolds.*

Anyone could be working with them.

'What's going on, Craw?'

She faced me, said nothing.

'What the fuck's going on?'

This time she leaned in across the table, hands still flat to it, fringe straying across her eyes. 'I think you need some rest, David,' she said quietly. 'Maybe a doctor too.'

'Don't lie to me.'

'I think a doctor would do you good.'

I glanced at the man in the green top again.

'Once you've rested, then we can talk.'

'Talk about what?'

'Talk about what's really going on here.'

My fists had balled together without me even realizing, my muscles tense, nerves shredded. I watched her as she leaned back in her chair again, running a hand through her hair, setting it right above the arc of her eyebrows. My vision blurred slightly.

Then my phone shattered the silence.

I looked down at the display.

Ewan Tasker.

I picked it up, eyes still on Craw. 'Hello?'

'Raker, it's me.'

'Is everything okay?'

'Yeah. They're both safe and sound.'

'Thank you.'

He paused. 'Are you all right?'

'Yeah. I'll call you when this is all over.'

I hung up, placed the phone face down again and looked at my watch.

It was 2 a.m.

Craw was examining me from behind her hand, her elbow to the table, her knuckles against her lips. Her face was unmoved, like a mask.

I scooped up the handset and stood, feeling unsteady on my feet now. My head was pounding. My stomach slithered, like something was moving inside it.

Craw gripped my arm. 'Where are you going?'

The man looked over at us again.

'I'm going to find out the truth,' I said to her.

She just stared up at me, hand still clamped at my elbow.

'Let go of me.'

'This is only going to lead to more trouble, David.'

'Then stop me.'

I ripped my arm away, looked again at the driver and walked out into the rain. As it pounded against my face, hard as needles, I gazed in through the glass at her. She was sitting at the back, eyes fixed on me, saying something to the man.

Another pop in my head.

Another wave of pain.

I headed to the car.

CHAPTER 56

By the time the sun bleached the sky, it was eight o'clock and I was sitting in a medical bay in A&E at Derriford Hospital, north of Plymouth. I'd ended up at the hospital after leaving Craw, my head getting worse every moment I was behind the wheel, until – at a set of traffic lights, four miles on – I'd blacked out. I'd been unable to think, unable even to drive straight, and by the time I arrived, I'd already been sick once. My shoulder was badly bruised, but there was no break. Of more concern to the doctors had been a gash to my head, at the base of my skull.

It had needed nine stitches.

As I waited to be discharged, I drifted in and out of sleep, desperately tired but unable to drop off. My head was full of static, full of conversations replaying over and over. In the hinterland between consciousness and sleep, I started to wonder what it was I'd seen and heard the previous night; how much of it was real, how much imagined. At 9 a.m., tired of waiting, I discharged myself, and as I moved outside, into the cool of the morning, it felt like everyone I passed was watching me, every whispered conversation carrying my name. At the car – looking worse than ever in the daylight – I surveyed the car park and saw shadows move inside vehicles, in reflections off the glass. I heard footsteps running off.

I heard my name spoken.

I let myself into the back seat and collapsed on to it, pulling the door shut. The car was freezing, smelling of burnt electrics and damp, and it instantly began to steam up as I lay there, face down. My shoulder throbbed, pulsing like a heart-beat. The stitches at the back of my head sent green shoots of pain upwards, into the dome of my skull. But I didn't care about any of that. I'd slept six hours in the last forty-eight. All I cared about was sleep. And finally, slowly, I let it take me away.

I woke to the sound of my phone.

Disorientated and chilled, I rolled over and hit my arm on the door. To start with, I wasn't even sure where I was. The skies were dark, thunderous. The windows had steamed up too, obscuring most of what lay outside.

Hauling myself up, I rolled my shoulder. It was stiff, but felt better. My head was still throbbing, though, a dull, repetitive ache, like a drumbeat. Clearing a patch on the glass, I remembered where I was: the car park at Derriford Hospital. Beyond the roofs of the cars to my left was the functional grey concrete of the main building.

I looked at my watch.

Three-fifty in the afternoon.

I'd been asleep for almost seven hours.

As I played catch-up, filling in everything I'd been too fuzzy to cope with earlier in the day, I felt the phone again, still buzzing in my jacket pocket.

I took it out.

A south Devon number.

'David Raker.'

'Ah,' a voice said. 'I was wondering if I was going to get an answer from you.' It was an old man, his voice a little cracked, a gentle wheeze playing out behind his words. 'Just woken up from your drunken stupor, have you?'

Suddenly feeling hot, I got out and breathed in the coolness of the day. There was no rain, just the reminders of the night before: puddles everywhere, water sloshing in the drains and the gutters, long-dead leaves scattered across the car park, reduced to piles of bronzed pulp. I scanned the area around me: a family getting out of their car, a woman walking to the pay-and-display meter. No one watching me. No one waiting.

'Who is this?'

'It's Alan Poulter,' the man said. 'You don't remember calling me last night? Three o'clock in the bloody morning. Next time, try calling at a decent hour.'

Poulter.

The doctor from Bethlehem.

Vaguely, in some distant part of my memory, I remembered calling him. I'd been in a state the night before: rattled from what I'd found out about Craw, woozy from the head injury, crippled by a lack of sleep.

'I'm sorry, Dr Poulter.'

'So you should be.'

'I wasn't drunk, if that makes it any better.' I felt around in my pockets with my free hand and removed my notepad. 'I was in a car accident. A minor head injury.'

'Oh.'

'Anyway, apologies.'

'That's, uh . . .' A pause. 'Don't worry.'

'Thank you for calling me back.'

I laid my pad on the roof of the car, pulling a pen out of the spiral binding. Then I looked around me again. *I've been watching you for a while now, and you've never had a clue.* The woman was attaching her ticket to the inside of her windscreen now. The family I'd seen were long gone. Otherwise, the car park was empty.

'I was hoping to talk to you about Bethlehem,' I said.

'I see. Who is it you work for?'

'I find missing people.'

'For the police?'

I thought about what the best answer would be to that. Poulter came from a time and a profession where confidentiality was paramount. Over the phone, and without the opportunity to get a sense of who he was, I opted for a lie. 'Yes,' I said. 'For the police.'

'I see,' he said again.

'So can I ask you about Bethlehem?'

'I prefer to call it Keel Point Hospital. The worst thing that happened to that place was when that religious nutter decided to rename it. As the years went by, the media, the locals, they loved the fact that it had this holy name on the front of the building, and – as they saw it, anyway – these unholy minds locked inside. They used it as a stick to beat us with. I'm sure they secretly did a little dance of joy when Silas murdered all those people in the kitchens.'

I gave him a moment to calm down, recalling the story of how William Silas had escaped his handcuffs and ended up killing and dismembering four staff, then pushed on. 'How long did you work there, Dr Poulter?'

'Twenty-nine years.'

'Were you there until it closed?'

'Oh no, no, no,' he said. 'I retired back in 2005.'

'Right. Okay. Well, I'm trying to find a man who may have had some kind of a connection to the hospital. I'm not sure he was a patient there, but – according to my information – you and he were in touch by telephone. His name was Leonard Franks.'

'Franks?'

'Yes. Leonard.'

Nothing on the line except the soft sound of wheezing.

'Dr Poulter?'

'He was the policeman, right?'

Bingo. 'That's exactly right, yes.'

'Yes, I remember him. Well, I read about him.'

'You mean, in the local newspapers?'

'Yes. He disappeared at the start of the year, didn't he?'

'On 3 March, yes.'

'Ah, right. Either way, I remember reading about it, because I thought to myself, "I'm sure I know that man from somewhere."'

'You knew him from the hospital.'

'I can see that now, yes.'

'But I don't think he was a patient of yours, was he?'

'Oh no. He lived in London, didn't he?'

'Yes. Unfortunately, Mr Franks's family haven't been able to locate him.' I paused and thought of Craw, but then instantly moved on, not wanting to get distracted. 'However, I believe you may have been in touch with him in or around the year 2000.'

'That's a long, long time ago, Mr Raker.'

'I realize that, yes.' I stopped, scanning the car park again. 'I don't suppose you recall what you and Mr Franks talked about?'

A snort. 'Absolutely no idea.'

'None at all?'

'It was *thirteen years* ago. We used to have conversations with the police all the time. They'd always be checking up on people they'd arrested; people who we were now treating. A lot of police officers don't like the fact that human beings suffer psychological problems and do unfortunate things because of them. They prefer things in black and white. It helps them sleep at night. So they used to call us a lot, double-checking patients – their arrests – hadn't taken them for a ride to avoid going to prison.'

'And Mr Franks?' I said, prodding him.

'I only remember him retrospectively.'

'You mean, from what you read about his disappearance?'

'Right.'

I decided to change the angle of attack. 'If I mention some names to you, could you maybe tell me whether you recognize them as patients?'

'I can't talk about individual patients, Mr Raker.'

'All of these people are dead.'

I looked at the list I'd made – Welland, Viljoen, Preston, whoever Kay was – and knew that only two of them were confirmed dead. But I kept going, anyway.

'It's unethical,' Poulter said.

'I realize I'm asking a big favour here, Dr Poulter. I'm not asking for details of what you discussed with these people . . .' I stopped. *Not yet, anyway.* 'It's simply a question of narrowing their movements down to Keel Point at the time you were in touch with Mr Franks.'

'I had a lot of patients in twenty-nine years.'

'But maybe we can just give it a go anyway?'

A long pause. 'Okay. If you think it would help.'

'I do,' I said. 'Thank you. Okay, so first: Pamela Welland.'

'How do you spell that?'

I spelled it out for him. I already knew this one was a dead end. Welland had never left London in her eighteen years, let alone left it for a psychiatric hospital in Devon.

'Hmm,' he said. 'I don't think so.'

'Are you sure?'

'Did she live down here?'

'In Devon? No. She lived in London.'

'Hmm,' he repeated. 'Her name rings a bell, but I'm pretty sure she wasn't one of my patients. How old is she now?'

'She was murdered in 1996, aged eighteen.'

'Oh. Well, she definitely wasn't one of mine, then. Would I have read about her death in the newspapers, like I read about Franks?'

'Quite possibly.'

'That must be it, then.'

'All right. What about Paul Viljoen?'

Again, I spelled it out for him. Again, he said no.

'Simon Preston?'

He considered it. 'No. That doesn't ring any bells.'

'Ever treat a patient with the first name Kay?'

'K-A-Y?'

'Yes.'

'In twenty-nine years? I couldn't say for sure.'

'You don't remember?'

'I'm seventy-eight, Mr Raker. I've been retired for eight years. I spent almost half my working life at that hospital. You can't expect me to remember everyone I treated.'

A few spots of rain began falling, dotting the roof of the car and the pages of my notepad. It seemed to sum up the direction this conversation was heading.

'You don't have *any* idea what you were calling Mr Franks about, back in 2000?' I asked again. 'Maybe someone he'd arrested had been transferred into your care?'

'That's the most likely possibility.'

'But you don't know for sure?'

'I'm afraid I don't.'

I flipped back through my notes, through the names of everyone connected to this disappearance, and felt a fizz of frustration.

'Welland,' Poulter said.

I tuned back in. 'Pamela Welland?'

'Yes. You said she was murdered in London?'

'Correct. In 1996.'

The soft sound of his wheezing came down the line again. I waited him out, looking off at the car park. A husband and pregnant wife were moving towards me from the direction of the main building. A blue Ford was entering the lot, a man at the wheel, a teenaged girl in the seat beside him. I watched them all the way into a space just down from me, and then returned my attention to the call.

'Dr Poulter?'

'I don't know,' he said.

'You don't know what, sir?'

'I don't know if this is really . . .'

'Really what?'

Another long pause. 'Really ethical.'

It took me a moment to catch up. 'You recognize her name?'

No response.

'Dr Poulter?'

'I shouldn't be talking about these things.'

'I understand that. But these are old cases, old crimes. All I'd appreciate knowing is, if you recognize Pamela Welland's name, maybe an indication of why.'

Silence.

Come on.

'Dr Poulter?'

'Perhaps.'

'Perhaps you recognize her name?'

'Yes.'

'From somewhere other than the newspapers?'

'Yes.'

My grip tightened on the pen. 'Where from, Dr Poulter?'

'I used to have a . . .' He stopped. *Come on. Come on, don't hold out on me now.* He cleared his throat. 'I used to have a patient. This lovely girl. Troubled, but lovely. She came to the hospital in a very bad way: she'd lost her two-year-old son in an accident, and then she and the father divorced, and she just got into a spiral she couldn't control. By the time I began treating her, she'd already tried to kill herself three times. The third time, she was in ICU for two weeks. She'd been so far gone, her vital organs had shut down.'

I wrote down what he said. 'Who was she?'

'You mentioned a Kay earlier.'

'This woman was Kay?'

'I don't know if it's *your* Kay,' Poulter said. 'It certainly seems too coincidental that you would mention Pamela Welland and then someone called Kay.'

'Kay knew Pamela Welland?' I asked.

'She used to talk about being very affected by a murder,' he said, as if he hadn't heard me. 'One that had taken place near to where she'd lived. Before she had her son, before her divorce, she'd been based somewhere in London. Greenwich, I think. She was originally from this part of the world, returned here after her son tragically died, but she was in London for a number of years. Anyway, when we talked about her time there, she always talked about being upset about this girl's death. She'd never talk about the reasons *why*, only that it had affected her. I always assumed it was the girl's age.'

I paused, pen hovering about my pad, not interrupting.

'I think maybe she was talking about this Welland girl.'

'Was that why you called Franks?'

He sounded confused.

'I really need you to think hard about this, Dr Poulter. Because Franks was the lead on the Pamela Welland case. Did Kay say something to you about the case?'

'No. No, it wasn't that.'

'Are you sure?'

'Positive. I think I might have been calling him to let him know how she was. I think he might have asked me to update him. It's so hazy, such a long time ago . . .'

'Why would Franks want to know how she was?'

'Honestly? I can't remember.'

I looked down at my notes.

'One thing you *could* do,' Poulter said, 'is speak to my successor at Keel Point. A man named John Garrick. I have his number here somewhere.'

'Okay. I'll take that. Thanks.'

He told me to give him a moment. Once he'd put the phone down, I minimized the call and went to the browser on my mobile, googling 'Bethlehem' and 'Dr Poulter'. I found a picture of him, at some kind of conference. He looked old, even then. Backing up, I did the same search for the name he'd given me: John Garrick. The picture I found of him was nothing to do with the hospital. Instead he was part of a local newspaper story, fronting a campaign to prevent the destruction of south Devon's nature trails. He was in his early fifties at the time the picture was taken, had shaved hair and a hint of grey stubble, with a sticker on his lapel that said, *Hello! My name is John.*

Poulter came back on the line. 'I have it here. John came in when they were already scaling back the kind of services we offered. They weren't hiring for full-time roles any more, they were hiring contractors. Dreadful shame. I mean, seriously, you can't run a hospital by filling it with part-timers.' He paused, a bitterness in his voice that echoed his comments about the media and the locals earlier. 'But none of that was John's fault. He was a very good psychiatrist. From what I heard, Casey liked him very much.'

'Wait, her name was Casey?'

'Yes,' he said. 'Kay for short.'

I flicked back through my pad until I found what I wanted: something Franks had written down in his diary that I'd never been able to fully put together.

UnID'd victim + CB?

Simon Preston had been the unidentified victim.

And now I'd found his girlfriend.

'What was her surname?' I asked.

'Casey's?'

'Yes.'

A brief pause, as if he was trying to draw the name from his past.

'Her surname was Bullock.'

CASEY

September 2011 | Two Years Ago

One Friday, towards the end of September, she drove down to Keel Point, parked up and watched from the beach as staff began transferring high-risk patients to the ferry.

Psyday, Casey thought.

Five hundred feet away from her, they marched patients off a transfer bus one by one, across a secure area, fenced in and connected to the jetty, into the ferry waiting in the water. Most of the patients were sedated and were helped in, but if they weren't too heavily medicated, the staff shadowed them into their seats. After they were on board, nurses would secure a patient and then return for the next. A security guard from the hospital and an armed police officer remained at the transfer vehicle the entire time, watching the process unfold, their eyes never leaving the patients.

There was no one else watching, just her. She sat alone on the shingle beach in the warmth of early autumn, sun peaking through the clouds, the sea blue and still.

Most of the patients moved quietly between the two vehicles, without much fuss, heads down, legs dragging. A couple more looked across the water, their eyes distant and drugged, but didn't react. One began crying as he saw what awaited on the other side of the causeway, great howls of pain, as if the hospital scared him. And then the last patient emerged, a man in his forties, with a ponytail and a black goatee, handcuffed at his wrists and ankles. Two hospital staff flanked him, one hand on either elbow, pushing him forward. As he came down the ramp from the transfer vehicle everyone tensed: the security guard seemed to fill out, the police officer's hand gripped his gun even harder.

'You know who that is?'

Casey turned, startled.

Behind her, at the sea wall that separated the shingle beach from the empty car park beyond, stood a man in his late thirties, thickset, chest and arms knotted with muscle. Physically, he looked like a bodybuilder, and yet he was pale and bloodless. He had a pair of sunglasses on, making it hard to tell exactly where he was looking, and was dressed in black, his boots dirty and mud-specked, the hood of his top up over his head.

Inside, she could see his scalp was shaved.

Casey didn't reply, and the man turned further in her direction, letting her know that he was waiting for a response. When he still got nothing, he removed his sunglasses and came forward a step, an odd, unsettling sensation gathering in her. She brought her bag in closer to her, like a defence mechanism. The man watched every inch of movement, his eyes tracking the journey of the bag, the flow of the muscles in her hand, the change in her breathing. She swallowed, shifted on the pebbles and got to her feet.

'You going somewhere?' he said.

'Yes.'

'I hope it wasn't me.'

She studied him. 'I prefer to be alone.'

A smirk bloomed on his face, then he pointed over her shoulder, back towards the ponytailed patient they were loading on to the ferry. 'So do you?'

'Do I what?'

'Do you know who that guy is?'

She didn't want to turn her back now, not to watch a patient being taken from one place to another. But when he got no response, when she didn't look at the patient, the man's eyes snapped back to her.

'Cat got your tongue?'

She felt a flutter of panic. Simon had always been aggressive, cruel, had called her names to try to suppress her. He'd grab her and shake her when she refused to back down. But Simon had never scared her. Simon had been heartless, but he'd been dumb.

This man was different.

'Take a look at him,' he said, stepping away from the sea wall, and she felt as if she had to, even though turning her back on him went against every instinct she had.

On the other side of the beach, inside the secure

fenced area, the patient with the ponytail and goatee was almost at the door of the ferry.

'That's Gary Corrigan.'

At the sound of his voice, she turned in his direction again. He'd stepped closer without making a single sound on the shingle. He was four, maybe five, inches taller than her and well built. In his smooth, pale hands, he held the sunglasses he'd been wearing. As he looked down at her, he moved them between his fingers, manipulating them, passing them back and forth between his thumb and ring finger.

Back, forward. Back, forward.

'The Richmond Park Rapist,' he said.

She found herself turning back to Corrigan without even thinking, recognizing the name from the news. By the time she realized what she'd done, she could feel him almost brush against her, disturbing the air between them. She turned slowly, heart hammering against the inside of her chest. He'd dropped to his haunches, his gaze moving from her feet, past her legs, and then above his eyeline, to her breasts and her face.

'What a waste of fucking time,' he said, his attention returning to Corrigan. 'Bring him all the way down here from London, stick him on the psych ward for six weeks, then take him all the way back to London again.' He looked at her, saw her confusion, and a smile cracked across his face. 'Oh, didn't you know? In two months' time, they're closing your little madhouse across the water there. It's too expensive.'

She looked away, off across the causeway to the hospital, back to the patients, now all loaded on to the ferry, then back at him. 'I never . . .' She stopped. 'No, that can't—'

'It can.'

He stood again, the height difference between them more marked than ever. He looked from her, to the ferry, then leaned in so close she could feel his breath on her face. She could smell his odour too: the stench of mildew, of unwashed clothes.

'That tedious little doctor you see, he'll be gone. This place, it'll be left to decay. And then what are you going to do? Crawl back to London?'

'Who are you?'

He shrugged. 'People used to call me Milk.'

Her gaze returned to the hospital. Could it really be true? Was it really closing? She remembered Garrick telling her a few months back that there were things happening at the hospital, but she didn't think he meant this. Why hadn't he told her? Maybe he thought she wouldn't be able to handle the news. Maybe he didn't even know himself.

And then she realized something.

She'd turned her back.

Suddenly, she felt his hands on the nape of her neck.

She froze, goosebumps scattering along her spine. When he felt her reaction, her repulsion, he pressed either side of her throat, digging the hard knots of his fingertips into the cartilage. 'Did you ever hear about what happened to your boyfriend?'

She felt his breath on her ear.

'Did you?'

'Let go of me.'

He pressed harder. 'Did you hear about Simon?'

She stopped moving; tried to look at him.

'I'll take that as a no,' he said.

'What about Simon?'

'He had his throat cut back in March.'

'What?'

'Ear to ear. That's what happens when you stray on to someone else's turf. He had a big mouth too, which didn't really help. Down here, he might have been someone. Up in London, he was rat shit. Nothing. A gnat.' He dug his nails into her neck and the words vanished instantly, carried off into the grey of the morning. 'Let me ask you something else, Casey.'

He even knew her name.

'Do you know how many women Gary Corrigan raped?'

She tried to fight him, tried to wriggle free.

His nails punctured her skin.

She flinched as he gradually drew her back to him, paralysing her movement, a spider cocooning its prey. 'You didn't answer my question,' he said.

She shook her head.

'Corrigan raped ten women. And do you know whose watch that took place on?' He paused, but he wasn't waiting for a response this time. 'An arsehole called Jim Paige. You know what's interesting about Jim Paige, Casey? He was best friends with Leonard

Franks, and there was this . . .' A pause for effect. 'Wait, I hope I'm not getting ahead of myself here. You've heard of Leonard Franks, right?'

She shook her head for a second time.

'Are you sure?'

'Of course I'm sure.'

'That's weird. Because your dead boyfriend seemed to know Leonard quite well. And you know what else he was crowing about in the days before his throat got cut? You know what he was saying, Casey?' He pulled her in so close to him, she felt his lips brush her ear. 'Simon was saying that everything he learned about Leonard Franks, he actually learned from you.'

CHAPTER 57

I headed into Plymouth, left the BMW at a long-stay car park, then paid for a hire car at a Hertz half a mile down the road. It was a small, black Vauxhall, but it would be better for now. The BMW was dying a slow, painful death, made worse by my not having the time to get it seen to. The more problems that I ignored and let develop on the car, the more conspicuous I made myself – and the more likely I was to get stranded somewhere. The added advantage was that no one I knew would be looking for me in a Vauxhall.

Not Reynolds.

Not Craw.

Before setting off, I transferred my wetsuit, torch and backpack across from the BMW. My plans to cross the causeway had been put on hold – but only temporarily. Low tide the next morning was six-seventeen. I wasn't going to miss the chance this time.

Next, I checked in with Tasker. The girls were fine, he said. When he was about to tell me where he was keeping them, I stopped him. 'I don't want to know for now,' I said. 'That way, I can't give up the information.'

'What the hell have you got yourself into now, Raker?'

'It doesn't matter.'

'It matters to me. It matters to the girls.'

'I'm okay, Task – that's the main thing.'

I told him I was going off grid for a while and that I'd call again in a couple of hours. Next, I tried phoning Murray. I wanted to ask her whether she recognized the name Casey Bullock. Poulter reckoned Bullock felt an attachment to the Pamela Welland case – or, at the very least, knew about it.

But the call went unanswered.

For a moment, as I listened to it ring, an alarming thought entered my head: I'd somehow compromised Murray. But then reality kicked in: I'd never mentioned to Craw that it had been Murray on the phone. Hanging up without leaving a message, I turned off my mobile and removed the SIM. I'd been surprised once by Reynolds when he'd tracked me through my handset.

It wasn't going to happen again.

I picked up the A38 back out of the city and followed it west for sixteen miles. It was slow going, like all roads were in this part of the world, and by the time I'd found the turning I needed – a B-road south that would take me all the way down to Keel Point – it was starting to darken again: evening took a grip, patches of sky fading, clouds disappearing, everything replaced by the ashen gloom of another winter night.

Halfway down, I took a quick detour east, towards Kingsbridge. On the edges of the town, I found the house that had once belonged to Simon Preston and Casey Bullock. It was a tiny semi-detached at the end of a scruffy cul-de-sac. The view was the best bit, the rear of the house backing on to rolling fields. The rest was plain but tidy: cut lawns, a freshly painted front door, an orderly driveway with a mid-range Ford parked on it. I paused there, engine running, studying the exterior, wondering how it might have looked when it had belonged to Preston. I guessed something less than this: something shabbier, more carious.

More reflective of the man who'd once owned it.

Living in the house next door was Andrew Stricker, the neighbour that Murray had chatted to on the phone. There were no cars on the drive, and no lights on inside. I wondered if it might be worth coming back, to take a run at him myself. But it would have to wait. I didn't want to stand still. Not now.

Continuing into town, lights circling the mouth of the Kingsbridge estuary, I parked up and headed down to the quay. A coffee shop was still open, a man wiping down tables out front that I didn't imagine had been filled at any point in the last month. Through the glass I could see it was virtually empty, which suited me fine, and – lined up, adjacent to the counter – were three iMacs. A sign above said, *FREE WIFI with every food purchase.* I could have used my phone to get on the web, but the less I used it, the more difficult I made it for Craw and Reynolds to find me. Plus I was hungry.

'What time are you open until tonight?' I asked the guy.

'Seven o'clock, mate.'

I looked at my watch. Six-fifteen. That gave me enough time.

Inside, I ordered a sandwich, some fries and a coffee, and then got an access code from the woman serving behind the counter. Choosing the Mac furthest away from the door, I sat down and logged in using the code, then went to Google.

I put in a search for 'Casey Bullock'.

Results were mixed: I got hits for the name, but mostly for Facebook profiles of women in other countries. At the bottom of the first page of results was a Twitter account that had Devon as its location, but when I went to the page, it was a shell: the default egg icon for its profile pic, following no one, followed by no one, not a single tweet.

I clicked through to the next page of results.

Halfway down, I found her.

A small story in a local newspaper, dated 26 September 2011.

At the top was a photograph of a woman. It was her thirtieth birthday. She was standing in front of a silver, heart-shaped balloon with '30' printed on it, one hand on its string, one on the back of a chair, a smile on her face. There was no indication of the year the picture had been taken, so I concentrated on her.

There was a kind of quiet beauty to her, almost a sadness, even as she smiled for the camera. Her auburn hair fell against her shoulders, but there was a clear view of her face. It was one that had aged before its time, blue eyes like a fading sky, wrinkles marking the hollowness of her cheeks. I started reading the story beneath.

Three lines in, my heart dropped.

I'd found her.

But I was two years too late.

LOCAL WOMAN GOES MISSING

A woman from Kingsbridge has gone missing in what Devon and Cornwall Police are describing as 'worrying' circumstances. Thirty-six-year-old Casey Bullock hasn't been seen for 48 hours, which police describe as 'highly unusual'. Ms Bullock, an outpatient at Bethlehem Psychiatric Hospital, was last seen talking to a man on Keel Point beach.

A police spokesman was keen to downplay the significance of her psychiatric care in relation to her disappearance: 'According to her doctor, and to the people responsible for her well-being, Ms Bullock was healthy, very lucid and absolutely aware of her actions. The care she was receiving at BPH had been ongoing for a number of years, and she had – prior to her disappearance – been extremely well. We are not currently exploring her hospital care as an angle of investigation. However, we would be keen to speak to anyone who saw her in the hours before she went missing on 23 September. In particular, a man in his late thirties, with a shaved head, who was seen in conversation with her on Keel Point beach.'

As Ms Bullock is an only child and both parents are deceased, police have been seeking the help of her ex-husband, Robert Collinson, who they are hoping will give them some personal insight into her disappearance. In a tragic twist, Collinson and Bullock's two-year-old son, Lucas, died in a drowning accident at a London park in 1999. When we contacted him, Mr Collinson cited it as being the reason the two of them had separated. 'I always tried to keep in touch with Casey, even after we split up,' he said, 'but she became increasingly isolated. I couldn't even tell you how long it's been since I last spoke to her. However, I'll do whatever I can to help the police, even if I sincerely doubt the Casey that I knew back then is the same as the Casey she is now.'

A spokesman for Bethlehem Psychiatric Hospital said they were fully cooperating with police. In July, local health authorities took the decision to close BPH because of spiralling costs and inadequate facilities, controversially not revealing the details of the closure to staff until last week.

As I returned to Google, my food and coffee arrived, but suddenly I wasn't feeling hungry any more. My stomach was a knot, a slow, crawling dread taking hold.

Casey Bullock had disappeared and never resurfaced.

Franks was missing.

All the things that might help paint a picture of what was going on were being put to bed one by one by Reynolds. The worst thing was, he was right there in the police description – age, appearance – and yet he may as well have been a ghost. Even the closure of Bethlehem worked in his favour.

And then there was Craw.

Franks had chosen not to reveal the identity of Simon Preston in his investigation of the drug murder – a wrong decision, although one he was likely to have taken for what he thought were the right reasons. It seemed certain from everything I'd heard and read since that he believed Reynolds to be involved in the actual murder of Preston, as an accessory, perhaps even as the man who had wielded the knife. And, if that was what had been firing him – a thirst to see Reynolds brought to justice – maybe he'd tried to track down Bullock, in order to find out more about Preston and his relationship to Reynolds.

Except Reynolds had got there first.

Yet there were still so many other questions, not least what Craw's motivation was here. So, instead of trying to figure it out, I set it to one side and did a fresh search – this time for 'Casey Bullock disappearance'.

I got the same story I'd just read, and a few other basic reprises in the days after, confirming she'd never been found. The truth was, at thirty-six, worn and weathered, and with a history of mental illness, Bullock wasn't the Broadway show newspapers wanted. They wanted Pamela Welland: a beautiful teenage girl, blonde-haired, blue-eyed, from a decent middle-class family, with her whole life ahead of her.

That sold newspapers, not Casey Bullock.

I'd seen it play out time and time again, over and over. A week after Bullock went missing – a week after the papers essentially *alluded* to the fact that she may have been taken by someone – her candle burned out and the story disappeared into the ether. I felt a pang of sadness for her, a measure of guilt too, at having once been a part of an industry that could so easily forget. And then my resolve hardened.

She'd been abandoned back then.

But she wasn't going to be abandoned now.

CHAPTER 58

Before I left the café, I checked my emails. There was one new message. It was from Melanie Craw.

I think you need to call me.
M

I sat there for a moment, staring at the screen, trying to second-guess her. It was clear she'd emailed because she hadn't been able to get me on the phone. That probably also meant she'd been unable to triangulate any calls I'd made since the last time we met. I logged out, my thoughts returning to the previous night when I'd found out that it was her police ID number at the top of her father's missing persons report.

I remembered, clearly, what she'd said to me at the end.

This is only going to lead to more trouble, David.

A lot of the rest of it was a blur.

The back of my head throbbed as I tried to dig out more memories. When I turned in my seat and looked across at the counter, I caught the woman who'd served me staring at the stitches.

I got to my feet, thanked her and headed outside.

Across the road from the café, right on the quay, was a phone box. I returned to the darkness, rain spitting, the wind bitter as it rolled down the estuary. The water was black, squares of light dotting the banks on either side, houses and pubs perched on its banks. Somewhere, four miles down, the estuary hit the English Channel.

In the channel was Bethlehem.

I stepped into the booth, fed some coins into the call box, then dialled the number Poulter had given me for John Garrick, the doctor who had treated Bullock in the years after Poulter had retired. It was for a mobile. After seven rings, the call switched to voicemail: 'Hello, this is John Garrick. Do leave me a message, and I'll call you back.'

'Dr Garrick, my name's David Raker. I'd like to speak to you about a woman called Casey Bullock.' I left it there, gave him my mobile number and ended the call.

Next, I dialled Craw's phone.

After the fourth ring, she picked up.

'Melanie Craw.'

'There's a café at Kingsbridge quay called the Coffee House,' I said to her. 'I'll meet you outside there in thirty minutes. Come alone and don't try to screw me over.'

'Raker?'

I hung up.

CHAPTER 59

Twenty-five minutes later, I saw her Mini coming in from the western edges of the town. I was on the other side of the water, looking across the estuary to the car park and café. From my position, it was initially hard to tell if she was alone or not, but once she hit the lights of the parking lot, the orange glow filled the vehicle, and I couldn't see anyone else with her. She switched off the engine, looked around her and got out. The night was cold, her breath forming in the spaces above her head. She locked up and headed along the fringes of the water to the coffee shop. It was closed now, its tables and chairs inside.

Outside the café, she paused, scanning her surroundings. The town was quiet, out of season and dormant. Cars passed steadily, otherwise there was no one around.

After a couple of minutes, she checked her watch. A couple of minutes after that, she got out her phone and checked that too. I wondered if she might be about to contact someone, but after the phone briefly illuminated her, she put it away.

I reassembled my mobile, waited another sixty seconds, then called her. As the phone buzzed in her hand, a muted white light blinking on and off inside her coat pocket, she lifted it out and checked the display. A second later, as she saw it was me, she looked around herself: to the parking lot, along the edges of the water, across the road to where shopfronts were just dark squares. Eventually, she lifted the phone up and answered.

'Raker?'

'Are you alone?'

'We need to talk.'

'Are you alone?'

I waited for anything that suggested she wasn't, an automatic reaction to knowing someone had followed separately. A look. A movement of the eyes. Instead she remained still, staring out to where a twelve-foot boat was moored against the walls of the estuary, rocking gently on the water.

'Yes,' she said. 'I'm alone.'

'Look to your right.' I watched her look further along the promenade, a road that ran parallel to the estuary. 'There's a sheltered area about half a mile along. It's got a set of benches in it. You see it?'

'Yes,' she said.

'I'll be there.'

'Do you realize what you've—'

I ended the call and headed for the shelter.

It was a hexagonal block, with a triangular roof, that looked out to the mouth of the estuary as it widened further down. During the day, people used it as a viewpoint.

But not at night.

Not in the middle of winter.

Craw arrived three minutes later, a mixture of anger and caution in her face. She stopped at a short flight of steps down, eyeing it, then me, then the shelter a second time. She was dressed in the same black parka, her hands in her pockets. Her short hair was clipped back from her face. Beneath the parka, she had a pair of black denims on, and black leather boots. She came down the steps, under the shelter. We both stood there, looking at each other, rain in the air around us.

Then she said, 'What the hell's going on?'

I stepped past her and looked back along the road. No one was following us. No one was watching. There were no cars for the moment.

We were alone.

'Is that some kind of joke?' I said to her.

She didn't reply for a moment, her gaze fixed on me. 'Are you all right?'

'No,' I said. 'I'm pretty far from all right.'

She looked me up and down. 'Do you even remember last night?'

'I remember.'

'Because it looks like you've got a pretty serious head injury—'

'I'm fine.'

'Are you sure?'

'Don't bullshit me, Craw—'

'I'm not *bullshitting* you, Raker. I'm trying to figure out what the hell's going on here. I mean, look at this place.' She waved her arms at the shelter. 'We're standing at the end of a promenade in the pissing rain, in a place that stinks of puke and booze.'

For the first time I felt a flicker of uncertainty. *Was this all an act?*

'Why did you lie to me?'

'*Lie* to you? What are you talking abo—'

'I know you passed on your father's missing persons file to Reynolds. What I can't figure out is why. So now you're going to tell me.'

'*What?* Are you *insane?*'

I didn't reply.

'Why the fuck would I give that scumbag anything?'

I took a sidestep out from under the roof of the shelter, trying to get some distance between us. 'Reynolds had a printout of the file among his things. It had *your* ID number at the top of it. I heard him talking to you on the bloody phone.'

That seemed to throw her.

She didn't say anything, eyes moving from me out to the water. The rain began getting heavier, beating a tempo on the roof of the shelter, disturbing the stillness of the water. Finally, she looked back at me. 'I'm not working with Reynolds.'

'Really? So how did that file magically end up in his possession?'

'Someone must have . . .'

'What? Used your ID?'

'Yes.'

I studied her. 'I asked you last night if it was hard to gain access to the database, and you told me it was. I asked you if anyone knew your login details – and you know what else you said to me?' I paused. She was trying to recall. 'You changed the subject.'

'So?'

'So you didn't want to answer me.'

'That doesn't mean—'

'You're lying to me.'

She shot me a look. 'Are you even hearing yourself?'

'You're denying you said that?'

'Why would I lie to you?'

'I don't know. Why *would* you?'

'I'm not lying to you. If someone's got hold of Dad's file, it's on the QT. I haven't given my login details to anyone – at least, not knowingly.'

I tried to see the deceit in her face. The previous night, it had seemed so clear to me. The way she'd looked. The way she'd spoken. Now there was no hint of anything. She was stoic, unreadable. If she was lying, I couldn't see the lie.

Or she'd never lied in the first place.

I checked the spaces beyond the shelter: the pavements, the path running along the banks of the estuary, the parking lot across the water. When I turned back to Craw, she was still studying me, eyes narrowed.

'Do you remember *anything* about last night?' she said.

'Enough.'

She took a step closer to me. 'I thought you were going to black out at one point. You told me something had popped in your head.'

I frowned. 'What are you trying to—'

'*Listen* to me: whatever you think's going on isn't going on. You honestly believe, in the cold light of day, that I'd pal up with an arsehole like Neil Reynolds?'

'You said—'

'I don't give a shit what you *think* I said. You know what you called me at one point last night?'

She stopped.

My head was swimming.

'You called me Derryn.'

I looked at her. 'No.'

'Yes.'

'Don't mess with me, Craw.'

'You've got stitches in the back of your head. You were virtually incoherent last night. Your vehicle looked like it had been rescued from the scrapyard. You were in a *car accident* . . .' She paused. 'I told you that you needed to see a doctor.'

I rubbed an eye, trying to recall last night.

Had I called her Derryn?

Was I really that mixed up?

She took another step towards me, a sudden, confusing sympathy in her face. 'This is why I hired you,' she said quietly.

447

Initially I was thrown by the change in her voice, but then I began to like the softness in it. For a moment, for the first time tonight, she was a different person.

'You care about your cases,' she continued.

She touched a hand to my elbow.

'But you're not fighting me. *I'm* not your enemy, David. Any energy you waste on me is energy you don't have for the real fight.'

I looked from my elbow to her face. She was a couple of feet from me now. I could smell her perfume beyond the freshness of the rain.

I studied her for a long time.

'David?'

As a smile passed across her face, I felt a strange sense of relief take hold. I didn't want her, of all people, to betray me. Despite our history, despite our differences and our run-ins, whatever else she'd been to me before, she'd been honourable.

'Look,' I said to her, the beginnings of an apology.

'It's fine,' she replied, hand dropping away from my elbow. 'The only thing I care about is finding out what happened to Dad.'

I nodded, contemplating my next move – and then my phone started buzzing.

Shit. I'd forgotten to switch it off.

Removing it from my pocket, I looked at the display.

A blocked number.

I went to switch it off, then stopped. *What if it's Garrick returning my call?* I held up a finger to

Craw, asking her to give me a moment, and retreated further from the shelter, into the rain.

'David Raker,' I said, answering.

'I don't know what you want or who you are,' a man's voice said, reduced to little more than a whisper. It sounded taut, threatening. 'But let me give you a piece of advice, okay? Forget Casey Bullock. For your own sake, just . . . forget her.'

I waited, his breath crackling down the line at me.

'Hello?' he said after a couple of seconds.

Hesitation now, and for the first time I realized he wasn't on the attack. He wasn't threatening me. He was warning me off. He was trying to help me.

He's terrified.

'Hello?' he said again.

I backed away from Craw, so she was out of earshot. 'Dr Garrick?'

Another hesitation, words forming and disappearing, as if he was speaking a sentence he wasn't sure he should commit to. And then finally, feebly, he said, 'Please. Please don't hurt me. I haven't told anyone, I promise.'

CHAPTER 60

Garrick paused on the line, his breath ragged and nervous. I glanced at Craw. She'd taken a seat on one of the benches, but was looking in my direction. The softness I'd glimpsed in her – that hint of a different person – was gone now, replaced by the woman I'd come to know much better. After eyeing me with suspicion, she removed her phone and started checking it. I turned my back on her and looked along the road. No vehicles. No people.

'Dr Garrick, I want to speak to you about Casey Bullock.'

'*Please*. I haven't told anyone.'

'What are you talking about?'

'I swear to God, that's the honest truth.'

'Wait a minute, wait a minute. I don't know what you're talking about, but I need you to calm down, okay?'

He sounded like he might be about to break down. But then I heard the line drift and the sound of a door closing. When Garrick came back on, he was more in control of himself, although his voice remained small and quiet. 'Who are you?' he said.

'My name's David Raker. I'm an investigator. I want to speak to you about Casey Bullock.'

'Why?'

'I'm trying to locate her.'

A pause. 'Are you serious?'

'Absolutely.'

Another pause, this one longer, as if he was trying to work out whether I was joking or not. 'Casey's dead.'

'Do you know that for a fact?'

'She hasn't been seen for nearly two years,' he said, 'and the man who came to see me about her, he was . . .' A long silence. 'He was the type who would . . .'

'The type who would what?'

'Who would hurt her. Who would hurt *me*.'

I knew instantly he was talking about Neil Reynolds, so the question wasn't who Garrick was referring to – it was why, after murdering Simon Preston, Reynolds had then gone after his ex-girlfriend.

'This guy came asking questions about Casey?'

More hesitation on the line. 'I don't even know who you are.'

'I realize that, but I—'

'You could be anyone.'

'I told you, I find missing people.'

'And I told *you*. Casey isn't missing.'

'It's not Casey I'm trying to find.'

That seemed to throw him.

I glanced at Craw. She'd finished checking her

451

phone and was looking across at me. We were on opposite sides of the shelter, rain coming down heavier now, cascading off the roof and through holes in the guttering. A car passed, headlights freeze-framing the boats out on the water. I covered the mouthpiece and moved closer to her, so she could hear me properly: 'I need to make a couple of calls.'

She didn't reply.

'I can meet you back at your car.'

Again, she eyed me with suspicion – but then she got to her feet and pocketed her phone. 'I don't want to be playing catch-up, Raker,' she said to me.

'I'll fill you in when I'm done.'

Her eyes lingered on me again, then she pulled up the hood on her coat and headed out into the rain, following the promenade back towards the centre of town.

I heard Garrick say something.

'Sorry, can you repeat that?'

'So if you're not trying to find Casey, then who?' he said.

'I'm trying to find a man called Leonard Franks.'

A hesitation.

'Dr Garrick?'

'I don't . . . He isn't . . .' He stopped. Now he sounded genuinely scared. 'I don't want anything to do with this.'

'Do you know Franks?'

'Please don't contact me again.'

'Dr Garrick?'

'I don't want to die.'

'You're not going to die.'

'You weren't there when this man came to see me.'

'I can protect you from him.'

'You can't.'

'I can.'

'You *can't*.'

Seconds from having him hang up on me, I realized there was no other way of coaxing him out. 'Look, I'm going to find out what happened to Leonard Franks whether you help me or not. That's what I've been asked to do. But, if you *don't* help me, I can't promise you won't be caught in the crossfire.'

I could almost hear him suck in his breath.

It was hard for me even to form the words: 'You're putting yourself at risk if you hang up on me. But if you don't, I can make sure you're kept safe.'

A stir of disquiet formed in the pit of my stomach: I didn't want to have to use his safety as a negotiating tactic. But this was the only way I could play it.

On the other side of the estuary, I saw Craw was already in her car, motor running, lights on. My Vauxhall was just down from hers. Even if she'd spotted it, she wouldn't recognize it, instead expecting to see my battered BMW.

Garrick had still said nothing, so I waited him out.

'*Please*,' he said eventually.

He sounded on the verge of tears. Rain drifted in, peppering my face, my coat. 'What I need to do is establish what's going on here – then I can try to help you.'

Silence on the line.

'Dr Garrick?'

'I'm scared.'

'I know. I understand.'

'He said he'd kill me if I talked.'

'Did this guy tell you his name?'

A long silence. 'How do I know you're not working with him?'

'At this point you don't.'

A snort. 'So I just have to take your *word* for it? I have to entrust my safety, the safety of my wife, my three sons, to *you*?'

'Let me paint the alternative for you: you don't help me, I don't find the man who took Casey Bullock, and you spend the rest of your life worrying about your boys getting snatched the second you turn your back.'

I heard him form words and let them go, one after the other, endless moments where he couldn't decide what was worse: placing his trust in a man he'd never spoken to before, who claimed to be an ally – or continuing to worry, every day of his life, that his family were about to be targeted by Neil Reynolds.

Finally, almost a whisper, he said, 'I didn't even know Casey had gone missing. I hadn't seen it reported. I hadn't read about it in the papers. No one even *cared* she'd disappeared.' A long, loaded pause, painful, palpable. 'So the week after she vanished – I don't know, this must have been early October 2011, I guess – I was waiting for her to turn up to her appointment. I always saw her on a Tuesday and a Wednesday. By that stage, she didn't need to be seen that often, but she requested it. She wanted it like that. That day was going to be the day I told her the hospital was closing. I was dreading it.'

'So what happened?'

'She didn't turn up. This man did. He didn't tell me his name.'

'What did he look like?'

I heard him swallow, another moment of panic, as if he'd entered a newer, even darker corner of the memory. 'I don't know . . . In his late thirties, I suppose. Five-ten or eleven. But broad. *Big*. Pale, shaved head. He had this . . . this odd way about him.'

Definitely Reynolds.

'What did he ask?'

'He asked me about Casey.'

'What about her?'

'He wanted to know what we talked about during our sessions.'

'And what did you tell him?'

'He had a knife,' he said, a tremor in his voice.

'So you told him everything you and Casey talked about?'

455

No response. Then I heard a sniff. 'I betrayed her,' he said, words smudged now. 'She confided in me . . . and I betrayed six years of her life.'

Unexpectedly, he started to sob softly. I felt sorry for him, but didn't interrupt, letting him have his time of mourning. It was clear, even from the short period I'd been talking to him, that Casey Bullock had meant a great deal to him.

When he began to recover his composure, I said, 'What, specifically, did this guy ask you?'

'He wanted to know about her past.'

'Her past with her ex-boyfriend Simon?'

He seemed unsure of how I'd made the leap. 'Yes. Yes, that, and everything else. Her marriage to Robert, the death of their son, her breakdown, her suicide attempts.'

'Did you discuss Leonard Franks with her?'

'Yes.'

'What did she tell you about Franks?'

'She said she was worried about him.'

'Worried about him how?'

For the first time, in the background, I could hear a noise – laughter – and then realized what it was: Garrick's children.

'I think she was scared of him,' he said.

That stopped me. 'Wait, she was *scared* of Franks?'

'Yes.'

I looked over to where Craw was sitting in her car. Inside, I could just about make her out, face half painted in the orange glow of the street lights.

'Why was she scared of him?'

'She never said.'

'She never told you?'

'No. I tried to get at what it was, over and over. I could see this great event in her past casting a shadow across our sessions. She lived in London for four years, and it was something to do with her time there. Something related to a case she saw in the papers.'

'The murder of Pamela Welland?'

A pause. 'How do you know all this?'

The silence was heavy with suspicion. I imagined, at this point, he was wondering whether he'd done the right thing.

'She was affected by the murder of Pamela Welland?'

He didn't reply.

'Dr Garrick?'

'Very affected by it,' he said after a while.

Poulter had said exactly the same thing. But neither of them had managed to get at the reasons behind it. All I had was the death of Pamela Welland, Franks as the man leading the hunt for her killer, and Casey Bullock – a woman for whom it had become more than just a passing interest. And, seventeen years on, the only two people who might know why were gone. Reynolds had buried Bullock where she would never be found. But I couldn't be sure what had happened to Leonard Franks. Not yet.

'Did she say Franks ever threatened her?'

'No.'

'But she was scared of him?'

'She said he made her "worried". That was her choice of words.'

'And she never said why?'

'No. I treated Casey for six years, and the person before me – Dr Poulter – treated her for almost six, and neither of us got a clear idea as to why she became so fascinated – if that's even the right word – about the death of that girl. As for this Leonard Franks . . .' He paused. I could hear laughter in the background again. 'Kids, give your dad some space, okay?' Another short pause. 'Let me put it this way: do you know how long it took for Casey to bring that man's name up?'

'Franks? No. How long?'

'Five years. That's five hundred and twenty sessions. Five hundred and twenty *hour*-long sessions before she found the courage to even as much as speak his name.'

'Did you tell that to the guy who came to see you?'

A silence heavy with remorse. 'Yes. He said he'd kill my *family*. I betrayed her, I betrayed Casey, but . . .' He paused. 'My family. I just . . . I couldn't bear to . . .'

. . . *live without them.*

There was no sobbing from him this time, but I heard him sniff, cover the phone and – for a second time – tell his kids to give him some space.

Then he came back on the line.

'I need to go, Mr Raker.'

'Did you ever think about calling the police?'

'About the man who came to see me? No way.'

'Why not?'

'Why do you think? I'm not putting my boys at risk.'

'What about Casey? What about before then, when she said Leonard Franks had scared her? Did you think about calling the police back then, on her behalf?'

'That was just the problem,' he said, and I heard some of the uncertainty return to his voice; a tremor of fear misshaping his final couple of words. 'I couldn't call the police – because she said the police were all in on it.'

CHAPTER 61

Craw got out as I approached, leaving her door open, the lights on, the heaters blowing. She stood there watching me, shadows at her face. I kept my expression neutral, but inside I was burning up. *I couldn't call the police – because she said the police were all in on it.* I didn't know whether that just meant Reynolds, or it meant him and Craw. Maybe Paige. Maybe Murray. Maybe even Franks. At this point, I didn't know who I could trust.

'Everything all right?'

I looked at her. 'Yeah, all good.'

Her eyes lingered on me, as if she could sense that hadn't been entirely the truth, but then she looked off into the parking lot. 'I don't see your car anywhere.'

'No. I left it about half a mile away.'

'Do you want me to drive you there?'

'No, it's fine. I'm already soaking wet.' I attempted a smile and hoped it looked convincing, then removed the ring with the keys to the cottage on them. 'Here.'

'What are they?'

'The keys to my parents' old place.'

She glanced at them. 'Aren't you coming?'

'I need to make a couple more calls.'

'To who?'

Just take the damn keys. 'There's a couple of leads I need to chase up. Once that's done, I'll meet you back at the house and we'll get everything straightened out.'

'"Straightened out"?'

It was the wrong choice of words. She eyed me again, mistrust written in every muscle on her face. 'I mean, I'll tell you everything I've found out, and we'll lay down a plan. One that doesn't involve me taking a detour to A&E.'

She nodded.

'Okay?'

She glanced at the keys, still being held out to her, then back to me. After a moment more, she reached over and took them. 'Okay.'

I gave her directions to the cottage. If she, or anyone else, turned the place over, they'd find nothing. I'd cleared it out earlier in the year when I'd moved back to London. Everything I needed I had in the car twenty feet beyond where she was standing.

'I'll see you later, then.'

She nodded again, her eyes still lingering on me – and then we both set off, moving in opposite directions.

She got back into her car.

I headed anywhere that wasn't with her.

CHAPTER 62

A mile and a half out of Kingsbridge, I found a public phone box, overrun by grass and half hidden in the shadows. I pulled up alongside it, turned off the engine and got out.

Inside it smelled of piss and damp.

The road was lonely, lined on both sides by high hedges, but the rain had stopped and now there was a break in the clouds, like a hole punctured in a ceiling. As I fed some coins into the slot, I could see moonlight escaping through the gap, illuminating fields further down, and then hinting at what lay beyond.

The ragged outline of the coast.

And then, across the causeway, Bethlehem.

I dialled Ewan Tasker's mobile and waited for it to connect. He picked up after a couple of rings, sounding suspicious. He didn't recognize the number.

'Task? It's me.'

'Raker?'

'Yeah. How's it going?'

'Everyone's fine. How's things your end?'

'Good.'

'You want to speak to them?'

'Please.'

I heard a muffled conversation, and then Annabel came on.

'Hello?'

'How you doing, sweetheart?'

'Okay, I guess.'

'I'm sorry about this.'

She didn't say anything initially, but then: 'Okay.'

'What have you been doing?'

'Getting Olivia to sleep.'

'Is she all right?'

'She's fine. She thinks it's a big adventure.'

But I didn't need to dig too far to find out what Annabel thought about it. The wind whined gently as it passed through the spaces in the telephone box, the cracks in its glass, its rusted-out frame. In the background at her end I could hear laughter on a television, a snapshot of domestic normality. Except even that was a lie. I'd dragged the two of them out of their beds in the middle of the night and sent them into hiding.

This was their normality now.

I'd made certain of that.

'Have you found the man you're looking for yet?' she asked.

'No. Not yet.'

'What happens when you do?'

'That depends.'

'On what?'

'On whether he's alive or not.'

She paused. 'And us?'

'You and Liv?'

'Yes. When you find him, can we go home?'

'That's the plan.'

'And this won't happen again?'

There was a mix of sadness and frustration in her voice that would have got to me even if she hadn't been my daughter.

'No,' I said. 'It won't happen again.'

Briefly, I could see my own reflection in the glass. *Another lie.*

'So where are you at the moment?' she asked.

My eyes moved to the coastline again, a grey smudge in the distance. The clouds had begun to knot together, gradually returning everything to darkness. 'I'm a couple of miles from Keel Point.'

'Keel Point? Oh. That's where the hospital is.'

'That's right,' I said, a little thrown. The fact that she knew about it surprised me, even though it shouldn't have: she'd been brought up only a few miles down the coast.

'You're not going across, are you?'

She'd asked it as a joke.

'I was thinking about it.'

'Seriously?'

'Seriously.'

A long pause. 'You're brave.'

'Why do you say that?'

I waited her out, but I thought I might already know what she was failing to put into words: people weren't the only vessels for memories. In my work, in the search for the missing, I'd been to places that had a resonance, a sense of what had taken place in them, even years after they'd been abandoned. It wasn't ghosts, it was something real and more powerful; as if a place could become scarred by its history.

Eventually, she said, 'If you're really thinking about going, you should cross at Parl Rock.'

'Where's that?'

'Another half a mile further down the coast. The crossing takes a little longer, but because of the sandbanks the water level never gets quite as high.'

I paused, wondering how she'd come to know that.

She seemed to sense my thoughts. 'I had some friends who went across, after it closed. They did it as a dare. I've got a brain between my ears, so I just watched from the beach.' She cleared her throat, as if finding it hard to articulate the words. 'On one side of the building, there are all these windows. Loads of them, all looking out to sea. I remember watching my friends head out there and thinking those windows . . . they looked like . . .'

'What?'

'It makes me sound crazy.'

'It's okay.'

A brief hesitation, then: 'They looked like eyes. Some had already been vandalized, smashed and broken, but lots of them were still intact – and when the moon, or the lights from the beach, reflected off the glass . . . it was like people were moving around in there.'

I looked out into the darkness.

'Just be careful,' she said.

'I'll let you know if I'm being washed out to sea.'

She made a brief, amused sound. 'Honestly, cross at Parl Rock. That'll make it easier. All you need to do to get there is follow the signs for Brompton Lee.'

'Okay, I wi—' I stopped. 'Wait, where?'

'Brompton Lee. It's the last village before Parl Rock. That was where my friends lived. The ones who went across.'

'What's in Brompton Lee?'

'*In* it? I don't know what you mean.'

'Houses? Shops?'

'Yeah. Uh . . . a pub. A post office.'

I removed my pad and flicked through the notes I'd made. Pretty soon, I found what I was looking for: what Franks had written on the scrap of paper and the pub flyer. What I'd found printed on the plastic tag I'd dug out of the ground on Dartmoor.

BROLE108.

I told Annabel I'd check back in a couple of hours, then hung up, powering on my mobile. I went to the web browser and searched for 'Brompton Lee post office'. After a couple of seconds, I found a picture of it in Google Images. It was a post office inside a general store. On the board above its entrance, in a thin serif, was

466

BROMPTON LEE GENERAL STORE AND POST OFFICE. Next to that was its phone number.

BROLE 577233.

When I scrolled down, I found its opening hours. Because of what else it sold – milk, bread, newspapers – it opened at 6 a.m. It was a stroke of good luck, as I could take a look inside and still get down to Parl Rock for low tide the next morning.

But that wasn't what caught my eye. Instead, what I zeroed in on was part of a list below the store's opening times.

Its facilities and services.

Including one hundred and ten post-office boxes.

CHAPTER 63

Brompton Lee was a mid-sized village south of Salcombe, set on the edge of the coast. It had maybe eighty homes, in a raft of different colours, two pubs, a butcher's, an estate agency, a tea room and a pharmacy. The general store sat on its own, midway through, an extension on its side doubling up as the entrance. The A-road in and out meant the village had good access to Salcombe, Kingsbridge, the surrounding villages and everything east of the Avon, which was probably why this post office had survived the government cull.

In the windows was a mix of foodstuffs, ice-cream signs and postcards of the local area. A sign confirmed its opening time as 6 a.m. I drove past, finding a spot about two hundred yards away. When I switched off the engine and the lights, the night washed in, and – except for the metronomic crash of the sea on the beach, eighty feet below – all I could see were squares of light from the village, hanging there in the blackness.

I got out, the night cool, and walked further into the lay-by, where a hole had been cut out of a thick tangle of ivy. Through it, I could see the vague outline of boats, drifting slowly across the channel, miles out to sea. In front of them, it was difficult to see anything.

But I knew the hospital was there.

A ghost marooned in the water.

I'd set my alarm for five-forty-five. As it started to go off, I shrugged off the spare coat I'd been using as a blanket, and sat up on the back seat. It could easily have been midnight. The sun wasn't going to be up until after eight, so there was absolutely no hint of light in the sky at all. It was as cold as a tomb too. The first thing I did was clamber into the front, start up the engine and put the heaters on full.

Ten minutes later, warm and awake, I locked the car and headed back into the village on foot, trying to keep my arrival as low-key as possible. The lights above the store were already illuminated, and forty feet from the entrance I could see a grey-haired woman in her sixties standing at the window, turning an Open/Closed sign around. I was at the door before she realized she had a customer, the darkness disguising my approach.

The store was small and cramped, shelves packed with produce. At the front, in wicker baskets, was fresh fruit. At the other end was a dark wood counter, a sweet display and the day's newspapers on top, then a cove beyond that, perhaps ten feet across. Inside was the only thing in the store that looked like it belonged in the twenty-first century: post-office boxes, built floor to ceiling. The antiquation hadn't quite been abandoned, though: the boxes were all housed behind a pair of old-fashioned saloon doors.

'Morning,' the woman said.

I smiled at her. 'Morning. How are you?'

'I'm good. You're up early.'

It was clear she didn't recognize me as a local, her eyes lingering on me a fraction longer than they should have done. She moved slowly, was slightly hunched, round and overweight, but she was switched on. There was a spark to her. At the back, through a glass sliding door behind the counter, I could see a man about the same age. *Her husband.* He was marking something off on a printed list. Next to him, on the wall, was a board full of hooks. From the hooks hung one hundred and ten keys, all secured behind a locked, reinforced-glass cabinet. They were spares for the PO boxes.

Each key had a red plastic tag on it.

'I'm just passing through,' I said.

'Ah. I didn't think I recognized you.'

'I've been in a few times before.'

She frowned. 'Oh, right.'

'Your husband helped me with my PO box.' I nodded to the cove at the back. 'My wife and I have just moved to a place on the other side of East Prawle.'

'Oh, *right*,' she said again. It was obvious she

didn't recognize me, but she tried to pretend my story rang a bell.

'Anyway, I'd better get on.'

'Yes, of course,' she said, gesturing towards the cove at the back. 'Do you need anything else? I can gather some stuff together for you in the meantime.'

I needed to keep her occupied while I had a look around, but sending her on a milk and bread run wasn't going to take longer than a minute. I felt around in the pockets of my jacket: the plastic tag, my notepad, my mobile phone.

My lock picks.

'That would be great,' I said. 'Thank you.'

I told her what I needed and then left her, making a beeline for the saloon doors. On the other side, I waited for them to settle back into place, got out my phone, then put in the number for the general store. When I looked out over the doors, I could see the woman was already at a refrigerator.

'What size milk do you want?' she asked, without looking at me.

'Just a couple of pints – thanks.'

I took in the boxes. They were standard-sized, all red, numbered 1 through to 110, and were built across three walls.

Box 108 was on the bottom row, right-hand side.

Returning to my phone, I called the number for the general store and placed the mobile back into my pocket. Somewhere beyond the cove I heard a ringing, then footsteps. They weren't the woman's, they were her husband's. As I dropped to my haunches at the lock, I heard him say hello. By the time he was saying hello a second time, I had the tension wrench in and was using the pick to apply pressure to the pins.

The man put the phone down.

In my pocket: the soft sound of a dialling tone.

'Brown or white?' the woman called over.

'Brown,' I said, adjusting the tension wrench slightly and feeling the pins settle against the pick. I looked through the slats on the saloon door and could see her at the wicker baskets now, choosing the three apples I'd asked for. Returning my attention to the box, I tried to work faster, but any excessive movement and everything reset – and then I'd have to start all over again.

Suddenly, beyond the walls of the cove, there were more footsteps and the sound of a sliding door. The husband was in the shop now too.

Steadying my hand, I closed my eyes for a second, trying to focus on what I was feeling rather than seeing. As I slowly drew the pick back out, I heard the two of them talking – the woman explaining to her husband what she was doing and where I was – and, when I opened my eyes, I could see the husband looking my way, head tilted, frown on his face. She'd repeated what I'd told her: that he'd help me set up the box.

Except he couldn't remember me.

Because it was all a lie.

He came out from behind the counter – and started to come towards me.

Damn it.

Suppressing the urge to withdraw the pick, I steadied my nerves and wriggled the wrench again. Tiny, fractional movements, but enough so that I could feel the pins dab against the pick, and the lock turn gently from left to right.

Come on.

The husband was six feet away.

Come on, come on.

The dialling tone in my pocket had turned into the constant whine of a terminated phone call. I checked through the slats.

Four feet away.

One pin left.

Slowly drawing the pick towards me, I saw the husband's feet come into view beneath the bottom of the saloon doors. Then the top of his head.

I'm not going to make it in time.

Shit, shit, shi—

The door of the box popped away from its frame.

Immediately dropping the pick and wrench into my opposite pocket, I opened the box and looked up over the saloon doors.

The husband's head emerged fully above it.

He smiled politely. 'Hi. How are you?'

I tried to look nonplussed, my hand snaking into my jacket and killing the sound of the phone. 'I'm good, thanks. Nice to see you again.'

He nodded, still smiling politely at me.

He didn't remember me, but he tried to pretend he did. With my hand still in my pocket, I pressed Dial, knowing it would call the last number.

Their telephone started ringing a second time.

The husband looked towards the counter and back to me, rolling his eyes. 'Sorry. I won't be a minute.'

I told him that was fine and then watched him go. Once he was far enough away, I turned my attention back to the box.

Inside was a foot-long mini-holdall.

The phone stopped ringing elsewhere in the shop as the husband answered. I heard his voice beyond the walls of the cove and an echo of it through my mobile. When he got no response, he asked who it was, annoyed, frustrated.

I dragged the bag out and slung it over my shoulder.

It was time to go.

CHAPTER 64

At the car, I dumped the holdall and the shopping bag on to the passenger seat, then followed the signs out of the village, towards Parl Rock. It was a claw of land that reached out into the channel like a finger pointing across the causeway. A narrow road took me halfway down, where a car park had been created inside a natural ring of slate and knotted quartz.

Turning off the lights, I sat in the dark for a moment, wondering what I was about to find. And then I clamped the torch between my teeth and unzipped the holdall.

It was full of money.

For a moment I just sat there, looking into the holdall, slightly dazed, my mind spinning. But then I reached in and pulled some out.

It was segregated into three-hundred-pound bundles, secured with paperclips. As I started counting through them, I found twenty separate bundles. *Six thousand pounds.*

Beneath the money was something else.

A mobile phone.

I took it out and powered it on. It was a three-year-old Nokia – no touchscreen, just a selection wheel. At first I thought it had been restored to factory settings, or maybe never even used. There was nothing in the address book, no texts, no calls, no web history. But then I started looking through the photos and videos.

It wasn't empty.

There was a single two-minute film.

I selected it and pushed Play.

At first it was hard to tell what was going on. The camera was struggling to focus in a poorly lit room, as fuzzy black-and-white shapes merged with one another, and then separated again. I looked at the timer on the video.

Fifteen seconds had already passed.

But then, a moment later, the picture snapped into focus.

The camera wasn't amazing, but it was good enough, and it became clear what everything was: the fuzzy black was the edges of the dark room it had been filmed in; the white, blurry shape it had been merging with was a television.

The person recording the video moved closer to the TV, the camera snapping in, out and back in again to focus on it, and this time there was a much clearer sense of what was being filmed: a TV show set in a pub. It was packed: people lined up at the bar, trying to order drinks; the tables – further back – were all occupied; and a small dancefloor off to the right was filled. The camera-phone video had sound, because I could hear the rustle of clothes, and the hum of electrical equipment, but there was no sound coming from the TV show.

It was on mute.

Suddenly, there was a clumsy fast-zoom in towards the left side of the screen, and for the first time I caught a glimpse of the phone's operator, frozen there in the black edges of the television.

It was Leonard Franks.

I've found you.

He was holding the phone out in front of him, his face claimed mostly by shadow, the room behind him indistinguishable and inexact. I heard him sniff once, then he moved away again, his reflection dissolving into the gloom.

Onscreen, the camera remained zoomed in on an actor at the bar, one elbow on the counter, one holding a beer bottle. He was talking to someone. Franks edged the zoom out again, more carefully this time, and there was an actress there too.

And then I realized something.

It's not a TV show.

It was security camera footage.

It was Pamela Welland and Paul Viljoen.

Franks adjusted his position and suddenly it became clearer. The scene was exactly as Murray had described: Viljoen, all muscle and brawn, trying to impress; Pamela Welland, blonde, petite, polite but disinterested. Franks's hand steadied, showing the two of them interacting, Viljoen trying his luck again after a knock-back, getting closer, his fingers flat to the bar, almost brushing against her arm. She smiled at something he said this time, and he smiled back. She looked at her watch. He asked her something else and she leaned in towards his ear – the first time she'd been that close.

But then it started to break up.

Slowly, the quality of the footage on the TV began to deteriorate. Interference sparked on the screen, disrupting the clarity of the picture. Franks tried to move in closer, but it made no difference. As Viljoen closed the gap again, between himself and Welland, a series of scanlines broke, moving bottom to top, and I realized Franks must have been filming this from an old VHS tape.

So how old is this camera-phone footage?

I paused the film and went to the video's data: Franks had shot the footage on 1 March 2013. Two days before his disappearance.

And yet the tape he was filming was much, much older.

I realized what that meant: he'd called Paige and Murray, not because he wanted a copy of the footage, but because he wanted a *better quality* copy of it. Better than the one he had here. But why? What was he seeing in these moments between Welland and Viljoen? What had made him rewatch it so many times his original copy – his VHS copy – had become so badly damaged? Why had he gone back and filmed it forty-eight hours before he vanished?

I returned to the camera-phone video Franks had shot and picked up where I'd left off, more scanlines pulling at the images of victim and killer.

There was thirty seconds left.

And that was when everything changed.

CHAPTER 65

Franks moved even closer. He was right next to the television now – maybe two or three feet away – but his attention had drifted from Welland and Viljoen. They were on the far left of the shot. Instead he'd focused in on the edge of the dancefloor area to the right, where four men and five women were gathered around a table. It looked like they'd come straight from work: the men were in suits, the women in skirts and blouses, in dresses, in trousers and jackets. The scanlines were even worse, the picture on the TV jumping, stuttering, the colours fading and retuning. The tape had been played over and over – but why?

A second later, I got my answer.

One of the women left the table, her back originally to the CCTV camera, and headed towards the bar. She was in a grey patterned knee-length dress and black heels.

I recognized her immediately.

It was Casey Bullock.

Franks didn't want the footage for Pamela Welland.

He never had.

He'd wanted it for Bullock.

On her face was a residual smile, left over from whatever had been the subject of conversation at the table. The tape floundered again, the picture descending into a mess of static and scanlines.

Against the silence of the camera-phone footage, I watched Franks move again, his finger brushing the microphone on the Nokia. Then, on the TV, he paused the footage.

Suddenly, Bullock was freeze-framed.

The timing of the pause was perfect, as if Franks knew exactly when to do it: two scanlines framed Bullock's face and shoulders, top and bottom, as she passed Welland and Viljoen at the bar. Above all three of them was a sign for the toilets. She was heading that way, but as she'd passed them – even with the deteriorating quality of the footage – I could see her attention had shifted towards them. Viljoen, partially hidden behind a scanline, had his hand on Welland's upper arm now; Welland's eyes were on his hand.

Bullock's eyes were on them.

We had a couple of eyewitnesses, including one in the bar that night, and they said they saw Pamela talking to a guy in his early twenties, Murray had told me when I'd met her and Paige in the hotel. *The witness in the bar said the guy was obviously trying to crack on to Pamela, but she didn't seem to be playing along.* At this moment, the way Welland's eyes were on Viljoen's hand, it looked like she wasn't happy

481

about it. And this moment was what Casey Bullock had described to police afterwards.

She was the eyewitness in the bar.

As the phone lingered on a close-up of her, paused mid-stride halfway across the pub, there was a noise in the mobile's microphone: a soft sound, like a gentle creaking.

A door moving in a breeze.

Or a chair being eased into.

Then the camera-phone video ended, plunging the car back into darkness. I sat there trying to take in what I'd just seen.

The money.

The footage of Casey Bullock.

Part of me was desperate to call Murray again, to find out what she remembered about Casey Bullock, about why Franks was interested in her – and why Bullock had become so scared of him. But then I remembered something John Garrick had told me.

Casey said the police were all in on it.

I didn't know if that meant Murray.

Instead, I switched on my phone, went to the browser and searched for Pamela Welland's murder for the second time. I spent ten minutes reading the true crime websites, clicking on JPEGs of front pages from the time, and accounts of the murder. I'd been through the same pages four days earlier, when Paige and Murray had first mentioned the case to me, and just like before, there wasn't much to go on. The case almost pre-dated the Internet.

But when I'd looked at it the first time, I'd never seen the truth lying there between the lines: the name of Bullock never came up, at any point, even during court coverage.

Because she'd been deliberately kept out of it.

Franks must have struck some sort of legal deal where her identity couldn't be reported outside the courtroom. But it wouldn't have stretched to police files at the time – or after. Which is why, fifteen years later, when Simon Preston was murdered, Franks stepped in and worked the case himself. Deep down I'd always known it, but now I knew it for sure: him taking on the drug murder never had anything to do with a lack of resources – it was because he knew, eventually, the death of Preston would lead investigators back to Bullock. So he cut the case off at the knees, and blocked the trail to Casey Bullock a second time.

But why would he do that?

Why had Franks frightened her so much?

I sat there, trying to form the answers. When I couldn't get a clear view on it, I turned and looked from the money, back in the holdall now, out through the windscreen, and into the darkness.

All I could hear was the unbroken rhyme of the sea.

After changing into my wetsuit, I made sure I had a torch, dry clothes and a drink, zipped up the waterproof backpack and headed down to the beach. The suit had come with a pair of neoprene boots, which provided some relief from the freezing morning air.

At the beach – a gentle sweep of sand about one hundred and twenty feet long, cut into a cliff that ascended eighty feet back up to Brompton Lee – I stopped, making sure I was alone. There was no natural light here, so – checking there was definitely no one around – I used the torch to direct myself down towards the rock, the beach smoothly sloping away to the sea, crabs scuttling off into the darkness as soon as the beam passed them.

A pathway had been smoothed out of the rock by decades of people climbing on it, all the way to its end, forty feet out in the water. Effectively, it had become a natural jetty. I got up on to it, its ridge about ten feet off the sand, then began heading out. Below me, as I passed the waterline, the sea started to slosh and gurgle around me, and I felt its coolness dotting my hands and face. Five minutes later, at the end, I shone the torchlight into the water and could see it was about four and a half feet deep.

I clambered down.

The temperature of the water took my breath away. I'd expected it to be cold but it was still a shock, so I paused there for a moment, adjusting to it – and then I began.

The tide came up to the midway point of my stomach, but the sea was relatively still, the weather benign. To my left, the sky had lightened, the blackness of night giving way to a soft charcoal blur. It was the first hint of morning, an hour and a half before the sun came up, and as the colour changed, so my surroundings became more visible.

The outline of Parl Rock.

The houses of Brompton Lee above that.

And then, finally, the island that lay in the water in front of me.

PART IV

CHAPTER 66

At six-forty, I reached the jetty on Keel Point island. My legs were burning, my skin slick with sweat. As I climbed on to it, it rocked gently beneath my weight, and I looked up at what awaited. Hidden in the twilight, most of Bethlehem's blemishes were concealed – but not all. Beyond two security fences – one a wooden barricade erected after its closure, the other the original mesh fence topped with razorwire – I could see the vast, east-facing wall of windows Annabel had described, three rows deep and twenty panels long.

Moving off the jetty and on to the approach road, I shrugged off my wetsuit and changed into dry clothes and boots. I left the suit hidden in a tangle of bushes, slipped the backpack on and started up. This close to the hospital, the size of the building suddenly seemed more intimidating, its façade reaching up into the shadows of the morning, so big it was almost impossible to take it in. The distant splinters I'd seen in its paintwork, as I'd crossed the causeway, were now huge clefts; the holes I'd glimpsed in its windows and roof – ink blobs from the mainland – were now gaping jaws. Its front was a cathedral of corrosion and memories, channelled into a fractured spire one hundred feet high.

I headed further up the approach road.

Then stopped.

There was a noise.

Beyond the initial wooden barricade, the mesh had started to bow gently. Midway along that, the glass panels in the single, lonely guard tower – twenty feet off the ground, its ladder sawn off at the halfway point – had been used as target practice for stones and debris. The guard tower's door was no longer secure either, flapping back and forth like a blanket as the breeze rolled in off the channel. Was that what was making the noise?

I heard it again.

Shining the torch into the scrub either side of me, I started wondering whether it might be an animal. It had definitely come from the left the second time. I bent down, arrowing the torch in through the knot of branches and leaves.

Something moved.

I got down even lower, so my face was almost flat to the road, and tried to pick it out. Then I realized: whatever it was, it wasn't inside the scrub.

It was on the other side of it.

Getting to my feet, I headed back down the road until I was almost at the water's edge, and moved up the other side of the scrub. For a moment, all the torch picked out were chunks of masonry, strewn among the long grass. As I continued moving, birds scattered, and then an animal shifted. I almost turned my ankle on a hidden cleft. When I slowed, readjusting my footing, something passed the very edges of the light.

I angled the torch back.

Finally, I found the source of the noise.

It was placed right up against the perimeter fence, half covered by grass and dried scrub. As the breeze passed across the island, it rocked gently, sounding a knock as it tapped against the wooden barricade. Two feet to its left, a square had been cut out of the wooden fence with a buzzsaw.

Unevenly, inexactly.

But, unless you were looking for the hole, you'd never find it.

My eyes instinctively drifted above the lip of the barricade, to the rows of windows on the eastern wall. From where I was now, I could see this side of the building more clearly than ever, its glass panels changing colour as day continued to break.

The gentle knocking sound came again.

Knock.

Knock.

I looked back to the source of the noise.

In the torchlight, next to the hole in the fence, was a boat.

CHAPTER 67

The space was about two feet high by the same wide. I pushed my backpack through to the other side, then scrambled in after it, shuffling beyond the wooden fence on my belly. There was a two-foot gap to the second, mesh fence, but a hole had been cut out of that too. I shuffled through the second space and scrambled up a four-foot grass bank – torch off – to a pathway running parallel to the building. The hospital loomed over me, as if it had suddenly become bigger.

Behind me, the boat's hull continued to knock gently against the wooden barricade. A seagull squawked in the sky above. Waves lapped at the island.

Otherwise, this place was silent.

I used the grey morning light as my guide. It was just before seven and, out to sea, daylight had begun to stain the horizon, bleeding and spreading. If I'd been watched all the way to the hole in the fence, there was no pretending I wasn't here. All I could do now was use the darkness that still remained to mask my position temporarily.

I headed around to the front entrance.

Adjacent to the oak doors, the building peeled off into a series of windows, all of them barred from the inside. The approach road became a driveway and formed a circle at the end, which had allowed the tractor-ferry to turn and come back. Above me were the crooked, broken remains of a stained-glass window.

I moved up the steps to the door – and then stopped.

It was already ajar.

Not much, but enough, a thin black line filling the gap between the door and its frame. I placed a hand against it, edging it forward, waiting to see what kind of sound it made. When it made none, I pushed at it again, and this time it made a doughy moan, like the whimper of an injured dog. Along the edge of the door, I could see chisel marks: the wood had splintered, and the lock itself had been removed.

But there was something else.

As the door came to a stop, I became aware of a series of short, familiar clicks – the same sound I'd heard at the house. At my feet, half disguised by the dark, was a thin wire, running out from under the door. Taped to the wall behind it was a small plastic case, like a walkie-talkie, with a series of LEDs. Another makeshift alarm system.

Reynolds.

He was here.

As I slowly started forward, more of the corridor

came into view: medical green walls; endless doors fading into darkness; tiled black-and-white floors, like a domino set. My heart was beating harder, my fingers crushing the flashlight, but after a while an unpleasant smell began to distract me: musty, medicinal, burnt.

There were no windows here.

Only doors.

The nearest one opened up into what must have been an administrator's office, a windowless space with a desk that had never been removed, and three rows of empty shelves. On the walls had been charts and planners, but they'd long since gone. I closed it, moved on a little way and opened another one: exactly the same layout, except for a series of concentric rings on the ceiling where water was leaking through from above.

I continued forward.

Beneath the soles of my boots, broken pieces of tile cracked and shattered. On the walls, pictures had been removed, leaving bright, unfaded green squares behind. There was nothing else, just paint-peeled walls, shedding like a skin, and light fixtures without lamps or bulbs.

The deeper into the corridor I got, the cooler and darker it became, and the stronger the stench of extinction: the building was decomposing, shutting down, leaking, falling away.

At a bend in the corridor, I stopped and looked back the way I'd come, shining the torch off into the gloom. I couldn't even see the entrance any more. But then, as I turned back again, something moved in front of me – beyond the cone of the flashlight.

I waited, heart pumping.

No movement.

No sound.

Screw this.

I switched the torch to its brightest setting, light erupting from it and arrowing off along the corridor. Forty feet down, the corridor split. The right-hand fork carried on into the bowels of the hospital, to the western and southern wings.

The left-hand fork dog-legged east.

I edged forward. The deeper I got, the more unpleasant the smell became. Wet and sour, it stuck to the inside of my nose and throat. When I tried to swallow, it seemed to come back even worse than before. As the smell deteriorated, the darkness got thicker, closing quickly, the spaces beyond the torch like the drapes of an infinite curtain. I could barely see walls four feet from me. Anything ahead of the torch was just a solid block of colour.

Eventually, when I got to the split in the corridor, I felt a murmur of disquiet, a realization that I'd been drawn too quickly into this maze. I thought of the boat out front, the alarm system, the know-ledge that Reynolds was *here*, waiting, watching, and it was like the air changed around me. It started to hum with a threat I was blind to, the memories of this place awakening, as if its ghosts were brushing past my body. When I tried to listen for any sound, any giveaways, there was nothing. Literally, no sound at all.

No dripping. No echoes.

What kind of place makes no sound at all?

Suddenly, something moved.

I brought the torch up from my side and directed it along the eastern corridor. More doors, all identical. The same pale green walls. The same black-and-white tiled floor.

But at the end was a lift.

Next to that was a staircase.

A shadow flickered on the wall next to the staircase, there and then gone again. At first, I thought it was the light from my torch, shadows forming and shifting as its glow pointed along the corridor. Then I became less sure. My stomach curdled as I subtly moved the torch from left to right.

The shadows on the stairs didn't change.

I couldn't affect them from here.

But someone on the next floor up could.

CHAPTER 68

I started up the stairs, keeping the torch angled down. Above me, for the first time, soft grey light spilled into the stairwell, on to the paint-blistered walls and railings. There was a thin layer of dust everywhere too, sheets of it, of plaster and shattered glass, all glinting under torchlight as if it were a covering of frost.

At the top, I paused, leaning out into the corridor. One way was nothing but a void: impenetrable, indefinite, like a coalface. In the other direction, the hallway ran for about one hundred and twenty feet, its design on repeat: ward after ward, set behind identical glass-panelled doors, most of which were pulled shut.

Most, but not all.

A few of the doors had swung open, revealing partially lit interiors. I could see the outlines of bed frames, some upright, some on their sides, some at a diagonal. In the doorway of one ward, a thin metal IV stand stood sentry, and I recalled one like it in Reynolds's photo. Just inside the doors of another, a bedside cabinet was tipped over. But one pattern was repeated over and over: each of the rooms had some form of light coming in.

Because these wards look out over the water.

This was the wall of windows.

I directed the torch in the opposite direction, where it was darker. There were no wards, just doors. Here, the hospital's decline seemed to be faster and more effective, as if being in constant shadow had accelerated its decay.

I headed in the direction of the wards.

As I passed open doorways, I peered through to where windows looked out over the causeway. Ahead of me, the corridor kinked right, an upturned chair lying in my way. Softly, there was the sound of wind now too, feeding in through holes in the walls, and through windows without glass.

At the corner, I paused.

The corridor seemed to go on for ever after the bend, ward after ward, door after door, the labyrinth unravelling.

Except, midway down, was something else: a set of double doors.

A day room.

I moved towards it.

The room was large, perhaps eighty feet across. On the far left was a window, its view looking out across the causeway. The glass was intact, although the wall above it had crumbled away to reveal hot water pipes. The entire room was covered in a layer of dust and dirt, of fallen insulation and cracked wall tiles.

But this room was different from the others.

Starting to the right of the window, and following one another, was a series of murals, painted directly on the walls. Each one was about four feet wide by six feet high, and had nameplates attached at the bottom, with the title of the painting and the name of the artist. As I walked up to the nearest one – a series of grey-blue stripes that looked like a hyena – I saw what they were: the work of patients. Next to the name of the artist was the name of the painting and a ward number.

'The Hyena' by Carl H, Ward East C.

I cast my eyes around at the others.

Directly across the room – on the side furthest from the window – one of the murals was partially obscured by shadows.

And yet something about it registered with me.

I stepped closer and raised the torch.

It was two hillsides, coming in from the left and right and meeting in the middle, both painted in emerald green. In the sky above was the sun, perfectly round, its beams coming down in parallel lines to where two crudely drawn figures, a mother and a child, made their way down the middle. The rays of the sun fell directly on them as they descended the valley.

I took a step closer, eyes fixed – not on the sky, or the sun, or the figures – but on something square and grey, perched halfway up the hill on the left side.

499

It was the remains of an old tinner's hut.

I looked down at the nameplate below the mural.

'Heaven' by Casey B, Ward East A.

CHAPTER 69

The mural was a version of Franks's photograph: the valley, the spire, the tinner's hut. Dropping to my haunches, I ran a finger along her name and removed some of the grime, my mind firing. But, before I had a chance to think about what this meant, to try to understand why Casey Bullock had replicated the location in Franks's photograph, I noticed something else: below the mural was a tiny air-conditioning vent, about six inches wide and three inches high. Its cover was on the floor in front of it.

And inside the vent I could see the end of a rope.

I reached in and grabbed hold of it.

The rope snaked off further into the air-conditioning system, but as I pulled on it, it became taut. *It's tied to something on the other side.* I yanked at it a second time, even harder, until the rope went rigid. And then I felt a shift in weight, a movement from back to front – except this time I realized it wasn't something in the shaft that I was moving.

It was the wall itself.

The entire wall panel was coming towards me.

I scrambled away, expecting it to fall on me. But it didn't. It rolled out smoothly, as if on runners. When I pulled it all the way out, I saw that was exactly what it was on: the wall panel had been cut away, supported at the back by a makeshift metal frame, and perched on two tracks, so it could slide in and out. Beyond it, in what was supposed to be the cavity wall, a space had been knocked through, about five feet high by two feet wide.

It led through to the adjacent room.

Shining the flashlight ahead of me, I moved in behind the wall and into the cavity space, and then through to the next room. It was totally dark. No windows. One door.

I tried the door.

Locked from the outside.

Sweeping the light from right to left, I could see it had once been some kind of supplies room. Shelving units were lined up in three banks of four, all the shelves empty. One of them had toppled over, hitting the nearest wall. There was dust everywhere, a sea of lint caught in the cone of the torch. There was a smell of damp, of rot, of a room that had been closed up from the moment the hospital was abandoned. When I glanced back at the door, no light escaped in under it.

No one could get into the supplies room.

Unless they came in through an entrance they weren't supposed to find.

I began heading further in. As I did, the air changed: it seemed to settle and become heavier, thicker, the smell changing too. It was no longer just damp and rot, but something more acrid and harsh, like burnt plastic. There was a gentle buzz now too; a constant, unbroken hum. I used the torch to zero in on it. It was a generator, battery-operated, sitting on its own against the back wall, about six feet from me. It hummed endlessly, the same noise, a burning odour drifting out of its plastic grille.

Something glanced my face.

I started, and looked up.

It was a light cord.

I tugged at it. Weak, yellow light rinsed out across the spaces around and behind me – but my eyes didn't leave the back wall.

Because it was covered.

Photographs. Maps. Tickets. Receipts.

As I moved again, getting closer, they seemed to multiply: occupying every available space, except for a small rectangle of wall, right in the middle, where a trestle table had been set up.

On top was a VHS player.

On top of that was a TV.

There was something beneath the table too, partially hidden in shadows. I brought the torch back from my side and switched it on, directing it to the space under the table.

Sitting on its own was an urn.

It had LUCAS engraved on it.

An odd feeling ghosted through me, as if I'd stumbled into something sacred – a memorial; a mausoleum – and then something caught my eye in a picture to my right.

I leaned in.

It was Casey Bullock, at least five years younger than the photograph I'd seen of her in the newspaper. She was holding her son. He was ten, eleven months old, dressed in a black-and-red winter jacket and a pair of denims. The boy was smiling, Bullock turned to him. Her expression said everything about how she felt about him, her eyes full, her mouth wide, the muscles in her face, the radiance of her skin.

Above that picture was a receipt.

Much of it had faded, but someone had taken the time to highlight the date and copy over it in biro.

7 February 1998.

At the top was the logo for London Zoo.

My eyes returned to the photograph. Immediately, it was obvious where Bullock and her son were: in the background of the shot, I could see the Casson Pavilion at London Zoo. And as my eyes moved further up the wall, past the picture of the two of them, past the receipt, I saw something else, obscured in shadows.

The black-and-red jacket the boy had been wearing in the photograph.

Then I realized what this place was: nothing here was random. Each vertical strip on the wall formed a collection of related items – sometimes a photograph, a receipt and piece of clothing; sometimes a piece of clothing and toy; sometimes just pictures, even paintings.

But all from the same day, or occasion.

As I moved further and further in, I saw the first two years of the boy's life charted, week to week: days old to twenty-four months; crawling to walking to running; the dark hair of his birth to the blond of his second year. In one – adjacent to the trestle table – he was staring in awe at the candles on a birthday cake, a train passing along tracks made from icing. The clothes he'd been wearing in the photograph were now pinned to the wall next to it.

At the trestle table, I stopped.

The TV was on, as if it had been used recently. There was no picture onscreen, but when I touched a hand to it, it felt warm. Below that, the VCR was on too, its time set to 00:00, flashing on and off slowly. An icon on the readout showed a tape was inside.

I pushed Play.

A picture kicked in.

The CCTV footage from the night Pamela Welland had died.

It was in terrible condition, worse than the version of it that had been filmed on the phone. Scanlines drifted from bottom to top constantly, the picture glitching, the colours rinsed out and pale. There was no sound, just a timer, running down the moments until Casey Bullock got up from the table and headed to the toilets. When she did, the footage became so badly damaged it was almost impossible to see what was going on.

The screen went black.

I raised my eyes.

High above the television, at the very top of the wall, was another picture, placed there in shadow, as if deliberately hidden. It was Bullock again, her son cradled in her arms. The boy – about a month old – was wrapped in a thermal jumpsuit, Bullock dressed for spring, in a scarf and raincoat. In the background were a spire and a tinner's hut.

Above that was a blank card, Franks's handwriting on it.

Instantly, I wheeled back to the camera-phone film I'd watched in the car before coming over. In the moments before Franks had ended it, I'd heard a creak on the video.

A door moving in a breeze. Or a chair being eased into.

But it hadn't been those things.

I knew that now.

It wasn't a breeze or a creak.

It was a sob.

Because, next to Bullock in the photograph on Dartmoor, was a younger Leonard Franks. He had one hand on the dome of the boy's head, one hand reaching off-camera as he took a picture of the three of them. He was smiling – and in his eyes there were tears.

He'd been crying at the video of Casey Bullock.

Just like he'd cried the first time he saw their newborn son.

THE END

October 2012 | Fourteen Months Ago

Casey left the house and walked down the road to where the phone box sat perched on the edges of the cliff. Two miles west, along the coast, she could see Keel Point island, out in the water. The hospital was a smudge from here, a collection of buildings barely visible in the dwindling light of dusk. But she knew it intimately, even eleven months on from its closure – its shape, its structure, its corridors. She didn't even have to see it.

At the phone box, she paused and looked around.

For three months, she'd slept in cheap hotels, in bed and breakfasts, in hostels, even on the streets – hunted, terrified – before this had finally become her home in January. Ten months on from that, some of the fear had gone, but not much. She'd been forced to establish habits here that she hated but knew were necessary. She'd only go out at dawn and dusk. She wouldn't use a mobile phone. She didn't send emails. She never told anyone what her real name was. Her neighbours on the floor above, a couple with a one-year-old daughter, thought her name was Charlotte. That's the name she'd told them to call her.

Charlotte.

Or Charlie, for short.

Yet, over time, she'd grown tired of the hiding. She'd never hidden from anything in her life. All the things she'd had to deal with – Lucas's death, her divorce, her spiral into depression, Simon – she'd faced down. Some journeys had taken longer than others. Some she'd never fully made. But she'd never hidden from anything.

Not until this.

She tried not to linger on the thought – on the realization that this was her life now – and fed a couple of coins into the slot. She looked around again, in case she was being watched. But, the reality was, the village was quiet. In truth, it was barely even a village. There were seven houses, two of them subdivided into a pair of flats. It was half a mile north to the nearest through-road. The only people who came down here were those who lived here. Visitors would make curtains twitch. Visitors got noticed.

That was why they'd chosen it.

She dialled the number she'd been instructed to, and looked out to the island again. Sun glinted in the windows on the eastern side of the hospital, some of them smashed already, its vast cream façade soaking up the late-evening colour.

Bethlehem was bleeding.

A couple of seconds later, a generic voicemail message kicked in. She waited for the beep and then said, 'It's Wednesday 3 October, 7.15 p.m.'

She hung up. As one coin tumbled into the dial box, another emptied into the coin slot. She slid two fingers in and pulled it out. It would be enough to make another call if she wanted to. A call to Garrick. A call to tell him she was okay. She wasn't missing. She wasn't dead. A call just to be able to talk to someone who wanted to listen to her.

Slowly, she raised the coin to the slot, her hand hovering there, head screaming at her, telling her all the reasons not to do it; heart pulling her in the other direction.

You're lonely, she heard herself saying.

Desperately lonely.

So she pushed the coin in and dialled his number. She knew his mobile off by heart. He'd given it to her after a while, and told her she could use it in emergencies.

But then, as it connected, she panicked.

As she listened to it ring, she thought of the voice-mail calls she'd been instructed to make. She thought of being cornered by Reynolds on Keel Point beach. She thought of how she'd got away from him in the hours after, of surviving thirteen months without him finding her – and she thought of the terrible risks she'd been taking by calling Garrick.

The risks to herself. To Garrick.

To his sons.

As Garrick's answerphone kicked in, she jammed

a hand on the cradle and killed the call, looking back at the village she'd become a prisoner in.

Better to be a prisoner than a corpse.

That's what Len had told her.

But she wasn't sure if she believed that any more.

Two days later, she got back to the house after making her call to the voicemail, let herself in and locked the door. In the hallway mirror, she caught a glimpse of herself: a 37-year-old woman who wore every single year of that time on her face. She'd long since stopped thinking of herself as attractive, but sometimes in the months before she had to go into hiding, she'd still caught men looking at her, holding her gaze as she passed them in the street. In those moments, she realized something of her past remained.

A glimpse of a younger life.

A better life.

She moved through to the kitchen. It had two entrances: one from the living room, one from the hallway. The flat was small, but despite its size, despite the way she had started to feel imprisoned inside it, it had a nice flow to it. She liked the way the rooms all connected. She might have liked the location if she got to leave it more often. She'd even grown to like the sound of the family padding around upstairs: their laughter, the girl's tears when she was upset, the way the mother could so quickly and quietly comfort her.

Casey had done that once, a long time ago, and as she thought of those moments, she allowed herself to drift. She sat down in the semi-darkness of the kitchen, and recalled those times that were gone and never coming back. That first train ride into London, reading over her interview prep, nerves coiling in her stomach. The day they called her at home in Devon to offer her the job. Cradling Lucas in her arms, three years later, in the hours after he was born. Turning her back for what seemed like a second and then hearing his screams for help. Burying him in the rain, his tiny coffin disappearing into the grave. And then the collapse of her marriage, the descent into depression – and coming out the other side. Sometimes she wondered if it might have been easier not to.

Then she heard a noise.

A click.

She listened again.

Nothing.

She inched around the kitchen table and looked through the archway, into the living room. She could see the edge of a sofa, and a side table with an empty cup on it. As she passed under the arch, her hand moved to the wall and she switched on the lights.

The living room was empty.

'I thought I'd let myself in.'

Her heart hit her throat.

She spun around, facing back into the kitchen.

Reynolds was standing in the doorway connecting the kitchen to the hall. He took another step. She automatically took a step back, the base of her spine hitting the wall.

He's found me, she thought.

Oh fuck. Oh shit. He's found me.

In the subdued light, his skin was chalk white, like a phantom. He smiled, holding up a big hand, as if that would be some kind of reassurance.

But it was the opposite.

There was no reassurance in him at all.

'Relax,' he said.

'What do you want?'

'I think we need to talk.'

'How did you find me?'

He smirked. 'Oh, it wasn't so hard. I knew you wouldn't be able to resist calling that doctor friend of yours. After all, who else have you got?' He paused, eyes widening. 'I've had a tracker on his mobile for over a year. He's so caught up in his own world, in his buzzwords, his amateur-hour psychology, he never realized. Thirteen months later, your weakness finally exposed you. You just don't like being alone, do you, Casey?'

'What do you want?'

'What do I want?' He took another step into the kitchen, hand reaching out for the counter. He pressed his palm flat to it, fingers spreading like an oil spill. 'We never got to finish our conversation. Don't you remember that? Our conversation on the beach at Keel Point? We were watching all those patients being loaded on to the fun bus.'

She just looked at him.

'Do you remember that?'

She nodded.

'Do you remember what I said to you? I said I wanted to talk to you, somewhere private, somewhere people couldn't see me with my hands around your neck. So we made an arrangement: I would follow you on to the moors. And we would talk.'

'You were taking me up there to kill me, to dump my car, to get rid of any trace I existed.'

Another smirk.

He took a couple of quick steps towards her, and before she could come out from against the wall he was two feet from her, leaning over her. He didn't touch her, but he didn't need to: he'd blocked off her route into the living room, and out into the hallway.

'You managed to lose me that day. I suppose you made use of your advantage: you know these country roads much better than me. I'm more of a big-city man myself. But, even so, when you lost me, when you didn't return to your house, I thought to myself, "She won't be stupid enough to go up against me. She'll come back here, because she knows what happens if she doesn't." And yet, there I was, day after day, week after week, sitting there in my car outside your home, waiting for you to return. And you never did.'

She swallowed. 'You would have killed me.'

'Yes,' he said, smiling. 'But, back then, I would have made it painless.'

Out of nowhere, a knock at the door.

'Charlie?' a muffled voice said.

Reynolds didn't move. He stayed there, standing

513

over her, looking down into her face. She glanced from him to the door into the hallway.

'It's my neighbours,' she said.

'Charlie?' the voice said again.

Another knock at the door.

'What do they want?' Reynolds hissed.

'They always cook a big stew on a Friday night.'

'So?'

'So they always bring some down for me.'

'Charlie?' the voice repeated. 'Are you there?'

Reynolds grabbed her by the throat, pinning her against the wall. His fingers felt as hard as bullets. 'Answer it. Get rid of them.' He pressed harder. 'Don't fuck with me.'

She didn't react.

'Are you listening to me?'

She nodded this time.

'If you warn them, if you shout out, if you run, I will kill them all: him, her, their girl. And I will do it all in front of you.'

He held her there a moment more.

'Are you listening to me, Casey?'

She nodded again.

His eyes narrowed – and then he let go.

Casey hurried across the kitchen, heart pounding, stomach knotted, but then hesitated in the doorway, looking along the hall to the front door. She could see the silhouette of the man from upstairs.

Anthony.

A nice guy. A nice couple.

A nice family.

They've got a little girl, Casey thought. I can't let Reynolds hurt her.

As she hesitated, as Anthony knocked on the door again, Reynolds came forward a step, fists at his side. 'Answer it,' he snarled. 'And get rid of him.'

She turned back to face the door.

'Charlie?' Anthony said again.

She walked along the hallway.

'I'm coming,' she said softly, her voice betraying her fear, tears slowly filling her eyes as she realized this was the end. She'd never been scared of dying. Not after Lucas.

But she was scared now.

And, in those final moments before she answered the door – before she took the food from her neighbour and closed off the outside world for ever – she thought of how Len wouldn't get a voicemail message from her tomorrow.

How he would realize something was wrong.

Realize Reynolds had forced her to confess everything.

And realize – inevitably – that the end had finally come for them both.

CHAPTER 70

It felt like the room had grown roots, pinning me to the floor. I looked up at the blank card, a letter from Franks to Bullock saying how much he missed his son, and then to the picture of the three of them: in 1997, Franks would have been forty-six, Bullock would have barely been twenty-two. I thought of her husband at the time, Robert Collinson, and wondered if he, even for a minute, had suspected that the boy wasn't his. I doubted it, otherwise their marriage surely wouldn't have continued for three years. From what I'd read, it had been the death of their son that had split them up. Except his son, the boy he spent two years bringing up as his own, had never been his.

He had been Franks's.

It all started on the Pamela Welland case.

Franks was the lead. Bullock was the witness in the bar. They'd come together by chance, by fate, whatever it was they believed in – and then I saw now that it became something more. But the pregnancy *had* to have been a mistake. She was already married to Collinson by that time, Franks had been

516

married for twenty-six years to Ellie, and their kids – their son, their daughter – had flown the nest: Carl was twenty-three, Craw was twenty-five.

Even older than Bullock.

My thoughts shifted to Craw, to whether she'd had knowledge of her father's secret life, to why she'd asked me to find him in the first place if that was true. And then I felt a pang of sadness for Ellie. She had no clue that the last seventeen years of her marriage had been built on a lie; that her husband's reasons for moving down to Devon might not have been because he loved the wide-open spaces of the county, like he'd told her – but because he loved another woman.

He wanted to be closer to her.

To the memories of his son.

She said he made her worried, Garrick had told me on the phone. *That was her choice of words.* But I understood now: Bullock wasn't worried about what Franks would do to *her*. She wasn't scared of him. She was worried *for* him. She was worried about their secret coming out. She felt no fear of him, and she never had.

She loved him back.

There were so many questions now, one after the other, that I realized I'd tuned out all the other sounds in the room. The mechanical buzz of the generator. The soft purr of the video and the television. The gentle crackle of the light bulb above me.

And something else.

I reversed away from the wall and looked back

along the storage room. The noise had stopped now. Tightening my grip on the flashlight, I returned to the false wall, to the hole in the cavity, crouched and shuffled through.

The day room was lighter than before: the sun was up, passing through the only window, washing in from the corridor, from the windows on the eastern wall.

I moved through the disturbed dust, to the double doors of the day room, and looked out. In both directions, it was quiet: a breeze passed me, from one end of the hallway to the other, coming in through the broken holes in the windows and drawing itself deeper into the hospital. To my left, the corridor carried on, one of the doors flapping back and forth. Twenty feet further along was the proper entrance to the storage room I'd just been in: as I'd expected, the doorway had been secured shut with a thick metal plate, making the false wall the only way in and out.

Slowly, I kept going, checking behind me every ten paces. I passed identical rooms, some closed, some open, some with furniture, some with none. The light seemed to change a little more every second, sun spilling in from everywhere, through the glass, through skylights, through breaches and schisms in the structure itself. A mesh of streams emerged in front of me, sunlight criss-crossing like laser sights, and then I got to another corridor, heading left in the direction of the island's southern tip.

I know this part.

The corridor had windows on either side, each of the windows made up of twenty separate glass blocks. The walls and ceiling were discoloured, peeling, paint marbled as it shed like a skin. And at the end was an open door, flanked by two stained-glass windows.

Just inside, an IV stand stood, covered in cobwebs.

Reynolds's photograph.

I moved towards the open door, pieces of old tile, of dried paint, scattering against the toe of my boot. At the door, I stopped, looking through the gap. The benches I'd seen in Reynolds's photograph were still in place, just like the IV stand. To the right of the room was an elevated platform, with a lectern on it. Above that was a circular window, entirely stained glass, with an image of Christ being tempted by Satan.

It was a chapel.

I placed a hand against the door and pushed. It was made from thick oak, similar to the one at the front entrance, and wheezed gently as it fanned back to reveal the rest of the room. But, as I started thinking about the reasons Reynolds might have chosen to take a picture of the hospital's chapel, I heard something behind me.

A soft crunch.

I went to turn – but then a hand locked in place at the back of my neck, and a knife slid in against my throat. The blade was so sharp it nicked my collarbone.

'Don't move a muscle.'

I held up my hands either side of me.

'You going to give me trouble?'

I shook my head, trying not to get my throat cut. But I was already moving ahead: I knew the voice.

And it wasn't Reynolds.

This man had a London accent.

The rasp of an old man.

I'd heard the same voice – before this, before everything that had happened since – in the home movie Ellie had shot of her husband knocking down a wall in their Dartmoor home.

I'd found Leonard Franks.

CHAPTER 71

'Leonard, I'm not your enemy.'

The knife dropped away a fraction.

He didn't reply, his hand still locked in place at the back of my neck, but as I said his name a second time, trying to soften my expression even more, I felt the knife drift even further out from my throat. An instant later, he shoved me forward.

I turned.

In front of me stood a pale reflection of the Leonard Franks I'd seen in photos, the ghost of the person I'd watched knock a wall down with a sledgehammer. The muscle he'd maintained into his sixties had gone; he was now a bleached, haggard old man, his clothes hanging off him, his skin drawn tight against the bones of his face. His silver-grey hair, so immaculately styled before, had grown out into an untidy, straggly mess.

He was an apparition, sallow and anaemic, even his tall frame giving way to a hunch, as if he'd spent the last nine months crouched in the darkest corner of the darkest part of this place. I thought, briefly, of the storage room, of the history on its walls, and realized maybe that *was* what he'd been doing. But then he raised the knife, almost jabbed it at me, a flash of steel returning to his face, and I could see not everything had gone. He was still smart.

He could still fight.

He could survive.

I held up a hand. 'Leonard, I can help you.'

'Who have you brought here?'

'No one. It's just me.'

'Don't lie to me, son.'

'It's true.'

He tilted his head slightly, as if trying to draw the real truth out of me, and then he waved the knife back along the corridor. 'Have you even *looked* outside?'

I frowned at him.

'Go.'

He waved the knife at me, gesturing for me to pass him and head back down the corridor. I did as he said. When I got to the hallway with the wards on it, I looked back at him, and he used the knife to tell me to head right. The whole time I was trying to figure out a plan. How to bridge the gap between us without getting a blade in the ribs. How to convince him I wasn't his enemy. How to get the answers I needed out of him.

'In there,' he said.

He was pointing to one of the rooms on the eastern wall. I made my way in, over more debris, past a rusting metal bed frame, to a window looking out across the water.

Down at the jetty was another boat.

Shit.

Someone had arrived after me.

I turned. 'I didn't come with—'

But he was gone.

Quickly, I moved out of the room and into the corridor, and – to my left – I caught a glimpse of him taking the stairs back down to the ground floor.

The shadows swallowed him up.

I headed after him. 'Leonard, wait.'

Taking the steps two at a time, I sprinted back to the split in the corridor. The sun had made it down in patches – enough to create a low grey light; enough to see him take the corridor south, towards the back of the hospital – but the night still ruled here. Thick, unyielding shadows clung to pillars, coves and doorways, to sudden changes in the layout of the building as corridors fed off into different parts of the maze. I upped my pace and followed, watching Franks move from dark to light to dark again – then fail to reappear.

Now all I could hear were footsteps.

Countless doors whipped past as the corridor started to bend, drifting away from the eastern and western sides of the hospital, and ploughing its own furrow south, across the island. I caught another glimpse of Franks ahead of me, there and gone. Mostly, all I could hear were the echoes of his movement inside a tunnel of doors that never ended. The deeper I got, the more oppressive the darkness became, the grey becoming clouded and murky, the walls closing in around me. With it came a smell: decrepit and stale, like old paper – and then something more ripe and overpowering. The stench of compost.

Soon, I realized why.

Without warning, it began to get light again, colour rinsing into the corridor via a pair of double doors directly in front of me, glass panels in each. As I closed in on them, I saw they were still swinging gently. Franks had gone through them.

I slowed up.

Through the glass panels, I could see the greenhouse, the distinctive triangular kink on the western wing of Bethlehem's layout. Sun streamed in, illuminating it, empty flower trays lined up in the middle. A gardening stool sat on its own, between two of them. Next to that were five chairs, stacked up. The greenhouse was forty feet from end to end, glass ceiling about thirty feet high.

I went to push open the door. Stopped.

There was no noise down here, no wind, no broken windows to pass through. It was silent. And yet I thought I'd heard a voice behind me.

I turned and looked back into the dark.

Nothing.

Glancing through the glass panel again, I saw only one way for Franks to go: at the opposite end, down a flight of steps. Above the door was a rusting sign that said, STAFF ONLY. *It must be the kitchens.*

The same noise again.

What the hell is that?

Stepping away from the door, I moved a few paces back along the corridor, still gripping the torch. I couldn't switch it on. Not any more. It let Franks know where I was.

And whoever else was here.

I kept going for another twenty feet, then stopped. Listened. Nothing. The hospital was so muted, the only thing I could hear was the soft buzzing in my ears.

But then it came again.

Louder. Closer.

A voice.

'David?' it said again, the word echoing towards me.

And then I realized who it was: Melanie Craw.

CHAPTER 72

The light from the greenhouse passed through the glass panels of the double doors and cast long, parallel rectangles across the floor in front of me. Beyond that, the corridor was opaque.

I heard her before I saw her.

She didn't speak again, didn't call out for me, but – gradually – I could hear her footsteps getting louder, rhythmic, steady, and then she appeared on the edges of the light, right at the apex of the rectangles. She stopped, half her face visible, her feet, some of her trousers. Everything else was still a part of the corridor, covered by the blackness.

'Hello, David,' she said.

I checked her hands. They were at her side, no weapons in them, one of them out flat against her thigh, the other balled into a fist.

'Craw. What the hell's going on?'

She nodded, as if she'd expected the question. Her skin was the colour of chalk, her hair a mess. She looked different, unexpectedly shabby.

She swallowed. 'Reynolds said you would be here.'

I felt a twist of betrayal. Deep down, a part of me had still clung on to the idea of her not being in on this; of her not working *with* Reynolds, but against him. But then I remembered what I'd seen in Franks's room upstairs: years of secrets, of duplicity. Craw was his daughter. They shared the same genes.

Anger burned in my throat, and the words were out of my mouth before I'd even processed them: 'You fucking liar. You said you weren't working with him.'

She blinked; said nothing.

'Where's Reynolds?'

I couldn't still the rage, or the disdain I felt for her. It was pooling in my chest, forcing me towards her. Even as I tried to regain my composure, told myself she didn't have any weapons, nothing to come at me with – that I didn't have to get angry to get the answers I needed – I couldn't suppress it. In that moment, I hated her for what she'd done.

She'd made me doubt myself.

Worse, she'd stabbed me in the back.

'Is Reynolds *here*?' I repeated, teeth gritted.

She seemed to start, as if jolted from a memory, coming forward half a step. 'You tripped the alarm an hour ago. But he's been on to you for a while now. He put a tracker on your mobile phone two days ago – after you crashed your car.'

A sudden realization hit me: I'd replaced my mobile once, when he'd managed to lose me on the Tube – but not a second time. In the hours after he'd cut my tyre, after I'd crawled out of a hospital bed with stitches in the back of my head, I'd lost my focus. I'd forgotten myself. I'd got sloppy. I never returned to those moments on Dartmoor. I woke from unconsciousness, watched him leave Franks's house, got my injuries repaired, slept them off and changed my car. But the case just kept coming and coming – and I never stopped to think about what he might have done in the time that I was out cold.

I thought I'd been smart keeping my phone off, removing the SIM, reducing the amount of calls I was making – but they were on to me from the moment I'd woken up after the car crash. Every time I switched on my phone, they had my location again. And when I'd used it that last time, in the post office, they knew I was in Brompton Lee – and they guessed I was about to cross the causeway. Tripping the alarm just confirmed it. Reynolds had always known there was a secret hiding in Bethlehem: it was why he'd taken the photos of the outside, of the chapel; why he'd set up the alarm in the first place.

The irony was, in the end it had gone exactly as I'd predicted: he waited until I was close enough to the truth about Franks's disappearance – and then he came for me. He needed a fresh perspective. He needed someone else to figure it out.

They both did.

'Why are you doing this?' I said to her.

She didn't react. She didn't do anything. Instead, she muttered, 'Have you found out what happened to him?' There was no expression in her voice at all: it was colourless, almost robotic. 'Have you found out what happened to Dad?'

I shook my head. 'Is that a *joke*?'

'I need to find him.'

For the first time, something registered with me. I looked at her hair again, messy and out of place; her clothes, dishevelled and spattered with mud; and then, finally, at her face. Had she been crying?

As if she'd read my thoughts, fear flashed in her eyes.

'Craw?'

'*I'm not working with him!*' she said quickly.

Momentarily confused, I took an instinctive step towards her. But then she jolted again, more violently this time, and staggered out of the darkness.

And, as she did, my stomach lurched.

Because she wasn't alone.

Behind her, hidden in shadows, was Neil Reynolds.

CHAPTER 73

The upper half of his face emerged, like a shark breaking the surface of the water. His forehead, eyes, a cheek, the ridge of his jaw. And then he stopped. He was an arm's length behind Craw, a gun pointing at the back of her head.

He jabbed the gun into her neck, drawing a wince of pain. When I made a move towards her, he shifted the weapon in my direction.

There was no lateral movement.

His aim was utterly still.

'I should probably make myself clear,' he said. 'If either of you do anything to fuck this up, I will put a bullet in your eye. So . . . did you want to be the hero, David?'

I held up both hands.

'I thought not.'

He turned the gun back on Craw, forcing her forward. As more of him emerged from the black of the corridor, looking bigger than ever, I saw he had a backpack on.

When Craw got level with me, Reynolds shifted her around to face me, so she acted as a shield between us. There was nothing in her face but fear now. The control was gone, the sobriety, every technique she'd mastered, every stoic expression she'd used to get on in the Met, nothing but history.

I felt a spasm of guilt as tears flashed in her eyes.

Reynolds's attention flicked between me and the doors to the greenhouse. When he looked at me again, he said, 'Is Franks here?'

I didn't reply.

His eyes narrowed and he jabbed the gun hard into the back of Craw's head. She lurched forward, coming towards me, drawing a sharp breath as the pain passed through her skull. But as I went to catch her, Reynolds clamped a hand on her shoulder and yanked her back in towards him. A second later, he had the gun on her again.

'Is Franks here?' he repeated.

I nodded.

Craw's face changed – shock, fear; a sudden, desperate need to see him with her own eyes – and she looked in through the glass panels. Reynolds did the same, briefly, before returning his gaze to me.

'Do it,' he said to Craw, even though his eyes were fixed on me.

Whatever he was asking her to do, she didn't.

He pushed the gun into the side of her head, forcing her to lurch to her right. 'I'm not playing games with you, you stupid bitch. Say *exactly* what I told you to say.'

His eyes returned to me.

Then, softly, as if practised, Craw said, 'Dad?'

'*Louder.*'

'Dad?' she repeated.

Reynolds kept the gun pressed against her head and used his other hand to gently push open one of the doors. When there was a gap of about a foot, he shoved her forward.

'Again,' he whispered. 'Louder.'

'Dad?' she called, and this time her voice seemed to echo, carrying off into the high-ceilinged spaces of the greenhouse.

Silence.

Reynolds pushed her through the doors, then gestured for me to follow her in. Once we were both beyond him, he took a step back and nodded to Craw. '*Again.*'

'Dad,' Craw said. 'Dad, it's Mel.'

I looked across at the steps down to the kitchen, thirty feet away, and then back to the doors. Reynolds had retreated into the corridor. I couldn't see him through the glass.

He was hidden from view.

'*Dad.* Please.'

'What's going on?' I said to her, keeping my voice low.

She swallowed, eyes on the kitchen, our backs to the panelled doors. 'He came for me at your house this morning while I was sleeping on your fucking sofa.' Her voice was taut, emotional. 'You told me you were going to *meet* me at the house, Raker.'

'I thought you were in on it.'

532

'I told you I wasn't. He's my *father*.'

I tried to clear the fog – the missing persons file with her ID on it; her forgetting to call my new number; every suspicion I'd had about her – but it was happening too fast.

'Is Dad really here?'

I looked from her to the kitchen steps, at least understanding something: Reynolds had used me to locate Franks, now he was using Craw to draw him out.

But it wouldn't end there.

This was just the start of whatever Reynolds had planned.

'Raker? Is Dad here?'

'Yes,' I said to her, 'he's—'

But, before I could finish, he appeared.

He came up the steps from the kitchen, knife in his hand at his side. I heard Craw take a sharp breath, at the sight of the man she hadn't seen for nine months, at the sight of a man so different from the one she'd known all her life.

But, halfway across the room, Leonard Franks stopped, eyes shifting beyond us.

A flicker of panic in his face.

Reynolds was inside the doors already, ten feet back from us, gun pointed in our direction. Franks – almost in the centre of the greenhouse, sunlight raining down on him – held up a hand. Then his eyes flicked to Craw again, anger flaring in his face as Reynolds moved in behind her and pushed the barrel against her head.

'Let her go, Reynolds,' Franks said to him. 'She's innocent here.'

With the gun still aimed at the back of Craw's head, Reynolds started shrugging off the backpack. He let it fall to the ground.

Inside, something metallic pinged.

'Slide your knife across the floor to me, Leonard.'

Franks did as he was asked.

Reynolds picked it up.

'Okay then,' he said, eyes on Franks, gun on Craw. He flicked a look at me, letting me know that, if I made an attempt to get to him, he'd be able to react. 'I think it's time to make a movie.'

CHAPTER 74

'**M**y name is Leonard Franks, and this is my confession.'

He sat in the centre of the greenhouse, the sun like a spotlight on him, drawn and tired, hair matted to one side of his face. He looked ten years older, shrunken, his eyes on the floor in front of him. Six feet away was Reynolds, standing behind a video camera on a tripod. He had Craw seated to the side of him, her wrists tied with duct tape behind her, her ankles bound, her mouth gagged. Air jetted out of her nostrils as she watched.

Reynolds had the gun to her head.

He'd placed me furthest away, parallel to Franks, so I could watch, but not in the camera's field of vision. He'd done exactly the same to me as he'd done to Craw, feet and arms anchored, a gag in my mouth.

'Start at the beginning,' Reynolds said.

He hadn't tied up Franks. There was enough distance between the two of them for Reynolds to get in a shot if he needed to. Franks didn't respond, eyes still on the floor in front of him. Reynolds took a sideways step towards Craw and placed the gun under her chin. Faster streams of air shot out of her nose, a tremor passing through her throat. And then a sound emerged: desperate, terrified, awful. Franks looked up instantly.

'Don't hurt her,' he said.

'Then start talking.'

This was another reason he hadn't tied Franks up: whatever his endgame was, he wanted it to look like a real confession, an admission Franks had chosen to make, not one where his hand was being forced. Except, of course, that was exactly what was happening – and it was even clearer now why Reynolds had brought Craw: she was the bait.

'Do you want me to hurt her, Leonard?' Reynolds said.

'I . . .' Franks stopped, glancing at Craw. Something shimmered in his eyes. *He's going to talk about Bullock.* And then, quietly, he started again: 'Casey and I, we cou—'

'Start with Pamela Welland,' Reynolds said.

'Okay. Okay.' He swallowed, nodded. 'In those first few days, we just couldn't find a decent witness. No one saw Paul Viljoen the night she died. He dumped her body in Deptford Creek, but he got lucky: he didn't leave a trail. We had a taxi driver who might have seen a car parked near the crime scene, but couldn't be one hundred per cent sure. We had a few leads, but nothing that would take us anywhere.' He looked up from the floor, to the camera, to Craw. 'But then . . .'

Reynolds used the gun as a prompt, pushing it hard into Craw's jaw.

'But then Casey came to see us.'

'Casey who?'

Reynolds already knew. He just wanted it on tape.

'Casey Bullock.'

'So why don't you tell Melanie who Casey is?'

Franks swallowed again and again, as if his throat were closing up. 'She came to us about a week after we found Pamela. She spoke to Murray initially, told her that she'd seen a photo of Pamela in the papers, and recognized her from the pub that night. She said she might have some information we could use. But she was scared.' He stopped, a twinge of sadness in his face. 'I mean, she was young. Twenty-one. She hadn't left Devon in her entire life, until she moved to London. She didn't know anyone.'

'But you sorted that out, right, Leonard?'

For the first time, Craw glanced up at Reynolds, confusion in her face, then at her father. In everything that had happened in the last thirty minutes, I'd forgotten something: Craw hadn't been upstairs to the storage room. She didn't know her father's secret yet.

'At twenty, she got married to Robert,' Franks muttered.

'Speak up.'

He cleared his throat. 'He was seven years older than her. I'm not saying she didn't love him, but

537

I think what she wanted was company. London gave her that. Robert gave her that. She told me once that, growing up, her mother was always ill, and her father was never there. She spent her childhood alone.' He paused, not meeting his daughter's eye. 'She thought talking to the police would end up making her lonely. She thought that her work colleagues would shun her, that Robert wouldn't support her.'

'But she talked eventually,' Reynolds said.

Franks nodded, eyes downcast. 'I told Murray to let me speak to her. Melanie was around the same age as Casey. I thought I could help her.' His eyes finally flicked to his daughter, and then away again. 'She didn't want to come to the station, so I went to see her at the flat she shared with Robert, and . . . I don't know, we just hit it off. I liked her. She was unsullied by life – but she wasn't dumb. She definitely wasn't that. I remember thinking to myself, "She's smart. Give it ten years and she'll have a great job."' A pause. At the end, his voice had fallen away as he faced down the reality. 'In her next life, I guess.'

'Speed things up, Leonard.'

He was still looking down at the floor.

'*Leonard.*'

'I persuaded her—'

'At the *camera*,' Reynolds hissed.

He glanced at me, off to his left, facing him but unable to help – and then he looked into the gaze of the lens. 'I persuaded her to tell us what she knew – and she did. She said she happened to be there that night at the pub, so we sourced the CCTV footage, and we zeroed in on Viljoen. But she was still scared. I kept reassuring her, over and over, that everything would be fine. I gave her my number and she just kept calling me. Sometimes she'd be in tears. By then, I'd . . . I'd really grown to like her.'

His eyes moved to Craw. She watched him, tears still glinting, but steadier, more contained. She'd caught a glimpse of where this was going now.

'After we charged Viljoen, and she realized she'd have to go to court, she kept calling me, telling me she was scared. She kept saying Robert didn't understand how she felt. I sat down with the CPS to talk about the case, and I told them that the only way we could be sure that she would give clear, concise testimony was if they kept her name out of the media. We had Viljoen's confession on tape, but the forensic evidence tying him to the scene was nothing better than passable. That made a believable witness like Casey, someone the jury could get behind, even more important.' He swallowed. Once. Twice. 'But sitting down with the CPS, pressing them for anonymity, I realized after they signed off on it that I hadn't been asking on her behalf. I could see what was happening between us.'

Craw flinched.

Franks began nodding, aware that she was ahead of him now. He was looking down into his hands, knotted together on his lap. Six feet from him, his daughter glanced at me, to see if I'd already known. I tried to make a sound through the gag, but when that failed, I just shook my head at her. *I didn't know until today. I swear, not until today.*

'So why don't you explain "what was happening" between you?' Reynolds said.

Finally, Franks looked up at Craw, his face an odd kind of blank. I'd expected a hint of an apology, some measure of contrition. But then I realized: *he doesn't regret it.*

He doesn't regret any of it.

'She got pregnant,' he said.

Craw hardly reacted. Instead, she sat there, motionless, her face impassive, staring into her father's eyes. Beside her, Reynolds looked disappointed. He glanced from her to Franks, and took a step forward. 'With *your* child,' he added. '*Say it.*'

Franks kept looking into the camera. 'With my child.'

This time it hit home with Craw: she took a series of short, sharp breaths, and moments later a tear broke from her eye. Franks didn't turn to her this time.

'I first saw Lucas when he was a month old,' he said. 'He was beautiful. I'd had all sorts of emotions in the months leading up to his birth. Panic. Fear. Regret. Anger. I was angry at Casey, and then I was angry at myself. I couldn't leave my wife, my family. I knew, if the secret got out – if people discovered that I'd got a *witness* pregnant – my life would be over. I'd get sacked. I'd get prosecuted. I'd probably go to prison. So I told her I wanted her to have an abortion.'

A snort of contempt, mostly for himself.

I glanced at Craw.

She'd closed her eyes to him.

'But Casey was never going to do that. Never. She wanted the baby. She told me that she understood the reasons I couldn't get involved, so she was going to tell Robert it was his, and if I wanted anything to do with my son, she would like that.'

He shifted in his chair.

The room was perfectly silent.

'One month after Lucas was born, she called to tell me Robert was away, and I picked her up and we drove down to Dartmoor. We ended up at this beautiful valley called Parsons Wood. Casey had gone there as a kid.'

Parsons Wood.

The place in the photograph; in the mural she'd painted.

He'd taken a picture of it on 35mm film, way back at the start when Lucas had just been born. Then, as that had started to fade, he'd taken a newer one, once he and Ellie had settled on Dartmoor. It was a pattern he tried to repeat with the CCTV footage of Casey Bullock: replacing an older, degraded memory with a newer, identical version.

'We went back once a month. I'd tell Ellie I was

in meetings all day, and unable to answer the phone, and I'd book a day off, and we'd drive down there. Leave at nine, be back for five, so no one – not Robert, not Ellie – would notice. In between our visits, she'd take these photographs for me, paint pictures of him, of the places the two of them went, and then she'd leave them for me in a storage facility off Holloway Road. She'd leave his clothes there too, once he grew out of them. I liked that.'

He stopped for a couple of seconds, thumb massaging a graze on his knuckle. 'When Lucas started getting old enough to remember me, we had to stop coming down to Dartmoor, in case he mentioned it. Instead, we'd meet in London parks, chance meetings that Lucas wouldn't take any notice of. But it was agony: I realized the older he got, the less I could interact with him. The more love I showed him, the more I made him laugh, bought him toys, picked him up and carried him – all the things I was *desperate* to do – the more likely it was he would say something to Robert. And if he did that, everything was over.'

Reynolds had moved away from Craw to a position behind the camera. In the changing light, he was bleached and still, sunlight reflecting in his hairless scalp, one hand on the tripod, one clutching the gun.

For a moment, the dynamic seemed to shift subtly: two liars, facing each other – one with a weapon, one confessing his crimes to a camera.

Then, unexpectedly, a tear broke from Franks's left eye. He didn't move, didn't react to it, just let it run down the middle of his cheek, through the grey stubble along his jaw – and then it was gone.

'The day I found out he was dead . . .' He glanced at Craw, who was watching him again, her own cheeks marked. 'At his funeral, I had to stand at the back, among all the people who would go away and forget about him the moment they left. *My own son*. And after it was over, I went home to Ellie, and I looked at her, and I thought to myself, "I don't even know what to say to you." She asked me about my day, started telling me about hers, and I just thought, "I don't care." But I couldn't say that. I had to stand there and listen, and pretend like it mattered, hours after burying my boy.'

Craw made a noise behind the gag.

Reynolds flicked a look at her, then returned to her side. 'Shall we see what your daughter makes of all this, Leonard?'

He ripped the duct tape away.

She sucked in a long breath, as if she'd never learned how, and I could see dots of blood had formed along the top of her lips. Despite the pain she was feeling, in all the forms it was attacking her, she didn't show it. Not any more. She just looked at her father and said, 'You lying piece of shit.'

He glanced in my direction and back to Craw.

Her face was taut, outraged, barely able to contain its disgust. His was different: clearly emotional, but measured too, almost relieved, as if this confession was one he'd written in his head, countless times over.

'Who are you?' she said to him.

She'd recovered more of her composure now, but her face was a mess, marked by tear tracks, by blood, by specks of dirt and mud. Her hair fell across her eyes as she tried to wriggle forward in her seat, to get closer to him: the man she'd trusted, perhaps above all others.

'Mel, I couldn't—'

'*Who are you?*'

A momentary flicker of pain in Franks's face, and then a slow solidification, like concrete setting. 'I understand,' he said, eyes back on her. 'But the thing is, that wasn't even the worst thing I did.'

CHAPTER 75

'After Lucas died, Casey went downhill fast.' Franks was forward in his seat now, hands in front of him, elbows on his knees. I glanced at Craw. She'd reined her emotions in but it had come at a cost: she was slumped back, binds locked tight, head against her shoulder, staring at the floor. For the first time there was a hint of a smile on Reynolds's face, behind her. This was what he wanted.

'Speak up, Leonard,' he said. 'This is the good bit.'

Franks's eyes lingered on Reynolds, as if he were contemplating making a move. But then Reynolds placed the gun against Craw's head again, his smile dropping away.

'Start talking,' he said.

Franks wavered for a second, then began again: 'Her marriage fell apart and she stopped returning my calls. About a month later, the hospital phoned me, telling me she'd been found at Lucas's grave, with her wrists cut. The doctor said it was lucky that she'd been found by someone. Five minutes more, and she would have been dead.'

I watched something move through him, like an aftershock; a tremor passing from arm to arm, from pelvis to throat.

'Eventually, she told them to call me. When I turned up there and looked at her, I tried to convince myself it was a one-off, that she'd get better. But then she tried to kill herself twice more, and I knew it would never end until I ended it. I knew I had to get her somewhere safe, somewhere she could be treated. I wanted her away from London too. She'd become unpredictable. Some days, she was catatonic. Others, this person I'd never seen, this ball of rage. All her anger, her grief, that put me at risk. So I suggested to her that she go back home to Devon. She resisted it, but I kept chipping away at her. And that was how she ended up here. My head told me it was the right thing to do, but I was just torn up inside.'

He stopped, looking around the room, and then continued: 'The first time I brought her here, they gave me a map of the hospital, with the location of her ward circled, with contact numbers and visiting hours. I remember I binned it as soon as I got back to the mainland. I mean, how could I take it home with me? What if Ellie had seen it? But when I wasn't with Casey, it felt like, when I'd got rid of it, I'd thrown away my only connection to her. So I developed this . . . *habit*. I'd draw the layout of this place, over and over, sometimes without thinking about it or realizing I'd done it, to try and remind myself that it was for the best. I could never tell anyone she was here, never write down her name, or speak of her. Drawing this place, it became a way of reassuring me that I'd done the right thing.'

Gently, the silence was broken, a breeze passing across the greenhouse, one side to the other. Above us, the sun emptied in, clearing out the shadows that lingered. And yet there remained a kind of darkness to Franks, to this man who had expected such high standards of others, who had taken cases like Pamela Welland's so seriously, and so personally, but who had been drawn so rapidly into a knot of lies.

Even so, something still didn't make sense: what was Reynolds's endgame? He was getting a taped confession of Franks's crimes, and ensuring the people who loved Franks the most were seeing who he really was – but why did he care about any of that? This had to be more personal.

As if sensing my thoughts, Reynolds moved, and the silence shattered: he grabbed a handful of Craw's hair and yanked her head back. Franks came forward on his seat, an automatic response, then stopped. But Craw hardly reacted. She seemed to have lost something: her fight, her fear. She just looked at her father, expressionless, inert.

'Let's speed things up,' Reynolds said, waving the gun at Franks. 'Casey went to the nuthouse for a year, and then when she got released at the end of 2000, she said she wanted to see a shrink more often than just the once every two weeks that the NHS were willing to fund. So you fronted up the cash – basically, as a way to buy her silence – and she started coming back here three times a week.'

Franks didn't say anything.

'Does that sound about right?'

He nodded.

'Does that sound about *right*, Leonard?'

'Yes,' he said. 'I started setting aside money for her, withdrawing cash often, but in small amounts, so it wouldn't raise any flags and its purpose couldn't be traced.'

It was why I'd never seen any anomalies in his financials.

'Your mum was very special to me,' he said quietly, looking at Craw.

Reynolds smiled. 'Is that why you fucked someone else?'

Franks glanced at Reynolds and then back to Craw. 'They were just very different people. Your mum is so much like you. So strong and . . . and . . .' He faded out. *He can't find the words to describe Ellie*. It was clear then, if it wasn't already, that he liked her company, the stability she brought. He loved the family they'd had together. But his love had changed for Ellie. He didn't love her like he loved Casey Bullock.

'I opened a post-office box in Brompton Lee,' Franks went on, face half turned in my direction.

'I used to keep the key at work when I was still at the Met, and drive down once a month to deposit her money. But when we moved to Devon, I had to keep the key somewhere Ellie wouldn't find it, so I buried it out on the moors. She was always finding things I'd forgotten I had.' A brief, fleeting smile. 'I've been using that PO box as a place to store cash over the past nine months . . . and other things that are important to me.'

He meant the mobile phone.

He meant the footage of Bullock.

I knew already why Franks had called Paige and Murray about getting hold of the CCTV tape. He wanted a better version. But now I was starting to see why he'd been in such a state: by that time, Bullock was dead, and Franks realized that the only way he could hope to remember her was through the footage of the night she'd – by chance – passed Welland and Viljoen in the pub. When he finally accepted he was never going to get sent a newer version of the footage from Paige and Murray, he recorded his original VHS copy using the Nokia I'd found with the money, just so he had *something* preserved on film.

Two days later, he disappeared.

Something else made sense now too: his constant sketching of Bethlehem's layout. The fact that – on the scrap of paper I'd found in his Moleskine notebook – his sketch also had 'BROLE108' written on it, suggested it was one of his earliest repetitions, made in the weeks and months after she'd started collecting cash from the PO box.

He was thinking of her the whole time.

He just couldn't write her name down.

Reynolds made a couple of adjustments on the camera, then came forward. 'Why don't you tell us about Simon Preston?'

Franks glanced at Craw.

Silence.

Reynolds sighed. 'Okay. I'll start then. Simon Preston was becoming increasingly problematic on the Cornhill estate in south London – wasn't he, Leonard?'

'You tell me. You were in bed with Kemar Penn.'

'Simon was a microscopically small fish in an immensely big pond,' he went on, not giving anything away in his face. 'He thought he could run the same kind of amateur operation up in the big city that he ran down here in sleepy Devon. K-Penn didn't like it, so he set his minions into motion and – boom – next minute, Simon's had his throat cut open.'

'You were one of those minions, *Neil*.'

Reynolds smiled. 'Not that day I wasn't.'

A look passed between them, an unspoken conversation – and then it hit me like a punch to the stomach. I tried to say something, forgetting I was gagged, and when Reynolds saw that I understood, he crossed the greenhouse towards me.

'I think David here has seen the light.'

He wriggled the gag free from my mouth.

I glanced at Craw.

She was staring at me, a frown on her face.

Then I turned to Franks. 'Reynolds didn't kill Simon Preston. You did.'

CHAPTER 76

His eyes lingered on me for a second – and then he gave a fractional nod of the head. Across the room, Craw reacted instantly. '*No*,' she said. 'No, Dad. Not this. *No*.'

Behind her, Reynolds just watched.

'Casey told me she'd started dating someone,' he began, head forward, turned in my direction, 'but she never talked about him. I didn't ask. I started to appreciate what it must have been like for her, having to watch me appear once a month at that post office in Brompton Lee. I'd spend thirty minutes talking to her and then I'd disappear back to Ellie. I didn't blame her for trying to move on.'

'Get on with it,' Reynolds said.

'They'd been dating five years when Preston found a box she kept in the attic,' Franks continued, not taking his eyes off me. 'It was full of things from her time in London, full of things he could use. He saw an opportunity.'

'He blackmailed you?' I asked.

Franks nodded. 'He collared me outside work one night. This was the middle of January, three months before I was due to retire. He tried to stop me, and I shrugged him off. I was late for the train, I wanted to get home. But then he called out from behind me, "Casey says hello."'

Franks stopped, his past shivering through him.

'He told me if I gave him a grand, I'd never see him again. So I did. A grand wasn't all that much. It seemed worth it. All I wanted was for him to go away.'

'But he didn't.'

'No. A month later he returned, and then again a week after that. He was threatening to tell the world about Casey and me, about Lucas. I took a big lump sum from my pension when I hit sixty in the February, and I started using that money straight away to pay for down payments on the renovations. So, after he came back again, I managed to hide what I was giving him in the housing fund. I just kept paying – a grand, then two, then three.

'I'd been at the Met thirty-five years, I had a lot of money in my pension. The lump sum I'd taken was six figures. But sooner or later I knew Ellie would start noticing. She'd start to see that the costs of the house weren't tallying up with what I was spending. After the third time he came back, at the start of March, after I watched him leave with even more of my money, I had this sudden moment of clarity. I thought to myself, "This is going to go on for ever. It's never going to stop until I make it stop."'

I glanced at Craw. She was watching us, pale and unmoved.

'So you killed him?' I said.

A long, painful pause. 'Yes.'

'Speak up, Leonard.'

We both looked at Reynolds. He was back behind Craw, the gun at the side of her head.

'And say it clearly. This is what I came to hear.'

'Yes,' Franks said, louder, eyes on Craw. 'I killed Simon Preston.'

'You cleared everything out of Preston's flat that he had on you and Casey,' Reynolds went on, 'and you made it look like a drug murder. Is that right, Leonard?'

He nodded.

'Is that *right*, Leonard?'

'Yes.'

'And why did you make it look like a drug murder?'

'I just wanted him to go awa—'

'*No*,' Reynolds hissed. 'I want you to start your answer by saying, "I made Simon Preston's death look like a drug murder because . . ."'

Franks flashed a look at him. Anger. Hatred.

But then Reynolds pushed the gun in hard against Craw's temple, her head jerking sideways, and said, 'You believe I won't do it, Leonard? You *really* believe that?'

Franks backed down, an acquiescence taking hold, his eyes lingering on Craw. As he shuffled back in his seat, like an animal retreating to cover,

I looked between the four of us, light streaming in, the crumbling walls of the hospital wrapped around us, and I wondered how this ended. *With blood. With death.* A confession, and whatever he hoped to achieve with it, would never be enough for a man like Reynolds. Even if he didn't kill Preston himself, he was still capable of it. He just buried his secrets better than Franks.

'Let's have it, then, Leonard.'

Franks swallowed again. 'I made Simon Preston's death look like a drug murder because I knew I could blame it on Kemar Penn. I killed Preston how Penn – and Penn's lackeys – killed: I cut his throat, and removed his identity. Preston had a load of cocaine hidden under the floorboards. It took me a while to find it, but I found it eventually, and then I took it out and placed it where it would easily be found in the kitchen.'

'Did Casey know?' I asked.

'No. She and Preston had split up by then. She didn't know he was dead until . . .' He stopped, looking across the room at Reynolds. 'Until you told her on the beach that day. But after Preston began blackmailing me, I called her and – in a roundabout way – tried to find out more about him. But it was like she didn't even know him.'

'Because she was protecting you,' I said.

He frowned. 'How do you figure that?'

'She never asked Preston to share anything, because she didn't want to have to share anything back. If no one knew anything about her, no one

555

knew anything about you.' I thought of Carla Murray. 'That's why her neighbours in Kingsbridge didn't even know her full name.'

'Very touching,' Reynolds said. 'But I think we've missed something.'

Franks eyed him.

Reynolds came forward a step. 'Detective Inspector Cordus took charge of the Preston murder, but he was a bit too clever for your liking, which is why you had to invent an excuse to take on the running of the case yourself.'

Franks seemed to slouch. 'Cordus barely looked at Penn. He saw anomalies, things I hadn't done to the body that had been done at other drug murders on that estate. So I had to step in. I told him that we were stretched, that I needed him on bigger cases – and I took it on. I worked his angles long enough to make it look convincing, but not deep enough to go anywhere. I brought Penn in and used him as a patsy – and I closed off any avenue to those potheads in the flat opposite who heard Preston call himself Simon.'

'And?' Reynolds said.

'And Casey remained off the radar.'

'No, not that.'

Franks stared at him for a long time, defiance in his face. But then his eyes flicked to the gun pressed against his daughter's head, and he seemed to remember that he didn't hold the cards here. Quietly, he said, 'After I retired, I ended up talking to Carla Murray on the phone one day. I can't even remember why she called. But we were just chatting when she mentioned that Cordus had decided to take another look at the case—'

'What case?' Reynolds snapped.

'The Simon Preston case.' Franks turned to me, as if he couldn't bear to look at Craw – but especially at Reynolds. '"Cordus thought he'd take another shot at solving it," she said to me. I just *froze*. By that time, Casey was okay, living above this old woman who used to watch quiz shows all day. I had . . . I hadn't *forgotten* her, but we'd both . . . Anyway, Ellie and I had retired, we were in a lovely part of the world. We were happy.'

'It was a lie,' Craw said.

He looked at her. 'It wasn't a lie. I *was* happ—'

'Get to the fucking point,' Reynolds interrupted.

Franks leaned forward into a shaft of sunlight pouring through one of the glass panels above his head. 'There were all sorts of rumours about Reynolds being dirty.'

I glanced at Reynolds. His eyes were fixed on Franks.

'When I retired, Jim Paige took over the running of the command, and when Carla called me, and mentioned the Preston case being looked at again, I got on the phone to Jim and said, "You need to take a closer look at Neil Reynolds's involvement with this." It was the only way I could think to deflect attention away from me, and I knew Jim would be responsive to it. I'd complained about Reynolds to him. I'd had Reynolds in a meeting room six, seven months before then, and told him I knew he was dirty.' His eyes turned to Reynolds, a flash of aggression in them. 'You *were* in with Kemar Penn, we all know that. You were in with him all over the city. I was doing the Met a favour.'

Reynolds smiled. 'So you lied?'

'It wasn't a lie. You were guilty.'

'I wasn't the one that killed Simon Preston.'

'But you've killed others.'

'Did you ever find any evidence that I was involved in anything?'

Franks said nothing.

'For the camera, Leonard.'

'No.'

'No what?'

'No, I never found any evidence you—'

'Neil Reynolds,' Reynolds said.

Franks took a long breath. 'I never found any evidence that Neil Reynolds was involved in anything untoward.'

'So why did Paige fire you?' I said to Reynolds.

He looked at me, as if he saw my question as some kind of trap. 'He didn't. I walked. Paige was never going to give me a chance, not after Leonard had finished bending his ear. Paige was in my shit from day one. It was only a matter of time . . .'

'Before someone found out you were dirty.'

He didn't reply to me. Instead he reached over and pushed the Pause button on top of the camera. It made a whirr as it stopped recording.

'And the file?' I said to Reynolds.

He looked at me.

A blank.

'The file that got sent to Franks at his house, the file that started all this – you sent it to him to draw him out, right?'

Again, he gave me nothing.

But it was the only thing that made sense.

'You were familiar with Preston,' I went on, 'because you'd been asked to scope him out by Kemar Penn; as a rival to Penn. But then you *really* started digging into who he was and you hit the jackpot. You found Casey Bullock. And then you found Franks.'

I stopped again, giving myself a moment to catch up, and remembered something Murray had told me: *There was never any talk of Reynolds being dirty in Trident, back when he was working gangs; not really any talk of him being dirty in Sapphire either. I mean, there was a lot of smoke, but no fire. Once he was put on a Murder Investigation Team, though, things changed.*

Instantly, it aligned. 'It was Franks who started the rumours about you, to deflect attention away from him. He was the one who ruined your reputation at the Met. *Franks* was the reason cops started looking at your cases in a different light.'

He blinked. 'Now you know.'

And as I saw that, I remembered the conversation I'd had with Healy when I'd called to ask him what he knew about Reynolds. *When Franks retired,* Healy had said to me, *the drug murder was a dead case. Yet, a few weeks later, Jim Paige finds Reynolds with his nose in Franks's casework. Why would he be doing that?*

Because Reynolds suspected the man Leonard Franks claimed to be – his principles, his integrity, his honour – was a lie. He wasn't looking for evidence of himself in the case – he was looking for something he could use.

A secret. A cover-up.

He was looking for revenge.

And that was what he found.

'You're clever, David. I could have killed you a long time ago. But I needed a fresh pair of eyes.' Reynolds began removing the camera from its tripod. 'I'd had a trace on Bullock's phone for a long time, but she lay low for the first three months after she managed to lose me that day at the beach. Hardly used her mobile at all. Every so often, I'd manage to triangulate her signal to a youth hostel or some shitty motel, but by the time I got there, she'd moved on. She didn't know I was tracking her, but she knew not to stay still, and while she never got in touch with Leonard on any of the numbers I had for him, I knew they were in contact. I knew he was advising her. And then, the following January, she disappeared for good. That was when he set her up in that place I finally found her in.'

He stopped, glancing at Franks, a snide twist to his face. 'But just before she went into hiding, she made a call to a phone whose signal originated from *inside* this hospital. She'd only made one other call to that number – and that was in the hours after she gave me the slip at the beach. I knew, even then, that the number probably belonged to Leonard, and it seemed pretty obvious in the days after she went into hiding that, during that second call, Leonard and Casey were nailing down the finer details of her disappearing act. What I could never figure out at the time was why – during that second call – his phone signal was coming from inside a hospital that had been closed for two months.'

'The signal came from the chapel,' I said.

He nodded.

Except, when he'd come across, he hadn't found any evidence of Franks in the chapel. Because the signal hadn't come from the chapel.

It had come from the storage room next door to it.

With that, something else slotted into place. What seemed like an age ago, I'd asked Ellie if Franks ever went out hiking by himself. *Sometimes he just liked to be alone out there*, she'd said. I'd wondered if he'd gone hiking at all, whether his journey might have been in the opposite direction, to the coast. Now I knew I was right: he'd been using the chapel as a place to hold his memories long before Reynolds had sent him the file. He kept returning here after the hospital closed, to build his mausoleum – a place no one would find – and he was here, at the altar of his son's life, the day Casey called him to finalize her new life in hiding. She didn't know she was being traced, perhaps thought a second quick call to Franks wouldn't matter now he'd organized a safe house for her, but it helped Reynolds make the connection to the hospital; to a building Franks was returning to, on and off, for months before he finally ran.

And then a building that became his permanent home when he did.

'Casey managed to hide for ten months at that house,' Reynolds said. His voice snapped me back into the moment, and I could see he was now clutching the videocamera. 'She managed to hide until her loneliness came back to haunt her last October. And then I went to visit her, and this time . . .' He glanced at Franks. 'This time I made sure.'

'You fucking bastard,' Franks said. 'Where did you bury her?'

A snort of derision. 'You just don't get it, do you? This bullshit reputation you built yourself at the Met; all the doe-eyed pricks in that place who worshipped the ground you walked on – and *this* is the truth. *You* lied, *you* killed. *This* is who you are. Now I'm going to make sure the world gets to see it.'

'The world?' I asked.

He held up the camera before returning it to his backpack. 'Any media outlet that wants it. And I'm pretty sure there'll be plenty.'

I shook my head. 'No one's going to trust you as a source, Reynolds.'

'*What?* It's all on *tape*. Once I've edited it down and created a little back story for how I got hold of it, people will be convinced. After all, I *am* a former police officer.'

'And all of us?'

'Well, I'll keep Leonard alive, because I want to see him playing hunt the soap in Pentonville. I want to watch his downfall.'

Franks looked at him. 'You're insane.'

'Why am I insane?'

'You think I won't tell everyone what you've done?'

'Who's going to believe you? You're confessing to getting a witness pregnant in one of the media's *favourite* murder cases. This is Pamela Welland we're talking about, not some two-bit pro spreading her legs for drug money. You compromised her case by fucking around with Casey Bullock, and now you've just told the world – *on tape* – you killed a man to prevent your lover's identity from getting out. You think I haven't spent *two years* preparing for this? Even if you tell them I'm involved, no one will find anything. They'll come and ask me questions, and find nothing. You're done.'

Franks seemed to shrink then.

Reynolds reacted with a flicker of a smile, then zeroed in on Craw and me, looking between us. He walked across to her, peeling the duct tape off the side of the tripod and placing it over her lips again.

Franks started getting up out of his seat. 'For the love of God, Reynolds – do anything you want to me, but she's done *nothing* to you.'

But then Reynolds stopped, raising a finger to his lips.

We all looked at him.

Silence.

Softly, there was a sound from the other side of the doors.

CHAPTER 77

The glass panels of the doors were perfect squares of black. There was nothing visible beyond them. Reynolds waited, watching, as if expecting the noise to come again. But it didn't. He looked from me, to Franks, to Craw and back to the doors. Keeping the gun pointed at Franks, he retrieved his backpack and took out the duct tape, then tossed it over. Franks caught it.

'Start tying your legs to the chair,' Reynolds said. 'Do it fast.'

Franks did as he was told.

Reynolds took the duct tape back from him, eyes still on the doors, and wrapped it around Franks's chest, his arms locked in place at his sides. Then he checked the binds on me and on Craw, folded up the tripod, picked up Franks's knife and zipped it all into the backpack. He glanced again at us – then moved swiftly across the greenhouse.

He paused.

Looked through the glass panels.

A beat.

Then he pulled one of the doors open and

slipped through the gap, gun up in front of him, like the bow of a boat moving through the night. A second later, the door fell back into place and he was gone.

I looked at Franks.

He was watching me, as if expecting me to say something, to add to the chorus of judgement. Across from him, Craw was just staring into space. She was worn, betrayed, incapable of even looking at her father any more.

'I disappeared to protect my *family*,' he said, but the words sounded impossibly hollow, even to him, and they drifted off into the sunlight, vanishing instantly.

A silence settled around us.

Drawn out, painful, like a period of mourning.

I looked towards the doors. The whole building seemed to have become still. No wind passing through the place. No birdsong.

A minute passed.

Two.

Craw's watch made a gentle beep and I realized it was eight o'clock on Tuesday 17 December. I'd started working the case the previous Thursday. Now, five days later, everything had changed: the course of the investigation, a family's life, their entire future.

I looked towards the door. Still no sign of Reynolds.

Do something.

Slowly, I started shifting my chair forward, across

the space between Craw and me. There were pieces of glass scattered across a patch of ground to her right.

Franks shot me a look. 'What the hell are you doing?'

I ignored him, concentrating on keeping noise to a minimum. Craw was watching me now too. I paused close to her, scanning the ground for the biggest piece I could find.

'He'll kill you both if he finds you like that,' Franks whispered.

'He'll kill us either way.'

Rocking my chair from side to side, until the legs began rhythmically leaving the ground, I felt the back of the chair bend slightly – and then it toppled over. I was ready for the impact, but it still hurt like hell: the ground was hard, full of jagged glass and uneven concrete, and although I managed to keep my head away from the floor, my shoulder bore the brunt. Pain lashed across my chest, reigniting memories of old injuries, of hitting a grass bank in my BMW, of knocking myself out, of accusing Craw of being in on this. I glanced at her as I lay there on my side, guilt blooming in my stomach, but although her gaze was on me, her mind wasn't. She was somewhere else.

Shuffling across the floor on my shoulder and hip – chair still attached to me – I turned, scooped up a sliver of glass and manoeuvred it around in my hands, so the point faced down towards my fingers. I started to saw away at the tape. I went slowly at first, careful not to cut myself, but then found a tempo, eyes fixed on the doors in case Reynolds came back. Sunlight broke through the clouds again, cutting down through the roof and forming a pale spotlight to the left of me. But the doors remained still, and the greenhouse stayed silent.

My wrist binds snapped loose.

Bringing the glass around, I cut through the tape at my ankles, got to my feet, then freed Craw. She nodded her thanks, wiped both eyes with the sleeve of her jacket and looked across the room at her father. So much passed between them, so much history I could never be a part of, or ever understand.

'Can I have that?' she said, gesturing to the glass.

I studied her for a moment, all the evidence of the past hour written in her face, her impassivity gone, her resolve challenged.

I handed it to her.

As she walked across to her father, I headed for the doors, coming in at an angle so I wasn't in front of the panels. I glanced behind me, once, and saw her cutting away at his binds, the two of them silent: he was staring down at the top of her head; she was crouched beside him, using the shard to free his ankles, not making eye contact.

I reached the doors.

Spreading my hand across the middle of the one on the left, I gradually moved it back, the soft squeak of the hinge carrying off into the darkness. My heart was banging so hard it felt like it was bruising my ribcage. Images flashed in my head – snatches of what lay ahead of me – and then I left the greenhouse and hit the musty, enclosed spaces of the corridor.

It was dark.

Quiet.

But it was empty.

Reynolds was gone.

CHAPTER 78

By the time we got to the front of the hospital, Reynolds's boat was half a mile away, just a mark on the water as it headed east along the coast. From where we were, against the still of the early morning, we could hear its motor, its whine becoming ever quieter, as it faded from existence. Reynolds was standing at the controls, one hand on the wheel, the hood up on his top, his face a flash of white inside. He looked back towards us, a smudge in the distance, and then the boat started passing the eastern edges of the bay's curves.

A minute later, he was gone from view.

For a moment, all three of us stood there, watching the empty causeway, sun on our backs, trying to work out what was happening, and what had changed Reynolds's plans. Then I suggested to Craw that she should remain outside while Franks and I did another sweep of the hospital. Her head, understandably, wasn't in the game, and she needed some time alone. Over the next hour, she was going to have to make some big decisions.

I went in, armed with my flashlight, and Franks followed behind me. For ten minutes we were silent, but as we got to the second floor of the east wing, approaching the day room – the false wall panel still open – I stopped.

'What happened to Casey?'

I heard him come to a halt behind me.

When I turned, it was like he'd become bound to the floor, unable to move, frozen by his unintended part in her death. 'Reynolds found out where I'd put her.'

'She was in hiding?'

'Yes.'

'How did you keep in contact with her?'

'I had two phones,' he went on, 'the one everyone knew about – and one that only Casey had the number for. After Reynolds cornered her on Keel Point beach, after she managed to give him the slip on the way up to Dartmoor, she called me on my other number. She was scared shitless. I calmed her down and asked her who the man had been, and she described Reynolds. And then she said he'd told her his name was Milk.'

'That was when you knew he was after you.'

He nodded. 'So I helped keep her off the radar for three months while I tried to find a permanent place for her. We met in person, or we spoke on payphones. Eventually, I set her up along the coast, in this tiny village, where I told her she wasn't allowed to go out during the day, she wasn't allowed to call me, she wasn't allowed to use her mobile phone at all. She had to dial into a voicemail I'd set up, same time every day, to tell me she was safe – and she had to do that until I gave her the all-clear. I wasn't sure when that was ever going to come. I wasn't sure what the end even was. But when Reynolds cornered her on that beach, that was when I realized the secret was out.'

'Did Simon Preston tell Reynolds about you and Casey?'

'Yes. He must have.'

'When?'

'I don't know. Maybe they came into contact before I . . .' *I killed Preston.* A long pause. 'Maybe Reynolds had been around to see Preston on behalf of Kemar Penn; to deliver a warning about straying on to Penn's turf. Maybe they got talking. Either way, once Reynolds knew about Casey and me, he got his ducks in a row, he waited until the time was right, and he sought her out. He wanted to use her to get at me. So I helped her stay hidden, and spent thirteen months wondering what the hell I was going to do next.'

'Did he ever seek *you* out in that time?'

'No. Never.'

'Why?'

'Because *she* was everything he needed. He could force her to tell him the truth. Manipulate her. Frighten her. Hurt her. He could coerce her, but he knew he couldn't hurt or frighten me. So, even after she gave him the slip, he didn't panic – he just spent those thirteen months waiting for her to make a mistake. And, once she did, he found out where she was and he forced her to tell him everything – and then he put it all in that file, and he . . .'

Murdered her.

He couldn't even say the words.

'When she stopped calling the voicemail at the end of October, I knew something was wrong. I stewed on it for a couple of months, thought about driving to the village and calling at the house. I was *desperate* to find out where she was, and what had happened to her. But I couldn't. It was too risky. And, deep down . . .' A gentle breath. 'Deep down, I knew she was gone. And, just as I was trying to cope with that, the file arrived.'

I gave him a moment. 'What did the file have in it?'

'Everything.'

'Your entire relationship?'

'Everything,' he said again. 'On the cover it said, "Confess your sins".'

'But why would Reynolds send it anonymously?'

'Because he wanted me to walk *myself* to the newspapers, to the media, to whoever the hell else wanted to hear about what I'd done. The file he sent me, it wasn't a threat. Not overtly. Not at first. It was an offer. It had everything in it – Pamela Welland, Lucas, Simon Preston, everything.' He stopped, swallowing. 'Inside, it said I had six weeks. If I didn't confess what I'd done before then, there would be consequences.'

I remembered the two calls Franks had received

from the phone box off the Old Kent Road. 'He first called you on 24 January to – what? – make sure you had the file?'

He nodded. 'Yes.'

Franks had received a second call as well, a week after he disappeared, from the same phone box. That had been his six-week deadline. Reynolds had been phoning to tell him, possibly to up the stakes – but Franks had pre-empted him.

He'd already gone.

'That was why you met Murray that day in the pub a few weeks after the file arrived; why you asked her if she'd seen Reynolds around.'

It was why he'd written 'Double-check 108' on the back of the pub flyer too: he didn't know whether the file was the end of what Reynolds knew – or just the beginning. Franks was reminding himself to make sure that the money he'd put in the PO box was still there, that neither that, nor the footage of Casey on the phone, had been compromised. But his habit of writing everything down, his obssession with detail, had left a trail: from the meeting with Murray, all the way to a post-office box in south Devon.

'I wanted to find Reynolds,' Franks said to me.

'You wanted revenge?'

'I wanted something.' His eyes moved to the wall, to the mural on it. 'The minute the file arrived, I thought about running. That was why I called Paige and Murray at the end of January, asking for a copy of the footage. I wanted . . .' His eyes flicked back to me, a flash in them. 'I'd exhausted the VHS copy I had; watched it over and over. So if I was going to run, I wanted a new copy. Wherever I went, I wanted to be able to see her.'

'But then?'

'But then, in the days after, my resolve hardened. I thought, "I'm not running, I'm not being black-mailed by him," and I started working through the file, trying to come up with ways to fight back against what he had on me. But there was nothing. I had nothing. I'm not sure Reynolds thought I'd have the balls to up and leave like that – leave my life behind, my wife, my daughter, my grandkids. That was why he gave me six weeks.'

'But you ran anyway?'

'What else did I have left?'

I looked at him. 'Apart from your family?'

'Don't fucking judge me, Raker.'

For a second, there was a nasty twist to his face, the shadows of the man that had lucidly, willingly, crossed the line into murder – and then it was gone again.

Franks had forged his reputation as a straight arrow, a man of morals, a cop who held others up to standards he'd never come close to meeting in the depths of his hidden life. I understood very clearly why Reynolds saw mileage in that. The concept of getting it all on tape made a certain kind of sense too: it was clean, dramatic, easy to process for the media – and it would utterly destroy Franks.

Reynolds was merciless, a cold-blooded fixer, almost certainly a murderer too. And yet, in getting Franks's confession on tape, he'd captured something true. He'd shone a light on the spaces between himself and Franks, and shown what divided them.

And, at points, there was nothing.

No division between them.

No difference at all.

CHAPTER 79

As we were coming back towards the front entrance, daylight washing into the corridor, a thought came to me. I turned to Franks, and he stopped.

'How exactly did you do it?'

'Do what?'

'Disappear like that.'

He nodded, glancing through the gap in the door where Craw was perched on the bank, looking out across the sea. 'We had a routine. Ellie liked a routine. That time of year, we started the fire about three in the afternoon, and it would start to die out about five, five-fifteen. That was when I tended to get up and get some more logs.' He sniffed, a smile flickering across his face. 'When I made up my mind I was going to go, I spent a week timing how long it took to get to the log pile and back. On average, it took thirty-two seconds. No time at all. But then I spent a week timing how long it took *Ellie* to do her things: fill the kettle, boil the kettle, get two cups, make the tea, bring it back. That took, on average, four minutes and twenty-seven seconds. The day I left, we'd gone to a bakery in Widdecombe and bought a carrot cake. I knew that would add on time for me.'

I looked past him, at the darkness of the hospital, at the doors dissolving into the shadows. As I met his eyes again, he nodded at me once, as if he understood what I was thinking. This was the end of a journey: from their dream home on the open spaces of Dartmoor, to a place full of memories and ghosts left to rot in the middle of a causeway.

'I bought a backpack, a change of clothes, some essentials, all for cash,' he said, 'and then left the backpack in the log pile. Separately to that, I'd stored about ten grand at the post office over there.' He gestured across the water, in the direction of Brompton Lee. 'It was part of that lump sum I took from my pension, so I wasn't concerned about people looking into my financials after I was gone. *Everyone* takes that lump sum when they retire. I mean, it's tax-free, why wouldn't you? Plus we were doing that kitchen extension, so that was a good disguise for shifting bigger chunks of money around.'

'But it was still light when you left that day?'

'Yes.'

'So how did Ellie fail to spot you on the moors?'

'Because I wasn't *on* the moors.'

'What are you talking about?'

'I was in the boot of our car.'

It seemed such an obvious ploy now, and yet at the time Ellie would never have thought to check. Why would she? They loved their house. They loved their retirement. As far as she was concerned, they loved each other. Why would her husband *ever* choose to pull a stunt like that? Parked at the side of the house, the car's obvious use was as a means to get away – not something to hide out in. Except this wasn't the retirement she expected.

This wasn't the husband she knew.

'And you waited until it got dark?'

He nodded, and this time there was a moment of sorrow in his eyes as they drifted out to Craw, hanging on her. I recalled the video of Casey Bullock he'd had on his mobile phone too. He loved them all in different ways; just not ways he could express.

'I waited three hours, until it was pitch black.' He stopped, seemed to waver. 'And then I got out of the car – and I left for good.'

CHAPTER 80

That was the last conversation I ever had with Leonard Franks. Shortly after, we crossed the causeway, back to shore. We chose a secluded cove as our destination, further down from Parl Rock and out of sight of people watching us from the coast. Craw sat at the back, saying nothing. She'd yet even to speak to her father, and he'd yet to attempt to engage her. As Franks guided the boat he'd kept hidden at the fence, back across the blue-grey water, I saw a slow change in his expression, as if a realization had taken hold.

He'd lost everything.

His wife. His daughter.

The woman he'd loved.

The son he'd hardly known.

And now, with Reynolds gone and the video in his possession, it was about to get even worse than that. Because leaving the island wasn't the end of the journey for Franks.

It was only the beginning.

I helped him pull the boat back on to the shore and then stepped away from the two of them – from father and daughter – as they stood there, facing one another on the cold, sun-speckled beach. After a couple of moments, I could see a change in Franks's eyes as a plan went through his head. He was going to run again. He was going to hide.

But Craw saw it too.

'Either hand yourself in – or I arrest you and take you in myself.'

He turned to her, disbelieving. 'Are you kidding me, Mel?'

'No,' she said flatly, unmoved. 'I mean it.'

'I'm your *father.*'

She shook her head. 'I don't know *what* you are any more.'

In the hours afterwards, Craw drove him to a police station in Totnes and waited while he handed himself in. I wasn't there at the time, so could only imagine what the moment had been like for her, for both of them, and knew the after-shocks would continue as the enormity of her father's crimes became clearer. But I'd admired her for doing what was right, even as she must have glimpsed the personal damage it would wreak.

At the same time that she was watching her father being led away, deeper into the bowels of that police station, I was arriving at the motel Ewan Tasker had been keeping Annabel and Olivia in, just off the M5. Reynolds wouldn't come after them now, I was certain of that. He had his tape. Franks was going to prison. That was his endgame.

So I collected them both, thanked Task again and drove them back home to Buckfastleigh.

I stayed with them for a couple of nights, and at five on the morning of Thursday 19 December, unable to sleep, I got up, went downstairs and made myself a coffee. When I came back through to the living room, I was surprised to find Annabel sitting there, with her feet up on the sofa, wrapped in a dressing gown.

'Morning,' she said.

'Morning. Do you want a coffee?'

She shook her head. 'No.'

I sat down next to her. 'Can't you sleep?'

She took a long breath, but didn't say anything. 'Belle?'

Her eyes were fixed on a photograph opposite, of her, Olivia and the two people she'd spent twenty-four years calling Mum and Dad. 'Things weren't always perfect with them,' she said quietly. 'We used to argue. Sometimes Mum – or, I guess, the person I thought was my mum – could be overbearing. I think maybe I under-stand why now.'

It was a veiled dig at me, and I didn't blame her.

'I'm sorry,' I said.

She turned to me. 'It is what it is, I suppose.'

'You were never in danger.'

'Are you certain?'

'Positive. I was just being sure.'

'And now?'

'Now you go on living your life.'

'And this won't happen again?'

'No,' I said, squeezing her arm.

But it was difficult to look her in the eyes as I said it.

CHAPTER 81

Three days later, I pulled into Melanie Craw's driveway in Wimbledon. It was lunchtime on 22 December. At the front of the house, she and her family had decorated one of the fir trees, looping lights around it, a wooden reindeer perched in the mud beside it.

But that wasn't the only thing outside the house.

Rows of photographers stood in a line at the fence. Even though there was no sign of Craw, no sign of her family, they jostled for position all the same, a series of news crews trying to create a space between them all where they could frame the house in the background. On the opposite side of the road, vans were bumped up on to the pavement, from Sky News, the BBC and ITV. As I passed into the driveway, journalists' hands palmed at the bonnet and the doors of the courtesy car I'd been given while my BMW was brought back to life. But once I was past them, I paused, got out and made a point of pushing the gates shut again. They fired questions at me – a wall of noise – but I said nothing, got back into my car and headed up to where Craw's Mini was parked.

She'd asked to meet on a Sunday morning because she said the house would be quiet. When I suggested she might want to spend the time with her family more than me, there was a pause on the line. 'It's fine,' she said. 'Mum's taken Mads and Evie out.'

It was the first time she'd ever mentioned her family without being asked a direct question about them. I knew her husband was called Bill, that her girls were called Maddie and Evelyn, but I didn't know much more than that. As I got out of the car again – the day cold but bright – I wondered if this was the start of an adaptation process for her. She'd based her life so closely on her father's, taken on his traits, his beliefs, his opinions – in her home life and in her work. Now she was five days on from hearing the real, terrible history of the man she'd loved. Maybe it was time to change.

She met me at the door, dressed casually in grey tracksuit bottoms and a hooded top, and a sea of camera flashes erupted behind us. I moved past her and she pushed the door shut, then gestured down, to the sunken living room. It was a little more untidy than before, kids' toys scattered across one side of the room, a stack of DVDs sitting in front of the TV. It looked more lived in, more natural. Perhaps that was purposeful too.

'Where's your mum taken the girls?' I asked.

'Ice skating at Somerset House.'

'Is she skating too?'

Craw smiled. 'No. Just making sure they don't break their legs.'

She made us both a coffee. When she returned, it was with two mugs and a pack of biscuits. 'I'm not much of a cook,' she said, 'so I hope you're okay with digestives.'

'Digestives are good.'

She smiled again, more fleetingly this time, and as we sat down on opposite sofas, a silence settled between us. This time, unlike our first meeting in the members' club ten days ago, it wasn't awkward – but it was pregnant with everything that had taken place over that time, and everything that was taking place now. It was clear she'd been crying not too long ago as well.

'Have you seen the news?' she asked.

I nodded. Franks was all over it. A copy of the video – edited, and presented how Reynolds had promised – had been delivered to every newspaper in the country; every website, every TV station. In every part of the media, on every Twitter feed, there were countless freeze-frames of Leonard Franks sitting in a chair, confessing his sins. He didn't look under duress. In the edited footage, he seemed strangely relaxed, almost comforted about being able to tell his story finally. Outside of the cuts was the truth of it, though: he'd done nothing on his own terms, even turning himself into the police.

'Any luck finding Reynolds?' Craw said.

I shook my head. As soon as I'd got back to

London, I'd been around to his flat and tried ringing the front buzzer, but without any answer. Then, at night, I'd returned and got into the garden and up on to the slanted roof where the window had been unlocked before. This time Reynolds hadn't made the same mistake: the window was locked, the latch down – and, inside, I could see the entire place had been cleared out.

He'd planned ahead, maybe even cleared the flat out in the hours and days before he'd headed down to Devon. Everything, all his planning, had been focused on one thing: securing the confession, delivering it to the media anonymously, then disappearing.

'What about you?' I asked. 'Have you found any trace of him?'

A sadness moved across her face. *Nothing.*

I wasn't sure, for the time being, what difference it really made. Even if she found him, what next? He'd pretty much admitted he was on the take in the moments before he left us in the greenhouse – but it would be her word against his. There was nothing on tape. No actual, usable evidence. Plus the confession that was playing on television now cleared Reynolds of any wrongdoing and admitted Franks had set him up. Reynolds was lying low, letting the confession speak for itself. Eventually, when he resurfaced, there would be difficult questions for him to answer, difficult questions for Craw too – about hiring me, about handing me police files – but I didn't raise either of those things with her now. First of all, investigators needed to get Franks's side of the story straight, and they were still locked away with him in a London station after he'd been transferred into Met custody.

Again, the house became quiet.

I thought about the things we'd talked through, in person and on the phone, over the past few days. Twenty-four hours earlier, I'd asked her why she'd come to Dartmoor that night at the house – curious now, not suspicious – and she'd told me.

'Cortez called, and said he'd seen someone there. That wasn't a lie. I never lied to you. I wanted to find Dad, as much of a mistake as that seems now. But things were . . . Things were difficult here.' She'd paused then, and I'd caught a flash of where the conversation was heading: *she meant things had been difficult with her marriage.* 'In truth, I wanted to get away. I'd had an argument with Bill on the phone, and I needed to give myself some time to think. I just completely forgot about you giving me a new mobile number. My mind was full of static from the fight, trying to think about where we went next. So I just called the mobile number I had for you – your old number – because I was too busy thinking about Bill. He and I . . .'

As she'd faded out, I'd said, 'You don't have to tell me.'

'I want to,' she'd replied, and I'd got the sense this might be strangely empowering for her, a change she was trying to embrace. 'He moved out in May. All the stress from Dad going missing, it was all having an impact. All we did was argue – work, kids, the idea of Mum moving back here, everything. So he doesn't come to the house. He picks the girls up outside, takes them out – but he never comes in. We just talk on the phone.'

'I'm sorry to hear that.'

She'd shrugged. 'Life can be tough.'

As I returned to the present, she leaned forward on the sofa and picked up her mug. There was a flash of fresh tears in her eyes, but she held them back. I thought for a moment how different she'd become in the past five days, the emotion weighing heavy on her, hanging from her face, from her shoulders, in her voice. And yet, strangely, it added something to her, something that had never been there before. For the first time, Craw was less rigid and programmed. I didn't wish any of this on her, but there was a slow change in her, as if she were being shaped in a different, slightly softer way.

'So what next?' she said.

But then, on the sofa beside her, her mobile phone began buzzing gently. She looked down at it and rolled her eyes. 'Speak of the devil,' she muttered.

Her husband.

'Maybe I should leave.'

'No,' she said, holding up a hand. 'No, I want you to stay.'

Her eyes lingered on me, those last five words hanging in the air between us, and I saw something in them: a vulnerability, a loneliness, a need.

I nodded. 'Okay.'

She got up and headed off towards the kitchen. It wasn't long before I heard the start of a fight, of raised voices, but then the kitchen door closed, and I was alone.

I got up, went to the windows at the front and looked out from behind slanted blinds at the media. They'd settled back into small packs. With no sign of Craw, no sign of her family, her husband, or of the woman Franks had arguably betrayed most of all – Ellie – they had nothing to feed on. Craw had said on the phone the day before that Ellie was doing okay, that she was putting on a brave face – but I wondered how quickly that mask dissolved in private. She was bright enough to see where this ended up: Franks on trial for his crimes, and her sitting opposite him in the courtroom, in the stalls, on the stand, looking at a man she didn't even know. I'd left it up to Craw to decide whether she also told police about the events at the hospital, about the room I'd found, full of memories of a second life. In the end, she'd decided not to. Maybe, lucidly, because without Reynolds, without a scrap of evidence about what he'd done, there would only be more questions; maybe, emotionally, and without caring to admit it, because she saw the room for what it was: a celebration, a funeral, a tomb. Whatever else Casey Bullock was, she ended up another victim: in life, in death, through the lies of Leonard Franks.

As I looked around, I could see the living room had changed in other, even more subtle ways since I'd last been here: as well as the toys on the floor, there were pictures out too, photographs of Craw's family, even of Franks. She'd put them all away last time I'd been here, separating her work life and her home life, just like her father had done countless times during his years in the Met. Again, just like the toys, just like her telling me about her husband, it spoke of her trying to shake off the shackles that bound her.

Close to me was a picture of Craw and her brother, Carl. They were five or six years younger, sitting together on a wall with Sydney Opera House in the background. Next to that was one of Craw and her daughters, Maddie and Evelyn. Beyond that was Craw and her husband, Bill, in happier times. He was older than her, his hair a frizzy mess, his salt-and-pepper beard thick and unruly. He was different from how I imagined him being. I'd imagined him as plainer, more sober, something closer to how she'd always been.

Just then, in my pocket, I felt my own phone start to buzz.

I took it out.

Murray.

I tried to imagine what she could want, and briefly considered letting it run to voicemail. But then I heard Craw in the kitchen, arguing with her husband, telling him he might actually want to come into the house once in a while, and realized she wasn't going to be done for some time. So I pushed Answer. 'David Raker.'

'You watching this?' she said.

'What?'

'Are you in front of a TV?'

'No.'

'I suggest you get in front of one.'

I looked around the room for a remote control and found it wedged between two cushions on the sofa. 'What channel am I supposed to be looking at?'

'BBC London News.'

I scrolled through until I got to the local news bulletin. Onscreen was a reporter in a windbreaker, standing in front of the Scotland Yard sign. At the bottom was a caption: FORMER METROPOLITAN POLICE OFFICER FOUND MURDERED IN SOUTH DEVON.

Instantly, something congealed in my stomach.

'What the hell is this?' I said.

The report cut away from the reporter to a helicopter shot of a crime scene. It was right on the edges of a shoreline, police tape marking out a square, a white tent erected on the sand. Waves washed in about twenty feet away. As the helicopter lurched left to right, buffeted by the wind, I suddenly caught a glimpse of something else, further out to sea.

Bethlehem.

'He washed in this morning,' Murray said.

'Apparently, he was out in the drink for four or five days. Naked. Rumour is, he was shot through the back of the head.'

Reynolds.

'It's definitely him?'

'Yeah,' she said. 'It's definitely Milk.'

Which meant he'd been killed while we were all still on the island.

And it wasn't him escaping in the boat.

CHAPTER 82

I told Murray I'd call her back and then looked around the room for something to write on. My pen and pad were in the car, and I didn't want to have to face down the media. On the other side of the room was a sideboard, with a series of family photographs on top. I moved across and searched its top drawers; in the third one along was a spiral-bound notepad and a selection of biros.

Behind me, on the television, the news report had moved on to something else, so I switched it off and used the silence to focus. Quickly, I started to write down everything I remembered about the day Reynolds was killed: the lead-up, the things he'd said, the things Franks had said, anything that didn't add up. Then, on the fourth page of notes, I got to it: the moment Reynolds had left the greenhouse after hearing a noise.

He'd been lured out.

Someone else had been there.

Instantly, another revelation hit me: the flat Reynolds had lived in, one side of it so different from the other. In the living room, there had been

a tiny TV on a cheap piece of flat-packed furniture, a cardboard box being used as a makeshift
table, a three-seater sofa with a pillow on it.

He'd been using the sofa as a bed.

Reynolds was living in that side of the flat – it
even smelled of him – while, on the other side,
it had been pristine, looked after, things had been
tidy. Shoes were lined up under the bed. It had
smelled pleasant.

Someone else had been living there with him.

A noise from the kitchen.

I looked across the room.

Silent. Still.

There's no phone conversation any more.

At a diagonal from where I was, on the other
side of the sunken room, the kitchen door fanned
gently, a breeze coming in from somewhere beyond
it.

The back door's open.

I placed the pen down and quietly moved towards
it. At the kitchen, I paused. Listened. I could hear
the sound of the wind passing gently through,
funnelled from the exterior door, through the
kitchen and into the living room.

Placing a hand on the door, I gradually inched
it back. The kitchen came into view. Granite worktops and black units running off towards a back
wall where utensils hung. A matching island in the
centre with pots and pans hanging from a hood.
The floor was polished oak, specked with dust and
grains of food. And, to the far right, across the

island was a door out to the side of the house, disguised from the media at the front.

It was open.

I headed into the kitchen, rounding the island.

Then I saw her.

'*Fuck.*'

It was Craw.

She was face down on the floor, behind the door. She'd been dragged there, a smear of blood charting her journey from one side of the island to the other. More blood was leaking from her nose and mouth, from a cut on her cheek. She'd been hit hard twice – maybe three times – with something heavy. I rolled her over on to her back and dropped my ear to her lips. She was breathing, but only just: shallow, wet, hoarse. 'Craw?' I said, straightening her chin. Her eyes were open, but glazed. 'Craw?'

No reaction.

I dug my phone out and called an ambulance. As soon as they answered, I gave them the address and hung up. She looked up at me, her eyelids flickering. 'Craw,' I said again, hand against one side of her face. Her blood was trickling over my hands, over my fingers. I couldn't tell where from any more: her head, her ear, it was all a mess.

Grabbing some tea towels from the island, I bunched them up and wedged them under her head on either side, trying to keep her propped up. The blood had been running into her eyes, blinding her, but now – momentarily – it stopped.

'Hold on, okay?'

She didn't react.

'*Craw.*'

She seemed to start, a tiny movement that rippled all the way through her. Her eyes shifted, left then right, trying to find my face.

'I'm here,' I said to her.

But she couldn't find me.

I took her hand, squeezing it once.

'Hold on.'

And then, in my back pocket, my mobile started ringing again. I reached around, one hand still entwined with Craw's, thinking it might be the paramedics.

I pulled it out and pushed Answer.

'David Raker.'

No response on the line.

I looked down at Craw, her eyes almost closed now, barely moving, barely even breathing. 'David Ra—'

'Don't be a hero, David.'

It took me a second to place the voice, even though I knew I'd heard it before. Then it hit me like a train.

It was John Garrick.

Casey Bullock's psychiatrist.

CHAPTER 83

I felt a sudden rush of blood. '*Garrick?*'
  I could hear a buzz on the line. He was talking to me through a speakerphone, as if in a car somewhere. When the buzz died, the gentle hum of an engine took its place.

'Garrick?'

'I'm sorry it had to come to this,' he said.

I felt completely thrown. Why Garrick? What did he have to gain here? Why attack Craw? As I looked down at her, my heart lurched: she'd blacked out.

'Craw,' I said to her. 'Craw, wake—'

'*I'm the one talking here!*' Garrick screamed, so loudly the speaker distorted, a high-pitched whine following in its wake. 'I'm the one speaking here,' he repeated, his voice normal again: calm, controlled, quiet.

'Why have you done this?' I said.

'I suspect you'll find out in time.'

'She's dying, you fucking bastard.'

'I know. I'm sorry.'

'Are you *insane*?'

'Why, are you an expert in the field?'

A long pause.

Then, cool, composed, he said, 'My plan was to come for you at the same time as Melanie, just now. Two birds, one stone. But when I looked through to the living room and saw you there, making your notes, I'd run out of time. Melanie didn't go down as fast as I was hoping. She fought hard. So I'll have to take care of you another day.'

I felt overwhelmed, my head crackling with noise: I couldn't understand his reasons, I couldn't see how Craw had become a victim, I couldn't rip my eyes away from her, her skin awash in blood, her body slowing to a halt. She was like a machine powering down – except I was fused to the machine, could feel its warmth fading, its movement stalling.

I could see the end coming.

'When I looked through from the kitchen,' Garrick went on, 'I remember thinking, "I bet he's already worked it out." Is that right? Have you worked it all out?'

'She's *dying*, Garrick.'

'Yes. I know.'

I squeezed her hand, trying to get a reaction from her. 'You don't give a shit that you smashed her head in? That she's dying inside the home her *kids* live in?'

'It's unfortunate.'

'You can't be serious.'

'I'm serious,' he said. 'I'm deadly serious. I feel sorry for those kids. I care about how this might affect them.'

'And if it were yours?'

'My what?'

'Your sons.'

A snort of derision. 'I don't have any sons.'

'You said—'

'I said a lot of things to you when you called me. That's what you have to do with smart people, David. Anyway, during the fullness of time, Craw's kids will be fine.'

'You tried to kill their *mother*.'

'I didn't try,' he said, voice even and soft. 'I'm hoping I did.'

I looked down at Craw. She was like a mannequin: waxy, motionless. I wiped blood away from her face, trying to get a reaction from her, but there was nothing. When I bent down to her lips, my ears to her mouth, I couldn't feel anything. No breath.

No sound.

Shit.

As I tried to find a pulse in her wrist, Garrick started talking again: 'Anyway, I expect you're thinking, "I get why Neil Reynolds wanted to see Leonard Franks brought to justice, but I don't understand Garrick's reasons." Is that right, David?'

I didn't answer, my fingers tracing the underside of her wrist. *Nothing.* I moved my forefinger and middle finger together, up and down, pressing harder.

Her blood slid against my skin.

'*David.*'

600

'I don't know,' I said.

'You don't know what?'

'I don't know what your reasons are.'

'Well, why don't you think?'

Finally, I got a pulse. Faint. Subdued.

But there.

Come on, Craw.

Hold on. Hold on.

'David.'

I tried to tune back in. *His reasons. His reasons. His reasons.* 'Something to do with Casey Bullock,' I said, eyes on Craw. 'You loved her too?'

Garrick burst into laughter, his first sign of any emotion. '*Loved* her? Oh dear. Is that the best you can do? All of this, everything I've worked for, and you think *that's* what it's about? Leonard Franks and I, facing off over who can love poor Casey more?'

I was barely hearing him now, my attention on the clock opposite me, on the wall. It had been five minutes since I'd called for an ambulance. It felt like fifty.

'Did you know I worked at the Met?'

Now he had my attention. 'What?'

'I used to work at Broadmoor on a Monday,' he said, his tone reserved, sober. 'Then I was down at Bethlehem on a Tuesday and Wednesday, and at the Met on a Thursday and Friday. At the Met, I was a consultant psychiatrist. You would have found out eventually, I expect, so we might as well put our cards on the table. Anyway, I got to see

601

the cult of Leonard Franks first hand, twice a week, every week, for the ten years I was posted to Scotland Yard. I used to look at him, look at the reverence with which he was treated, and I actually used to find myself thinking, "I wish he knew who I was." Can you believe that? I'm actually embarrassed even saying that out loud now.'

'So you attacked Craw to – what? – get at *Franks*?'

'No,' he said. 'Not quite.'

'Then why?'

'Do you care about her – is that it?'

'She's innocent.'

'You know what your problem is, David? You're easy to get at. Your daughter makes you weak. Craw's kids made her weak. Any ties of any kind make you weak. You can be targeted, manipulated, ground down. That's why you've got to cast them off.'

'Are you hearing yourself?'

'Very clearly.'

I didn't give him the satisfaction of an answer, even though vengeance was burning in my throat. Instead, I felt for Craw's pulse again.

Hold on. Hold on, just a little longer.

'Are you still there, David?'

'She's got about five minutes, Garrick.'

'Yes,' he said, cool, dispassionate.

'That's it? "Yes"?'

He didn't reply to start with, then: 'Let me recount a quick story.'

'I don't want to hear—'

'One day, about five years into my stint at the Met, a policeman was referred to me, and just started laying into Leonard Franks. This guy absolutely *hated* him.' He paused, letting me catch up, but I knew who he was talking about: Neil Reynolds. 'I sat there across from him, thinking, "I agree with you. I hate him too." So, after a while, I began to encourage that side of him – just to see where we went.'

'You hated Franks because he was *popular?*'

Another burst of laughter. It was such a change from how he conducted himself the rest of the time, the noise sent a chill down my back.

'Oh, David. Dear oh dear.'

'Then *why?*'

'I'd sort of fantasized, I suppose, about what it would be like to harness someone like Reynolds,' he continued, sidestepping the question, 'but I didn't do anything about it for a long time. Then I started to remember things Reynolds would say to me in sessions, right up until he was fired, about how Leonard started rumours about him being dirty—'

'He *was* dirty.'

'About how Leonard was trying to ruin his career—'

'Reynolds isn't the victim here, Garrick.'

'Everyone is a victim of Leonard Franks.'

'How are *you* a victim?'

He didn't reply.

Distantly, finally: sirens.

Hold on, Craw. Hold on.

'Poor Neil,' Garrick said.

'You felt sorry for Reynolds?'

'Yes. He was a tragic figure.'

'So you shot him in the back of the head?'

'Yes, that was sad,' he said softly, prosaically. 'But he was a loose end.'

I looked down at Craw. *So is she. And so am I.*

'I waded across the causeway in a wetsuit, I managed to draw him out to the front of the hospital and then I shot him. Once I dumped his body, I dressed in his clothes and returned to the mainland in his boat. I think even you will admit that was rather clever.'

The sirens were in the road now.

'Oh, is that sirens I can hear?'

I didn't reply.

'I think it's time to go.' He cleared his throat, like he was reciting a speech. 'Two things: don't try to trace this mobile. It's pointless. This phone, this SIM, this number – I won't ever use it again after this call. There'll be nothing left of it. The second thing . . .' He paused, no variation in his tone, voice barely above a whisper. 'I think it's best you don't mention my name to the police when they get there. You might look like you're trying to deflect attention away from yourself.'

I paused. 'What are you talking about?'

'Neil Reynolds.'

'What about him?'

'I decided to call the police – anonymously, of course – to let them know that Franks had been living in that hospital since he disappeared. It seemed the decent thing to do. Then they can find Leonard's room full of memories too.' He paused for a long time, deliberately drawing it out, and in the silence that followed I felt a tension grab hold of me. 'I also told them that you were the one who killed Reynolds.'

'They won't believe that.'

'I think they will, actually.'

My stomach lurched. 'Why, what have you done?'

I heard the ambulance pull on to the driveway, the voices of newspaper journalists and TV crews rising in a crescendo, screaming at it, wanting to know why it was here.

'I've hidden the murder weapon in your house.'

And then he hung up.

CHAPTER 84

I secured Craw's head, made sure she was conscious, and then used the blood I had on my hands to draw an arrow in the living room, pointing the way to her body. When I returned to the kitchen, her eyes were glazed and unresponsive. I bent down to her ear, whispering her name, trying to get some sort of reaction from her. Out on the driveway, I heard voices at the door. 'Craw,' I said softly. 'I'm sorry, I've got to go.'

Nothing.

'Hold on. Okay?'

Nothing again.

'Just hold on.'

My car was still on the drive, my jacket still in the living room – but I couldn't worry about those now. If the police weren't on to me already, they would be before long. Garrick had made sure of that. Now the only way to head it off was to find him.

I took her hand and squeezed it gently. As the doorbell sounded, I got to my feet, washed my hands, wrists and arms, and rolled up the sleeves on my shirt to disguise the bloodstains. I paused at the rear door to look back at her, at the carnage around her.

All of this for Leonard Franks.

I headed out, pulling the door shut behind me, and found myself in the gap between Craw's house and her neighbours'. A tall side gate disguised my position from the media and paramedics out front. At the rear was a long garden with a five-foot fence at the bottom. On the other side of it, I could see people walking, and hear cars.

A road.

I made a break for it across the lawn, scaled the fence and landed on the other side. As a couple of people eyed me, I headed in the direction of Wimbledon Park.

Moving south across the park, I heard more sirens. This time they belonged to the police. I tried to remain focused, but panic was already taking hold. Craw wouldn't be able to tell them anything. Not now. If her injuries were bad enough, maybe not ever.

I was boxed in: fifty journalists had seen me enter the house and never come out again. My courtesy car – easily traceable back to me – was parked outside her house. Garrick had swept away anything implicating himself, but ensured the opposite was true for me. He didn't have to read too far back into my history to know how things would play out with the police. I'd crossed swords with them before. There were cops at the Met who'd been waiting for a reason to bring me down. Garrick, anonymously, had just given it to them. He'd manipulated me, and my history – and yet I still couldn't get a clear sight of his reasons.

I'd eventually seen Reynolds's endgame.

But I couldn't see Garrick's.

At the south-west corner of the park, I left its boundaries, headed along Church Road and turned left, in the direction of the Tube. It was Sunday, cold but clear, and the sun was out, none of which played in my favour. Good weather meant bigger crowds. With my head down, I kept moving, intermittently switching from one side of the street to another to lessen the chances of people seeing my face. If Garrick had called the police about the weapon twenty minutes ago, that meant they were probably turning up at my house now. If he'd hidden it relatively well, to make it seem less obvious, that gave me another ten minutes, fifteen maximum. That meant I was a quarter of an hour away from having my name and description wired out to every police radio within a five-mile radius of here.

I need to get out of Wimbledon.

Ahead of me was the Tube station. I went straight inside, past the gateline and down to the platform.

The next train was two minutes away.

Retreating to the furthest corner, I kept my eyes on approaching passengers while trying to form a plan of attack. Where did I head next? Where did I begin to look for Garrick? As I tried to come up with something, my mind kept returning to the carnage I'd left behind me: to Craw, to the moments before I'd found her, to news of Reynolds washing ashore, to the media baying for blood outside the front gates. The minute I snapped back into focus, I began to drift again, still trying to come up with reasons why Garrick had done this, why he would go this far, how he'd gone from treating Casey Bullock to killing Reynolds and trying to do the same with Craw.

All in order to expose Leonard Franks.

It didn't make sense.

As the train rumbled into the station, I found a seat at the end of an empty carriage and began trying to clear my head. *Think*. But, thirty seconds later, as the train lurched into action and we passed out into the sunlight, I let the warmth carve in through the windows and take me away again. I let my mind turn over, moving back through my conversation with Garrick, playing it, rewinding it, playing it, rewinding it, trying to see what lay in the spaces in between. His phrases. His choices of words. His explanations.

His slip-ups.

My eyes snapped open.

Don't try to trace this mobile. It's pointless. This phone, this SIM, this number – I won't ever use it again after this call. There'll be nothing left of it.

He wasn't just going to dump the phone.

He was going to turn it to liquid.

CHAPTER 85

The warehouse off the Old Kent Road looked worse than ever in the daylight. The others, the ones still operating, were closed up too, shut down for the weekend, but they at least had evidence of a pulse. The one at the end was dark, dormant, a sepulchre built of steel.

Garrick must have left his car somewhere else, so he wouldn't draw attention to the fact that he was there, but, as I approached, it seemed unlikely anyone would notice, even if he had. It was deathly quiet, the noise from the Old Kent Road fading behind me, the buzz of the Overground line – passing across the top of the railway arch – a soft murmur.

There were windows at the front, but they were whitewashed, giving no view out or in, so I headed all the way around to the steps I'd climbed just over a week ago. At the bottom, I paused for the first time and looked up: the door had probably been locked from the inside, which meant, to get in, I was going to have to pick it for the second time.

I moved up the steps, feeling them bend beneath

my weight. At the top, I looked around, removed my picks and started on the lock. Every few seconds, I stopped, listening for any movement on the other side, but it was silent. Four minutes later, as I felt the door bump away from the frame, I opened it a fraction and looked in.

Darkness.

Pocketing the tension wrench and the pick, I searched around in the scrub at the side of the warehouse for something I could use as a weapon. Discarded in a bunch of brambles, six feet away, was what looked like a snapped table leg. I moved back down and picked it up. It was damp, a little rotten along its edges, but it would be good enough.

I pulled the door all the way open.

There wasn't as much heat this time, but I could still feel a change in temperature. He might not have been burning a lot, but he was burning something. In the air, there was the soft whiff of smoke, of ash, of melted plastic. I moved inside, pulled the door closed, and faced along the corridor. The entrance to the warehouse was shut. I inched forward, checking the office on my left. It had remained unchanged since my last visit.

At the warehouse door, I paused again, placing my ear to it. On the other side I could hear a gentle hum and the pop of the kiln. Nothing else. Wrapping my fingers around the handle, I gently pushed it away from the frame and looked through the gap.

Fire licked at the throat of the kiln, casting a watery yellow glow across the floor in front of it. Caught in the light were three boxes, one already empty, the other two full of things waiting to be erased from memory. As I opened the door further, I could see the table on the far side, where Reynolds had set up his laptop: in front of it was a chair with a blanket on it. On the table itself was a Coke can and a paper Burger King bag.

No sign of Garrick.

I pushed the door all the way back, and it swung soundlessly open. With daylight creeping in through the whitewashed windows, the shadows of the warehouse weren't as deep and as long as the first time I'd been here. I couldn't see everything, but I could see enough to know he wasn't here. So where was he?

I looked towards the boxes in front of the fire.

Maybe he's gone to get more.

Moving inside, I headed for the kiln, looking back over my shoulder to make sure I was still alone. At the table, I picked up the Coke can. Empty. Inside the Burger King bag there was no evidence of food: no cartons, no wrappers. The only thing left at the bottom was a sachet of tomato sauce. I looked for a bin close by, to see how recently he'd eaten, but there was no bin, and no rubbish. *It could be left over from the last time he was here.* Except, beyond the smell of the kiln, there was the lingering stench of fast food.

I turned and looked into the kiln.

Paper burned. Files. A mobile phone.

He'd done exactly what he'd promised.

I dropped to my haunches and started going through the boxes. Appointment diaries. More files. Photographs.

I grabbed a selection of pictures. They seemed to be a chronicle of his working life. I cast them aside and, beneath, found a picture that was much older. Garrick in his mid twenties, hair slicked down, boyish, studious. He had a name badge: Dr John W. Garrick. He was standing next to an old man wearing dungarees and a shirt, his beard long and grey, his hair shoulder length but tied into a ponytail with an elastic band. There was such an uncanny resemblance, it had to be his father.

Beyond them, in the background of the shot, was a smudge of orange.

The kiln.

His father was a glassblower.

I looked at the warehouse around me. It all belonged to Garrick. His father had run the glass-works out of here – and then, when that had closed, he had left the building to his son.

My eyes returned to the picture, studying his father – and, as I did, something stirred in my thoughts.

Do I know him from somewhere?

I cast my mind back across the last week to every photo I'd seen, to every newspaper story. The old man would probably be in his late eighties or early nineties now – if he was alive – but I couldn't remember reading anything about a man of that age.

I moved on, hoping things would pull into focus if I sidestepped away from them. I dumped the pictures back in the box, then started to go through the patient files.

They all belonged to people he'd treated at Bethlehem.

Midway in, I found Casey Bullock.

Clipped to the front page, her face looked out at me. She was younger than when I'd seen her in the newspaper account of her disappearance, but the loss was there in her face, clawing at her eyes, shadowing her expression. As I flicked through Garrick's notes – the way he described her – it was clear that he'd felt a connection to Bullock.

So is that what this is all about?

Jealousy over her relationship with Franks?

He'd denied it on the phone and, as I read on, I could see confirmation of that here too. Garrick didn't feel the same about Casey Bullock as Franks did – but he felt something. Not love, not even friendship exactly, but something more than just a clinical rapport. I got the sense, in a way, he'd harboured hopes of saving her – and not just from her illness. From her dependency on Leonard Franks.

Clunk.

I looked back towards the door.

And then a memory formed: when I'd been in

here the first time, I heard the same noise. A deep, resonant sound, almost industrial. Dropping Bullock's file back into the box, I stood and moved slowly across the warehouse, back in the direction of the door.

In the corridor, there was nothing.

The main entrance was still closed.

I stood there for a moment – ten seconds, twenty – and, when the sound didn't come again, I moved further into the corridor and began checking inside the office.

It was empty.

Clunk.

I spun on my heel and looked back towards the warehouse. It had been louder this time. Gripping the table leg I'd pulled from the scrub, I edged back to the door.

Stopped.

Directly ahead of me, caught in the light coming through one of the whitewashed windows, I saw a shadow moving. It had been cast left to right in the glow from the kiln, and spilled across the floor towards the loading doors. It was black, shapeless.

But then it formed.

Garrick.

From his shadow, I could tell he was kneeling at the boxes. I could hear him sorting through the files inside, tossing paperwork into the fire, the crackle as the pages instantly disintegrated, and then the same again: over and over.

When I got to the door, I stopped.

My mind was firing, trying to figure out how he'd got inside, whether there was a back entrance I'd missed both times I'd been in. But I knew I hadn't. There was no other way in except through the loading doors, and those were still padlocked from the outside. And yet, as I peered around the door frame, I saw Garrick hunched in front of the boxes, his back to me, pulling piles of paper out of them and disposing of them in the kiln. A second later, his phone went off.

He pulled it from his pocket and looked at the display, eyes narrowing. Then he stood. He cleared his throat and took two long, deep breaths.

What the hell is he doing?

Another pause. 'Hello?'

I watched him as he listened to whoever was calling. He seemed to shrink a little, become smaller, more vulnerable. 'Yes,' he said, his voice soft and weak, a tremor of emotion passing through it. Yet his eyes stayed the same: focused, unmoved, unaffected.

Because it's all an act.

'Oh no, no, no,' he said, and he began to pretend to cry, moving across the warehouse, sniffing, heading in the direction of the loading doors. 'Yes. I will try to get there as fast as I can.' There was something in his face now, something I recognized.

And then it came to me.

His father.

I'd been trying to work out why I recognized Garrick's dad. But it wasn't his father I recognized: it was Garrick himself. I thought of the picture of the two of them, the way his father had looked – long hair, unruly beard – and then I cast my mind back further, to the minutes before I'd found Craw dying on the floor of her kitchen.

I thought I'd only ever seen one photograph of Garrick up until now, the one I found online after Dr Poulter had first given me Garrick's contact details. In that one, he'd had shaved hair and a hint of grey stubble. But now I realized I'd seen a second picture of him too, without even knowing it – and, in this one, he'd had long hair and an unruly beard, mimicking the way his father had looked all those years ago.

The photograph had been in Craw's living room. And it had been of her with her husband, Bill. John W. Garrick.

John *William* Garrick.

Bill.

Garrick was Craw's husband.

CHAPTER 86

I retreated, almost stumbling, into the semi-darkness of the corridor. Once Garrick was gone from view, I backed right up against the wall – heart thrashing in my chest, head thumping – and let everything fall into place around me. It was like a bough breaking.

I understood how Garrick had got hold of Franks's missing persons file: he hadn't stolen Craw's login, or anyone else's at the Met – he'd simply lifted the file from her possession. He knew all about Craw coming to me, from minute one. It was why Derek Cortez had told Craw he'd seen someone at the house on Dartmoor three days before I arrived there, before the case had even got off the ground. It was why the mobile phone conversation I'd overheard Reynolds having with someone at his flat felt so much like Craw: she was keeping Garrick abreast of the case, and he was passing the information on to Reynolds. They'd had arguments, constant disagreements, but – with Franks gone and Ellie unable to cope – Garrick remained the only person she could talk to about it.

Even their marital problems seemed a calculated move by him: if he was absent from her life, he was absent from her thoughts; if there were problems between them, he knew she'd try to hide them from public view. That meant she wouldn't try to include him in any search for Franks. That meant no photographs. That meant no trail to him. He was hidden because, when it came down to it, Craw was so much like her father.

I gripped the length of wood, images flashing in my head: everything Garrick had done, all the damage, all the violence – and then I remembered how he'd left his wife.

The mother of his daughters.

Taking a deep breath, I moved back to the door, fingers wrapped so tight around the club it felt like it might snap in my hand. At the frame I paused and looked around it.

He was standing at the kiln, watching me.

'Ah,' he said calmly, 'I thought it might be you.'

'It's over, Garrick.' I moved into the warehouse, the heat from the kiln gathering around us. He'd worked his way through two of the boxes, the last memories of whatever he didn't want the world to see, burning to cinders. I looked at him. 'Or is it Bill?'

A flicker of surprise. 'So you've finally caught up.'

'You're done.'

'*You're* the one the police want.'

'You're the one burning files.'

He glanced at the one remaining box. 'There's

nothing incriminating in here – apart from the phone I called you on earlier. This is all house-keeping. The less paperwork you leave behind, the fewer questions can be raised about you.'

'"Leave behind"?'

His expression twitched. 'A slip of the tongue.'

'Are you going somewhere?'

'Maybe for a short while, until everything dies down.'

'And your kids?'

'They've got used to not having me around. Melanie and I haven't been living together since May. They have their grandmother. Plus they'll be provided for.'

I shook my head. 'You think they want *money*?'

'You think they don't?'

'They're kids.'

'And your point is?'

'They want you. They want Craw.'

He shrugged again. 'Yes, well, I just had the hospital on the phone and it sounds like the next time we'll all be seeing "Craw" is in a pine box.' He paused, his voice soft but clear, barely more than monotone. 'No?' he said. 'Nothing? I thought this would be the point at which your superhuman powers of morality kick in.'

'Are you even aware of what you've done?'

He nodded. 'Unfortunately, I am.'

'You killed the mother of your *children*.'

'Ah,' he said. 'There it is.'

I made a move towards him, and he immediately

went for the inside of his coat. A second later, he had a gun in his hand. *Reynolds's gun.* I stopped, six feet away.

'So the gun's not in my house at all,' I said.

He shrugged. 'I just needed to distract you for a few hours.'

'To do what?'

'To make sure things were watertight.'

'And then?'

'And then I suppose I would have had to kill you.'

As I studied his aim, I expected him to waver, to show some sign of being uncomfortable with the gun – but he wasn't. He was steady.

'Let me ask you something,' he said, eyes not moving from me. 'I met Melanie at a house party in 1989. We dated for three years, and then in 1992 we got married. Do you know how many times in over twenty-four years together – in two decades of marriage – Melanie ever came to *me* for advice? Bearing in mind, for a moment, I was her husband.'

I just looked at him.

'Never,' he said. 'Zero times. Our marriage – if you can even really call it that – was defined by one thing, on repetition: Leonard Franks. When they were still up here in London, before the move down to Devon, I'd get home from work and Melanie wouldn't be here – she'd be over at their place. At weekends, it was him she wanted to spend time with. She'd leave the kids with Ellie and go and play golf with him. She'd call me in the evenings to say she was going to be working late – and then I'd see Leonard pulling up outside and dropping her off, and find out they'd all been out drinking: her, him, every other starstruck moron at the Met who thought Len was the second coming. The two of them always made a point of never discussing work, even when they were out drinking like that, as if that were some incredible achievement. But they talked about everything else – literally *everything* and would never share any of it. Can you imagine how frustrating that becomes, David?'

'So killing her makes it better?'

'Over the course of twenty-four years,' he said, ignoring me, 'it just builds and it builds, until . . .' A brief, distant look. 'Until, finally, you snap.'

'Well, you snapped all right, Garrick.'

'If I hadn't done it, she would have found out what I was doing eventually,' he said, and smiled – but it was sad, as if it carried the weight of bereavement. 'You know,' he went on, 'I bought Leonard this pen for his birthday one year, this beautiful, gold-nibbed Caran d'Ache Léman fountain pen from Switzerland. This was back when I was still trying to understand how to muscle in on their territory, when I still cared about becoming part of their clique. Melanie told me I didn't need to – maybe she meant that I shouldn't; that he wouldn't like it – but I did it anyway. I ignored her, and I gave it to him, and he was very polite, thanked me, told me I shouldn't have. About six months later, we were round there for dinner, and I happened to find it in one of the kitchen drawers, dumped there with the ninety-nine-pence biros. A four-hundred-pound pen.'

'You know how pathetic you sound?'

'Really?' He made a *hmph* sound, like he was processing what I'd just said. 'You know, I removed that pen – there and then – and claimed it as my own. I carried it through years of sessions with patients. *Years.* And you know the first person who ever guessed the importance of that pen to me?'

I didn't reply.

'Casey Bullock,' he said. 'Did you know Leonard bought her a dog?'

'What?'

'A dog,' he said. 'I had my fountain pen, and she had her dog. Bear, she called it. It was such a Leonard way of dealing with a situation. Their child drowns in a lake, and Leonard tries to fill the gap that's left behind with an animal. I mean, Casey seemed to like the dog. In fact, she was very upset when it died. And then when she eventually told me everything – about her affair with Leonard, their child, all the secrets, all the lies – after it finally all spilled out of her after years of sessions, I sat there utterly stunned and thought, "What a mundane gift for such an elaborate liar." A dog.'

He paused, backing away from the kiln, and went to the table. He perched on its edge, gun resting on his lap. Next to him the empty Coke can rocked gently.

'Living with her was like living with him,' he said quietly. 'The older she got, the worse she got. She never shared anything. She never told me about her day. All we used to talk about was what she wanted done around the house, about the girls and their fucking homework. That was all we had.'

'And now you don't even have that.'

He flashed a look at me, but his tone didn't change: flat, quiet. 'You're so perfect, aren't you? A perfect widower, a perfect dad. You think because you had some horny teenage romance twenty-five years ago that you're now an expert father?'

'No,' I said. 'I'm no expert.'

His eyes lingered on me for a long time. 'I hate him.'

A long silence, as if he were reassessing that statement.

'Actually, that's not true,' he finally continued. 'I hate him even more than that. Sending him that file in January . . . I would have loved to have been there when it arrived, when he looked at the envelope and figured it must have come from the cold-case people at Plymouth – and his face when he opened it up and his world fell apart. That was a great piece of timing. I didn't mean it to be so perfect, because I didn't know he'd been in contact with them about taking on freelance work. But he deserved it.' He looked at me, taking a long breath. 'The truth was, though, I started compiling that file long before he ever thought about taking on freelance work. It was eight months in the making. Do you know what started it off? Do you know what made me reach out to someone like Neil Reynolds, and get his help in compiling it?'

'What?'

'One night the June before last, nine months before Leonard magicked himself into thin air, we were at their place on Dartmoor. He and I were out front, sitting around a barbecue. He never let me cook. Even when they came to ours, Melanie would always let him take charge. He'd help himself to my tongs, to my cutlery. When we went down there, I just slumped into a chair and tried to drink my sorrows away. It was the same that day as it had been every year I was married to Melanie. The same as always: I didn't know what to say to him, he didn't know what to say to me – just this unspoken tension. Anyway, I knew all about his indiscretions by then – Casey had already told me everything – and the more I had to drink, the more I chewed on it, the more I wanted to call him out on it.'

He eyed me for a second. 'I looked at him and thought, "You're a fucking liar." I *hated* him, just as much as Reynolds hated him. More. His public persona, it was a sham. He wasn't that man. I saw the *real* him, even before Casey started telling me about what he'd done. I saw the real Leonard Franks every day of my miserable marriage. The way he treated me, the way he looked at me like

625

I was something on his shoe. It ate away at me, until finally, we were standing over that barbecue, and I cracked. I said to him, "Are there any circumstances, any circumstances at all, where I might be good enough for you or for your daughter, Leonard?" After I said it, I stood there frozen, scared about what his response would be, but also somehow relieved that I'd actually got it out.'

'And what did he say?'

'He said no. He said to me, "You're not the man I wanted my daughter to marry. You're not the man she deserves. You're not good enough for her, John." He always called me John, not Bill. I hated the name John, even though I used it for work. It was my father's name, and he was a man just like Franks: never happy with who I was, or what I wanted to be.' He looked out at the warehouse, gesturing to the spaces around him. 'Like I was *ever* going to settle for a life blowing glass.'

His voice raised just a fraction, but then, a second later, it settled back into the same tone: 'That's why Leonard started calling me John. He knew I didn't like it. I'm sure he secretly loved the fact that Melanie decided to go with Ellie's surname, even after we got married. And after it was all out in the open, after he told me I wasn't good enough for his daughter, I knew it was over. Not for me. It was just the start for me. But I knew it was all over for him – because I was going to go after him. I was going to show the world who he really was.'

'You think it was heroic?'

'It was, in a way.'

'You're delusional.'

A twist of animosity, there and gone. Then he shrugged. 'The chances of me working at Bethlehem at some point were always high. When it was still open, there were only four high-security psychiatric facilities in the entire country, and I was moving between them all the time. But Casey actually becoming one of my patients . . . it was fate. I was seconded down there, at the same time I was doing two days a week at the Met, and when Casey finally told me why the Pamela Welland case had meant so much to her, it was perfect. It took five years for it to all come out, every detail, but it was perfect.'

'And Franks never knew?'

A snort. 'Leonard never showed a moment's interest in what I did. Not a moment. He never once came to see me when I was at Scotland Yard, even to say hello. Towards the end, Melanie was exactly the same. They knew I'd spent years doing contract work at facilities all over the country, but if either of them had made any effort, if Leonard had spent a single second asking me about my work, he would have found out I was down at Bethlehem. He'd have realized I was down there at the same time Casey was being treated.' He studied me, wiping a sheen of sweat from his forehead. 'But you know what the most damning indictment of him is? He never even bothered asking *Casey* who her doctor was. If he had, he could have stopped all of this before she confessed. She gave him Poulter's name back at the start, but Leonard never bothered asking again. That was so typical of him. He loved her, don't get me wrong, but I think a part of him was happy, knowing she'd been packed off to the nuthouse, unable to create any problems for him – the sort of problems she'd created for him when she'd tried to kill herself.'

'And Reynolds?'

'I kept in touch with Neil,' he said, matter-of-factly, 'even after he was fired, because I saw something in him that I might be able to use later on down the line. He was angry, but he was disciplined. And when the time was right, I told him all about Casey and Leonard, about their son – and he told me about his own suspicions.'

'You mean about Franks killing Simon Preston?'

He nodded. 'And you think *I'm* the bad guy.'

'You're both pond life.'

'He's the one who killed Casey.' He drifted for a second, and for the first time it was like he'd lost his focus. 'I liked Casey. She was smart. She was a challenge to get at. I spent over five years trying to get to know her, how she thought, why she was so willing to let her life drift by while she lived with worthless dogshit like Simon Preston. And then, when she finally told me about Leonard, about everything that had happened, when I found out that *that* was the reason – that she was, in her naivety, protecting Leonard, and his reputation – I sort of . . .' He stopped; a genuine flash of pain. 'I sort of felt betrayed.'

Clunk.

Garrick didn't move, even as the sound came again. I looked around at the warehouse: to the spaces beyond the empty shelves, to the loading doors, back to the corridor. When I turned again to face him, he'd come forward, gun up in front of him. There was about eight feet between us.

Too far to try to go for him.

'Well, I guess this is the end,' he said. 'I had to be quiet when I got rid of Melanie because gunshots tend to arouse suspicion in suburbia. But here . . .' He looked around. 'It'll just go down as industrial noise.'

Clunk.

It sounded right on top of us, and this time there was a minor movement of his head, eyes swivelling right, as if the proximity of the noise had surprised even him. And, as his body adjusted, the gun moved fractionally side to side.

This is my chance.

Ducking, I charged him.

A gunshot sounded.

It happened so fast I barely had time to think, and it was only as I made contact, knocking him into the table, both of us going sprawling across the floor of the warehouse, that I felt an old pain bloom in my shoulder, forking across my chest like a lightning strike. He was six feet from me, on his side, facing away, the gun beyond his grasp.

He started scrambling to his feet. As I moved, my chest heaved. I was struggling to breathe. I went at him again, straining every sinew, using the table – on its side now – to get to my feet.

This time my direction was off, but I got enough of him. I grabbed him as he bent for the gun, and we stumbled forward, past the kiln, into the back wall. We hit it hard, Garrick in front of me, face on. I'd managed to use part of him to cushion the blow, but as I rolled away – feeling the heat of the fire above me – I still felt dazed: blood leaked from a wound in my arm, old bruises were throbbing, my head lurched like a sinking ship. I looked across at Garrick: he was slumped, blood on his face, his nose bent and broken from hitting the wall face-first. His eyelids fluttered briefly, as if his body were trying to restart.

He was alive, but unconscious.

I forced myself on to all fours, sucking in deep breaths, then paused there for a moment, trying to suppress the nausea in my throat.

It'll pass.

It'll pass.

It didn't, not fully, but as I used the half-wall circling the kiln to get to my feet, I stood and breathed in again. Gradually, I started to gain control of myself.

And then I noticed something.

Under the kiln was a switch.

CHAPTER 87

The switch was between two sets of runners. It hadn't been visible when I'd been at the front. I bent down and shuffled in closer: it was like a light switch. No markings. Just on or off. I reached forward and flicked it down.

Clunk.

The kiln began to move.

It made a gentle whine as it shifted back, the fire still burning inside it. For a few seconds – as I stood there, holding my shoulder – all I could see was more of the polished concrete floor. But then, slowly, a thin black line started to show itself. Inside five seconds, the line had become a rectangle.

Inside ten, the rectangle had become a hole.

The kiln reached the end of its runners with another *clunk*, and revealed all of the hole: four feet square, the blackness showing a set of rickety wooden steps.

I moved to the lip of the hole.

There was nothing visible beyond the halfway point of the ladder. I looked around the warehouse for a torch, but Garrick hadn't brought one with him, and all I had was a torch app on my phone.

631

Something soured in my throat as I dropped on to my backside and placed my foot on the first step of the ladder. Not nausea any more: disquiet, growing and clotting every moment I looked down at what lay beneath me. Gingerly placing my foot on to the next step down, I realized why Garrick hadn't bothered bringing a torch.

On the wall, just inside the hole, was a light switch.

I reached in and turned it on.

Below me, a single light bulb erupted into life, scattering a creamy glow across a concrete floor. There was dust everywhere, debris from the kiln too: flecks of paper, tiny chunks of wood, pieces of discarded electrical equipment. On three sides, the walls were close up to the ladder. On the fourth, a thin corridor snaked off into the shadows.

I paused there for a moment, my arm crackling with pain, my lungs feeling like they might be about to close, and looked across the warehouse to where Garrick lay.

What have you done now?

I headed down.

The further I got, the colder it became. By the time I was on the ground, the heat of the kiln was completely gone. Ahead of me in the shadows, despite the light from the bulb, it was hard to see anything, but somehow I got the sense the space was big. As I inched forward, my footsteps echoed slightly and the walls felt like they parted, dropping off into the darkness. A few feet further in and I started to be able to smell something.

It was sweet, not sickly: not perfume exactly, but something close. And, on the back of that, there was something more familiar. At first, I couldn't quite place it.

Then it clicked.

I stopped, goosebumps scattering up my arms.

Fast food.

I felt something change inside the room, as if the air had been disturbed, like there was a shift in the shadows – and then a hand grabbed at my face. Nails clawed at my skin as I stumbled back, clipping a wall. When I lost my balance, a weight came with me, one hand still clamped on to my jaw, the other trying to dig their way into my neck.

I hit back: one punch to whatever part of the body I could get to, and then another. Whoever was on top of me wheezed, the air shooting out of them, but it was only after I managed to push them off – scrambling back into the light – that I realized something.

It was a woman.

I removed my phone and shone it out into the darkness. In the far corner, she was lying on her side, in the foetal position, a half-eaten burger, an empty packet of fries and a plastic cup of Coke four feet away from her toes. She was dressed in what amounted to rags: torn jeans, a frayed fleece, one sock, no shoes. Her hair was a mess: greasy, dirty, a tangle caked to her face. At her left ankle was a chain, secured to the rear wall.

As she lay there crying, I moved closer.

'It's okay,' I said to her. 'I'm not going to hurt you.'

Above her was a series of metal pipes.

She'd been hitting them. It wasn't just the movement of the kiln making the noise. It was her trying to get someone's attention.

I held out a hand.

'It's okay,' I said again. 'It's over now, Casey.'

CHAPTER 88

I spent Christmas with Annabel and Olivia in Devon, and when – the day afterwards – they began a slow tour of their extended family, I ducked out, headed back to my parents' old cottage and sat at the window, watching the sea. I imagined my mum and dad in the same place years before, sitting across from one another at the same table, admiring the same view.

On 27 December, I took a drive along the coast. It was a freezing cold day, wind buffeting the car as I wound my way down to Keel Point beach, and once I'd parked I kept the engine running, turned the heaters all the way up and switched on the radio.

They were still talking about Leonard Franks.

The police hadn't yet confirmed charges against him, but they would come soon enough. He'd been all over the TV for a week, his taped confession playing on repeat, and now Garrick's involvement had elevated it to something even more. The story had burned brightly for seven days – now it was going supernova. For the media, there was no better tale than a twisted, deadly family feud, and this was all that and more. The victims along the way – Craw, Casey Bullock – were almost footnotes: heading news bulletins, dominating front pages, was the story of Leonard Franks versus John Garrick.

As I looked out at Bethlehem, like a shipwreck in the channel, I kept returning to the moments after I'd found Casey Bullock in the cellar. I'd managed to free her of her binds, prising the ankle clamp away with a pair of shears from the warehouse, and for a moment we paused there, either side of the room, her eyeing me, waiting for me to come at her again. When I didn't, when I kept telling her she was safe, repeating it over and over, there was finally a shift in her expression, a soft acceptance, and she began to cry. I didn't approach, just waited, and then – a couple of minutes later – she regained some of her composure, and I asked her if she felt ready to leave.

She said that she did.

In the warehouse, she'd paused, staring at Garrick, still slumped against the back wall, unconscious. By then, we could already hear sirens: I'd called the police while I'd been looking for the shears. She ran a hand across one side of her face, mud and tears smearing, long strands of matted hair slick against her skin, and then she turned to me, eyes narrowing, as if she couldn't understand why I would come here and do this.

'What's your name?' she said.

'David.'

She didn't reply straight away, her gaze moving between me and the hole she'd been kept in. 'I thought no one would ever find me. I thought I was going to be there for ever.'

'Do you know how long he kept you down there?'

'What date is it today?'

'It's 22 December.'

A hint of more tears. 'Fourteen months.'

And then she told me about the day Reynolds had come for her – at the place Franks had set her up in – and how her neighbour had started knocking on the door.

'Except it wasn't my neighbour,' she said.

'It was Garrick.'

She looked at me, wondering how I'd made the leap, but it suddenly seemed so clear: he'd sent Reynolds to get rid of her – but, ultimately, Garrick hadn't been able to go through with it. *I liked Casey. She was smart.* He'd denied he felt anything deeper for her, and maybe that was true, but he'd become emotionally invested in her as a person, her decisions, her life; and the line between doctor and patient had blurred. *When she finally told me about Leonard, about everything that had happened . . . I sort of felt betrayed.* It was such a mess, so complex: he liked the woman who loved the man he hated. He knew what had to be done, but he couldn't go through with it – so, instead, he told Reynolds he would take care of her. And how else could he hide her from view, without hurting her, than by making her a prisoner?

I doubted Reynolds knew she was still alive – even when he was occupying the warehouse himself – otherwise he surely would have seen the risks and attempted to do something about it. So, as far as he was concerned, the day Garrick took her away from her hiding place was the day Casey Bullock died.

When the police finally arrived, I watched them enter the warehouse, looking at me, at Casey, at the boxes of files and photographs waiting to be burned, at Garrick on the floor, his breath hoarse, and I had a moment of clarity. All the death, all the lies, all the suffering, and what it came down to in the end was loss: for Franks, the woman he loved but couldn't have, and the son he knew only in passing; for Craw, the father she'd idolized and would never know again; for Garrick, the wife who abandoned him, and the father-in-law who rejected him; and for Bullock, the life she'd dreamed of, and the death of a son she'd loved, above all else.

A trail of wreckage.

A map of broken hearts.

Before I headed back to London on 28 December, I made two phone calls. The first was to Carla Murray to see how she was. She was abrupt, unemotional, unwilling – even now – to speak ill of Franks. But her pain, her sense of betrayal, was there, unspoken, unmissable. She said she'd talked to Jim Paige on the phone, that he was calm and rational about everything, but we both knew it was a show. It was all a show. The two of them had been hurt badly.

The second call was to Ellie Franks, to see how she was doing. She too remained resolute for a while, but then it began to get on top of her – all the news reports she'd had to endure, all the lies she'd had to try to process over the past nine days – and she broke down. As I listened to her cry, I thought about something she'd told me the first time I met her: *Len said to me once, 'Sometimes you just have to let people go.'* He was talking about a woman he'd had an affair with, about the son he'd had to watch being buried from the back of the church – and yet, in the end, it had probably been one of the most honest things he'd ever said to his wife.

I sat beside her bed as the sun came up, cutting through the blinds at her window. It was 3 January and one of the male nurses was busy taking down Christmas decorations.

She was sleeping on her side, pale and still, IV gently dripping, heaters humming. In my lap, I held a photograph: Casey, with her son. I'd managed to persuade the investigating team to release one picture for her.

At just before seven-thirty, she began to stir, making a gentle moaning sound as she rolled on to her back. I watched her surface, her eyelids flickering, her fingers pushing the blanket away from her. As she opened an eye, I looked down at the photograph again, at the face of a mother and the memory of her son, then returned it to my jacket pocket. She clocked the movement, realizing someone was beside her, and turned to face me.

A hint of a smile broke across her face, although much of her skull remained obscured by bandages.

'Morning,' I said.

'I see you caught me looking my best again.'

I returned the smile. 'How are you feeling?'

She took a long, deep breath, her eyes like a projector: doubt, pain, grief, worry, relief. Then, finally, Melanie Craw said, 'I guess I feel like my life starts here.'

CHAPTER 89

Everything is connected. It took me a long time to realize that. After my wife died from a disease I couldn't fight for her, I spent two years drifting, propelled by the ghost of who she had been. All that I did in that time, every case I closed, every killer I found, all the darkness I faced down, was driven by her. Her ashes may have been scattered long ago, taken by the wind and washed away by the rain, but what she had been to me remained.

I found my calling in missing persons because I soon realized the families of the lost were just like me: wandering a road without boundaries, searching for answers in the dark. In the end, whether I walked their loved ones to the front door, or returned them as memories, dust and bones, I always brought them back – and I always closed the circle.

When Derryn died, I refused to believe there could be a reason. Perhaps, in a lot of ways, I still don't. But, as my grief slowly subsided, I started seeing things with more clarity, moments in my cases that might have escaped me before: links between events, connective tissue binding one person to the next. I saw actions from one decade echoing through to the next, and saw how you could drift from people, become so distant from them it seemed impossible you would ever meet back in the middle. But then you did.

You were bound to them.

Perhaps even, in some small way, responsible for them.

The café was at the eastern end of Lower Mall, on the fringes of the Thames. When I arrived, Colm Healy was on a stool at the window, hands flat to the counter in front of him, eyes following two rowers as they passed under Hammersmith Bridge.

He'd barely changed in the fourteen months since I'd last seen him in the flesh: tall but overweight, his red hair thick and messy, his shirt bursting at the stomach, his expression dogged, tired, distressed. He wasn't wearing a tie, and his jacket was on the back of the chair, but he'd rolled his sleeves up, as if preparing for something. He turned as I approached, and we shook hands, then he offered to get me a coffee. I couldn't recall the last time he'd done that, and immediately, perhaps cynically, wondered what the real reason was for him inviting me here. In the days before I'd put the Franks case to bed, I'd told him I would call him to arrange something. But, in the end, he'd called me instead.

After my drink arrived, we talked for a while

about Franks, about Craw, about the things the media had reported, and then a sudden greyness seemed to grab hold of him.

'You all right?' I asked him.

He nodded. 'Yeah.'

'You sure?'

'I'm *fine*,' he said.

I left it there, looking over at the river. It was 8 January, and there was fresh snow on the ground. In front of us, the sun winked through the naked branches of an oak tree.

'How's the security gig going?'

He didn't respond.

When I turned to him, he was looking down into his empty coffee cup. His hand was around it, wedding band still on, even though his wife had left him three years ago.

'Healy?'

'It's not,' he said.

'It's not what?'

'It's not going.'

'The security job?'

He nodded.

'You mean you left?'

He shook his head, then looked up at me. A movement in his face. 'There never *was* a security job. I lied. I can't get a fucking job anywhere. The guy I pretended was the other security guard, the one I told you on the phone was always checking up on me . . .'

I just stared at him.

'He's just a guy I bunk with in the shelter.'

'You're living in a *homeless* shelter?'

He looked out through the window; nodded.

'Why the hell didn't you call me?'

'I called you today.'

'I mean, *before* today.'

'Yeah, well . . .' He stopped, taking a long breath, and it was like something shivered through him. 'You want to help me? I got something you can help me with.'

'What?'

He sat there, unmoved, staring out at the river. 'You know the point at which my life *really* started going down the shitter? It wasn't when Gemma left me. It wasn't even when I found Leanne. I mean, don't get me wrong, that messed me up. You shouldn't outlive your kids.' He cleared his throat, and when he glanced at me, I could see his eyes had welled up. 'What messed me up was those two girls. The twins. They were the start of everything. I couldn't find the bastard who killed them, I couldn't find a fucking *trace* of that arsehole *anywhere*, and from there my whole life got flushed: my marriage fell apart, my daughter was murdered, I got fired from the Met, and *now* look at me. I'm living in a homeless shelter, pretending that I'm working a security gig. I'm pathetic.'

'Healy—'

'No,' he said. 'Don't tell me I'm not. Don't lie to me.'

We sat there in silence for a long time.

And then, as I finished the last of my coffee, he swung around on his stool, some measure of composure back in his face, and he said, 'You want to do something for me?'

'This wasn't what—'

'You want to *do* something for me, Raker?'

I studied his face, the lines in it, gouged out by the journey of the last three and a half years; from the moment he'd found the girls, this was the path he'd been walking, these were his scars, this was where it was always going to end up.

Another broken heart.

'You want to do something for me?' he said again. 'Help me find the man who killed them.'